Like Wind Through Hollow Bones

A Fantasy in 12 Articulations

Book One of the Hollow Bones Trilogy

Michael Phillips Mann

Wandering in the Words Press

Requests for permission should be sent to Wandering in the Words Press:
2131 Burns St, Nashville, Tennessee, 37216
www.wanderinginthewordspress.com

PUBLISHED BY WANDERING IN THE WORDS PRESS

ISBN-10: 0989153959
ISBN-13: 978-0-9891539-5-9

First Edition

For my two Greatest Inspirations

Dylan and Holland

Thank you for Being who you Are

Thank you for Shining your Light in the World

CAST OF CHARACTERS

Cary Walker – a Reluctant Hero
Taylor Walker – Cary's Son
Ally Profett – a Namayan Warrior
Simon Boon – a Fugitive Reporter
Freddy Blake – a professor of ancient languages
Ksama – Anucara of Sh'ele
Syrgala – First Speaker of the Parisad
Sidra – an Assassin
DevaSurya – a Grace, The Queen of Light
Raj Satya – a Grace, Scion of The Queen of Light
Nelson Profett – First Member of the Namayan Council
Tristan Warner – Second Member of the Namayan Council
Teo Kirten – Third member of the Namayan Council
Emma Profett – a Healer, a Matriarch, an Angel
Sam Berns – a short Short Order Cook
Harvey Whitt – a Professor of Archeology
Renee DiRosa – a Cafe Entrepreneur
Madeg Shope – a Wildman Scribbler
Druid Cuervo – a Crazy Neighbor
David Johnson – a Cherokee Community Leader
Billy – a Cherokee Elder, a Hollow Bone
Arthur Walker – Cary's Father
Clovis Plowright – a Retired Tobacco Farmer
Murtaugh – a Scary Catacomb Dweller
Apavarita Varsah – Protector of Earth
Rahni Sisyah – her Acolyte and Assistant
Elias Carver aka Memsalemn – a Sumerian
Miranda Carver – Elias' Wife
Gareth Stokes – Carver's Chief of Operations
Cyrus Layton aka Nanoshe – a Sumerian
Ian Cord – Layton's Chief of Operations
Leon Hess – a Tech-Mercenary
Various Men of Hench
Ras Graal – Lord of the Grastar
Ripu Dasi – A Grastar General
Panii Visam – A Grastar Assassin
A Vast Horde of Grastar Warriors

FIRST ARTICULATION

a bow and a warrior

an angel and a demon

bad guys

an escape

a reporter

demigods and a crystal

a very old story

Present Day

The scream was coming. Cary Walker had glimpsed the evidence of its rising for the past five years, and the knowledge terrified him. But on this late mid-March afternoon in the Black Mountains, the scream still lived only in his shadows.

At 42 years old, Cary stood 5-foot-9 and was soft, round and pasty. He placed a newly purchased bow, along with three arrows and a leather case, in the back of his dust-caked Lexus RX300. The bow's black lacquered limbs and gilt handle gleamed like an invitation on the SUV's gray carpet. A relatively safe instrument of death for Cary to own. Far safer than a gun.

When he slammed the rear door, his love handles shook over the waistband of his olive chinos. A saggy, black sweater covered the telltale jiggle. Cary's hazel eyes had once been piercing and inquisitive; now his gray-brown hair swung across them like a curtain. From behind that curtain, he'd watched as his life spiraled further and further into the unknown.

But the scream was coming.

He stepped out from the shadow of a small billboard that announced the Appalachian Storytelling Festival. The sun's low rays struck him blind. When he opened his eyes, a girl stood between his Lexus and a mud-encrusted International

Scout as if she had materialized from a ray of light. That was the first time he saw Ally Profett.

Ambient sounds in Cary's head kicked up a few notches in volume. These constant tones—ranging from a high-pitched squeal to a low, humming throb—had developed near the end of the summer, five years ago, when Cary had still worked at Lilly in Atlanta. *Tinnitus*, Doctor Stano had called it—a nice, simple diagnosis. Cary had not told her about the voices that murmured and argued constantly in the shadow of these sounds. Sometimes he believed he could almost make out their words, could almost imagine what they were arguing about. He twisted his index finger in his right ear and shook his head, trying to release the noises the way a swimmer releases trapped water. Or at least make them quieter. But the sounds remained, and so did the girl.

Not a hallucination, then.

She was just over 5 feet tall, even in her calf-high combat boots. An olive drab spandex suit compressed her curves into a tight hourglass. The sun transformed her auburn hair into a halo of fire. She was probably only 19 or 20, but she had ancient eyes as green as ground moss. Those eyes transformed Cary into glass. She could stare straight through him or shatter him into a million shards, depending entirely upon what she wished. Cary could only stand and wait, silent and stupefied.

His right hand reached for the pendant hanging from a rawhide thong around his neck. A spray of scrimshaw dots pocked the talisman's surface; he rubbed his thumb over them in a familiar, calming gesture and grimaced at the sharp ache in his wrist.

Ten minutes later, Cary floated along the curves of Highway 197 toward home. He drove without thinking and was bouncing across the wooden bridge to his driveway before he was fully aware that he had left the parking lot at Winter Star Trading Post. He hadn't noticed the black Suburban he had passed as he turned onto 197, or the man inside who had raised a cell phone to his cheek.

He didn't even remember the girl backing away so that he could open his door. She had disappeared into the shadows with the same magic she had conjured to materialize from the light. One moment Cary had been standing there hypnotized by those eyes; the next, he was creeping down the mile-long ruts that hugged the banks of the Cane River.

Maybe she was a hallucination after all.

Inside the house, Cary reclined in a soft window seat overlooking the river. Steam rose from his forgotten cup of coffee. A gentle breeze played random melodies on wind chimes. He nodded once, twice. Yet, even as he fell into dreams, Cary struggled to awaken from the sleep of lifetimes.

***

Water lapped at his cheek, rushing into the recesses of his mind, enlivening unused spaces. A pale sliver of light arced near his face, and the river rushed past his eyes, sparkling in the lingering light.

How did I get down here?

Two voices argued nearby. A red wave of sun rolled through the valley, and the rasp of metal sliding on metal rang out. A body flew backwards over a tall copse of mountain laurel. The man was gigantic, at least 8 feet tall. He wore a golden breastplate, a skirt-like garment fashioned from wide leather straps, and sandals with long lashings that crisscrossed his muscular calves. His thick right hand gripped a shining gladius. And he had wings. Huge, white-feathered wings. *Angel wings.*

The angel crashed into the river. Droplets of water, dirt and blood filled the air like rising snow. He rolled backwards and up to his feet as his enemy leapt over the bush.

She was small, with dark blue skin and pointed ears. *A demon.* The demon wore only a gray loincloth and swung a kukri in her left hand. Her wiry body floated with lethal grace, and her unshod feet slapped into the water, sending aloft fresh droplets. The red sun transformed the particles into a bloody mist.

The angel sliced a shining scar through the steam. The blue demon deflected the attack with a graceful parry. They stared into each other's eyes, trembling in impasse. Cary watched from the shore at their feet.

"You will never have him," the angel hissed.

"I will," said the demon. "Eventually, he will come to me."

The angel stumbled back, freeing the demon's kukri to cut an arc that would separate Cary's head from his body. Cary raised his arm to ward off the blow. Light reflected from the blade. His soul burned with the effort of attempting to rise.

***

Cary awoke in the window seat. A low slice of sunlight cast red lines across his face. He massaged his unsevered neck. An anxious vortex in his chest prodded him to remember, but he recalled only the red haze floating above the river.

Steam still spiraled above the coffee. Beside the cup, a spandex wrist brace lay open like a dark pair of wings. Cary had left it there two days before. He reached for the brace, flexed his wrist, shook his head, and retrieved the coffee instead. With that gesture, the remnants of the nightmare melted into the air like the steam above his mug. Only his unanchored fear remained.

The dull ache in Cary's right wrist had begun the same summer as the noises in his head—and the nightmares. He never remembered them, only knew that they waited in his shadows like some tentacled beast. He had not revealed these dreams to Doctor Stano either. For Cary, it was enough that he could pinpoint the moment at which his mind, his will, and his life had begun to disintegrate. No reason for anyone else to know.

Cary took the bow, the blue-feathered arrows, and the case from the rear of the Lexus and carried them down rickety wooden steps to the river's edge. Venus and Jupiter shone pale beneath an early risen, three-quarter moon. He counted out 20 paces from the broad side of his old fishing shed and stuck the arrows into the rich silt. Directly above him, a raven watched with cocked head from the branches of an ancient yew that stood on the embankment, its roots exposed by years of erosion.

The bow was more difficult to draw than he'd expected. Pain sliced at his wrist. His arm trembled. Slowly, like pulling a trigger in reverse, Cary released the string.

"Ow! Shit!" The harsh string raked across his face. The arrow flew left of the shack, glanced off a boulder, and careened aloft to splash 30 yards up river.

His thumb ached and his cheek burned. He nocked the second arrow. This time, he kept his face well away from the bowstring and released before he had reached full draw. The arrow soared over the shack and disappeared into the underbrush 50 yards away.

"Double shit."

To his left, just out of reach, the first arrow floated downstream. Its taunting blue feathers flashed in the current until he lost sight of them in the river's fading, silver surface.

The moon and evening stars formed an axe forged from light in the darkening sky. The fishing shack loomed in defiance. Cary smirked.

Can't hit the broad side of a barn.

The last arrow stood alone in the dirt. A last hope. He nocked it and considered the weathered shack for a long time. One minute. Two. Three. His chest quivered on the verge of exploding, or collapsing into nothingness. Cary raised the bow slowly. Past the horizontal. Sound roared in his ears. Garbled voices shouted from the frontiers of sanity. He dropped to one knee to aim higher still, until the point was vertical, aimed at the sky itself. He drew the string, held it as tight as he held the scream building in his throat. By sheer will, he forced his eyes to remain open. His fingers relaxed, and his head cranked back, mouth wide, teeth bared. He released the string, and his voice with it. The scream filled his ears and forced away the inner sounds. But this was not the scream that was coming. This scream was a choked and choking thing.

The arrow disappeared into the blue. Cary's oxygen ran out, and his strangled scream died. He rose on unsteady legs, closed his eyes, stretched his arms wide, and pressed his heart against the sky, offering his life to fate, or perhaps only to the high swirling winds.

On his inner screen of thought, he imagined the tiny missile climbing higher and higher, exhausting its energy, pausing for a moment as if in contemplation, reversing trajectory in the empty expanse, and plummeting back to earth, hungry for a target. Cary clenched his eyes tighter and pulled his shoulders farther back, pressing his chest ever closer to the heavens. The arrow of his imagination fell toward his offered chest, inexorable. Closer. Faster. At the last moment, before the razor-tipped head buried itself in his flesh, a hand snapped out from the fringe of darkness and closed on the shaft, halting death. Was it his own hand, or someone else's? Divine intervention? He could almost feel the point of the imaginary missile pressing against the skin covering his breastbone before the mystery hand arrested it.

Seconds later he heard the small *thunk* of the real arrow plunging into the real earth. Only then did breath return to him; he gasped aloud, and his eyes flew open in the same moment.

The arrow had landed very near. He pushed aside foliage, but gave up after a few moments. Cary unstrung the bow and zipped it into the leather case. There would be plenty of time to find the lost arrow later when he needed it. Perhaps it was better for the moment that he didn't have any more arrows to play with. Deeper thoughts of what he had just done, and why, flitted away into the dark edges of consciousness.

Dusk hovered over the mountains. He climbed the steps, settled onto the soft ground moss at the edge of the drop-off, and dangled his feet in the air. The music of the river washed over him, competing with the internal voices for his attention.

"You're aiming the wrong way," the girl said.

Cary scrambled to his feet, nearly stepping off the embankment in the process. She caught the collar of his sweater and pulled him back from the edge at the last moment.

"Where did you come from?" he asked. He tried to catch his breath. "I didn't hear a car." She looked familiar, but he couldn't quite place her.

"I need you to come with me," she said.

She stood between him and the house, tapping her foot and glancing at the driveway. *Of course.* The same young woman he had seen outside of Winter Star. Bits of ground moss and twigs clung to her red hair. A gust of wind whipped a fiery strand across her eyes. She tucked it with its sisters behind her ear. Dried blood rimmed her left nostril. Mud darkened her olive knees. Wild ferns tossed to and fro at their feet while, high above their heads, the branches of poplars and hemlocks engaged in leafy sword fights. Three parallel scratches extended from the left side of her nose down to just below her ear, giving her the incongruous appearance of having stopped halfway through putting on war paint. The lowest scratch deepened to a true cut where it approached her carotid artery. Teardrops of blood trickled from the cut and ran down the side of her neck, disappearing inside her collar. Cary reached toward her cheek. She stepped back before he could touch her.

"I'm sorry," he said. "I didn't see you were hurt. Come inside. I've got a first-aid kit somewhere."

She traced her fingertips along the scratches and shook her head. "Doesn't matter," she said. "We have to leave." She trotted past him up the sloping lawn to the deck.

Cary didn't move.

"Are you deaf?" she yelled over her shoulder.

Her feet were drumbeats on the wooden porch. She disappeared into the house. Cary followed.

"What are you talking about?" Cary said. "Are you in trouble? I'll call the police."

"Police can't help," she said. "Get your shit. Only what you can carry." She shoved his green canvas coat into his arms. "Here," she said. "No time to explain. We have to go. Now."

"Whoa. Time out," he said. "Get a grip." *Funny, me telling someone else to get a grip.* Still, he shrugged into his coat and slapped his thigh to locate his car keys. "Look. I don't even know you. I never even saw you before today."

Her boots tapped out quick, muffled thumps on the thick carpet.

Cary's hand sought the comfort of the pendant hanging from his neck. "Why should I believe—"

"Okay," she said. "Fine. My name's Ally." She grabbed his hand and shook it several times. "Nice to meet you. Can we please haul ass now?" She pulled him out onto the deck.

"But I don't—"

"Geez! Will you listen to me? Big, ugly bad guys are coming here. And. When. They. Get. Here," her index finger stabbed his chest with each word, "They. Will. Kill. You. Or worse." She drew a line across her throat, crossed her eyes, stuck her tongue out and let her head sag to the left. And then, as incongruous as it seemed, she laughed at her own silliness. "And me," she said. "Get it? They'll kill us both."

Cary tried to wedge those statements into the map of the world he thought he lived in. Somewhere nearby, a truck engine growled. High beams sliced open the twilight and swept across the tree line; a black Suburban rounded the last switchback and came into view a quarter of a mile away.

"This way," Ally said.

She clamped her slight hand around his wrist. Her strength surprised him; she almost pulled him off his feet. They half ran, half staggered to a thick wall of rhododendrons behind the house.

How could she know about this place? The entrance is completely overgrown.

Ally pushed her way through dense leaves. Two granite dolmans jutted up from the earth like jagged teeth.

"Wait, wait, wait." Cary held up his hands. "There's no way out this way. There's nothing but forest. And it's almost vertical."

"Duh," she said. "How do you think I got here?"

"You came over the mountain?" he asked. "No wonder you—"

The truck engine fell silent, and all four doors opened.

"Besides," he whispered, "how do I know those people are here to kill me? It's probably just one of my neighbors. Or someone who took a wrong turn and ended up down here." He searched her eyes for assent, but found none. "It's happened before." He studied his shuffling feet.

The doors to the Suburban slammed shut. Cary began to push his way back through the rhododendrons toward the house. Then, above the murmur of the river, he heard the unmistakable *clack* of a handgun slide and the metal *ka-chunk* of a pump shotgun.

Cary froze. Distant voices echoed from the driveway.

"Are you insane?" someone said. "Put those guns away."

"Oh, right," another voice answered. "Forgot."

Then, heavy footsteps splattered toward them up the muddy driveway.

***

Elias Carver pressed a remote control and rose from the embrace of a black Cube Chair. The white wall in front of him slid away in opposing directions, revealing the infinite Pacific Ocean. He stepped out onto a cantilevered balcony. His loose, black pants and white shirt rippled in the wind. Still two hours above the horizon, the descending sun burned the white veranda to gold.

Carver raised a slender, black cell phone to his lips. Layton answered on the first ring.

"Do they have Walker yet?" Layton asked.

"Happening as we speak." Carver smiled, anticipating Layton's next reaction. "But…there's a wrinkle. They…uh…ran into…Profett's daughter in Burnsville."

"What the hell was she doing there?" Layton asked. "How did they find out about Walker?"

"A question," said Carver, "that I intend to have answered." He raised his glass to the horizon. "Here's to hoping she doesn't also know why."

"You mean she's still alive?"

"I'm told they drew blood," Carver said. "Almost cut her throat, in fact. She dropped one of Stokes's boys like a rag doll."

"Which one?" he asked.

"Boyette?"

"That guy's huge!"

"Didn't even see how she hit him. He's only now getting some feeling back in his legs. She'd disappeared before he hit the ground."

"Damn. Too bad we can't just shoot her."

"Yeah, well, we know how it turns out when we try that. What's happening with your venture?" Carver asked.

"Cord thinks they're in D.C."

"*They*, meaning…?"

"The whole Council," said Layton. "All nine of them."

"The entire *Namayan* Council is in one place. And we know where?"

"Only that they're in D.C."

Carver remained silent.

"Do you think we're going too far?" Layton asked.

"Do you mean breaking The Accords?"

"Well," said Layton, "we haven't killed one of them… haven't even tried in…I don't know…at least—"

"Doesn't matter," Carver said. "Everything's different now."

"Yes," said Layton. "I suppose we are off the map."

Carver laughed. "We've never been on the map. Besides, once we eliminate the Namayan, who will be left to retaliate?"

"Um…have you forgotten about Dossey?" Layton asked.

"Of course not," Carver hurled his glass out over the

balcony. It descended like a falling star, gathering sunlight as it fell to the sea.

"How do you think he found out about us?" Layton asked.

"I don't want to talk about Dossey," said Carver. *Not yet, anyway.*

Layton waited.

"Where are you?" Carver asked. "I can hear the ocean."

Layton's laugh was dry. "I don't think," he said, "that I am quite yet ready to become that friendly."

"No," said Carver, laughing silently. "I suppose not." He watched the ever-sinking sun.

"Still—"

"Yes," Carver said. This time he let Layton hear his laugh. "It is nice to be talking again, Brother." He tossed the phone onto the Cube Chair. It disappeared as it landed, black falling into black.

***

"Seriously," Ally said. "I need you to haul ass." She jerked Cary's wrist, and he stumbled into a locust sapling, shaking baby leaves thirty feet in the sky. The thunder of footsteps rumbled to silence. An osprey screamed somewhere upriver.

"In the back," someone shouted.

"We'll never get out this way," Cary said again.

"You need to trust me." Ally pushed through a thick wall of leaves, still dragging Cary in her wake.

"Mr. Stokes," shouted a voice near the house. "Check out these footprints. Looks like that little bitch is with him."

"Bitch?" Ally whispered. "That guy's an asshole!"

"How did she get here ahead of us?" asked the same man.

"Doesn't matter," said Stokes. He was just under 6 feet, wide and thick like a moving wall. His head was completely bald. "Now we can finish her, it being open season and all. Mr. Carver will be pleased. But don't let her size fool you. You saw what she did to Boyette. And whatever you do, don't pull your gun unless you plan to eat it."

"You?" Cary whispered. Ally shrugged.

Somewhere on the ridge above them, a limb broke with a loud crack. She continued to pull Cary up the stone path. Cary planted his feet like a mule.

"Are you crazy?" he said, no longer trying to keep their location a secret.

"You have to trust me," she said again. She looked into his eyes, and he suffered the same paralysis he had experienced in the parking lot. All around them, dark leaves softened the moonlight to an ambient glow. Cary nodded once and let himself be pulled forward.

They entered a circular courtyard of slate. Spokes of red fieldstone radiated from a black slab in the center. At the left rim of the circle, two small boulders supported a split walnut trunk, forming a bench; behind the bench, a granite wall sparkled in the moonlight.

"Wow," she said. "Beautiful."

"Um…thank you?"

Unbroken moonlight bathed the clearing in yellow. Suddenly, the calm was obliterated by a large man crashing through the foliage at the far edge of the circle. Cary looked over his shoulder, but Ally had disappeared. The man's heavy hand closed on Cary's throat. *Game over.* The man keyed a transmitter clipped to his epaulet, but before he could speak, his grip went limp, and he dropped straight down like a derelict building. Ally was behind him.

"Where the hell did you go?"

"Help me get him into the bushes."

"Is he dead?"

"Never killed anybody," she said. Her fingers traced the wound on her neck.

They lugged the man out of sight.

"Wait," Cary said. "Don't you want to get his gun or something?"

Ally smiled. "No guns. Besides, it's more dangerous to him if he keeps it." She winked and pulled Cary across the courtyard to the granite wall.

"How did you do that?" Cary asked.

"Do what?"

"Do what?" Cary said. "Disappear! That's what. And—you know—whatever you did to that guy."

Ally shrugged. "Just stuff I can do. Now, quiet." She slipped her right hand to the small of Cary's back. Her strength kept him from trying to resist. That, along with the knowledge that she had done something terrible to some guy named Boyette. Not to mention whatever violence she had performed on the man they had just concealed in the bushes. While Cary tried to imagine what these things might be, Ally shoved him a few feet to the left.

Again he was surprised by her strength. But not as surprised as he was when they suddenly plummeted into a hole in the earth. They slid along an oblique wall for a few seconds before they landed, still on their feet.

How could I not have known this was here?

The air was cooler underground. Sounds screamed louder in his head, amplified in the mystery cave. A single shaft of moonlight half lit their faces. Cary's world threatened to collapse in upon itself, inner nightmare combining with outer. Terror gathered in his throat like a volcano about to erupt. His mouth opened.

"Quiet, I said. They're very close." Her voice was scarcely a whisper, but it seemed to double and triple there in the darkness, like several Ally's speaking at once.

A thunder of boots approached above them, then faded as the footsteps passed by. Soon, only the muffled roar of the river remained.

"Who are you?" Cary asked.

"Nobody. A storyteller."

"Oh," he said without thinking. "Are you here for the festival?" Even in the darkness he could feel her looking at him like he was an idiot. "Right," he said. "I guess not." Another set of footsteps rumbled across the courtyard. "Well, *Señorita* Storyteller," Cary whispered, "this is the part of the story where I tell you that we're trapped in here. It's just a matter of time."

"We'll be fine," Ally said. "But you have to trust me."

"You keep saying. Why should I? And who are these people? Why—"

Ally's hand rose, a wispy ghost in the darkness. She pressed her palm to Cary's forehead, gentle, tender, almost regretful. "Later, dude," she whispered. "Right now we have to get out of here."

Cary hesitated.

"Look. I've already saved your ass. If I hadn't gotten here in time, you'd be dead, or more likely, eviscerated, then dead."

"Why? This is insane." He tried to swallow. "What do you mean, eviscerated?"

Maybe this isn't really happening at all. Maybe I've finally dropped off the edge. He laughed, remembering the edge she had just pulled them over.

"What could possibly be funny?" Ally asked.

Should I tell her she might not be real?

No.

Definitely not.

"Nothing," he said. "Sorry. But what do they want with me?"

"Don't know. Only knew who. Not why."

"Well, how did you know that, then?"

She weighed her responses. "You wouldn't believe me," she said finally. "I just knew. I only realized how serious this was when they tried to kill me, too." Again she traced her fingertips along the cut on her neck; her voice shrank in the darkness. "They've never tried that before."

"Before? You mean you know these guys? Who are you? Okay, so your name's Ally. And you're a storyteller? Whatever that means. But, I mean, who are you really?"

"Not now," she hissed.

"But—"

"No. We've already wasted too much time. You'll either have to believe me or take your chances with them."

"Not much of a choice."

"True," she said. "Get ready, then, because this is the part of the story where it's all about to change."

"What's about to change?"

Ally drew a deep breath and let it out slowly. "Everything. Everything you ever thought was real."

"Too late," he mumbled.

'Saahreee," she sang, her voice taking a nasal tone. Then her laughter rang like bells against the close walls of the cave.

"You're crazy," he said, but he laughed with her.

"You should know, of course."

"What the hell's that supposed to mean?"

"Not now," she said. "Here. Check this out. Look closely." Her open right hand rose into the lone shaft of moonlight. The light itself appeared to gather in her palm.

Outside the cave, someone sounded the alarm. "Over here. There's a cave."

"I told you," Cary said.

"Tell me you trust me." Mesmerizing moonlight continued to pool in her open hand.

Cary could not look away.

"I…I trust you," he said.

A flashlight beam swept across the cave entrance above them. Boots scrabbled against the stone opening. Bad men were coming down. Ally's fingers drew inward until her fingertips and thumb pressed together to form a single mass.

"Good," she said. "Sorry. This is going to hurt."

Before Cary could form the question, Ally's hand snapped forward and popped him once in the center of his forehead just above the eyebrows. She was right. It did hurt.

"You hit me," were the words his brain queued up, but his mouth produced no actual sound. She lowered his limp body into the darkness. A hurricane filled his ears, drowning out even his inner voices and…was that…was she…singing? Light brighter than desert noon penetrated his eyelids.

Then God flipped the off-switch, and the light became shadows. The wind and the rushing songs of the Cane River echoed away to silence. In the dark distance, tires cried on a freeway as Cary's embattled mind fell into the inner worlds.

Before Time

~

Ksama

Dawn is scarcely an hour away. A young woman leans out from the lip of an alley's shadow and surveys a small park called Tirtham Commons. She is young, 24 years old. Her face is soft and full like her body, and her skin is the color of dusty rubies. She has long, dark hair that normally cascades in thick ringlets down her back, but not tonight. Tonight her hair is bound, contained, protected. She wears midnight blue trousers and a tunic. Across her back, she carries a sword called *DevaRada*, God's Tooth, and a leather sheath holding a large crystal named *Sh'ele*. She is Ksama, *Añucara* of Sh'ele, keeper of one of the Sacred Stones of Uktenah. And she knows that she is being hunted.

Somewhere nearby, a soft footstep dislodges a pebble. She freezes. Every sound in the night might be one of Syrgala's assassins. Ksama is afraid, and with good cause. But she has taken a vow.

Across the green space, past the reflecting pool, an open sloop bobs unconcerned and unmolested on slight waves. Its name, *Varuna*, adorns the square stern in golden script. Ksama allows herself a smile; in her short life, she has already learned the importance of names.

She has almost made it, almost escaped. She needs only to cross Tirtham Commons, untie the Varuna, and escape upon the water. If an ambush is to come, here it will be. She touches the pommel of DevaRada and steps into the open. A vertical column of moonlight reflects from the calm surface of the pool. The world is as peaceful as an unfettered heart. Perhaps her caution has been unjustified.

Seven Hours Earlier

Ksama fidgeted at the eastern arc of the table, weary of this endless fight. She gathered her dark curls with a leather strip. She was the youngest member of the *Parisad*, the Council of Añucara, Keepers of the Stones of Uktenah. Syrgala, First Speaker of the Parisad, was shouting. Again.

Miles below the floor, the earth growled. Crystal goblets danced on the table. Syrgala stood, and his sturdy chair crashed to the stone floor. He was a huge square of a man, over 6-feet tall, and nearly as wide. The thick plume of his gray topknot quivered; his voice filled the chamber as fully as he had filled his chair.

"Do you feel that?" he asked. His eyebrows jumped like caterpillars on a stove. "We must take control of the stones now. We must redirect their power and avert this disaster. If we do not, then the *Apsara* will die."

Sumna, the oldest member of the Parisad, lifted his ancient head. Wispy white hair fell across his milky blue eyes. He rarely spoke anymore. Ksama often wondered if he was fully present at their meetings or off wandering in the inner worlds, perhaps preparing for his next life.

"The First Canon forbids such actions," Sumna said, his wizened voice scarcely more than a whisper. "You know this, Syrgala."

Several others murmured assent.

"Do you not understand?" Syrgala said. His pink face flushed deeper. "We adjudicate these laws. They are not written in stone. Can you not see that they no longer apply?

19

You hold the power of the Gods in your hands, and yet you cower in its presence like mewling infants!"

Ksama closed her eyes.

The power of the Stones of Uktenah was measureless. Twelve equally balanced quartz points, each over a meter long, were arrayed in a perfect circle. A 13th stone held the center, anchoring their singularity. The array transmitted a continuous wave of energy from which their entire continent drew power, unlimited and free. And dangerous, if not used wisely. The Canons of Uktenah, written before time was called time, protected them all. Not just the Keepers, but the Apsara, as well.

The First Canon was simple: *The Stones of Uktenah serve all, never one.*

When Ksama had been chosen as an acolyte at the age of 4, her first discipline had been to create the *Pravarna*, a cloak of protection that shielded her from her crystal, Sh'ele, and from the temptation to use it for herself. At this task alone, she had toiled for eight years. Since then, she had worn the Pravarna like a second skin. The Canons of Uktenah were more than written in stone. They were etched into the heart and mind. They were inscribed upon the soul.

The Parisad's tedium raged on, an angry murmur beneath the serene surface of Ksama's thoughts. The melody of a single flute filtered through her reverie and danced above the angry voices. Ksama's heart followed the song for several minutes before she realized that its source was not confined to her inner hearing, but was here, physically present in the chamber. She opened her eyes.

How can they continue to argue? Can they not hear? Can they not see?

A solitary woman stood in front of the western wall; her pale hands danced upon the ivory flute that disappeared into the shadow of her blue hood. One by one, the members of the Parisad attended the summons. When all argument had ceased, the woman paused and raised her head. Her cowl fell away. White hair surrounded her translucent face like an ice storm. Her pale blue eyes captured the essence of light in the chamber.

"*DevaSurya*," someone whispered. The Queen of Light. Queen of the Graces.

The air in the chamber slowed. Space and time echoed with the melody of her flute. A second figure stepped from behind the Queen. He lowered his blue hood to reveal an ivory face framed by golden curls.

Raj Satya, Ksama thought. *The Prince of Truth.*

It was believed that the Graces revealed themselves to the Añucara only in dreams. According to the Sutras, the world of matter was too dense for them. Most of the Apsara had ceased to believe in their existence. But here they stood, not merely one of the Graces, but the Queen herself, accompanied by her scion, the TruthSpeaker.

To what frightful end have we brought ourselves? Ksama's thoughts disappeared like clouds when Raj Satya began to sing:

Love has fallen to the night
Truth sleeps now in darkest light

His voice was a chime, echoing in the tall chamber. The council sat stunned until Ksama spoke.

"Please," she said. "Tell us what you mean." She met the Queen's eyes for less than a second, and Ksama's heart threatened to burst with the collective passion of a world on the edge of annihilation. DevaSurya, the Queen of Graces, raised the flute to her full lips, while the TruthSpeaker resumed his song:

Life descends with fiery wake
To die beneath the burning lake
Precious One, Chosen One,
In deepest shadows lie
Masked until the timeless time,
When only you shall rise
To Sacred Purpose even I
Shall not presume
To prophecy

None of the Parisad observed the departure of the
Graces. By the time they had returned to their senses, the
chamber had darkened to twilight. Ksama, like the Graces,
had long since slipped silently from the room. The remaining
members of the Parisad resumed their argument with
revitalized fervor, now debating the hidden meanings of Raj
Satya's song. Ksama had no need. Even as the TruthSpeaker
had sung, Ksama had silently answered with a sacred vow to
Sh'ele:

*I promise to hide you and protect you, now and forever, until you
rise.*

From millions of miles away, even as Ksama shaped her
promise, someone was watching.

Present Day

Carver leaned out over the white pipe railing and listened to the attenuated voice on the cell phone. His face was a calm mask; his knuckles matched the rail. Far beneath his feet, sun-red waves crashed into the escarpment, and salty mist rode the updraft to moisten Carver's waiting face. He inhaled the ocean and let it roll out of his mouth like his own personal tide.

"That's considerably disappointing," he said finally, and dropped the phone onto a chaise.

Carver had almost forgotten the sensation called worry. He did not remember the last time he had been actually worried about anything. Whenever that had been, the circumstances had certainly involved Layton and their game. At times, the stakes of their little game had reached vast proportions. When that happened, people died. Not Carver and Layton, of course. Though once, very long ago, he and Layton had come very close to killing one another. Those days had long passed.

"Perhaps," he said.

No. Only others died when the stakes were high. And the stakes were higher now than they had ever been. Except for in the beginning, a moment so clouded in the mists of history that it seemed mythical even to Carver, who was half of the myth itself.

People were supposed to have died today. Yet they had not.

Now this man, Dossey, had arisen out of nowhere and insinuated his way into their game. Dossey's presence, as well as his offer, had raised the stakes. Worry had been reborn. A perpetual thought now ran through Carver's mind like a subliminal ticker tape:

How does he know who we are? How could he know our true names?

Carver turned back from the railing in time to see his wife, Miranda, glide through the French doors with a gleaming martini in each hand. Her thick blonde hair swirled in the wind, and her white silk dress billowed behind her like a cloud. The setting sun infused the delicate fabric with fire.

My God, how beautiful.

He cupped her elbows in his hands, gently, so as not to disturb the drinks, and pulled her close. In his time upon Earth, Carver had cultivated the many textures of cruelty. He had watched himself perform *cruelty* the way an actor portrays an arch villain. But given enough time, cruelty, like all things, becomes stale. Carver had accumulated time. He overflowed with his own history. He looked into his wife's indigo eyes, the most amazing eyes he had ever seen, really, and thought, not for the first time, *You don't deserve the cruelty of my secrets. One day soon, I will tell you who I really am.* As always, in the same instant, he wondered if telling her this truth would be the greater cruelty.

Miranda handed him his martini.

He kissed her, let his lips linger, not opening his mouth, just feeling their soft fullness. "Thank you, my love," he said.

"Anything wrong, darling?" she asked.

"Oh…no." He waived a dismissal toward the telephone. "Just a project not going well." He sipped his martini.

"Do you want to tell me about it?"

"I don't even want to think about it," he said. He fell into the chaise, caught her wrist, and pulled her down to him. Icy vodka splashed her wrist. "Watch the sunset with me."

She snuggled her way to comfort; he licked away the cool liquid from her warm skin.

From behind Miranda's shoulder, Carver scanned the darkening horizon. Her hair parted like a curtain. A red shaft of sunlight stabbed his eyes.

Failure.

Miranda nuzzled and nestled in his lap. The bloody sun sank beneath the distant ocean. An exquisite moment. And yet that single thought continued to erupt.

Failure.

Cary Walker and Ally Profett had escaped, and now they were God knows where. At least Layton's team was closing in on the rest of them. The Namayan Council had been meddling in their affairs for thousands of years, and they had developed skills that made them virtually untouchable. But Carver had finally imagined a viable plan to eliminate them. Once they were gone, the world would open to him completely.

Nevertheless, they still had to find Walker. He was the real key. Dossey had been very clear. Only Walker knew the location of the crystal. If it was truly as powerful as Dossey had said—even by half—their power would quantum leap from planetary to limitless. Once they controlled the crystal he would deal with Dossey. And Layton? Carver had no intention of letting him…

"Elias, my love?" Miranda said. "Where are you?" Carver raked his hand through her hair.

"Out there somewhere," he said. "Can you forgive me? It's so beautiful."

"Of course, my love," she said. Miranda settled deeper into Carver's arms, lowering her head to his shoulder. Carver pressed his cheek into her neck. Her body relaxed into sleep. The last sliver of sun sank into its watery grave, resting until it was time to rise again.

***

Near the western end of Davis Islands, The Ponce De Leon apartment building overlooks downtown Tampa. In the office of his ninth floor apartment, Simon Boon sliced a pair of stainless steel scissors through the *Chicago Sun-Times*. The excised story was buried on page eleven of the Metro section: "Authorities Puzzled by Empty Grave." The Chicago PD had no leads and no clue why anyone would steal a body.

Simon's desk, an inch-thick slab of tempered glass atop two mahogany file cabinets, was uncluttered except for the newspaper. Above the desk, a neatly spaced grid of cork board squares displayed a dozen similar clippings, though few of them heralded from such august publications as the *Sun-Times*. Simon had arrayed the stories in chronological order, left to right, with quarter-inch margins between each story. The margins were exactly a quarter of an inch. Simon knew this because he had measured them.

Simon was 36. His sandy hair lay pasted across his head in a comb-over that didn't fool anyone, not even himself. Persistent strands broke loose from the façade and fell across his eyes. His clothes, brown pants and a white, short-sleeved shirt, looked like he had slept in them for a week, but it had really only been one night. The bottom of his shirt pocket was Rorschached from leaky pens. He was over six feet tall, but perpetually stooped forward, gathering himself around his soft middle to look about 5-foot-8. The toes and heels of his shoes were scuffed down to bare leather, and his socks hung limply around his ankles. Simon was the only spot of lint in his otherwise perfectly dusted life.

He affixed the *Sun-Times* article to the right of an *Enquirer* story that warned of a cult of ghouls operating in San Diego, and below a clipping from the *Star* that detailed the sighting of *Chupa Cabra* in Miami. The *Chupa Cabra* sighting had been linked to the discovery of an open, empty coffin.

Simon's brown leather desk chair groaned when he leaned back to scan the cork board. But his briefcase held the article that interested him the most. The freshly interred body of Eric DelGado, 17, had disappeared from Jose Marti Cemetery in West Tampa nearly six weeks ago. Eric had been the son of a high school friend, and this article had provided Simon's initial impetus. He had compiled the others, dating back two years. All the missing bodies were of victims who had died in their late teens or early 20s. Now, as unlikely as it seemed, as unreliable as most of the sources might be, Simon believed he had discovered a pattern of grave robbings. He had even begun to lurk—and he felt certain that *lurk* was the appropriate word—around various Hillsborough County cemeteries in the dark of night.

Maybe this is a waste of time.

He sighed, laced his fingers behind his head, and settled his heels onto the desktop.

"Simon's Reporting Rule Number 37," he said. "Investigative reporting involves wasted time."

An answering meow from the other room drew his attention. He turned his head and tipped the tender balance of the chair. The inevitable backwards tilt began. Simon kicked out with his feet, tried to catch his toe on the underside of the desk; failing, he tried to shift enough weight to his lower half to bring the chair forward. It teetered for a precarious moment on the brink of balance. He flailed his arms and legs in the air like an upended dung beetle and thought briefly of Gregor Samsa.

The thud shook the entire ninth floor. Still in the chair, reclining now rather than sitting, Simon heaved a deep sigh and rolled slowly to his knees to check for broken bones. The thick carpet had cushioned his collapse. He was not seriously hurt. Best of all, no one saw. Not even the cat.

Simon stood and straightened his unstraightenable attire as the wall clock in the living room chimed out ten bells.

"It's 10 p.m.," he said. 'Do you know where your children's bodies are?"

Time for Simon to hunt body snatchers.

SECOND ARTICULATION

a killing field of dreams

a dragon man

a hobo council

a lost boy

a UPS delivery

sustained lurking

body-snatching, preppy poets

a bobbing boat

Present Day

Moist clover tickled Cary's cheek. A huge, green field. Plumes of black smoke billowed in the near distance. He sat up.

Broken bodies littered the landscape. Death's perfume ascended into the smoky sky. A murder of ravens wheeled endless circles and screamed corvine secrets to one another in the clouds. Thick mist advanced from the fringes of the killing field like a freshly risen army of angry souls.

I know this place. Manassas. First or second? How do I even know that?

Cary stood on trembling legs. Drumbeats pounded in his chest. Wind whirled about him, scattering the mist. Would the wind drive away the horror, or lay it bare? He tried to look away, but his eyes gaped like empty graves. A bugle call dopplered high to low like a Viking battle horn.

Evil was coming, but Cary was too exhausted to move.

***

He awoke under an Army Surplus sleeping bag in the back seat of a Ford Taurus with his head cradled on his canvas coat. The driver's window was open, and March air raked across his face. Concrete seams thumped under the spinning wheels.

The dark dream faded to full black. Cary gathered the

sleeping bag around his shoulders and sat up.

"Where are we? Whose car is this?"

"Mine," Ally answered. "Ours." She pointed out the front window. In the distance, the tip of the Washington Monument floated above a dense fog. Yellow moonlight painted it gold.

"Foggy," said Cary. He shivered, not sure if from the cold or from something else. He wrapped the sleeping bag closer still. "Why are we in D.C.?" *And how the hell did we get here?*

"Some people here might be able to help us," Ally said. She pressed a button on the armrest. Her window glided up.

"Hasn't been my experience," Cary said. Ally laughed.

You laughed like that in the cave. Like bells. How long ago was that? How long must it have taken us to drive to D.C.? I don't remember the drive at all. Only bad guys at my house, and a cave. Wait... How did—

"Not those people," she said. "Other people."

What was I just thinking?

"Who?"

"People you wouldn't expect." She laughed again.

The rhythmic click of the road tugged at Cary's memory. "I think I was dreaming." He rubbed the heel of his hand against his forehead. "Hey! You hit me."

"You were trying to scream. That's why I opened the window. To wake you up. Do you remember it?"

"Remember what?"

"Duh. Your dream?"

"I don't think I want to." He explored his forehead with his fingertips, expecting to find a bruise. There was none. "Why did you hit me?"

"What are you talking about? I didn't hit you."

They passed the beltway interchange. Washington drew into his universe.

"I have some questions," he said. He slipped over the armrest between the bucket seats and settled into the passenger side.

"I have answers," said Ally. "You're probably not going to like them."

***

"All this lurking might just be paying off," Simon Boon said to the night. He lurked at the moment in his gray, '84 Volvo 240 and watched through a trusty pair of Nikon binoculars. A shiny, black Range Rover killed its lights and turned left into Jackson Heights cemetery. The Rover backed up to a large mausoleum near the center of the park. Stark moonlight washed the graveyard to black and white and gray. Two boys walked into the crypt, calm as strolling into a Circle K for Twinkies and Dr. Pepper.

"Damn. Aren't you guys even a little bit scared? Gotta be spooky work."

He disabled the dome light and opened the door.

"Didn't you brats ever see *Night of the Living Dead*?"

Fifty yards from the Lurkmobile, Simon slunk through an opening in the fence and up to the concrete mausoleum. The slide of stone on stone inside the crypt was as clear as a sound effect from *Creature Feature*. He lay on dew-soaked grass and peeked between the concrete louvers.

A battery-powered lantern cast sharp shadows inside the stark white tomb. The kids were teenagers—early 20s at the most. Both wore polos and khakis.

Least your wardrobe matches the Rover. Where's the black lipstick and multiple piercings?

Instead of Goths, they were Greeks.

Grave-robbing frat boys? WTH?

One of the boys stood over 6-feet tall. His dirty blond hair swung back and forth across his forehead. Huge biceps stretched the sleeves of his Ralph Lauren Polo beyond factory specs. Simon half expected an Austrian accent. The other boy was a 5-foot-3-inch wire. But he was in charge. They had already removed the coffin from its niche and placed it on the floor. Each of them held a pry bar.

"Percy," said the little one. "You ready?"

Percy? You've gotta be shitting me. That would make you Byron?

"Hey, dude," Percy said, "I'm waiting on you here." *Alas, not Austrian. Typical Florida polyglot.*

They stuck their bars into the seam, and the lid swung up easily, blocking Simon's view. The scent of cloves rushed into the night air.

"Jesus," said Percy.

"Told you," said Byron.

***

Ally navigated government-gray streets lined with the dark skeletons of buildings past. Shadow people in brown brick doorways awoke to momentary life as the Taurus rolled by.

"How did we get away?" Cary asked.

"What are you talking about?"

"Back at my house? Bad guys? Guns? And I'm sure you hit me." He rubbed his thumb across his forehead again.

"I didn't hit you. And that's your question? How'd we get away?"

"Well, the first one."

"You don't remember?" Ally studied the cryptography of the street.

"We went into a cave. I didn't even know it was there, and...you sure you didn't hit me?"

A wave of vertigo passed through him. If he had not been sitting in a car, he would have hit the ground like a rock. Staccato sounds and images peppered his mind like a drum beat from the abyss: a glass knife driving into soft skin; blood spurting. Ally in the cave, her fingertips pressed together. The clash of swords, the twang of a bowstring, the thunk of an arrow finding the earth, the squawk of ravens, the snap of bone, the roar of the wind, a lesser scream that had arrived and a greater scream that was yet to come, and a million other indefinable noises. He teetered on the edge.

"I'd remember if I hit you," Ally said. Her voice drew him back from the brink, and the mental barrage skittered away. "And believe me, *you'd* remember." She turned left down a darker street. "It wasn't a cave. More like a tunnel. Sort of. I'll tell you all about it. But first, tell me about that walkway. And the patio. Where did those come from?"

Her voice soothed him. He found himself wanting to answer her, wanting to tell her his story. He shook his head. In the distance, a siren cried.

"The patio," he said. "I did that. Me and my son, Taylor. Five years ago. We laid that courtyard...but...but I never saw any caves, much less a—"

"You have a son? I didn't know that."

"Feels like a long time ago," Cary said.

"Where is he?"

Cary studied his hands. "I'm not sure, really." His voice accumulated distance. "He was in school. College. Dropped out in the middle of the fall." Cary raised his eyes to look at Ally, but only made it half way before his gaze dropped. "The truth is...we don't really talk that much. Not for a long time. The only reason I knew he wasn't in school is his mother called to see if he was with me."

"Aren't you worried about him?"

"I...I'm not sure." Carcasses of buildings lumbered past the car like the hulking shades of dinosaurs. "I guess..." Cary's left hand found its way to his wrist, and he tried to scrub away the rising pain. "I guess I'd at least feel better if I knew he was all right." He reached for his wallet. "I've got his picture..."

Ally slid the Taurus against a tall, granite curb bordering a huge empty lot. "We're here."

On either side of the lot, husks of buildings waited their turns to collapse. Ally double wrapped a green scarf around her neck and stepped out of the car. Up and down the block, phantoms slipped back into the safety and anonymity of their doorways.

"You want to go in there?" Cary asked.

"Here be the place, matey." She hooked her arm inside his elbow and leaned close. "Come on," she added. "You can protect me."

Broken slabs of concrete marked the border between street and no-man's land. The skeletons of last year's weeds swayed like straw men blocking their way. High on the crumbling remnants of a brick wall at the rear of the lot, shadows danced like wraiths. Someone had a fire going back there.

They parted the sea of dead flora and crossed over into a different world. The fire lived in a rusty, 55-gallon drum near the back left corner of the lot. Red-orange shafts of light spilled from random holes in the barrel, and steam gushed from the spout of an enamel coffee pot hanging from a rebar tripod above tongues of flame. Several shapes shifted to and fro around the glowing cylinder. A ribbon of smoke, laden with the acrid tang of petroleum, burned Cary's nostrils.

Doré. Divine Comedy.

Cary choked back a cough.

The shadowy shapes resolved into distinct individuals. Nine of them. Homeless. One man stood guard. He wore a black wool greatcoat over a gray hooded sweatshirt. His hands, partially covered by dingy, fingerless gloves, rested interlaced upon his belly. Yellow streetlamps cast deep shadows into the vertical folds on either side of his mouth and the lacework wrinkles around his eyes. At one time in his life, this man had smiled. Often. Now he leered at Ally, his face a lascivious, ochre mask. Steam rose from his nostrils and disappeared into the night.

A dragon man.

Deep in Cary's mind, a beastly roar joined the muffled background noise.

The other eight men stepped in and out of the firelight, mumbling guttural incantations that echoed with the rumblings in Cary's head. Cary struggled to keep the inner soundscape from merging with the outer. Ally leaned in close.

"What the hell are they doing?" Cary asked.

"That would take way too long to explain. Ask him if we can share their fire." Her voice anchored him to the moment.

"Are you insane?"

She giggled. "You have to ask him if we can join them, or he won't acknowledge you."

"Why?"

Ally pressed her hands together in front of her heart and bowed her head. "Even in these modern times, the old ways must be observed. And, besides that, sometimes the only answer is 'That's just the way it is.'" She thumped him three times on the chest with two fingers. "Guess. What. Dude. This is one of those times."

"What are you talking about? This is just a bunch of...weird dancing bums? What possible difference...?"

Ally's eyes became the center of gravity to Cary's vision. *How the hell does she do that?*

He struggled to unlock his gaze, struggled to speak, aware all the while that this tiny battle was a waste of time. He would eventually do what she asked. At the exact moment he reached that conclusion, Ally smiled and nodded once.

"Art of War 101," she said. "*Sun Tzu.* Never fight a battle you don't know you can win." She smiled. "Unless, of course, you're willing to make a sacrifice for a higher cause."

"What? How did you know that I was—"

She raised her eyebrows and tilted her head toward the sentinel. The old man waited while the others continued their catatonic song and dance. Cary shrugged and cleared his throat. Once. Twice. The man ignored him. Ally jabbed a firm elbow into Cary's ribs.

"Excuse me," Cary said. The man continued to take no notice. "Excuse me," Cary said, a little louder. Still no response.

Ally let loose an exaggerated sigh. "Just say it."

Cary shrugged. "I wonder if we could...uh...share your fire?"

All of the figures stopped and turned their collective attention to Cary. A shiver that began somewhere around his knees shot straight up Cary's back and out the top of his head. His teeth chattered. Ally giggled again. The guardian stepped forward and looked directly into Cary's eyes. For a timeless beat, Cary was both here in a vacant lot staring into this homeless man's face, and outside of Winter Star two days ago, lost in Ally's gaze. Time's edges grew soft; Cary was a living jigsaw puzzle with missing pieces. An all-too-familiar whorl of terror spun inside him.

Ally bounced on her toes like a rocket about to lift off.

"You are welcome," the man said. His voice echoed inside Cary's head.

Did his lips move?

Instead of panic, acute awareness surged through Cary's body. Crisp night air washed over his bare face and hands. His feet felt rooted to the ground, like they had, well, roots. The terror that had, moments before, threatened to draw him into perpetual darkness, now burned away like fog at sunrise.

Centered. I've never felt so centered. And solid.

"Thank you," Cary managed.

The man held Cary's gaze, but he extended his arms in front of him. And just in time, because Ally had already launched herself into the air. The man caught her like a rag doll and gathered her to his chest, finally turning his attention from Cary to her.

"Lethe," he said. "It's wonderful to see you." His long arms engulfed her, and she became a little girl in his embrace. He kissed the top of her head and drew her closer. After nearly a minute, she slipped back to earth and straightened her coat.

"Cary Walker," she said. "I'd like you to meet Nelson Profett. My Father."

***

Taylor Walker stood on the corner of Ashley Street and Kennedy Boulevard in downtown Tampa. Warm March wind coursed through the 20-year-old's greasy hair. Green paratrooper pants and a gray sweatshirt that had long ago assumed the uniform colors of the street draped over his gaunt, 6-foot frame. His ravaged Doc Martens might once have belonged to Frankenstein's creature. A wild, wispy beard failed to conceal his thin jaw; his sea-green eyes were all but lost in the shadow of his brow. A knotted red bandana encircled his neck. With dirty fingertips, he worried the perpetual itch in the notch at the base of his skull.

An ocean of finely dressed humanity—attendees of the final night of *Phantom of the Opera* at the Performing Arts Center—flowed around him from north to south. Across Kennedy Boulevard, Mopheit Tower, a 33-story sandstone cylinder, rose into the Tampa night. Two spotlights on its roof cast enigmatic beams into the void of space. At one time, Taylor had wondered why its spotlights were aimed to the sky. Now he no longer cared. They were the most beautiful lights he had ever seen, matched only by the flashing "Walk" sign on the other side of Ashley.

The pedestrian river parted and flowed around him. No one paused to speak. The light changed to "Don't Walk," and the human river froze.

The drug was called "Nirvana." At least, that was the street name. He had no idea what its pharmaceutical name had been. Jackie Blue hadn't told him. Taylor had taken the drug nearly six months ago, on September 17th, the same day he had happened to run into Jackie. The sidewalks had been crowded that night, too.

Initially, Nirvana had brought on the normal rush, the sweet, rising anticipation in the belly and the perma-grin that he knew from mescaline or X or acid. But instead of the expected amusement park of the mind, an overwhelming oneness burned through him.

They named this right. I have got to get some more of this!

Even as those words had risen to the surface of his thoughts, certainty had risen in his mind. Getting more Nirvana would not be necessary. From that night forward, Taylor's entire world trembled in a precarious and elegant balance; every object, every idea in this huge, pulsing universe vibrated in perfection, just as it was. The effects of this drug would never wear off; they would be with him until the moment of his death. And that final countdown had already begun. The drug itself was killing him. The chemical compound had begun to take his life the moment it had made contact with the saliva on his tongue.

And it was worth it. Death, too, was a perfect vibration.

That same night, Taylor had first heard the Angel.

"The world is beautiful now, is it not?" she had said. Her voice rang like a choir in his private cathedral. Taylor had pirouetted around and around, searching the endless faces for the person who had spoken to him. But none of them had known what he knew. None of these mortals understood that he had transformed into a different order of being. Only the bearer of that voice had known.

"Yes," Taylor had said. "Where are you?"

"Such things no longer matter," the Angel had said.

"Then *who* are you?" He searched for the right words. "*What* are you?"

"Ahhh, a much more significant question. All seek the one true answer, do they not? For you, I am that answer. In the time you have left, we will discover that answer together."

Now, over six months later, she was with him almost constantly.

Taylor stood on the corner and observed all the poor, rich losers gift-wrapped in their precious cloth. They waited like robots, in complete ignorance. His heart reached out to them.

"How can they not see the beauty?" he asked. "How can I show them what I know?"

"Watch them closely," said the Angel. "You will see why. Tonight I will show you something new, something wonderful."

***

"You're sure they were Carver's people?" Nelson asked.

Ally huddled between Cary and Nelson; the three of them leaned forward to soak in as much warmth as they could from the fire. The other men sat in two groups of four on either side of them. Cary found himself wondering whether they were real or only phantom props in his own dark tableau. He didn't think he had ever actually had a hallucination, but he was increasingly unsure about the solidity of his reality, especially in the last 48 hours. They all drank steaming cups of black coffee from enamel mugs that matched the hanging pot.

If this is a hallucination, it's really well constructed. Maybe outfitted by Williams Sonoma?

Cary had no idea he was sitting around a hobo campfire with 10 of the most lethal people on the planet.

"Without a doubt, Daddy," she said.

Cary found it odd to hear this woman, who had saved his life and walked him through some tunnel he hadn't even known existed—*Did that really happen? And she hit me. I know she hit me*—calling someone "Daddy."

She took a long pull on her coffee. "I sort of...ran into...Giles Boyette in Burnsville."

"More than ran into, from what I heard," Cary said.

Nelson waited.

Ally's voice grew a little quieter. "He tried to kill me."

The group remained silent, digesting this last information.

"And?" Nelson asked.

"He won't be able to walk for a while."

Nelson nodded.

"But...who's Giles Boyette?" Cary asked.

"He works for Gareth Stokes, Elias Carver's Chief of Security." He turned to Ally and shrugged his eyebrows toward Cary. "How much does he know?"

"Nothing. Less than." She laughed and then hesitated. "Almost."

"What?" Nelson said. Ally stared at the fire.

"I had to bring him out through the Tangle." The cold night air tightened around them.

"If you recall," said the man to Nelson's right, "I predicted this would turn out badly." His voice was low and resonant, and his long chin protruded from the shadow of his hood. Three men sitting next to him murmured assent.

"This situation has nothing to do with that, Warner."
Nelson's voice remained calm, but it contained a reservoir of
animosity.

Palpable tension pulled at Cary's mind, tearing him in two
directions, one toward Warner and the other to the group of
men to his left. He suddenly became aware that, even though
these nine men were one group, two distinct factions existed,
and he was sitting between them.

The man to Cary's left inched forward; he tilted his head,
creating the illusion that only shadow lived behind the edges
of his hood. He paused, waiting, perhaps with respect.

"Teo," Nelson said, "you have something to contribute?"

Teo lowered his hood. He was in his early 30s, with a
shaved head and a five-day beard. His round face, framed by
a cowl, gave him the appearance of a young friar. But there
was no mistaking the power in his eyes. He might have been
years younger than Warner, but he was every bit his equal.

"Perhaps their attack on you was a mistake?" Teo said.

Ally unwound her scarf. The gash on her neck had
scabbed over. Several of the hooded figures caught their
breath at the sight of her near fatal wound. "No mistake," she
said. "Besides, we heard Stokes give the order to kill me."

Cary nodded.

"I told you, Nelson," Warner said. "I told you it was a
bad choice. She just can't handle them."

Ally exploded to her feet and jabbed her finger toward
Cary. "What do you call getting him out before they captured
him, huh?" A collective gasp emerged from the group. Cary
thought he saw a ghost of a smile pass over Teo's face. Ally's
tiny frame managed to loom over Warner. "What would you
prefer?" she said. "That I let them take him rather than risk
revealing one of our precious secrets? Where would we be
then?"

"Alethea," Nelson said. His quiet voice was a gavel.

Warner pulled his hood back, slow and deliberate,
releasing a dark, silver mane. He returned Ally's stare but
remained seated.

Ally bowed her head and sat back down. "I'm sorry, Father," she said. Then she looked at Warner and continued in a formal tone. "Forgive me, Warner. We have had a long and difficult journey. We barely escaped with our lives. And truly, none of us knows where we would be if Cary had fallen into their hands."

Warner lowered his head slightly, masking his face in shadow. But his potent eyes remained locked on Ally's.

"Hold on a second," Cary said. "What the hell are you people talking about? Who is this Carver guy, and what could he possibly want with me?"

Several hooded heads turned in his direction, and a giggle escaped from his lips.

Nobody expects the Spanish Inquisition!

Ally held Warner's gaze for another moment and then glanced at Nelson before she, too, turned to Cary. "I told you, we don't really know. All we know is that you have something that they want."

"Something important to them," Warner said.

"Important enough to break The Accords," added Teo. He looked at Ally. "Important enough to kill you." Cary thought he saw a spark pass between them.

"We've been watching...Carver...for a long time," Ally said.

"Long time," added a man on the far left.

Ally smiled before continuing.

"Yes, a really long time. And another man, Cyrus Layton, his enemy—"

"Adversary," Warner said. "There's a significant difference."

"True," Ally said. "We watch his adversary, as well. That's what we do. Mostly." She looked directly at Warner. "That's what *I* do."

Cary shook his head once, twice, trying to throw off the improbability of these fables.

"I don't understand," he said finally.

Nelson reached around Ally and placed his hand firmly on Cary's shoulder. "Don't worry, son. It's only going to get worse."

All the men laughed again, even Warner. But he stopped abruptly. "They followed you," he said.

The group quickly stuffed bedrolls and coffee mugs into backpacks.

Warner shook his head once and slung his pack over his shoulder.

"No way," Ally said. "They must have already known where you were."

Warner impaled her with a long, curious stare before turning to Nelson. "We'll discuss this at the next site." Eight of the men trotted toward the back wall, dispersing in several directions with choreographed precision. A light flashed in the back left corner.

Warner turned to Nelson. "Are you coming?"

"I'll find you there," Nelson said. "I have unfinished business with my daughter."

Warner shook his head again and trotted away. He passed a solitary figure before disappearing into the shadows. Teo stood alone at the edge of the darkness and looked back at Ally before he, too, turned and disappeared.

***

Simon squirmed on the grass, angling for a better view through the concrete louvers.

"Holy crap," Percy said. "I've seen this guy. He looks better dead than he did when he was alive."

"They all do," said Byron.

All? This is good news. Well, good news in this context. Isn't it?

"Put him in the van," added Byron. "I need to get home. I've got an Economics study group at eight."

Economics? Study group? You gonna bring cookies? What kind of pansy-ass grave robbers are you guys, anyway?

"How much am I getting again?" Percy asked. He lifted the corpse onto his shoulder and carried it to the rear door of the Rover. Byron opened a can of red spray paint.

"Hundred bucks a body," he said. "Hey! Careful! No

broken bones."

Percy lowered the corpse onto a sheet of Visqueen in the back of the Rover. "Shit," he said. He dusted off his hands. "A hundred a pop? Let me grab a couple more."

"No," Byron said. "It's not like that. Can't be just anybody."

"Any...*body*." Percy laughed.

Keep your day job, kid.

"Ri-i-i-i-ight," Byron said. "Anyway, only the ones they tell us. The ones they ask for." He pointed to the coffin. "Put that back, will you?"

"Too bad," said Percy. He hoisted the coffin like it was an empty cardboard box and slid it back into its niche. "Where are we taking him?"

"You won't believe it," Byron said. "Be ready in a sec."

Byron replaced the marble cover and then shook the can of paint. The clatter echoed off bare concrete. He painted something across the niche door. Simon tried to see, but the louvers were too slanted.

Percy and Byron climbed in the Rover and pulled away. Simon ran on tiptoe directly toward his Volvo. No time to look for the hole in the fence. He'd have to climb it. His belly flopped like a great wave with each step.

I have got to get in better shape.

The Rover's brake lights flared as the boys turned west onto Lake, toward Nebraska Avenue and Hooker's Row.

"No way," Simon rasped. "Not necrophiliacs."

He hit the fence at a full run and scaled it in one fluid move.

Wow. Not bad.

But the top bar sagged under his bulk; jagged wire caught the side of his trousers and suspended him halfway over. He kicked his legs like an upended palmetto bug.

Wasn't I just doing this at home?

Simon's pants gave way, ripping open the left pocket. A burr on the fence top sliced into his hip. His lungs emptied when he thudded to the ground. He lay on the moist earth, trying to suck air while the low roar of the Range Rover receded into the East Tampa night. When he finally sat up, the most sapient comment he could muster was, "Shit!"

Simon limped back to the mausoleum. The crypt reeked of fresh paint. Red graffiti covered the niche. It looked Arabic. Drops ran from the edges, making the design look like it had been painted with fresh blood.

"Helter Skelter," Simon said. "Only weirder." He took several pictures with his digital. "But maybe less dangerous." He dropped the camera into his coat pocket. "At least...so far."

Simon Boon, Hunter of Body Thieves, plodded back to his car, whistling "The Worms Crawl In." His pocket flapped back and forth, keeping time as he walked. Simon shook his head and laughed.

Whistling in the graveyard. Whistling in the freaking graveyard.

***

"This way," Nelson said, "but be quiet."

He trotted toward the shell of an old brick building to the left. Ally grabbed Cary's hand, dragging him along. Cary let himself be pulled yet again.

I'm sensing a theme here.

Nelson led them behind a ragged boxwood hedge overrun with volunteers. He shoved his shoulder against the brick wall, and a door swung inward, creating a dark mouth surrounded by thick, square teeth. When he pressed the door back into place from the inside, the bricks meshed together perfectly, and the portal was virtually undetectable.

They climbed three flights of wooden stairs, feeling their way in the darkness, emerging at last into a room that took up the entire top story. Portions of the ceiling had long ago collapsed, and the swollen moon painted the wooden floor a pale gray. Cary produced a soft whistle.

Nelson pressed a finger to his lips. "Quiet, I said. They're very close."

Ally said that. Those exact words. In the cave.

Once again, the threads of Cary's memory attempted to merge with the present, and reality's veil threatened to fall away. He clapped his hands to his ears, trying to shut out the staccato din in his brain.

Maybe I'm strapped down somewhere in a loony bin, pumped to the gills with Thorazine. Maybe I don't even exist at all.

Ally's hand lit on his shoulder, and the madness flew away. "You okay?"

He nodded.

They crept to an empty window frame and watched a UPS truck jerk to a stop behind the Taurus. Eight swift shadows poured from the back.

"You guys expecting a delivery?" Cary asked.

"Quiet!" Nelson and Ally hissed in unison.

The operatives deployed in silence across the lot. Another man eased out of the front and sauntered to the fire barrel. He was 6-foot-9, slightly curved, and thin as a rapier; his fluid strides seemed not to touch the dingy earth. While the others searched the weeds and shadows of the perimeter, the tall man performed a cursory examination of the ground. One by one, his subordinates joined him, each shaking his head. The leader lifted the coffee pot from its hook, sniffed it and tossed it into the barrel. A thick plume of steam billowed above the fire and died as abruptly as it had been born. The tall man nodded once. The soldiers double-timed back to the truck, shades disappearing into shadows. As he stepped up to the driver's seat, the leader lifted a cell phone to his ear. Not a single word had been spoken during the entire operation.

Ally slid down to the floor with her back against the wall. "Worse than we thought," she said.

"A lot worse," Nelson said.

"Why?" Cary asked. "We got away. They didn't find us."

"Yeah," Ally said. "There's that."

"Then what's the problem?"

"The problem is," Nelson said, "that knife of a man who ruined my coffee pot was Ian Cord. Those men don't work for Carver. They work for Layton."

"What does that mean?" asked Cary.

Ally stared at him for a long moment before speaking. "Carver and Layton are working together."

"In a period of less than two days," Nelson said, "they have attempted to kill both of you, and they came here most likely to kill all of us." He closed his eyes and ran both hands through his hair, pulling it tight at the back of his head. "They're trying to eliminate the Council," he barely whispered. "What is it that you have, Mr. Walker?"

"I don't have anything," Cary said. *Not even my mind.* "Well," he added, rubbing his wrist, "at least they didn't notice your car."

Ally returned his gaze. Her face relaxed into a wise and weary smile. The rumble of an approaching diesel engine shook the floor. All three watched as a tow truck latched on to the Taurus and pulled it away.

Before Time

~

Ksama

Ksama crept through the labyrinth of alleyways in the waterfront district, Sh'ele bound tight to her back in a black leather sheath. She held close to the brick walls of the Port Complex, slipping through shadows, advancing in silence. The nearer she approached Q'Tal Harbor, the more her footfalls blended with the beat of waves and the cries of night birds.

She had heard no sounds of pursuit, yet her intangible senses assured her she was being hunted. This was no surprise. Even in the light of the Graces' song, Syrgala would have remained entrenched in his dark scheme, and he had an army of operatives at his disposal.

She had formed her plan even as Raj Satya had sung. Only yesterday, while dangling her feet in the reflecting pool in Tirtham Commons, Ksama had admired the open sloop moored to the seawall in Q'Tal Harbor. She had closed her eyes and imagined climbing into the cockpit, hoisting the canvas, and sailing west across the Nameless Sea into forbidden waters.

The Apsara had charted and sailed trade routes to the east for thousands of years. The western waters were different.

Mysterious. Unknown. In ancient Apsarian mythology, Myrtu, the Living God of Death, lingered eternally on the western horizon, where the sun died each day. Though they were a sophisticated people, the Apsara retained this primitive taboo. Few sailors ventured out of site of land to the west. Perhaps the taboo was reinforced by the reality that those few who did sail into the Nameless Sea often did not return.

Her plan was simple, then. After slipping out of the chamber, she had hurried to the Temple of Uktenah, deactivated the mounting bracket, and retrieved Sh'ele. She would carry Sh'ele to the *Varuna* and voyage west. Somewhere in the vast, mysterious seas she would find *Asita*, the Islands of Dreams.

Ksama had first seen visions of the Islands of Dreams when she was a small child. In the powerful landscape of her developing mind, she traveled frequently to Asita: it became her inner sanctuary.

Her teacher, Dayate, had asked her, "Does Asita exist only in your inner worlds, or is it also somewhere in the physical? Perhaps by imagining it so strongly you bring it into existence?"

Ksama had not known the answer. She knew only that, during her travels to her inner worlds, she had seen Asita then as clearly as she saw the City of Light now. The image had never faded from her thoughts:

A ring of dark, mountainous islands embracing an inland sea.
An inlet, almost invisible in the face of a black slate cliff.
Two red-tailed hawks circling above the entrance.
A waterfall so high that it appears to pour from the clouds.
Stone steps that wind upward to the sky.
A ziggurat carved from living rock.

Now she could only hope and trust that the island existed, and that she could find her way there. If she succeeded, Ksama would have to conceal Sh'ele. The power signature of the crystal would act as a beacon, calling out to its counterparts. If Syrgala had managed to acquire just one of them, then his followers would have no trouble finding her, no matter how far away she sailed.

But these were problems Ksama would confront after she found Asita. Once there, she would find some way to hide the crystal, to protect it, to keep it hidden until, as the TruthSpeaker had sung, it would rise to its own sacred purpose. If Ksama's own end came before that resurrection, then Sh'ele's hiding place would pass into the Eternal Mysteries. No one would ever find it.

Perhaps that outcome was as desirable as any.

Present Day

"Look to their eyes," said the Angel. "Their true eyes. Not the two, but the one."

Taylor studied the man beside him. He was in his mid 50s, with a silver-streaked head of black, wavy hair. A dark smudge blotted out the center of his forehead.

Dies cinerum. Ash Wednesday. How did I know that? I never studied Latin.

But Ash Wednesday was weeks past. And this smudge moved. A pyramid-shaped shadow between the man's eyebrows, its tip invisible beneath his skin, spun in slow, counterclockwise revolutions. It was more than a shadow, really. It was the absence of light. Taylor pressed his attention into the darkness, and the spinning slowed.

Everything slowed. Then all movement stopped.

The songs of Taylor's world became a lethargic buzz. He observed the rest of the frozen walkers. A shadow pyramid hung at the center of each forehead.

Taylor pressed his index and middle fingers to his own head. The skin was tender, almost painful to the touch, like he had pulled a scab off a fresh wound. His fingers passed easily beyond the barrier of skin and bone to touch...*electricity.* He pulled the fingers out.

"Yes," she said. "Yours is gone. I have removed it. You are almost ready to join me. Do you wish to become one with me?"

51

"More than anything," Taylor said.

"Go to the park, then. Wait for me there."

All around him, humanity hung suspended in the temporal void. Then, like a wave catching up with itself, Taylor-time and world-time reconciled. The songs of the city shifted from a low, humming chant to a symphony of noise, an audible tidal surge of footsteps, conversations, engines surging and dying, car horns braying, and tires soughing on smooth concrete. The pedestrian light shifted to a vibrant white. *Walk*, it commanded, and the people flowed over the edge of the curb and into the street, sweeping Taylor with them like a freshly fallen leaf in a river. But a leaf that knows.

***

Simon braced his hands on the windowsill and scanned the Tampa skyline. At the far edge of downtown, a TPD helicopter circled Jackson Heights. Its 20-million-candle-power spotlight searched streets and alleyways for illicit purveyors of sex acts and mind-altering substances.

Closer to Simon's apartment, the two spotlights atop Mopheit Tower searched heaven for unknowable answers.

Simon peeled off his ruined pants and tossed them in the garbage. A raised, red welt decorated the full length of his left thigh. He assaulted it liberally with Neosporin and collapsed into a worn, beige Lazy Boy. The lanky, gray tabby jumped into his lap.

"Hey! Freddy Krueger!" Simon said. "Watch the razors." Woodstein turned circles and finally settled into a purring ball—albeit one with claws.

"So," he asked the cat, "what do we actually know? Some unknown weirdoes are paying Percy and Byron a hundred bucks a pop for dead bodies. Specific bodies." Woodstein blinked, indicating complete comprehension and utter indifference.

"The body looked better dead than alive. I can think of a lot of people I'd say that about. My editor. Couple of ex-girlfriends." He closed his eyes and lay back. Woodstein shifted again to find the sweet spot. "Byron said 'they all do.' They all look better? That's got to mean something. Right?" The cat didn't respond—unless a yawn can be construed as an answer. Simon stood abruptly, launching Woodstein onto the floor. The feline glowered and then turned his back.

"Sorry, Woody." Simon settled in at his desk and created a preliminary list:

> *Known:*
> *$100 per body.*
> *Only designated bodies.*
> *They drove west. Toward downtown? St. Pete?*
> *Wealthy—Prob. Parents' Range Rover—Prob. Percy's*
> *Weird Graffiti*
>
> *Questions:*
> *Why would someone want specific bodies?*
> *Why do they look better dead?*
> *Where did they take it?*
> *Are they stored there, or are they only brought there?*
> *Who are these kids? Wealth=Jesuit, Tampa Prep, Plant*
> *   HS, UT*
> *What does the graffiti mean?*

"Looks like I don't know shit."

Simon plugged the camera into his computer and printed copies of the picture. Definitely a word of some sort. Middle Eastern. At the bottom of the page he scribbled: *Call Freddy B.*

***

Taylor flowed across the street. Finely dressed theatergoers stared or pretended not to see him. *Just another street crazy.* He had become accustomed to this reaction months ago. He allowed the disapproving current to sweep him along, then he veered off and climbed the narrow alleé to Mopheit Park, nine feet above the street. He settled in, a young Buddha under a crape myrtle Boddhi Tree, and watched the oblivious crowd scurry along beneath him.

"I am here," said the Angel. Her voice had come from inside his head, as always. But this time it had also come from somewhere behind him.

"Where?" Taylor asked. "Where are you? I can't see you." He spun in a circle, still sitting. A community of the homeless talked and laughed at the rear of the park. Too far away. His eyes turned again to the spotlights atop Mopheit Tower.

"Are you up there?"

"Here," she said.

A glow—soft at first, like an unblinking firefly—emanated from the dark center of the plaza and grew to a brilliance that only Taylor could see. The light lifted him to his feet and drew him into its core. Amorphous radiance coalesced into two enormous wings. At their center, the figure of a woman shone with the brilliance of a thousand suns. She enfolded him with her wings—and many, many arms—embracing him as a mother cradles a beloved child to her breast. From the corner of his eye, Taylor glimpsed a chitinous shape skitter away at the edge of the darkness. He squinted to see, but the itch at the back of his head became an ice pick. He slammed his eyes shut. The Angel pressed her soft hands to his face. The pain departed as quickly as it had arrived.

"Very soon, now," she said. Her song was his personal balm. "Very soon we will be one. I have promised you, have I not? Are you ready to know the truth?"

"I am ready," Taylor said.

"Revelation," she sang, "begins like a single leaf falling at the threshold of autumn, like a floating particle of rain at the edge of the storm. Draw closer to me now, and I will whisper your True Name. Do you desire to know your True Name?"

"My True Name," Taylor said. "Oh, yes. Please. How do I come closer? What is my True Name?"

"Open your eyes wide. Relax now," she whispered. "Relax and I will tell you who you are."

The human awareness that once was Taylor began to drain away as blood pours from the neck of a Levitical Lamb. His mind emptied, and the Angel's siren whispers echoed in the ensuing vacuum, preparing to reanimate the shell with nascent identity.

And yet, somewhere, hidden in the folded shadows of consciousness, Taylor remained, cowering in the darkness, watching as a frightened child watches for the arrival of the beast, or of God.

***

Carver sat up in bed, a fluid shadow in the night, instantly awake and alert. His phone was about to ring.

Why would Layton call me at, he consulted the blue glow of the digital clock, *3:13?*

Miranda breathed evenly, shifting the silk sheets with each breath. The mattress rose and fell in increments too small to see. But Carver felt them. She did not stir when he slipped from the bed and out of the room.

Carver relaxed his mind, allowing it to soften and merge into the glowing entanglement that extended in all directions beyond the borders of his personal universe. Shining threads connected him to the thoughtforms of the world; he navigated to a familiar strand, the filament that articulated to Layton. Fear surged in Carver's gut, but this fear was not his own. He observed it, measured its texture and intensity.

Carver had been the architect at *El Mirador* when he had met the Olmec *brujo*, Azatlán. The *brujo* had initiated him into *La Maraña Luminosa*, the Tangle of Light, the unbounded network of nodes and filaments connecting all beings, all energies. Azatlán schooled him in the art of dancing upon the shining strands of other's thoughts, desires, and fears. Carver had learned to venture out upon that network, like a spider upon its own threads. Still, even after all these years, he did not know how to open the LightGates and travel along them with his physical body. Only the Namayan held that secret.

But if what Dossey said was true, Walker's crystal would give him that power, and much more.

Initially, Carver had been unable to differentiate the thoughts and emotions of others from his own. Azatlán had taught him to separate his own vibrations from those of other people, and thus to bathe fully in the ocean of another being's presence, as in a dream, when the dreamer is both the observer and the actor.

He bathed in the anxiety that flooded through him now. Layton was worried. This in itself was nothing new. Layton was always worried about something. But the intensity of this feeling was...dangerous?

Carver's mind ventured farther along the filament, into the nodes that articulated him and Layton to Cary Walker and Alethea Profett. However, even though Carver could not penetrate the borders of their worlds, he could still see that they were not the source of Layton's anxiety.

No. Something new had developed, something significant enough to disturb Layton's quantum field. At its edges, spikes of anxiety erupted like storms on the sun.

Carver's mind receded from the jagged landscape of Layton's fear while his body stepped out onto the balcony. A steady heartbeat of waves thrummed against the base of the cliff. Their rhythm vibrated upward through the rock face and tingled the soles of Carver's feet. A slightly imperfect moon cast a milky path on the water, a moonlight aisle that beckoned him to nameless lands.

Carver smiled. *Here there be monsters.*

The Unknown had always been Carver's favorite place on the map—even if he had sometimes found himself sailing over the edge.

"You never know how much is enough," he said to the moon, "until you know how much is too much."

Life continued to become more interesting.

He settled into the chaise lounge and wondered if Layton had ever learned about La Maraña. Perhaps Layton knew that Carver was waiting for his call, just as Carver knew that

Layton was, even now, activating his phone. It didn't matter. Soon, now. Just a few more seconds.

Carver answered before it rang. He held the phone to his ear and waited. At the other end, across the continent, somewhere on the Atlantic—though Carver could not determine where—Layton mirrored the silence for a time, then finally spoke.

"Do you already know?"

Carver considered the question. "Apparently not."

"They found Ubai. And the Prototype."

Damn. "You worry too much about insignificant details. You always have."

"This is not insignificant," said Layton. "If they find the stone—"

Ah, well. No getting around it now. "They won't."

"Of course they will," Layton said. "And when they do—"

"I moved it," said Carver. "Years ago."

Silence.

Layton's breathing belied his measured containment.

"You have the Benben?" Layton asked.

Carver laughed. "Why do you insist on calling it that?"

Layton ignored the question. "We agreed it would remain buried. Where is it?"

"Somewhere safe," Carver said.

"I'm beginning to remember why I stopped trusting you."

"Don't you think," Carver said, "that if I had wanted to use it, I would have killed you years ago?"

"You should have told me."

"I thought it was best not— "

"You should have told me!"

"You're right," said Carver. He took a deep breath and released a sigh just loud enough for Layton to hear. "I should have told you."

"There are still the inscriptions to consider."

"Let the diggers dig," Carver said. "By the time anyone is able to decipher them, if they ever succeed, you and I will already be in possession of the crystal. By then their knowledge of us will be insignificant compared to our power.

But…remind me again, Brother," said Carver, "why you felt compelled to have our histories chiseled in stone."

Layton laughed. "It seemed like a good idea at the time."

"Vanity," Carver said, "is the *Druaga*'s favorite sin." But he was laughing, too.

"Let the Lord of Demons concern himself with his own sins," Layton said. "When this episode has concluded, he will be working for us."

"Perhaps," Carver replied. *Or perhaps he will answer only to me.*

"I'm sending you the file now," Layton said. The phone went dead.

Carver's gaze fell once again into the beckoning pathway of light upon the moving sea, an aisle more sharply defined now that the moon had fallen nearer to the horizon.

He locked his office door behind him and brought up the web page on a large, transparent monitor suspended from the ceiling. An image popped up, the familiar apex of a ziggurat protruding from a sea of ancient sands. The article began beneath the photo:

AP: Baghdad: Today archeologists revealed that they have found what is believed to be the oldest ziggurat ever excavated. The tip of the structure was uncovered as a result of a bomb dropped by a US Navy F-25 in Southern Iraq, 40 miles southeast of Nasiriyah, near Ur.

"We're obviously very excited," said Jada Ellis, senior field researcher at the Royal Archeological Society. "This temple predates Ur by at least a thousand years and is likely the oldest such structure on the planet. We may literally be looking at the first great temple ever built. I mean, this is a very sophisticated structure, using quarried stones so precise that they did not require mortar. It's a miracle the bomb didn't damage it."

The temple Ellis refers to is a step pyramid, or ziggurat, measuring an estimated 60 feet from base to apex.

"One of the truly amazing features of this find," said Ellis, "is the condition of the site. This building appears to be virtually pristine. I've never seen anything like it."

Dr. Ellis's team has yet to venture inside the structure, but, based on the dimensions, she expects to find similarities to later pyramids, specifically the Khufu structure that dominates the Giza plateau and the Djoser pyramid, believed to have been constructed by the Architect, Imhotep, at Saqqara around 2600 B.C. The excavation is expected to be completed within three months. Plans to venture inside remain uncertain. "I can't wait to see what we'll find when we do," said Ellis.

I'll bet you can't. Carver closed the file and returned to the balcony. Behind him, dawn crested the Trinity Alps and cast a fiery blush across the ocean, setting the waves aflame.

Imhotep. A golden oldie. And Saqqara.

He laughed.

What a mess that was.

The moon floated above the horizon, a ruby ghost about to sink to rest.

But, eventually, all things must rise again.

THIRD ARTICULATION

hejira to Ybor

metempsychosis

another old story

an interloper

Qellepoth

a confrontation

Present Day

Saturday, D.C. awoke under an icy blanket of fog. Cary and Ally followed Nelson through a labyrinth of back streets, vacant lots, and gutted buildings. They climbed into a retired Checker, and he drove them to an underground parking facility in Arlington.

"Do you know where we are?" Nelson asked, grinning.

"Um…like, no?" Ally said.

Cary waited.

"You have the privilege of standing in the *Deep Throat* garage," he said.

"Daddy!" Ally said. "It is not!"

"Is too."

"Is not."

He pointed to a square concrete pillar. "Is too. Happened right over there."

Ally rolled her eyes and then looked at Cary. "Don't listen to him. He's always saying stuff like that."

"As you wish," Nelson said. He stopped next to a faded gray, '75 LeSabre adorned with splotches of red primer.

"Great," Ally said. "Another land barge."

"It's fast," Nelson said. "And solid. Emergency packs in the trunk." Ally popped it open. She tossed one to Cary and slung the other over her shoulder. "So," Nelson said. "Where are you planning to go?"

"Safe house in Ybor," she said. The slamming trunk echoed off smooth concrete.

Nelson smiled. "Should be safe there."

"Duh," Ally said. "Hence the name?"

"Did I raise you to be a smartass?"

Ally stared.

"Okay, okay." Nelson held up both palms. "Stupid question."

"Tampa?" Cary asked. He looked hard at the cold floor.

"Something wrong with Tampa?" Ally asked.

Cary hesitated. "No. I was just curious why we need to go so far."

"We need to see someone there," Ally said. "I'll tell you about it on the way."

Nelson's eyebrows rose, but he remained silent.

Ally looked at her shoes, then up at Nelson. "Daddy?" she said. "I'm sorry I was rude to Warner."

"The man's an ass. Always has been. I love him anyway. But we knew there'd be more trouble about you. He never liked it. That's why I kept you a secret until it was too late for them to do anything about it."

"What are you talking about?" Cary asked.

"Lethe can fill you in as much as she likes," Nelson said. "Right now you need to get the hell out of Dodge." He looked at the car and grinned. "But...you know...in a Buick." Again, Ally's eyes threatened to find the back of her skull. "Cord's probably gone, but he's always been thorough. He'll have left someone to watch for you."

"I still don't understand—"

Ally shook her head. "Let's get going. Bye, Daddy. Love you." Nelson lifted her off the ground.

"I love you, too, Daughter," he said, and lowered her to the concrete. Nelson offered his hand to Cary. "If we were different people," he said, "I would probably be telling you to take care of my daughter. But, well, perhaps you will be able to watch each other's backs."

***

The short, round TPD officer emerged from the South Tampa mausoleum writing notes in a black pad. His sky-blue shirt squeezed him like a sausage wrapping, and when he lowered his arms, they hung out from his sides like penguin wings.

"Yo, Maretti," Simon called.

"Yo, Boon," said the cop. "What brings your useless ass around here?" Maretti's tan said Sunshine State, but his accent said the Bronx. "This don't seem like your kind of story."

"What you got?"

"You know." Maretti smiled. "Just your routine grave robbing."

"Getting a lot of those, are you?" Boon asked, smiling back. Maybe Maretti really didn't know what was going on.

"Funny you should ask," said the cop. "Second one this week. Probably some new gang initiation crap. Some sort of graffiti in there. Punks got to find something weirder to do every year."

Simon said nothing at first, but his heart quickened. *Wait. Just wait. Don't want to seem too eager.* "Mind if I have a look?"

Maretti consulted his pad and then flipped it closed. "No problem. We're about done. You doing a story on this?"

"Maybe."

"Well, next of kin ain't been notified, so keep the kid's name out of it."

"Okay."

"And keep my name out of it."

"No problem."

The burial chamber was dark and cool. Small, square doors lined the stone walls from floor to ceiling. A burnished aluminum coffin gaped open and empty on the black tile floor. The nape of Simon's neck tingled with fear and excitement at what he knew he would find.

And there it was, scrawled above the shattered door of

the empty niche. The dripping red script, same as at the other site. Simon snapped several pictures.

Definitely send these to Freddy.

Simon and Freddy Blake had spent four years together at Jesuit High School. Four years in hell, they called it. In retrospect, it didn't seem so bad. Worse hells had long since come and gone. Freddy had remained with the Jesuits and studied ancient languages at Loyola, and then at Georgetown. Currently, he acted as chair of the Ancient Languages Department at the University of Tampa.

The room darkened. Maretti stood in the doorway. "You done here?"

"What gang is this supposed to be?" Simon asked without looking up.

"Nobody's recognized it so far. Street punks saying they got nothing to do with it. We'll get it out of them."

"You guys don't know anything at all about it?"

"Like I said," Maretti answered. "Why? You holding out on me?"

"No. Fishing expedition. You holding out on me?"

"Would I do that?" Maretti asked. "I mean, one of the guys said it looks like Hebrew, but nobody's taking that seriously, since we ain't got no Jewish street gangs, if you know what I mean."

***

Along I-95, spring struggled to awaken from winter; the farther south Ally and Cary drove, the more it succeeded. Weekend traffic congested the freeway, everyone traveling somewhere with a purpose, all completely unaware that this car contained two people who were hunted, whose lives were marked. And Cary still had no idea why. He had, instead, more questions than he could name.

"Why does he call you Lethe?" Cary asked. "And why do you talk differently with all those homeless guys? And what was the trouble your father was talking about with Warner?

And what—"

"Whoa, whoa, whoa," she said. "Slow down there, Hoss. One question at a time. First, my name. It was a joke. Your turn. Tell me about that bow."

"Wait a minute," Cary said. "I'm the one with the questions."

Ally's face became a creepy mask. "Quid pro quo, Clarice," she hissed.

"Do you ever take anything seriously?"

"Seriously?"

Cary grabbed his head with both hands. "Geez. Yes. Seriously."

Ally smiled. "You're alive, aren't you? Now, tell me about that bow."

"What?"

"Back at your house? Hello? You were playing Cherokee roulette?"

"Oh," he said. His hands fidgeted for a moment, then sought the necklace.

"What was that about?"

"Not Cherokee," he said. "It's not an Indian bow. And I never shot a bow before, okay?"

"Don't get touchy." She accelerated around a semi on an upgrade. "So why'd you get one in the first place?"

"Don't know, really," Cary said. "Went into Winter Star one day a few months ago, and there was this war shirt hanging on the wall."

"A war shirt?"

"Yeah. You know," he said. "Battle vest? Like they used to wear into battle? That's what caught my attention first. It was amazing. All leather. Really old, too. Had this red handprint on it—right hand, with a star on the palm. I thought about buying it, too, but that seemed a little overboard. The bow was hanging over it, even though, uh, like I said, it's not really a Native American bow, which is a little weird I guess… I don't know. It's stupid—crazy." Cary tumbled his necklace in his right hand like a die. The rawhide strap danced on his collarbone. "Hey! Wait a minute," he said. "You were in the parking lot that day. By my car. What were you doing—"

"What's stupid?" she asked.

"What?" He let the necklace fall back into place under his shirt.

"You were telling me about the bow," she said. "You said something was stupid."

"The bow," he said. "Right." He tried to massage away the pain in his wrist. "It's like...it felt like...like it was speaking to me. Like it already belonged to me and wanted me to take it home." He looked out the window. "I *told* you it was stupid."

Ally gripped his chin between her thumb and fingers and turned his face toward hers. She looked away from the road long enough to find his eyes. "That's not stupid."

"But...what were you doing at Winter Star?"

"Just one of them cosmic co-inky-dinks, I suppose," she said. "What kind of star?"

"Huh? You mean Winter Star?"

"No. You said there was a star on the vest."

"Oh. Right." Cary's eyes looked to the horizon of the past. "Six points. A blue star with six points. Painted right in the palm. But not like the Star of David. This was longer at the top and bottom. And it looked..."

"What?"

"It was a really good painting, because, even though it was really old...it...it looked like it was actually glowing. So, what were you—"

"*Ally* is short for *Alethea*," she said.

"What?"

"You asked why Daddy calls me Lethe."

"Oh," he said. He cast about in his mind. His submerged thoughts tried to scramble their way to the surface. Whatever they had been, they couldn't quite reach the light of consciousness. "So," he said, giving up. "What's the joke?"

"Huh?"

"You said it was a joke."

"Oh," Ally said. "Right. Alethea. It means truth. Truth is very important to us. But—"

"Us?"

"My family...the Council—"

"The council? You mean those homeless guys your dad was with."

"I'll get to that in a minute," she said. "You wanted to know why he calls me Lethe."

"Right. Right. Go ahead."

"It was a joke... I think. Because when I was in training, I—"

"Training?"

Ally cut her eyes away from the road long enough to impale him. He held up both palms.

"Sorry, sorry. I'll stop interrupting."

"Sure you will," she said. "Anyway, when I was in training, I used to forget a lot. So he started calling me Lethe."

"I don't get it."

"The River of Oblivion? Hades? The Dead drink from the waters of oblivion to forget past lives?" Ally tapped her knuckles on his forehead. "Hello? Didn't you ever read mythology?"

Cary yawned and stretched. "I forget."

"Ohhhhh, I get it." She slapped her thigh. "It has a sense of humor after all. But seriously, I've always wondered about how easy it was, how my name so perfectly shortened to that particular nickname. It was almost like he'd had it planned when he named me."

"What do you mean?"

"I don't know. Almost like it was part of my training to have a name that could mean 'truth' and 'forgetting.' Especially that kind of forgetting."

"What kind of forgetting?"

Ally glanced over at him. "Do you believe in reincarnation?"

"I'm a scientist," said Cary. "Well," he added, his voice losing the anchor of certainty, "I *was* a scientist."

"Okay then. Do you believe in the science of reincarnation?"

"Of course not."

"All right. How about entanglement?"

"You mean *quantum* entanglement? Of course."

They bounced across the threshold of a long bridge, and the LeSabre began to climb. Late afternoon sun reflected off the mud flats of the Savannah River. From beyond the horizon, a paper mill saturated the atmosphere with an acrid stench, turning the air to slow poison.

"That's how we escaped," Ally said.

"What?" He turned back to her.

"At your house." She paused long enough to check his reaction. "There was a cave. But not really a tunnel. It was a gate. Of sorts. We call them LightGates. That's why Warner was so pissed. I'm not supposed to even tell anybody about them, much less take you into one."

Cary stared at Ally as if she had just sprouted antennae. "Next you're going to tell me there's an alien conspiracy behind it all." He crossed his arms and stared out the passenger window.

"Well," she said. "Since you brought it up…"

"Stop it. Don't you think it's about time you told me a little of what's really going on here?"

Ally considered the request for nearly a minute.

She sighed.

"I don't suppose it could hurt anything at this point," she said. "Besides, you're obviously not going to believe me anyway. But not 'a little.' If I'm going to tell you anything, I may as well tell you everything. Even though I'm *forbidden*—like that word means anything now."

"What do you mean?"

"I mean all the rules have changed. Nothing's the same. And when that happens, you have to figure out the new rules. If you follow the old rules, you get lost. Or dead."

"You told me that would be the case," Cary said.

Ally looked at him, not comprehending.

"Back in the cave. You said everything was going to change."

"No," she said. "Not what I meant. I mean that all of my rules have changed."

"Well, if it's any help, I'm probably more likely to believe the truly weird now that I've been pursued by various unknown killers and met a secret council of the homeless. But I don't want to hear about any damn aliens. All right? And no wormholes through the earth."

"As you wish," Ally said. "We'll save those for when you're ready."

The Buick bounced across decaying Georgia asphalt as they approached Florida. "I wonder why it is," she said, "that the interstate always sucks when you get close to the border?"

Cary shrugged.

"Okay," she said. "Here goes. But try not to feel like you're in an Indiana Jones movie." Ally took a deep breath. A steady line of headlights streamed north on the opposite side of Interstate 95. She sighed again. "I'm a member..." She paused a moment and then continued. "I am a member of an ancient, secret society. We're called the Namayan. We've been a continuous line of Watchers—"

"Watchers?"

"I'll get to that. Our order was founded in Sumer, the region we now know as Iraq, when two men began to—"

"Sumer?"

"Yes."

"You're talking about *ancient* Sumer?"

Ally reached over and patted him on the cheek. "Is there any other kind of Sumer?" she asked.

"You don't have to be a smartass."

"Saahree... But I kind of do. Part of my training." She rubbed her eyes with the heels of her palms and ran her fingers through her thick hair, pushing it back off her face. "Anyway," she continued, "the Namayan Order began when... Oh. Wait. I'll just tell you about Carver and Layton. Then it'll all make more sense."

"Sure it will," Cary said. "Go ahead. Wait. By the way, how old are you?"

Ally considered the question. "A thousand, give or take," she said with a straight face. Cary was almost inclined to believe her.

***

Forty miles due east of Ally and Cary, Cyrus Layton scanned the moss green Atlantic from the stern of the *Nammu*, a 50-foot Beneteau. Behind him, the lights of Tybee Island twinkled to life in the dusk.

So Carver had taken the Benben from Ubai and hidden it somewhere.

I should have expected as much.

Carver's act had shifted the balance of power considerably. But it had also removed the twinges of remorse that had been marinating within Layton's own contingency plan.

His cell phone vibrated, and he pressed it to his ear. "Speak."

"I'm in Tampa," said Cord. "Still haven't found Walker's kid. Last time anyone saw him was September. Even his ex-girlfriend doesn't know where he is."

"What else?"

"Apparently he used to get high a lot before he settled down and got serious. But he had a regular connection." Cord's palm pilot beeped. "Guy named Jackie DiSpenza. They call him Jackie Blue. 'Cause of the song."

"No shit," Layton said. "I thought maybe he was a Smurf."

"Right. Well, anyway, seems somebody saw the kid with this DiSpenza guy back in September, just before he went underground. So we're, uh, we're looking for him."

"Tell me that's not everything," Layton said. "Please."

"We have a line on where the Council went."

"That's sounding better. Keep looking. When you find them, inform Stokes. Their plan is already in place."

Layton closed the call. The phone rang again before he

had removed his finger from the button.

"Speak," he said again.

"Mr. Layton." The voice was, as always, attenuated, but it still held a hypnotic strength. Layton sat in the cockpit and looked upon the endless waves. *Who the hell are you, really?*

"Mr. Dossey," Layton said.

"So," Dossey said. "Now you know just how much you can trust your so-called 'brother.'"

"How did you know about…"

"Mr. Layton. Have you not yet realized that there is nothing I cannot find out? You should be more concerned about your partner's treachery than my sources."

"Perhaps that is true."

"Make no mistake… Carver will move against you. He already has the Benben. All of its power is at his disposal. Do you think when you have found Walker and located the crystal that your brother will share this new power with you? Meanwhile, my army grows larger every day. My offer still stands."

The outgoing tide in Savannah Harbor gently rocked the *Nammu* at anchor. Her mast tilted back and forth like a bony finger wagging at the empty sky.

"I'm listening," Layton said.

***

A telephone booth. All Taylor needed was a telephone booth.

The cavern in his chest ached to be filled. When the Angel had revealed herself, when she had whispered to him his True Name, Taylor had experienced an immediate surge of…completion. But a new emptiness spread within him the moment the Angel's image began to fade.

He had left Mopheit Park and walked for hours—aimless, yet on a quest. An idea, an image, floated in the dark waters of his unconscious. *A telephone booth.* All of his answers waited within the safety of a telephone booth. He searched through the night and into the next day: past the Ice Palace and the Florida Aquarium, past the giant cargo ships in Port Tampa, through Ybor City and north into Seminole Heights, all the way to Sulfur Springs and the unlit lighthouse, where he folded himself inward and sat all night.

During his journey, Taylor passed several phone booths, but he saw not a single one. Like many who find themselves on a quest, he was unable to locate the object of his desire, not because it was well hidden in the world, but because it was well hidden in his own, private universe.

***

"Okay," Ally said. "I'm going to tell you this story the way it was first told to me. This story is my oldest memory."

Cary waited.

"Okay, here goes." She took a deep breath. "The Story of Memsalemn and Nanoshe: Once upon a time there lived a boy—"

"Wait a minute," Cary said. "Are you kidding me? Once upon a time?"

"Hey. I'm trying to tell a story here."

"Saaah-reee."

Ally tried to use *the look*—as Cary had begun to think of it— but she had to turn her focus back to the traffic.

"Suppose I could continue?" she asked.

"Oh, by all means," Cary said. *At least this is fun.*

"Fine," she said before continuing:

> *Once upon a time there lived a boy named Memsalemn. When he was 3, Memsalemn fell into a terrible fever that neither his mother nor the Ashipu could identify. While the doctor and his mother tried to heal him, Memsalemn dreamed the dream of the Garal Seed, a tiny speck floating high above him in the desert sky.*
>
> *Memsalemn tossed and turned for weeks, lost in his dream world. He walked day upon night in the burning and windless*

desert, and the Garal Seed floated above him.

Sometimes it descended closer to the earth, casting a cool shadow on the burning sand. Memsalemn would run to fall into that shadow and reach for the seed. But then it would rise into the heavens, once again becoming a tiny speck in the endless sky. Memsalemn knew that if he could just reach the seed— just touch it—he would be saved. Not only would he survive this trial, but he would also become a great king. Day after day he pursued, and day after day the seed eluded his grasp, taunting him from its unreachable place in the sky.

Until finally, it crashed with a great whump into the desert sands.

And it began to grow.

"Into what?" Cary asked.

"That part comes later," Ally said. She opened a plastic bottle of water and took a long drink. "You have to tell a story just right—or else."

"Or else what?"

"Or else it sucks."

"How do you know all this is real?"

"Shut up," Ally said.

Cary raised his eyebrows. Ally pushed on before he had time to generate enough sarcasm to throw at her.

"And now," she said, glancing at Cary, "we return to 'The Story of Memsalemn and Nanoshe,' which is already in progress."

For the rest of her life, Memsalemn's mother, Mevarah, told the story of how her precious child had danced for weeks at the door of death while she cooled his brow with holy water and prayed to Enmeduranki to remove the Hand of Darkness that held him in its deathly grasp.

"She prayed to Jimmy Durante?" Cary asked. Ally backfisted him hard on the shoulder.

"Ow!"

"For your information," she said, "*Enmeduranki* was a Sumerian God-King. He who connects heaven and earth. A high member of the *Annunaki*." Ally raised her eyebrows. "But," she added, "now that you mention it, there is also a Sumerian God named *Enki*, and Jimmy Durante did do that song 'Inkadinkado.' Never know. Could be a connection. Maybe Jimmy Durante was an alien." Her face remained serious.

Cary made a mental note to never play poker with her.

"Shall I continue?"

Cary nodded.

After nearly four weeks, Memsalemn's fever broke, seemingly of its own accord. Memsalemn—weak, frail and sweating—opened his red and burning eyes.

"It was a flower," he said, and drifted into a calm, healing sleep.

The dream returned over the years, always bringing with it a sense of urgency and endless toil. But Memsalemn never revealed this dream to anyone. Not even to Mevarah.

And the dream evolved. Now when the seed fell, gardens spread from its impact like the ripples from a pebble tossed into a calm pool. At first, the gardens were small, but they grew larger and larger.

When he was midway through his 24th year, Memsalemn married. On his wedding night, as he slept in the early morning hours, exhausted after a night of pleasure with his bride, Lyah, he watched the Garal Seed float in the sky. He knew that it would fall. It always fell. But for the first time, Memsalemn knew where he was, and where the seed was going to land.

He stood on a ridge above a lush valley just south of Uk-Anbar. The Valley of Ubai. He had traveled here only weeks ago to hunt lions with Lyah's brother, Nanoshe. The seed fell so rapidly that flames trailed behind it, and when it crashed to the earth, the garden spread in all directions, to the horizon and beyond.

Then Memsalemn rose into the air until he could see the

entire world floating in a black sky. But he wasn't alone. His brother in marriage, Nanoshe floated in the sky next to him. The buffeting winds of creation rose from the earth and shook them. Memsalemn tried to speak to his brother, but his words were lost in the great gale.

He awoke sobbing. Lyah cradled him against her soft chest, rocking him back and forth, stroking his brow like a mother to her child.

The wedding feast began that day at noon. Nanoshe approached Memsalemn with a traditional offering of shredded lamb in mint sauce.

"You are welcome into my family," he said. He stared for a long time into his new brother's eyes before he spoke again. "Now, when do you and I return to Ubai to find what our shared dream has revealed?"

Memsalemn smiled and nodded. Of course. This made perfect sense. "Right away," he said. "As soon as possible."

"Okay," Cary said. "Hold on. Back up. Really. How do you know all this?"

Ally cut her eyes and infused her voice with a Gypsy accent. "It is written," she said.

"Stop screwing with me now."

"No," she said, and unleashed that ringing laugh again. "I'm serious. This really is all written down."

"Where?"

"A book." She shrugged. "Maybe I'll show it to you one day. Do you want me to go on? It is a good story, isn't it?" she asked. "Whether it's true or not?"

They zoomed past an exit for St. Augustine. A creepy billboard with a photo of a mummified fetus advertised Ripley's. Cary had not yet decided to believe Ally's story, though there was clearly more going on here than he could understand.

"Keep going," he said. "You're right. It is a good story."

***

Simon pressed the "Retrieve" button, and his answering machine spoke.

"Simon, it's Freddy. I may have something for you. But not over the phone. And not at my orifice."

Orifice? Simon winced. *Professor of Ancient Languages, indeed.*

The message continued. "I have office hours 'til six. Meet me at Bean Cellar around 6:30. Call me if you can't make it."

The Bean Cellar was one of those rare cafés that had successfully resisted the Starbucks assault, having burst from the earth like a caffeine-enriched mushroom in the loam and shadow of an old college. It lived on Platt Street, a few blocks from the University of Tampa. Simon was a regular.

He parked his Volvo halfway down the block, in front of a '20s bungalow that, only last year, some ascending entrepreneur had regentrified into office space. The home had promptly become infested with attorneys. Hungry lawyers, along with undergraduates, comprised the bulk of the Bean Cellar's customers. Simon liked the place anyway.

Over the years, the essence of espresso had seeped into the walls, floor, and ceiling, transforming the Bean Cellar, through caffeine alchemy, into coffee itself. A tall, polished counter covered the entire right-hand side. A dozen students huddled in the center of the room at a battered array of bistro tables. Nine plump, cream-colored booths cradled the remaining walls; the place was a giant, padded cell. *Not a bad idea—considering the clientele and the vast amounts of caffeine they consumed.* Six Tibetan temple bells hung on a black silk cord inside the glass door of the café. They chimed the news of Simon's arrival.

Freddy sat in the back left corner booth drinking a cappuccino. He wore tortoiseshell horn rims and a gold tweed jacket with brown elbow pads. Obviously taking the professorial persona seriously. Foam stuck to his upper lip; he looked like a *Got milk?* ad for academics. Simon passed his digital camera to Freddy and slid into the opposite bench. Freddy dabbed the foam from his lip with a cloth napkin and then scanned the new images on the camera's view screen.

"It's Hebrew," he said. "*Qellepoth*. Means 'shells of the dead.' An empty body not occupied by a soul. Big, bad evildoers. They survive by sucking the Holy Light out of pure souls. Sort of like spiritual vampires."

"What the hell does that mean?" Simon asked. "Why are these grave robbers writing this word, what was it…"

"Qellepoth."

"Qellepoth," Simon repeated. "Why are they writing this where they steal bodies?"

"How the hell should I know?" Freddy asked. He took a long pull on his cappuccino. "Maybe it's like those vampire kids down in Fort Myers a few years ago. You remember that?"

Simon nodded. "Did a story on it." He looked back toward the counter. A girl with jet-black hair gathered into 15 or 20 arbitrary pigtails leaned on her elbows, absorbed in a weathered copy of *Les fleurs du mal*. Her skin was paler than the white cotton tank she wore.

"Hey, Mary," Simon called. Mary had long ago won Simon's Secret Award for Most Striking Eyes in the Universe, a fact he had largely kept to himself. She folded the page corner and looked up. Her smile banished all traces of the darkness she was trying to present.

"The usual?" she asked. Simon nodded. He turned back to Freddy.

"So what's all the secrecy about?"

Freddy took a sip and wiped away a fresh line of foam.

"Something spooky happened with one of my students. Fall semester I had this kid in my Intro course. Leo Cruickshank. He was a little flaky, but had a real passion for the old words. And he liked me. You know how they are when they latch on to somebody they think has the answers. But then, all of a sudden, he disappears just before exams."

"So maybe he didn't study."

"No," Freddy continued. "He was the second one that semester. And the first was a friend of his."

Mary brought Simon a cup of Bean Cellar's "Atomic GoJuice," *Cafe Cubano* laced with a quad shot of espresso. Simon held the sugar jar over the cup and poured an endless stream of crystals into the brown liquid.

"Seriously?"

"I like to get that sucrose quicksand at the bottom." Simon stirred the concoction like a potion in a cauldron. He took a test sip and sighed. "Perfect. I'm guessing there's more to the story of Leo Cruickshank?"

Freddy nodded and lowered his cup.

"Haven't seen the guy since, what, Thanksgiving probably. So, yesterday, I'm sitting in my office researching this symbol for you, and in he walks. At the very moment I find the word. He's got this weird-ass look on his face, like he's struggling with what to say, like maybe he's doing something he's not supposed to. And he finally looks down at the picture and says, I swear to God, 'Be afraid of the Qellepoth, Professor Blake.'"

"So, maybe he just knew the word. Maybe he's Jewish. Maybe he was just messing with you." But Simon wasn't convincing Freddy any more than he was convincing himself.

"I don't think so," Freddy said. "I don't see the kid for what...four months? And he shows up right then and says something out the ass like that? And now he's everywhere. I've probably seen him a dozen times in the last 24 hours. If I was in a spy novel, I'd feel marked for death."

Right on cue, the temple bells slapped against the glass door; Freddy's face grew as pale as Mary's.

"What?"

"That's him," Freddy said, staring into the depths of his cup. "He just came in the door."

***

Ally banked the LeSabre through the exit loop from I-10 to US 301. Several truck stops lit up the early evening brighter than dawn.

"And now," she said, "back to our exciting story."
Cary rolled his eyes, but listened nonetheless.

Memsalemn and Nanoshe stood together on the rim of the Valley of Ubai.

"What is it called in your dream?" Memsalemn asked.

Nanoshe hesitated.

Both men looked down into the valley where they had hunted only weeks before. Memsalemn thought about the trip. Had there not been a strangeness about the day? The circular valley had seemed to glow from within, a soft light that rose from the earth rather than fell from the sky. His neck had tingled almost constantly, and he had expected to flush a lion at every moment. But neither of them had encountered a single beast.

"Giral," Nanoshe finally replied.

Memsalemn nodded. Close enough.

Nanoshe searched the abundant puffs of clouds. "Do you think the seed will really fall?" he asked.

"No," Memsalemn said. He stepped off the ledge and descended the slope. "I think it already has. A long time ago." He looked back over his shoulder. "And when it did," he said, "it made this valley."

At the exact moment they stepped onto the valley floor, Memsalemn clapped his hands over his ears. Nanoshe was only a second behind. Both men collapsed to their knees.

A soundstorm roared inside their heads. High-pitched squeals pierced their brains like a thousand needles.

These frequencies danced upon a low, pulsing hum, an audible texture that was more than just a sound. This lower tone phased in and out in a steady, wave-like rhythm. Gradually, Memsalemn and Nanoshe fell into phase with the pulsing hum, and soon the shrill sounds no longer overwhelmed them. Instead, the frequencies formed intricate songs within songs that drew them ever onward to the deepest point of the valley, the geometric center. There, a pitch black, pyramidal stone lay at the center of a small depression. Nothing grew within a hundred feet of it. From the moment that they stood in its presence, the stone began to teach them things that even today are unimaginable by most people.

"Wait a minute, wait a minute," Cary said. "Didn't I see this in a movie? Only, wasn't it a black monolith?"

"Of course. What do you think that movie was really about, anyway? Where do you think Arthur Clarke got the idea for that story in the first place? It was a misunderstood, or rather, a partially glimpsed, vision of this story."

Cary shook his head and tried to focus on any aspect of this fantasy that might actually be true.

"So it was a meteor," he said. "I can accept that. Meteors often form rough pyramids when they burn. And the Valley of Ubai was the crater it formed when it crashed."

"Yes," Ally said. "But it was more than a meteor. It literally was a seed. Of knowledge. Sent by someone with a specific purpose. The knowledge gave Memsalemn and Nanoshe powers. Chief among them, whether you wish to believe in reincarnation or not, was the ability to reincarnate without drinking of the River Lethe, without partaking of the Waters of Oblivion. And they have been using that power ever since."

"That's ridiculous."

Ally half growled, half sighed.

"I mean, okay, suppose I even accept the idea of reincarnation. Which I don't. Then how would Carver and Layton be able to remember who they are—were. How would that even work?"

"That," she said, "is one of the best kept secrets of the last few thousand years. If we knew that, then maybe we could stop them. Maybe we could keep it from happening."

Cary dropped his face into his hands for a moment and then looked at her again. "So who sent the seed then?"

"If I remember correctly, you didn't want to hear about any *damn aliens*."

"Holy crap! Next you'll be telling me there are fairies!"

Ally smiled. "Ahhh, the *Tuatha*. Careful," she said. "They're listening all the time. And they don't like to be called fairies. They prefer *AosSidhe*." She flicked the turn signal, and its rhythmic clicks beat time to the silence. "There's an entire kingdom of them surrounding your house, by the way," she added.

"Jesus!"

"No. Just the *AosSidhe*. Jesus lives somewhere else entirely."

She let loose her tinkling laughter and pulled the LeSabre into a battered Shell Station that multitasked as a fried chicken joint and an ice cream parlor. They gassed up the land barge, bought stale coffee in Styrofoam cups, and continued on down the highway, deeper into the tropical darkness. Despite the decayed caffeine, Cary dozed with his head wedged between the seat and the window.

Before Time

~

Ksama

Across Tirtham Commons, the *Varuna* bobs on easy waves. Ksama has only to cross the open ground, untie the boat, and sail away. But there is still the matter of crossing the exposed terrain.

Sh'ele hangs heavy on her sweat-soaked back. A sudden breeze blows in off the water, cooling her and lifting her spirits. The fishy tang of salt air burns her nostrils. Only a few steps remain, but they are the most dangerous, the most vulnerable.

Doesn't matter. The park is the only path to the boat.

With her right hand, Ksama reaches over her left shoulder and touches the pommel of DevaRada. Like a soft shadow, she steps into the light. The *Varuna* dances high on the turning tide. She indulges in a preliminary sigh of relief, even as the thunder of charging feet rushes to her ears.

Two dusky red *Ugra* lope across the park, open jaws anticipating flesh. They are already almost upon her. Ksama spins to her right, freeing her blade and using the weight of Sh'ele as a counterbalance. The lead Ugra dives into the air.

How she loves the Ugra. The grace and power of their strides. Their unconditional loyalty. In ancient times, the Apsara domesticated these beasts and trained them to protect their temples. Now they mostly live as pets, companions. These have been trained only to kill. And Ksama is their prey.

With DevaRada, she traces a lethal line across the air. Tears sting her wide-open eyes.

I'm sorry.

The arc of her sword severs the beast into two halves that fly over her head, anointing her with warm blood. The two pieces splash into the pool behind her, staining the water black in the moonlight. The second beast follows the same trajectory as the first. Ksama plants her feet and reverses her blade in precise choreography with the Ugra's flight. Again she thinks, *I'm so sorry*, as the creature impales itself on her sword, pounding her to the ground.

How she loves the Ugra. How she hates killing. Her training has taught her reverence for all lives. These are the first she has ever ended.

Her back burns where she has landed on Sh'ele. Ksama struggles to her side and pushes the Ugra off her chest. A cloaked figure steps from the shadow of a *Berebole* tree.

"Sidra," she says. "Of course it would be you." The assassin pulls the cowl down, revealing tightly braided blonde hair burned to ash by the moon. Sidra's face is a mask of arrogant beauty. In her left hand, she cradles a short stick, perhaps as long as her foot. In her right, she twirls another, this one the length of her forearm.

"Give me Sh'ele," Sidra says, "and I will let you sail away in your little boat." With each word, Sidra closes the distance.

Ksama has devoted her life to prayer and contemplation toward the stewardship of Sh'ele. Her martial training has been perfunctory, a vestige of the time when the Añucara needed such skills. Sidra has devoted her life to death's sacred arts. The *Sieghke*, the sticks she wields, are her favorite weapons, her lethal toys.

"I cannot beat you, Sidra." Sidra laughs, genuinely amused at the notion that Ksama should feel the need to state the obvious. "But," says Ksama, rising slowly, "neither can I relinquish my duty." She swings DevaRada in loose figure eights behind her, drawing infinity in the bloodstained air.

Sidra smiles. Perhaps this conversation will at least prove to be amusing.

Present Day

Taylor squatted on his heels in a phone booth outside the Swan Motel on Nebraska Avenue. Night was freshly born; a few Early Bird Special hookers walked first shift along wide, broken sidewalks.

Why am I here? I came here for something.

The phone seemed a likely candidate. But he could not imagine whom he might call. Or why.

Taylor's bones ached. His skin burned; his blood was on fire. Buried deep beneath his new identity, memories struggled to rise. Familiar, soothing faces. A woman. A man. And a number. It floated like a bright planet on the border of his mind-space, but whenever he focused his inner gaze directly upon it, the number receded into shadow.

If the dial tone had answers to Taylor's puzzle, it withheld its secrets; soon the hum faded and was replaced by a voice. Not the computerized operator voice, but one that was soothing, hypnotic.

"It is time," the Angel said. "Are you prepared?" Taylor released the handset. It banged once against the metal booth, then swung back and forth, an ugly pendulum beneath a black metal box.

"Yes," Taylor said. A warm tide of peace and certainty flooded his body.

A multi-dimensional map formed on his inner screen:

past Ybor City, through downtown Tampa, across the Brorein Bridge, along Bayshore, and into Hyde Park.

Edison Avenue.

"Do you understand?" asked the Angel's voice.

"Yes," he said. Taylor left the booth and walked south on Nebraska. The voice stayed with him.

"Who are you?" she asked. Taylor did not immediately reply. Ideas crashed into one another, creating a storm in the ocean of his thoughts.

"Who are you now?" The Angel's soothing voice shifted to frequencies of command.

Taylor! his hidden thoughts shouted, but the shout evaporated as quickly as it had formed. Even so, Taylor foundered for a long time in the churning seas of that thoughtstorm before he finally provided the answer that the Angel required.

FOURTH ARTICULATION

night breakfast

Pop-Eggs Sam

a tiny dragon

zombies

a 12-year-old dream

Ybor

red on red

fell beasts

battle

I have become death

Present Day

The LeSabre's right front wheel slammed into a pothole, and Cary's head bounced off the window.

"What the hell?" he said.

"You were drooling," Ally said. "And snoring."

Cary rubbed his burning eyes. "What were we talking about?"

"Memsalemn. Nanoshe."

"Right," Cary said. "Mem… Carver and Layton. So you're telling me they're, what, a couple thousand years old?"

"Try 7," she said. "But not their bodies. Their bodies are both 53. Their minds…well…those have been aware in a continuous link for over 7,000 years."

Cary rolled his eyes. "Jesus," he said. "Welcome to the funny papers."

"What?"

"Just something my father used to say when he heard something ridiculous. This pretty much lands in that category."

"Right. Of course it does. So does the existence of LightGates." Ally took a sip of her coffee and grimaced. "There are more of those, by the way."

"Then why are we driving?"

"Everything has a price," she said. "We can't afford the price of using the LightGates right now."

"Right," Cary said. "And what's the going toll on LightGate travel?"

Ally sighed. "Detection," she said. "Then big, ugly, mean guys. With bad breath."

The shifting lights of oncoming cars played across her face. Cary turned away, leaned his head back on the seat, and closed his eyes.

"Look," he said. "I'm sorry. It's just that—all this reincarnation stuff—I just can't believe I lived before right now. It's inconceivable."

"Did you ever think that maybe there's more going on in the world than what you can see? Maybe someone else is pulling the strings."

"Who?"

Ally paused. "Well, that's the real question, isn't it?"

Neither spoke for several miles. Then Cary broke the silence.

"What did you mean when you said all of your rules have changed, too? You've known about this stuff all your life—not that I believe any of it anyway. But we're just talking here."

Ally nodded. "Remember when Warner said Carver and Layton are adversaries? It's more than that, really. They've been playing a game of control with each other right from the beginning. First, it was small and local. In their village only. But the more they learned, the bigger their game got. They've been playing against each other on a planetary scale since global communication became available. Especially since computers. But they're not supposed to join together. And the Namayan are never to be targeted. These are ancient agreements we all abide by. Keeping the silence from people like you is another."

"People like me?"

"You know, ordinary, everyday people who think the world is just a normal, old place without LightGates and 7,000-year-old Sumerians running around playing chess with the planet? But, like I said, I've reached a point where the old rules no longer apply. Some of them, anyway. Besides, since they want you for something, you obviously don't fit into the category of 'normal, everyday person' anymore. So you get to know. My decision. Even if you don't believe. When the rules change, you've got to change the way you play the game."

"Right," he said. "Like making a girl a Namayan."

"Figured that one out, did you?" she said. "But that wasn't part of The Accords. It was more like a male tradition. I guess no one before my father ever thought a woman could do it. Some still don't. Obviously."

"Then why did he think so?"

"Ahhhh," she said. "That's an entirely different story. The Namayan have an inner guide. A teacher, sort of."

Cary rolled his eyes.

"Well, we certainly can't do all of this by ourselves. Anyway, one day when I was 5, I was playing with my baby doll, Blondie Jan Sky, and my golden picture frame, and…"

"Blondie? Jan? Sky?"

"Hey, now," she said. "Don't you be talking trash about BJS. I've still got her, and she'll kick your ass."

"And…" he said, "you played with a picture frame?"

"Oh, I don't know. I used to just sort of walk around and hold it at arm's length and look through it and pretend that what I was looking at was a picture. It was all gold and ornate. It made the world…prettier, I think. Anyway, I was looking through the frame, and I saw my father sitting in his recliner with his eyes closed. And here's the really cool part. I suddenly knew what he was doing. I just knew. That's the only way I can explain it. I could see that he was having an inner conversation with someone. His lips weren't moving, but I could just see it on his face. And here's the really, *really* cool part: I could eavesdrop. And suddenly I could see them…somewhere else."

"How?"

"I don't know how. I just could, okay? Daddy was talking to a woman. She was the most beautiful thing I'd ever seen. An angel." Ally stole a glance at Cary. "But no wings. She and

Daddy were in a huge glass bubble. There was this beautiful, colored wind swirling all around outside. Daddy was sitting in his recliner just like he was in the living room. But he was in both places. She was walking around, working at various things. And she kept calling his name. 'Nelson,' she said. 'Nelson. Remember where you are.' He'd look from side to side and shake his head. And I suddenly realized that he couldn't see her. He was looking for her. His eyes were all scrunched up like he was in the dark. Then he took a deep breath and seemed to become more focused, there with the woman, and in his chair at home."

"'Remember your dreams tonight, Nelson,' she said, and he nodded, staring off into space with this goofy grin on his face. 'I will speak to you in your dreams.'

"Then she turned and winked at me! Her face literally filled my vision. It was the weirdest thing. Without stopping her conversation with my father, she talked to me at the same time. I was in both places at once, just like he was. I was still sitting on the floor at home, holding Blondie Jan Sky and watching Daddy through the picture frame, and I was sitting on the floor in that bubble room. Oh, my God." Ally's eyes glistened. "Her voice rang like a bell. It was so beautiful I started crying."

She wiped her eyes with the back of her hand.

"Then I asked what was her name."

"And did she tell you?"

"She did. *Apavarita Varsah.* But it was too hard for me to say. So she said 'I am the Hidden Rain in your heart, Little One. You may call me Pava, and you can visit me whenever you like. You need only remember my face.'

"When Daddy opened his eyes, I was sitting there, not making a sound. Tears were pouring down my cheeks. And it was so weird. For the next few minutes I saw everything twice—just before it happened, and then again when it actually happened. Like an echo, only a before-echo. Does that make sense?"

"No," Cary said.

Ally shot him a quick glance. "Anyway, *infidel*," she continued. "Daddy rushes over to me and picks me up and says, 'What's wrong, sweetie? What's wrong?' over and over. He thought I was hurt or sad. I don't know. He kept patting me on the back. And it was like being in a house of mirrors, only with sound, too, because I was hearing and seeing it all twice. Finally I say, 'Nothing, Daddy.' He hugged me tight, and I nuzzled my wet little face into his neck. And then I said, 'Pava says I can come visit, too, Daddy.'"

"I bet that got a reaction," Cary said. Ally looked at him curiously before turning back to the highway.

"It did," she said. "And when I told him what she looked like and where she lived, he was even more blown away. It was probably then that he realized I could do some of the really hard things about this job better than he could, better maybe than anyone ever had before. See, the Council had gotten so focused on the danger part that they didn't notice how much the world had changed."

"Danger? I thought you said Watchers weren't supposed to be targets."

"We're not. But it isn't easy keeping track of these guys. You run into some nasty stuff. And sometimes their operatives get pretty rough, even if they know they can't kill us. Couldn't, that is."

"Like Cord? And what's-his-face. Stokes."

Ally pressed her fingers to the scab on her neck and let out a deep sigh. "Yeah. And all their bad boys, too."

They rode in silence for a while. The rhythmic clicking of the tires lulled Cary into a sense of calm. *Why not?* It was certainly no weirder than LightGates, though that at least had some scientific foundation.

"So this...Pava person...this is the guide you told me about?"

"Mmhmm," Ally said.

"And you—what—speak to her regularly?"

"Well, yeah, all the time." Ally frowned. "Well, not exactly. Not like I did when I was a kid. It's a lot harder now.

Takes more concentration. Have to rely more on intuition. When I was a kid, I could just...I don't know...be there with her. Now...not so much. When I really, really want to bad enough, I still feel like I actually go to her, to where she is, completely. But it takes every ounce of my energy. Like going into a trance. So, mostly, I just trust that she's there guiding me, even though I don't see her."

"So," Cary said, "where is she? Somewhere..." He held both palms up and shook them. "Wooooooo...on the Astral Plane?"

"No, silly," Ally said. "She's on Venus."

"Give me a break."

"As you wish."

They continued down Highway 301 in silence. Signs for Silver Springs invited them to adventures in glass-bottomed boats.

"But...why?" Cary asked, eventually.

"Why *what?*"

"Well, why do you do this? Why does the Council exist? Why did you start watching these guys in the first place?"

"I think, initially, our founders believed they were evil," she said. "We weren't always only watching them, see...at first we were trying to stop them. We have a very violent history. That's why The Accords were created. That's why we have to learn to kick ass." She smiled.

Cary closed his eyes and leaned back against the seat rest. "They do seem pretty evil. If evil really exists."

"Oh, evil exists. Count on it. But it's tricky, you know? Bad people doing bad things...that's easy to figure out. The real problem is the evil that masquerades as good. And good that looks at first like evil."

"I don't know if I could tell the difference." Cary tuned his attention to the murmurs in his head. They battled on, angry and unintelligible. "At least not all the time."

"Me neither," she said. "But I do know I'm getting hungry. How about some breakfast?"

Cary stared into the Central Florida darkness. Breakfast for dinner? Why not? Everything else had been turned upside down.

***

Leo Cruikshank spoke to Mary, but his gaze remained fixed on Freddy and Simon. He was maybe 19, thin, with dark, oily hair and thick eyebrows that all but achieved oneness. His baggy shorts hung to mid-calf, and his ragged, gray Old Navy sweatshirt looked like it was made of oilcloth. His shoes had been, at one time, black Converse All-Stars, but they had transformed into little more than tattered sandals. He reached behind his head and scratched the base of his skull.

Simon turned back to Freddy. "Why are you so spooked?" Simon asked. "Play benevolent professor. You're the Chair of the Department."

Freddy laughed. "Right," he said. "It's easy to be the Chair when you're the only professor actually *in* the department." But the color had flowed back into his face. He nodded and waved at Leo, beckoning him over to the booth.

"Leo, this is my friend—"

"Hello," Leo said. Leo Cruickshank's eyes glittered with an eerie sparkle; when you looked into them, it was like looking at someone galaxies away, not at all at the person standing in front of you. "You're a reporter, aren't you?"

"Simon Boon." He extended his hand. "Yes. How did you know?"

Leo shook his head once, like he was trying to clear it. He pulled a curved-backed chair up to the end of the booth and sat. "I must have read your mind," he said, and laughed. "Or maybe it was one of your articles."

The kid was weird, all right, but not dangerous. Just flaky. Spaced out. Maybe he was high. His eyes sure looked like it. They had a creepy fire behind them.

"Are you planning on coming back to school?" Freddy asked.

Leo thought for a moment. School was clearly the furthest

thing from his mind. He shook his head again, only slightly.

"Are you sure you're okay, Leo?" Freddy asked.

Leo brought his gaze to bear on Freddy. "Yeah. Fine. Just need some sleep. Too much partying." He laughed softly. "Just need some sleep."

Leo Cruickshank stood abruptly, looming over the table. His chair slid back and teetered on its rear legs before thumping to all fours; his creepy-fire eyes fixed on Simon's digital camera. Leo opened his mouth to speak, took a step back to leave, looked again at the camera, then stepped forward. Simon and Freddy waited, mouths hanging open in stunned silence, while Leo performed his bizarre dance: open mouth, step back, look at camera, step forward, repeat. At last Leo turned and walked away without managing to give voice to the thought that apparently writhed in the abyss of his mind. Jangly temple bells heralded his departure.

"Weirder and weirder," Freddy said.

"Did you see the way his face changed when he was looking at the camera?" Simon asked. "It was like he was trying to remember something, and…and then someone passed an eraser over his mind." An army of goose bumps began their journey up Simon's spine. He rolled his shoulders to shake off the feeling, but it wouldn't go away. "It was almost like, almost like…" He didn't want to say it. It was too impossible.

"Like he became a shell?" Freddy said. Simon began whistling the well-known tune.

Freddy groaned. "No, no," he said. "Not the *Twilight Zone*. It's passé."

"Well, what then, Oh Master of Pop Culture?"

Freddy drained his coffee and smacked the cup down on the table. He whistled the theme from *X-Files* and raised his eyebrows.

"Oh, yeah," Simon said. "'Cause *that's* cutting edge."

But all the joking in the world could not fully banish the aura of creep that Leo Cruickshank had spread upon the table.

Simon took out a small notebook.

"By the way," he said, "who was the other student that dropped out?"

"What?"

"Leo's buddy," said Simon. "The other kid who stopped coming to class."

"Why?" Freddy asked.

"I don't know. Might turn out to be useful. I never know what's going to be useful until I need it and it's not there. So I tend to just ask whatever comes to mind."

Freddy thought for a moment. "Oh yeah," he said. "I remember. Walker. His name was Taylor Walker."

***

The Big Wheel Eatery, "Breakfast Served 24/7," was a stainless-steel diner that had originally opened on Kennedy Boulevard in Tampa in 1953. Thirty-one years later, the building-slash-vehicle had transmigrated through geographical metempsychosis—as such diners were designed to do—to a forlorn stretch of State Road 84 just east of Wildwood, 30 miles south of Ocala.

Ally and Cary sat opposite one another in a booth facing the parking lot. They were on display but had a clear view of their car. A trade-off, like most conditions. They turned Buffalo China cups right side up. The green Naugahyde booth had seen better days. Sometimes *original condition* was not such a good idea. They were the only customers.

A frayed wire of a man appeared at the end of the booth, pencil and pad in one hand, glass coffee carafe in the other. His white T-shirt and half-apron were stained red, yellow, and brown from a full day's cooking. He sported a three-day-old five o'clock shadow that could strip paint; his countenance suggested that he would probably prefer to do so rather than prepare another meal. With a flick of his pink tongue, the cook licked the tip of the pencil and looked past them through bloodshot eyes.

Ally stuck out her hand. "I'm Ally," she said. "This is my

friend, Cary. What's your name?"

The man focused on her, set down the coffee, and wiped his hand on the apron, a courtesy that had mixed results at best. He shook first Ally's hand, then Cary's.

"Sam," he drawled out in two syllables.

Ally's smile was warmer than the asphalt out on 84, and Sam softened visibly in its presence.

"Are you having a good day, Sam?"

Sam actually considered the question. "You know," he said, "since you ask, it actually ain't been altogether bad." His smile turned him into a little boy. "Now, what can I get for you folks?"

"I'll have two pop-eggs, Sam," Ally said. "Grits, bacon, a biscuit." She looked at Cary.

"Pop? Eggs?" Cary asked.

Ally favored him with a sage nod.

"Okay," Cary said. He turned to Sam. "I'm too tired to think. Same for me."

Sam filled the Buffalo cups and left to prepare their night breakfast. Crackling bacon and sizzling eggs echoed throughout the little diner.

"We were talking about reincarnation," Ally said.

"God save me." Cary laid his head on the table.

"It will," Ally said. "But listen. This is important. It's important that you understand this so we can figure out what's going on here."

Cary raised his head. "Okay. Fine. So when you reincarnate, you forget everything. Like your name. Lethe. Waters of oblivion. I get it. But Carver and Layton are different because they don't have to forget. How about you? Do you have to forget?"

"Definitely," she said. She blew a puff of steam off the top of her coffee. "That's why all the training."

"I still don't believe in reincarnation."

"Of course not," Ally said. "Of course you don't. What was I thinking? You can't actually see it, so it doesn't exist. Empiricist Pigdog! But you actually can see it. It's all around you. You just don't want to."

Sam arrived with two plates balanced on his right arm and the coffee pot in his left hand.

"Hey, Sam," Cary said. "Got a question for you. You believe in reincarnation?"

Sam straightened his back and lifted his chin, still balancing the plates and the coffee. "'Live,'" he recited, "'so that thou mayest desire to live again — that is thy duty — for in any case thou wilt live again!'" Sam winked, leaned forward a bit. "That there's Mr. Nietzsche."

Ally giggled. Cary rolled his eyes. Sam deposited the breakfast, topped off the coffee, and departed without another word.

Cary looked at his plate. "These are *over easy*," he said.

"Exactly," Ally picked up her fork and grinned.

"But why do you call them 'pop eggs?'"

"Maybe," she whispered, cutting her eyes left and right, "it's because my dad used to make them for me. Get it? Pop eggs?" She pierced each perfect, round yolk with the corner of her fork. Yellow liquid oozed from the centers and pooled at the edge of her grits. "Or maybe not." Ally winked and then used her biscuit to stir the grits and eggs together.

They devoured their night breakfast in silence.

Ally mopped her plate clean with the last morsel of biscuit. "I think," she said, "that I know why they're after you."

"What are you talking about?"

"Tell me about your necklace."

Cary retrieved the talisman from beneath his shirt and cradled it in the crook of his first two fingers. His thumb lingered over the tiny indentations, and his eyes sought the distance, like he was trying to read a forgotten language in Braille. The movement aggravated the ache in his wrist; he tried to massage it away with his left hand. There he sat, across from Ally in the Big Wheel Eatery, "Breakfast Served 24/7," right hand massaging the pendant, left hand massaging his wrist. He looked almost as if he were in prayer.

"Where'd you get that necklace?" Ally repeated.

Cary looked at the talisman. His eyes were lost, like he was walking in a dark dream.

"Found it," he said at last, and returned to his secret world. Distant sounds and a cast of invisible characters vied for his inner attention, drawing him further away from Ally. Empty breakfast plates littered the terrain between them.

"Where? Come on, Cary Walker. Tell me a story."

Cary looked at her, and for a moment he didn't know who she was. Or where he was. He blinked twice, returned partially to this world.

"You're the storyteller," he mumbled.

"Everybody," she said, "is a storyteller. Especially to themselves. You just have to be really careful which of your own stories you believe. So, tell me this one, and we'll see how much of it you believe."

"Well, okay," he began. "It is an interesting story, actually." The more he spoke, the more his voice and mind inhabited the present tense, though, he was enmeshed in a story of the past.

"It was the summer Taylor and I put in the walkway and courtyard. Well, mostly I did. Taylor had discovered *Doom* and *Duke Nukem,* so he was logging a lot of screen time saving the world from bad guys and scary aliens.

"Started off taking rocks from the river, but carrying them up the hill was kicking my ass, so I tried to find as many as I could near where I was working. So I'm working, and one day I find this stone slab just laying there in the dirt. It was a perfect rectangle with squared edges, almost like it had been crafted. Maybe 4-feet long and 2-and-a-half wide. Once I managed to pick it up, I realized, eventually, that it actually had been shaped, carved maybe. And it was covering a stone box that was sunk down into the dirt."

"Eventually?" Ally interrupted.

"Right." He took a sip of coffee. "On account of the snake."

"Snake?" Ally asked.

Sam appeared at the end of the booth. He retrieved the empty plates and pulled a hand-scrawled, green and white bill out of his apron. It floated soft like a leaf to the table. He screwed himself up into recitation posture.

"'Our birth'" he said, "'is but a sleep and a forgetting. The soul that rises with us, our life star, hath elsewhere had its setting and cometh from afar.'" He offered up a shy smile. "That there's Mr. Wordsworth." He departed with the plates, trailing clouds of glory.

"Are you paying him?" asked Cary.

Ally giggled. "You were telling me about the snake."

"Right. Big, black thing. Scared the shit out of me. Almost dropped the stone on my foot. Fell backwards on my butt. Rolled in a bunch of poison ivy trying to get away. Took me the rest of the summer to get rid of it. Anyway, when I finally calmed down, he was just sticking his head out of the hole looking around. I swear, damn thing stared at me like he wanted to tell me something. And..."

"What?" Ally asked.

"It's pretty weird." He stared into his coffee.

"Then it's in perfect company. Tell me."

"Well," Cary said, "when it first came out of the box, it..."

"What, already?"

"It looked like it had legs. Okay? But that's impossible."

"What? Like a centipede?"

"No, no. That might have made sense. Sort of. No. I know it's impossible, but I can still see it. Two in front and two in back."

"Like a dragon." Her voice was barely a whisper.

"No," Cary said. "It didn't have wings. And it definitely didn't breathe fire."

"Not all dragons have wings."

"Please," he said. "Let's not get tickets for the Existence of Dragons Pavilion until we leave the Reincarnation Emporium."

"As you wish," Ally said. "What happened next?"

"He just slithered up the mountainside and disappeared

into the ferns. Slithered. No legs. Must've been the shadows. Anyway, I checked out the rocks, mostly to make sure that there weren't any more snakes. That's when I saw there was a box. And a pouch."

"A pouch?"

"Yeah. I didn't know that's what it was at first, though. There was a leather pouch, all covered with mildew. I took it up on the porch and opened it—very carefully, I might add. I was still pretty freaked out. It was nasty on the outside, but inside it was like it had been put there yesterday."

"And that necklace was in it?"

"This necklace and a bunch of dried leaves. Like tobacco or something. It smelled really good. Kind of like cloves. And some little crystals and colored rocks. I've still got it all back at the house. I washed the pouch with some saddle soap. Had some kind of squiggly drawing on it. I put everything back in the pouch except for the necklace."

"What'd you do with the rock?"

"Well," he said. "Once I realized it was covering a box, I put it back on top. I don't know. Seemed...right somehow. That same squiggly design was scraped into the rock at the bottom. I figured some Cherokee had gone to a lot of trouble to make that thing. Like a time capsule. So I didn't want to dig it up. But I still used it. I just laid the courtyard around it."

"So," she said, "there's a container sunk into the earth under that courtyard?"

"Yeah," he said. "It's the rectangular stone right at the center. And get this. I mean, I know snakes can get into small spaces and all, but that thing was tight. I mean tight. I couldn't see anywhere a bug could get in, much less a snake."

"How big was it?"

"I just told you, 4-feet long by..."

Ally held up her hand. "Oh, believe me," she said. "The size of the box I remember. How big was the snake?"

"Oh, him. He was big. Probably 9 feet. Looked like an indigo, but they don't really live up in the mountains much. At least, I've never seen one. Well, except for that one."

"We should get going," she said. "Can you drive the rest of the way?"

Cary nodded. Ally left a twenty on the table.

Sam was waiting by the front door.

"Y'all be careful out there on that Bhavachakra Highway."

Ally smiled and gave him a hug.

"Bava whatcha?" Cary asked.

"Nevermind."

When they were in the car, Ally asked, "Can I see it?"

Cary hesitated, then hooked his thumbs into the leather strap and lifted the necklace over his head. The pendant was about an inch and a half long and three quarters of an inch in diameter. A small loop of silver extended from one end for the thong to pass through. She ran her fingers over the design, feeling it the way she had often seen Cary do.

"I think," she said, "this is what they're after."

"What makes you think that?" He started the car, but waited for her answer.

"Because," she said at last. "I had a dream about it."

"When?"

Ally stared into his eyes.

For an instant, the separation between them seemed, to Cary, immeasurable. The infinite space was filled with a multitude of swirling sounds: the roaring wind, voices shouting in argument, a distant symphony, and a single flute—all merging, yet separate, in the singularity of that instant. Cary shook his head. The distance collapsed, and she filled his vision.

"When I was 12," she said. "Twelve years ago."

***

Taylor left the lighthouse and careened south to downtown, drawn toward, but still resisting the pull of his new center of gravity. He walked the six miles of Bayshore Boulevard back and forth twice, resisting the Angel's command to follow his internal map, to turn away from the water and head inland. His feet were bleeding from blisters, but he did not feel the pain. Saturday late night joggers and in-line skaters zipped past him in both directions. As he approached the bridge to Davis Islands for the third time, he could no longer fight the attraction that pulled him away from the bridge and toward Hyde Park. The last of his resistance slipped helplessly into the dirty bay.

He passed through the wall of wealth that lined Bayshore, walked past the renovated residences of regentrified Hyde Park, through the underpass of Selmon Freeway, and into the as yet un-regenerated streets. Dark and dingy bungalows, built in the '20s and '30s to last forever, now teetered on the verge of collapse. Yet a warmth, a certainty, drew him onward up Edison Avenue almost to Kennedy Boulevard, where small bands of boy prostitutes congregated, but not quite that far. He came at last to a 1920s brick apartment house.

Four men and four women in their early 20s were assembled like a prayer on the porch. A woman stepped forward from the group. Tears poured from her smiling eyes. "Come in," she said. "We've been waiting for you. We'll take care of you." For the first time in his life, Taylor felt completely at home.

***

The temple bells rang when Simon and Freddy exited the Bean Cellar. Night had settled in; the chambered heat of the Florida day rose from the streets and into the cooling air.

"So," Freddy said, "are you planning at some point to tell me what this is all about?"

"At some point," Simon answered. "Once I..."

He came to an abrupt halt a few steps away from the curb. Halfway down the block, three kids leaned against a low brick wall, two young men on either side of a young woman. They stood in the yellow circle of a street lamp next to Simon's Volvo and stared up the block at Simon and Freddy.

Just staring and scratching the back of their heads.

"Cree-pay," Simon said. "Some of yours?"

"Never seen them before. And UT's a small place. Could be high school kids."

"They sure seem to have itchy heads."

Freddy smiled. "You, uh, need me to walk you to your car, big guy?"

"Actually, where are you parked?" He continued to stare at the—he had begun to think of them as zombies—by his car.

The zombies stared back.

"I walked over from campus," said Freddy. "Maybe you should give me a ride."

"Great minds stink alike."

They walked the half block to Simon's car. "How's it going?" Simon asked the kids. All three suddenly found the sidewalk very interesting.

"Whatever," said the girl after a long moment of indecision.

Simon had the urge to shout, "It's alive! My creature *lives!*" but thought better of mixing movie metaphors and pissing off the fine young weirdos, all three of whom continued to scratch the backs of their heads.

"Try Head and Shoulders," Simon said to the girl.

"Selsun Blue's better," Freddy said.

Simon shook his head. "Uh uh."

"Yeah huh," said Freddy. "Says so on TV, so it must be true."

Simon pressed his key fob, and the door locks clunked open.

"She was an articulate little thing," Freddy said after he had closed the door. "All that fancy book-learning must be paying off."

"And you thought Leo Cruickshank was a freak," Simon said. He pulled the Volvo away from the curb.

"Listen," said Freddy. "I'm going to see if I can learn any more about this Qellepoth stuff from the other students. I'll give you a call if I find anything out."

"All right. I'll give you a call, too, once I figure out a little more about how this fits in."

"You've got my cell," Freddy said. "I keep it on 24/7." He smiled. "In case my sweetie gives me a bootie call."

"I should be so lucky." Simon looked in the rearview mirror. The three kids watched until they were out of sight and then disappeared down an all-but-invisible alley.

***

Gareth Stokes called Carver from the rear compartment of a Westwind Astra somewhere over Georgia. Two of his crew slept in the main cabin. The rest were on call in D.C.

"We're en route to Tampa," he said. "Your boy Layton's first team is already there. Cord must have found Walker's kid."

Carver had taken the call in his study. Miranda had gone sailing for the day.

"Did Cord inform you of this?" Carver asked.

"Not on purpose." Stokes laughed. "One of my guys is, how do I want to say this...friends...with the wife of one of Ian's main operatives."

"Ah," said Carver. "The treachery of women. Never fails. Good work. What's the plan?"

"They're at the Harbor Island Hotel. We'll set up there too and make contact. Figure out what he's up to and make sure we stay on top of it." Stokes paused.

"Something else?" asked Carver.

"Well, maybe it's just all the years of being on opposite sides of the fence, you know, but I still don't trust that guy. Or his boss. Even if we are supposed to be working together now."

"I would say," Carver replied, "that your suspicion is quite on target, Gareth. Don't turn your back."

"Count on that."

"And," Carver said, "be ready. I may find it necessary to return to our more familiar relationships on a moment's notice. If we make that move, I want you and your men prepared to act before Layton can."

Stokes laughed. "That would truly be a pleasure."

"Very well," Carver said. "Inform me as soon as you know what's going on."

"As always, sir. Goodbye."

Carver propped his elbows on his desk and rested his head in his hands.

Tampa.

Walker's kid was there, and now Ian Cord knew exactly where. It seemed unlikely that Walker would choose now, while he was on the run, to try to find his missing kid.

Carver raised his head. Miranda watched him from the doorway. The light behind her offered inviting glimpses of her silhouette underneath the white shift.

"I thought you were sailing."

"I missed you too much. I turned around and came back before I even got to the harbor." She shrugged, a graceful, effortless movement; the shift slipped off her shoulders and floated to the floor. Her eyes smiled, then her lips; she turned and walked slowly to the bedroom. Without a word, Carver followed.

***

"How long have you known?" Cary asked.

"Actually, I've been pretty sure for a while, but I didn't want to..."

"How long?"

Ally hesitated. "Since the day outside Winter Star," she said. "Since I first saw you. You were holding that necklace in your hand, rubbing it like you always do. But—"

"I don't *always* rub my necklace."

"Ha!" she said. "You're kidding, right? It's like your worry stone or something. I'm surprised there's anything left of it."

Cary smoldered in silence. They had left The Big Wheel and driven the last two hours without speaking, until, as they had reached the outskirts of Tampa, Cary's question had finally exploded.

"You should have told me," he said.

Traffic thickened as they passed the Tampa Greyhound track and, of all things, a land-bound lighthouse miles from the sea, where only hours before Taylor had sat cross-legged, his back propped against its dingy base.

"I couldn't," Ally said, finally. "I wanted to, but what if I was wrong? And once I was pretty sure…well by then we were so busy staying alive that I…I just didn't think about it."

"Even if you were wrong," Cary said, "you still should have told me." He focused on the traffic, using it to block her out.

"We're going to a place called Ybor City," said Ally. "It's—"

"I know how to get there," he said. "Where in Ybor? It's Saturday night. The streets are closed."

"How do you know that?"

Cary glowered at the road. They completed the journey in silence.

Ybor City's streets were awash with yuppies and drunken college students. Locals observed the show from cast-iron balconies cantilevered over brick sidewalks or from rooftop patios. Cary parked the LeSabre in an above-ground garage on 15th Street off 7th Avenue.

"Where?" he said.

"Just how long are you going to stay mad at me?" Ally asked.

Cary took the daypacks from the backseat and handed one to Ally. He studied the concrete floor.

"You ever notice how parking garages all look the same from the inside?" he said. "D.C. or Tampa. Or freaking Sumer for all I know. Like parking garages all over the world are a single place, and they only become different when you step outside. It all seems to blur together." He met her eyes.

"I'm sorry. It's just that this is all so diff—"

Ally fell against him, wrapped her arms around his waist, and sobbed against his chest, soaking his shirt with her tears. Without fully realizing what he was doing, Cary wrapped one arm around her shoulders and stroked her hair with his other hand. Cary had not failed to notice how attractive Ally was, but she stirred different emotions in him.

"Don't worry," he said. "Don't worry. It's going to be all right." And he believed it—just as he had believed it the countless times he had performed this same dance and spoken these same words to Taylor. He was struck by the irony of how easy it was to believe his soothing assurances when he said them to Taylor, or now to Ally, but never to himself. Still, he did believe that everything would be all right.

He just didn't know how.

They left the garage and found 7th Avenue, Ybor City's party Mecca. The flow of festivity swept them along, deeper into the heart of drugged and drunken revelry. Cary draped his arm over Ally's shoulder.

Ybor was just starting to cook. Various brands of loud, throbbing music competed for their attention. Twelve blocks later, they heard the fiery cry of a guitar pouring down from The Blues Ship across the street. Ally steered them into the dark entrance of a narrow, brick canyon next to Blue Devil Tattoos; the burning guitar faded to a muffled throb.

"This way," she said. "We're up here." A smoky breeze tailed them into the shadows.

The safe house was a large studio above Blue Devil. Cary followed Ally through a doorway softened by decades of grime and layers of paint. Narrow brown stairs opened onto a small landing of white hexagonal tile. Lime-green plaster walls flaked away from wood lath nailed over red brick. Layer upon layer upon layer. *Everything is a palimpsest. What stories could these walls tell?* The ceiling was 20 feet.

A tarnished brass bed leaned against the left-hand wall. Ally bounced on the springy mattress, launching a swirling dust storm into the thick air. Two giant ceiling fans spun like indolent propellers, resentful of having to work in the tropical heat. Even in the swan song of March, temperatures already hit the '90s at mid-day, and the room had no air-conditioner. But the fans and the high ceilings kept the apartment surprisingly comfortable.

"I guess this is me." Cary sank into the soft cushions and tattered quilt on a threadbare, beige sofa. He had never felt more comfortable.

"You want the bed?" Ally asked.

"No, no," he said. "I'll suffer through."

The far end of the studio offered a kitchenette with an antique gas stove. Next to the stove, an even older refrigerator hummed and rattled. French doors opened onto a wrought iron balcony. Cary unfolded himself from the couch when Ally pushed open the doors. Night sounds flooded the room. They leaned over the railing, just a couple of locals watching the weekend invasion.

The party that had just borne them down the avenue continued to eddy and flow beneath them, but their perspective of it was entirely different. The balcony offered safety and detachment, neither of which had been available on the street.

"It's beautiful from up here, isn't it?" Ally said.

"I was just thinking that."

Ally followed the multicolored flow of the crowd. "Sorry I freaked back there. I do that sometimes. Not very professional, I guess."

Cary smiled. "It did surprise me. Don't worry about it. Everybody loses it sometimes."

Across the street, near the open front of a restaurant called Carmine's, a small crowd had gathered around a thin, shirtless man in wide, striped pants and red suspenders. He was juggling three flaming batons. Farther up 7th, in the open front of the Empire Club, a muscular man in a black, sleeveless tee poured golden shots of Cuervo into the willing mouths of college students and spun them in an antique barber's chair.

"So," Cary said. "Are you going to tell me about this dream?"

The latest victim of the barber chair stood and immediately collapsed, to the great delight of his companions.

Ally sighed. "Maybe the weirdest dream I ever had. I'm in a maze of cobblestone streets, chasing someone. A woman. And... I can see her back. It has this weird tattoo on it."

"And she has the necklace?"

"No. I don't think so. I think she *is* the necklace." Ally pulled the pendant into the light so that the design was visible. "This was the tattoo on her back. Sort of. I mean, it was different too, because it was all connected, like a dot-to-dot. But it was the same design. Told you. Weird. But that's dreams for you."

"But...how did you recognize it? Especially after all that time?"

"Something about the way the sun hit you that day. I could see the design on the necklace as clear as I ever saw anything. Besides, I've been looking for this design ever since the dream." She let the necklace fall back against Cary's chest. "It was disturbing. Not just because it was weird, but because I think I wanted to hurt her. I think I wanted to kill her. And I think she wasn't just the necklace. I think she was you."

Cary tried to take all of this in. Eventually he gave up and turned to words that could make sense to him. "So why are we in Tampa, then?"

"I know someone here. A professor. An archaeologist. He might be able to tell us what's so special about your necklace. We'll go see him Monday."

***

They told Taylor that they were called the Qellepoth, and they existed only to serve his needs. When he first arrived at the apartment on Edison Avenue, two women had showered with him, bathing him. Their actions were reverent, not at all sexual. Caitlin was in charge. She was thin and tall, with dark hair cut like a boy and big brown eyes that spoke more clearly than her words. Her friend, Meghan, was smaller and blonde, with sparkling blue eyes; Meghan was Caitlin's right-hand girl. The other Qellepoth hung back, waiting for orders.

Caitlin and Meghan dressed Taylor in red silk pajamas and a red robe with a black insignia on the back. They settled him on the old crimson couch in the front room like a king on a throne. Scented candles and sticks of incense burned on every available surface, saturating the air with an exotic mélange of perfumes. Taylor remained on the sofa, red on red, nearly invisible in the deep cushions. His servants entered only to bring him cups of freshly brewed tea.

Hunger was a faded memory. The herbal infusion that Caitlin and Meghan urged Taylor to drink provided everything he would need for the time remaining. They kept the brew bubbling in the kitchen; even with the burning incense and candles, a pungent scent like freshly ground cloves permeated the apartment.

The visions had begun shortly after he had drunk the first cup. With only a slight drop in his stomach for warning, like that first moment a roller coaster slips over gravity's ledge, Taylor found himself tumbling end over end in a deep red cloud, a living mist. All around him horrible, blood-red monsters clawed their way in and out of sight, in and out of existence. The mist itself was a sea of hatred and lust for carnage.

Grastar. They were called Grastar. The name resounded in the caverns of Taylor's brain, but he had no concept of how he knew this.

The Grastar beasts had four muscular arms and wide hands, each with 16, claw-tipped fingers. Their gargoyle faces were squat and flat with square mouths and rough, cube-shaped teeth. But Taylor caught only glimpses of their horror; the monsters took solid form scarcely for a moment, coalescing out of the red vapor long enough to glower at him and then dissolve back into the mist. Poisonous rage radiated from their eyes. They yearned to tear each other to pieces, to tear him to pieces, yet they were not corporeal long enough to accomplish either.

Most fantastic of all, they feared him. Each time one of the beasts formed in his presence, Taylor first felt its rage wash over him and then watched it cower and dissolve; Taylor's dominance was unquestioned.

Throughout the night and over the following days, Taylor slipped in and out of the vision. Each time the room shimmered and dissolved into the red mist, the monstrous bloodlust migrated a little deeper inside Taylor's soul. As each of the creatures cowered before him, Taylor's own lust for power grew. Almost immediately, he began to long for that sinking feeling in the pit of his stomach, the sign that he was about to slip into this other world where he was becoming a god.

And yet...

...the young man, the boy, the child that had spent 20-odd years becoming Taylor Walker, the little boy that had held his mother's and father's hands, that boy now clung to a thread, a fine filament of light connected to a receding reservoir of memory. In that reservoir, like a soft glow hiding among shadows, a different vision persisted:

Mother. Father. Safety. Love.

The child held that vision close to his heart. Hidden. Protected. Cherished. And he waited.

***

Simon dropped Freddy at UT and then crossed Tampa Bay to Davis Islands. Two more zombies, clones of the ones that had just scared the crap out of him and Freddy, watched from the corner as he turned onto Aegean.

"I say again," Simon said, "creee-pay."

At least none of them were staking out the front of The Ponce. He screeched up to the curb and, just to be safe, checked the rearview mirror before he got out. Aegean was deserted. He glanced up nine stories to his bedroom window.

"Hell-lo," he said. Light escaped from the edges of the white mini-blinds. "I'm pretty sure I didn't leave you on. And I'm definitely sure I didn't leave the blinds down."

To go up, or not to go up? That, definitely, is the question. Or to call the cops. And tell them…what? That I think I turned my lights off when I left. Unless someone's actually in there.

He had just about decided to risk going up when movement drew his attention to the palmettos at the base of the building. Simon tensed.

Like I could actually fight off these psychos.

He reached back for the door handle. Woodstein trotted out of the bushes, tail high in feline aplomb, and slunk over to the car.

"And just who let you out, my little love?" Simon gathered him up. Woody purred like a miniature jackhammer, and Simon's heart beat a tic slower. He looked up to his window just in time to see the blinds fall back into place.

"Well, shit," he said. He hugged Woodstein close to his neck and pondered the situation for another moment. "Okay," he said. "Definitely don't go up. What now?"

A young man stepped out from behind the bushes on the corner half a block up and simply stood there, arms limp at his sides. Simon backed into the car and turned over the starter, never taking his eyes off the man. Woodstein climbed onto the rear deck and curled up. Another man stepped around the corner behind them.

"What?" Simon yelled out of his car window. "Do you guys actually study old horror movies or something?" He gunned the engine and sped past the one in front. The man turned, watched, but made no move to follow.

"Tres creepay" he said. "Simon's Life Rule Number 11: Don't go into your apartment if teenage zombie creepazoids await."

He raced across the Davis Islands Bridge and turned onto Bayshore toward downtown. Several deep breaths dropped his pulse to 150 or so. Less than a quarter of a mile down Bayshore, he whipped into a pullout next to a large pirate ship.

Across the channel and beyond Tampa General Hospital, the Ponce De Leon stood stark and white against the starless night.

"Haaaaaarrr," he said.

***

"His name's Harvey Whitt," said Ally. "Teaches Archaeology at USF."

"I still don't see what could possibly be important enough about this old hunk of…whatever it is…that these guys would want it. Weird dream or not. I mean, so maybe it's 150, 200 years old. Some Cherokee buried it. So maybe it's worth something. But not that much. Not enough to kill for."

"Well," Ally said, drawing the word out, "that's why we go see Harvey. We should be pretty safe until then. There's no reason they would think we came here."

"Maybe," Cary said. He watched the crowd swirl and drift in clumps along 7th.

"What do you mean, 'maybe'?" Ally said. "Is there something I should know about?"

"Ask your girl, Pava," Cary said. "I'm going to bed."

He reclaimed his berth on the sofa and snuggled into the cushions. Ally turned off the lamp. Cary lay in the darkness, staring at a distant ceiling he could not see, but knew was up there. Muffled songs of Saturday night rattled the window panes. Despite the long drive, or perhaps because of it, his nerves were too tightly wound for him to relax.

"Hey?" he said.

"What?"

"Sorry I was an asshole. Thanks for saving my life."

Ally waited almost a full minute before she replied.

"You're welcome," she said. "Now go to sleep. We'll see Dr. Whitt on Monday and hope that he can help us sort this out."

Cary rolled to his side. He had not thought of the sounds and voices in his head for—he didn't know how long—hours at least. The moment he remembered them, they arose once again. For some reason, perhaps in comparison to what he had experienced in the last few days, their presence didn't seem to be quite the curse he had imagined. The pulse of the blues from across the street blended with his interior soundscape. Cary drifted on melodies he had not known were hidden there. He slid along the terrain of those songs into his world of dreams, and as he fell deeper into that world, he was able to make out the arguing voices in his inner worlds. They were arguing about him.

Oh my God. How could I not have known this?

By morning he had forgotten all that he had heard while falling asleep.

Before Time

~

Ksama

Ksama cherishes no illusions about this fight. Sidra is the most fell of the warrior class in Apsara. Her skills are legendary. Ksama cleaves only to the sanctity of her promise.

Sidra circles closer, extending the small stick in front and twirling the other behind her hip. She pirouettes to the right, closing the last bit of distance. The first blow of the long stick strikes Ksama's left shoulder. Sidra continues her spin and booms the end of the short stick like a hammerhead against Ksama's cheek. Bone and tooth shatter, and the iron gush of blood floods her mouth even as she strikes out with her blade. But Sidra has already stepped behind her, and DevaRada kisses only the air. With three quick strikes, Sidra pounds the back of Ksama's right shoulder like a drumbeat, numbing it and almost causing her sword to fall. Sidra rakes the long stick across the back of Ksama's legs, driving her to her knees. Ksama swings blind as she topples, begging God's Tooth to bite flesh. Instead, her wrist slips into the closing trap of the Sieghke. The long stick suspends her arm's momentum while Sidra hammers down with the other, full speed, full force. Ksama's arm snaps clean, three inches above the hand, just above the Mark of Uktenah inscribed on the inside of her wrist.

DevaRada rings like a desolate bell when it strikes the blood-moist ground, but the sound is lost in Ksama's endless scream. Her right forearm swings back and forth, a horrible, fleshy pendulum. She doubles forward, cradling the agony against her chest. The entire battle has lasted less than 15 seconds.

Ksama's world is a red-hot wound. She clenches her eyes tight, tighter still, trying to summon the blackness of oblivion, trying to force away the scarlet pain. In the distance, a soft voice speaks. Soothing or taunting? Ksama can't tell. Her bindings are loosened, and a great weight is lifted from her shoulders. The fresh evening air cools her uncovered back.

She sighs. Relief. But the relief is wrong. Soothing. But wrong. She rocks back onto her heels, labors to raise her head, to force her eyelids to part, though she fears more agony will flood her vision. Instead her eyes lite upon Sh'ele. The crystal lies exposed on the ground, its leather sheath flayed open like dark, useless wings.

A fine mist begins to fall, coating the glittering facets. Near Sh'ele's base, four smaller crystals have broken off— three stubby nodes and a spike that shines like a diamond icicle in the moonlight.

Sidra assesses Ksama the way a cat considers a rat that has outlived its capacity for amusement. The two women kneel on opposite sides of Sh'ele like worshipers engaged in mutual prayer, rather than adversaries in a game of death.

"It would appear," Sidra says, "that God's Tooth will find nothing to bite this night."

Profound stillness accompanies the inevitability of death. Such are the paradoxes of human existence. The peace of this perfect moment floods Ksama's heart, and all is well. Shafts of moonlight infuse the falling mist, lighting up Sh'ele like a looking glass. Ksama studies Sidra's inverted reflection in the widest of the crystal's facets. Sidra's mouth is moving, but Ksama does not hear. Instead her ears tremble with the roar of wind, though the night is still. Above the wind, or woven within it, the tinklings of a thousand tiny bells ring one upon another as each molecule of mist falls with sublime clarity onto Sh'ele. She has never felt so…present.

Ksama has no plan, only her failing vow of protection. Yet all is perfect as it is. Silent acceptance of her death. Perfect peace. Surrender. The most graceful and noble moment of her life, even in the certainty of defeat.

Ksama lets her languid fingertips trail over Sh'ele's shining face, tracing a line across Sidra's image, across the reflection of her neck. Her eyes meet Sidra's in a sorrowful gaze; her mouth quirks into a half smile. She continues the sweep of her good hand down the length of the glowing crystal, a most elegant and peaceful gesture. And in the peace of that moment, with an empty mind and a full heart, Ksama retrieves the crystal spike that is propped against Sh'ele's base and drives it, true and deep, into the left side of Sidra's throat.

"It would appear," Ksama rasps through her pain, "that God has many teeth."

An exquisite set of contrasts bursts to life within Ksama, and she floats in their tensions. The overarching pain in her dangling arm. The sweet iron mélange of blood mingled with saline air. The scrape of fresh cuts where the crystal spike has pierced her palm. The rhythmic spurting from Sidra's neck washed black by moonlight. The cadenced draining of life splashing again and again on Sh'ele's moon-bright surface.

The stunned astonishment on Sidra's face.

Their eyes meet one last time in a moment of respect, resignation, and acceptance of each to her fate. In that instant— barely more than a breath really—they make a contract to revisit these events, a pact to find mutual balance in another place, when time exists. Sidra nods once and slumps backward, her face a mask of forgiveness.

A sob explodes from Ksama's throat, followed by a rain of tears. Tears of relief, tears of grief. She surveys the results of her work. Her sacred commitment to serve life has come down to this.

"I have become death," she says. Then a warm wave carries her into oblivion.

Present Day

The *Jose Gaspar*, Tampa's own Ship of Fools, rocked easily on the ebbing tide, having accomplished its yearly invasion of Tampa only weeks before. The vessel was moored a quarter mile from the Davis Islands Bridge. Simon needed to get farther away, but even though his pulse had returned almost to normal, he couldn't stop his hands and knees from shaking. His cell phone gleamed like a talisman on the seat beside him.

"Okay," he said, "if I call the police then they'll want to know why I think these guys are after me, and my exclusive's blown. If I don't, then I can't go back to my apartment."

All of the clippings were in the apartment, but Simon's green canvas briefcase, containing his laptop and the notes from all his research, lay on the passenger side floor.

Woodstein hopped over the back seat and climbed into Simon's lap.

"Looks like we're going Kerouac, Woody."

It took Simon three attempts before he was able to force his still trembling fingers to dial Freddy Blake's number.

He got Freddy's voicemail three times before he gave up and drove to an ATM. He continued to call Freddy the rest of the evening, and for the next few days. But Freddy never answered.

***

Half a week later, a little after 2 a.m. Wednesday morning, Taylor leaned against the dirty glass panel of a phone booth. He pressed the handset against his chest, trying to force it through bone and skin directly into his heart.

The Angel's instructions had been very specific. He was to go to the apartment. He was to remain there. Servants, the people he now knew as the Qellepoth, would care for his every need.

Mixed with this memory was the newer vision, the one that had begun his first night with the Qellepoth. The place where demons with four arms arose out of hell to devour him, then cowered instead before his majesty. The World of Red Clouds, where the new Taylor had risen to become their God of Fear. The world where the monsters had already known his true name.

But only minutes ago, Taylor had remembered a lovely dream, an entire, encapsulated lifetime in which he had been a child, a student. When and where had that been? He longed to return to it. A number echoed in his empty hall of memories; this number held the answer. He had risen abruptly, still dressed only in his red robe and silk pajamas. A handful of loose change had accumulated on the table by the door. While Caitlin had toiled in the kitchen over a fresh pot of tea, Taylor had swept the coins into his pocket and stumbled out. He stood now in a phone booth in the parking lot of the Travelodge at the corner of Kennedy and South Boulevard.

He deposited eight quarters into the slot and willed his index finger to rise and press the buttons. Electronic pulses echoed in his ear. Once. Twice. After the third ring, voicemail answered. A familiar voice. Tears pooled in Taylor's eyes.

"Leave your message. I'll call you back."

Taylor heard his own voice speak from a great distance. "Daddy?" He had not called his father "Daddy" for more than 10 years. "Daddy," he continued. "It's..." He had to think for a moment, had to focus, before he could say, "It's Taylor. I'm sorry, Daddy. I'm sorry." He listened to his own story unfold there in the phone booth. He poured his hidden heart into his words.

I'm Taylor. I'm talking on the telephone to my father. Save me... Daddy...Mommy... I'm lost... I'm in trouble. Save me. Please save me... Please...

He did not know what he needed to be rescued from. Only that he was lost.

Neither did he know how long he talked or what he said. Night creatures passed by and looked at the strange man in the bathrobe and pajamas talking on a payphone. Sometimes Taylor waved to them. Then an electronic voice interrupted him, demanding more money for more time. But his pockets were as empty as his palace of memory. He held the phone to his ear, weeping against closed eyes, long after the phone had begun to beep.

When Taylor opened his eyes, Caitlin was there. Two men he had not seen before were with her. Caitlin opened the door to the phone booth, her eyes full to the brim, her voice trembling.

"Come with us," she said. She took his hand and pulled him into the gentle air. The men, one a small student-type in a black polo, the other a potential linebacker, supported him at the elbows. Taylor let himself sag, knowing their hands would keep him from falling. "Come with us," Caitlin said. "We'll take you home now."

Michael Phillips Mann

FIFTH ARTICULATION

an archaeologist

a tobacconist

almost Godzilla Roll

Cohibas

aliens

Irkalla

adrift

Present Day

Dr. Harvey Whitt, it turned out, had been in Urbana, Illinois, at a conference and was not due back on campus until mid-week. On Wednesday, Ally and Cary parked the LeSabre in the shadow of the USF Sun Dome and walked across campus to Cooper Hall, a brick classroom building gone gray and dull with lack of funds.

The single elevator was a cross between a creeping time capsule and a vibrating death trap. It took a full minute to rise two floors, and another 30 seconds to settle enough for the doors to lumber open.

"No wonder all the students were taking the stairs," Cary said.

Whitt was a tall, roundish professor in his mid-60s. Sartorial. Dapper, in fact. He wore a Harris Tweed jacket and sported a red bow tie over a crisp, white shirt. In place of a matching silk handkerchief, the tip of a red lacquered chopstick poked out of his breast pocket like an inquisitive serpent. The professor's soft, square face reminded Cary of a jumbo marshmallow. Whitt looked like he had never in his life soiled his hands in ancient dirt. But looks, as they say, can be deceiving.

"Alethea!" Whitt said, holding his arms wide.

Ally let herself be engulfed in Whitt's bulk.

"Child, I haven't seen you since you were running around

in diapers." Whitt's deep, rumbling voice carried the moist resonance of chronic bronchial infections. The stale aroma of depleted tobacco escaped from the tweed when he moved.

Cary found it hard to imagine Ally running around in diapers. She seemed to have just sprouted from the sea, born whole like Venus on the Half Shell, only with a more interesting—and more dangerous—retinue.

"Let's see what we've got," Whitt said after Ally had performed introductions and Cary had, somewhat reluctantly, handed over the necklace. Whitt reached across the lab table and pulled a magnifier light over the talisman. He turned the pendant several times, taking extra time with the ends.

"Can't tell too much from a cursory examination," he said. "But look at this." Whitt removed the chopstick from his shirt pocket and pointed to the end of the piece. The red lacquer tip looked like a bloody finger under the glass. "See the difference in textures here between the side and the end?" His ham-sized hands deftly manipulated the chopstick, drawing attention from one texture to the other. "And look at this line between them. Here."

"What does that mean?" Ally asked.

Whitt pointed again to the end. "Well, the artifact itself is probably bone of some sort or another. Deer. Or buffalo. It's been polished, so it resembles ivory, but look at the surface." He turned the pendant slowly. "Ivory has a grain. No grain here. Definitely bone. But this part on the ends is something else entirely. A composite. Or a compound. Maybe ground-up horn or antler mixed with resin to form a sealer. And see how the silver loop is embedded into the composite?"

"Why would somebody do that?" Cary asked.

"Maybe just to make the ends smooth. Seal the marrow. Make the piece prettier." He hefted the necklace in his hand, taking its weight and measure with his palm. "Where, might I ask, did you acquire this?"

Ally looked to Cary and raised her eyebrows.

"I found it," Cary said. "Near my house in the mountains. Western North Carolina."

Now Whitt's eyebrows drifted upward. "Really? Extremely interesting. That would indicate that the piece would be Aniyunwiya. Um…Cherokee." He continued to weigh the pendant in his hand. "This is definitely not Cherokee. It's too…well, primitive is not necessarily the correct the word. Maybe primal?"

"What about the markings?" Ally asked.

"Scrimshaw technique of some sort," Whitt said. "The surface is polished down and then scratched or pierced in a design. Then the bone is dipped in ink or stain. The ink washes off the polished sides and soaks into the softer scratches."

"Oh, I know what scrimshaw is," Cary said. He looked at Ally. She nodded. "But what do they mean?"

Whitt cleared his throat with a great, wet rumble. "Don't have a clue, do I?" He turned the pendant upside down. "Looks a little like a constellation. I have…a friend…who teaches in the astronomy department. She might be able to help."

"Harvey," Ally said. "You old dog. You've got a girlfriend!"

Whitt's marshmallow face turned pink.

"Well," he said. "I guess I do." He cleared his throat again. "So, can I keep it for a few days? I could show it to her. And carbon date it while I have it."

Cary snatched up the pendant before he even knew his hand had moved.

"Whoa, Gollum. Chill out," Ally said. She turned to Whitt. "Do you have to keep the piece to date it? I mean, could you take scrapings or something?"

"Well, yes, I could." Whitt perked up a bit. "That's what I'd do anyway." He paused. "And I suppose I could take photographs to show Emily…um…Dr. Young." He looked at Cary. Cary nodded and handed the piece back. "You know, though," Whitt mused, "this is really heavy for bone." He took the necklace to a small electronic scale. "See? Twenty-one grams. Way too much, even factoring in this composite."

"What does that mean?" Cary said. "Why would it...I mean...how could it...be heavier than it's supposed to be? If you're right about what it's made of."

Whitt looked closely at the talisman. "I wouldn't be surprised," he said finally, "if you opened this up and found something else inside it."

***

Taylor reclined on his soft, red throne. Caitlin and Meghan sat on either side of him. A fresh cup of tea steamed on the round table. Meghan lifted it and offered it to him.

"Drink this now," she said. "Catie and I will be back in a minute." The two girls disappeared into the kitchen.

Taylor stared into the golden brown liquid. Powdery residue swirled at the bottom of the cup. Meghan's and Caitlin's hushed voices carried through the thin walls.

"He's different from the others," Caitlin said.

"I know," Meghan said. "Everyone else was so...I don't know. Happy, I guess. But he seems so sad. Lost."

"Maybe he's just the first one we've seen like this. Maybe there's others who aren't happy about it either. We're only one cell. There's supposed to be lots of other cells. All over."

"Catie?" Meghan said.

Suddenly she sounded like a scared little girl. Her voice grew softer, but the walls and the distance dissolved a little more with each sip of the tea. Taylor heard every word.

"Yeah?"

"Do you still want to take it?"

Taylor drained the last sip of his tea.

"I'm not sure anymore," she said.

"Me neither," Meghan said. "I kind of want to go home."

***

Harvey Whitt had promised answers within a week. Cary and Ally used the time to lie low and recuperate. On Saturday

129

afternoon they ventured out for a stroll down sunlit Seventh Avenue. Across the street, four Cuban patriarchs played dominoes at a wrought iron table on the tile veranda in front of The Columbia Restaurant. Heavy brown cigar smoke mingled with the ubiquitous aroma of roasting coffee.

Ally stopped to look into a large, plate glass window. Gold lettering, 6 inches high, arched across the glass: *Almengual Tobacconists, Est. 1923.* Inside, a stout Cubano with a dark, shiny head and a thick, steel-gray mustache leaned back in his wooden chair and read *La Gaceta.* Four glass display cases with mahogany frames. held cigars in various shapes, sizes, and shades of brown. A battery of hand-made humidors lined the inside window ledge, and a large sepia-tone photograph of Don Vicente de Ybor hung high on the back wall.

"You, uh, want a cigar?" Cary asked.

"What?"

"Just wondering why you were staring into a cigar store?"

The old Cubano closed the paper to turn the page, opened it wide, and leaned back in his seat. Even in the noise of the street, they heard the chair springs whine in protest. Ally continued walking.

"What was that all about?" Cary asked.

"Nothing. I don't know," Ally said, still lost in her reverie. "Just an interesting shop."

Early afternoon sunlight filtered through metal balconies, casting bright grids on weathered brown cobblestones. Ally and Cary passed in and out of shadows on Seventh Avenue.

"But…nothing dangerous, right? That guy wasn't one of the bad guys, was he?"

Ally laughed. "No. I suspect he was just your regular old Cuban tobacconist. But it was a very interesting shop."

The hour had almost reached four; shadows of old buildings nipped at their feet. In the week they had been hiding out in Ybor, Cary had resurrected his lost love for *café con leche,* scalded milk mixed in equal proportions with Cuban coffee. Locals called it *media-media:* half and half. Cary bought two cups at Carmine's. He and Ally sat on a wood and iron bench in the plaza adjacent to the Cuban Club.

"This beats the hell out of lattes."

"You've been here before," Ally said.

Cary stared at the red brick patio. He nodded, looked up at her for a moment, and then rekindled his interest in the bricks.

"Why didn't you tell me?"

"I don't know," he said. He finished his coffee and looked around for a garbage can. None was visible. He worried the empty Styrofoam cup with his fingers. "Hey," he said. "Why don't you tell me about that alien conspiracy now?"

Ally raised her eyebrows. "What do you want to know?"

"Start with where they're from."

"I don't know," she said. "Nobody knows. But they live on Jupiter."

Cary's laugh burst out like a cough. "Nothing can live on Jupiter," he said. "It's…"

"Nothing human," she said. "Besides, technically, Jupiter's not a planet. In fact, it wasn't even an original part of our solar system. They brought it here, or it brought them here, and…"

"Whoa," he said. "Hold on. This is like a really bad science fiction story."

"It's not *that* bad a story. Besides, I told you before, where do you think all those sci-fi stories come from? You really need to get this. There is nothing, no story written, no story told, no movie made, that isn't happening somewhere. The act of telling it brings it into existence."

Cary looked at her like *she* was an alien.

"If that's true," he said, "then how do you know *we're* not just part of some story? How do you know anything is real?"

She looked into his eyes for a long moment. Then she shrugged. "I don't."

"Okay…?" he said. "But, just for the sake of continuing this discussion, let's move on to areas I can't easily refute with science. What do these aliens want? What do they have to do with the assholes that want my necklace? What are they called?"

Ally looked into his eyes. *My God. Are you actually starting to believe me a little? Cool.*

"Tell you what," she said. "I'll answer one of those questions for now. But first, you answer mine. Why didn't you tell me you'd been here before?"

Cary shrugged. "It was a long time ago," he said. "I'd just broken up with the love of my life. Thought she was, anyway. I had a friend who lived here, so I hitchhiked down. Did grunt work. Under the table. No records. Just crashed in his warehouse for a year or so."

"You know," she said, "for just an average guy, you have a lot of skeletons in your closet."

"I don't have any closets," he said. "Much less skeletons."

The sun had fallen lower, and shadows consumed the light in the plaza.

Ally stood. "Nothing to be done about it now," she said. "You like sushi?" She pointed to a purple neon sign, hanging in front of a renovated warehouse a block down the street: "Sushi on 7th."

"Sushi," Cary said, rising, "is the food of the gods. Godzilla Roll. There's this place in Asheville that makes the best Godzilla Roll in the world. I'd eat it for breakfast if they opened that early."

"Why don't you get us some takeout? I need a half hour or so to think. I'll see you back in the apartment."

Cary followed her. "Wait a minute," he said. "You were going to answer one of my alien questions."

Ally turned back. *Better. Definitely getting better. Waking up. Starting to remember. Definitely a good thing.*

She nodded.

"Okay. But I don't know that much about them. My inner…voice told me they were coming, that they were dangerous." She downed the last sip of her coffee. "Grastar," she said. "They're called the Grastar."

***

Carver drove a silver M45 along the Pacific Coast Highway to his private airfield 30 miles south of Arcata. The flight to Tampa would take less than an hour in the prototype Hydrogen Pulse-Jet.

The smile that lit his face was only half his own. A call was about to come in. The man who would be on the other end was excited. Happy. It was the content of this call that Carver had not yet received that had him already zooming down the highway. He activated his earpiece a second before the phone buzzed.

"Already on my way to the jet," he said. "I believe you have some good news for me?"

"One of these days," Stokes said, "I'm going to figure out how you do that."

"Better that you don't," Carver said. "So. You found them?"

"General location only. They're hiding out somewhere in Ybor City. We're on the way to meet Cord there now."

"Have a driver waiting for me at Tampa International."

"You want me to meet you?"

"No," Carver said. "I want you on the chase. These two have already slipped away too many times. I'll call you when I'm on the ground. Once you have acquisition, take them to the tower. Use the underground entrance."

Carver turned off the phone and concentrated on the drive. He let the big Infiniti climb up over a hundred; the car gripped the curves like it was tethered to the road. In a matter of minutes, Carver would be ripping open the sky, the Pulse-Jet's silent, mach 7 scream trailing at a great distance. And then this part of the game would be over.

***

Ally stood just inside the doorway to the balcony, cell

phone pressed close to her ear. Cary's footsteps resounded in the narrow stairway.

"Thank you," Ally said. "You probably saved our lives. He's back. I have to go. Be safe." She tucked the cell phone back into a concealed compartment in the bottom of her bag.

Cary walked through the door carrying a brown sack full of sushi. Oil darkened the bottom. Ally had begun to pack, but Cary was too preoccupied to notice. He sank into his makeshift bed and stared into his own shadows.

"What's wrong?" Ally said. "Did something happen?" She tossed Cary's pack to him. "Whatever it is, you'll have to tell me on the way. We have to get out of here." The pack landed in his lap and slipped to the floor.

"My son," he said, not moving.

"What?"

"My son. Taylor." Cary stared at the pack. "He's in trouble."

"So are we," she said. "Come on. We have to get out of here now. Before they...Wait... How do you know your son's in trouble?"

Cary struggled to pull his attention back to the present. Ally stood before him, tapping her foot.

"I checked my messages," he said. "On my way to the sushi bar."

"You what? Oh my God! Of course."

"What?"

"Nothing. Never mind. Come here." She cracked open the French doors and pulled him out onto the balcony.

"My son is in trouble. I have to find him." He paused. "He's here. In Tampa. In Hyde Park. He gave me an address."

"No closets, huh? Looks like I'm not the only one with secrets." She scanned the crowd.

"There," she said. "Look at those two."

A matching pair of beefcakes loitered in front of The Empire Club. They were large, excessively muscled, and wore black polos over black BDU pants.

"I don't see anything wrong with them," Cary said. "Couple of gay weightlifters dressed like twins. We *are* in Ybor City."

"Watch the one on the left," she said.

Cary observed the man. He and his partner held post on the corner and scanned the street. Cary was about to say that a lot of people like watching crowds, when the man pulled his collar up toward his mouth and said something.

"Damn," Cary said.

"No shit, doofus," Ally said. "All right. Good news is they don't know where we are, or they'd already be kicking in the door. Bad news is, that guy's talking to someone, so there's at least one other team out there. We've got to go now. But we've got to keep an eye out for the other team. They'll be watching for us."

Ally led the way downstairs and into the alley that led to Seventh.

***

Taylor waited. Something important was happening now. He could feel it. Something was coming. Someone. A visitor. And with the arrival of that visitor...

Completion.

This part of the story would be over soon, and Taylor would receive his reward.

Oneness.

Nearly an hour ago, Caitlin and Meghan, tearful and earnest, had explained to him that they had to leave now. But not before Caitlin had stood next to him on the sofa and spray painted a sigil on the wall behind him. The scent of fresh paint still lingered in the air, mixed with incense and cloves.

Taylor knew that sigil; it was etched into his soul. He did not even have to look to know its shape and magic.

He had not seen or heard the Angel since he had arrived at the apartment on Edison Avenue. But the vision of the Red Cloud World had resumed almost as quickly as Caitlin had fed him more tea. He saw that world now as an overlay on this one, like a double exposed picture. Taylor could place his attention on either world. Here in the reality where he had passed his dwindling life, the empty shell of a room glowed with wan candlelight; in the Red Cloud World, a flurry of activity was underway. The beasts stood before him in a long line. Each would bow low, then stand and strike its huge barrel chest with all four fists and let loose a deafening roar. Taylor rested on his throne in both worlds. In one, he reveled in the obeisance of his subordinates. In the other, he awaited completion.

Tonight, it would come.

***

Cary leaned out from the lip of the alley's shadow and surveyed Seventh Avenue. Never in his life had he been on the run like this. Nevertheless—his posture, the alley and the shadow of the building, the tingling in his gut that signaled danger, the incongruous excitement of it all—he found this drama both centering and uncomfortably familiar.

The crowd was thickest in the middle of the street; Ally and Cary could just make out the shape of the two men in front of the Empire.

"Where are we going?" Cary asked. Ally pointed to another narrow passageway across Seventh.

"You go first," she said. "Just weave among the crowd, and keep your face turned away from them. We'll just have to hope that the other team doesn't see us."

Cary was about to step out into the street when Ally grabbed the collar of his sweatshirt and pulled him back in.

"Over there," she said. The other team stood two blocks up in the opposite direction. They were flanked. "We'll just have to risk it," she said, giving him a little nudge. Cary hurried across the street; Ally followed. Neither of the teams saw them.

"But where are we going?" Cary asked again.

They paused just inside the opposite alleyway. Cary looked up to their apartment. Two men stood on the balcony scanning the crowd. Cary's hand tapped Ally's shoulder at the same moment that the men saw them. One was Cord, the other Stokes. In a strangely calm movement Stokes spoke into the microphone at his lapel. Then, he smiled, popped a piece of Godzilla Roll into his mouth, and waved at them.

"Shit!" Ally said.

"I just made that call 45 minutes ago," Cary said. "How the hell did they find us so fast?"

"They were already here. Your son, Taylor. They'd have been watching, hoping you'd show up."

She ran into the alley, pulling Cary behind her. They took a left into another passageway. Ally pulled up short at a gray door and jerked a set of lock picks from her pocket.

"What are you doing?"

"Don't talk," she said, working the picks furiously. "Damn! Come on!"

The tumblers fell with a clunk, and they slipped into the cool darkness of Almengual Tobacconists, Est. 1923. She pushed the door closed only a second before both teams converged on the alley from opposite ends.

"This way," Ally whispered.

Cary followed her into a storeroom. The strangely pleasant, almost nurturing aroma of tobacco permeated the *tienda*.

"My grandfather smoked cigars," Cary said.

"Here," Ally said. "Help me get this drain open."

The heavy, bronze grate was tarnished to a beautiful verdigris. Raised letters across the center bar identified the manufacturer as *Irkalla*. Together they pried it open and stared down into the dark pit.

"We're going in there?" Cary said. "Isn't that going to lead to sewers?"

She looked at him, and as she opened her mouth to speak the words, he nodded and spoke them with her.

"Trust me."

Ally smiled, took a black MagLite Mini from her bag and dropped into the hole. Cary lowered the two bags down and then followed. He pulled the grate back over them. The moment it settled into place, the back door to Almengual's flew open.

***

Stokes and Cord had rendezvoused with the two teams in the alley.

"They're in one of these stores," Stokes said. "That bitch can get in anywhere. Check the locks."

Six men fanned out and began scanning the door handles.

"Here," said Mercer, a wispy blond man whose coiled posture made him look like a cobra about to strike. His mouth was perpetually pinched into a cross between a frown and a sneer. He pointed his penlight at a door. The dark metal of the handle had been scraped away in several places, leaving silver trails.

"She was in a hurry," Cord said. He gestured to his two men, and they took off at a run to cover the front of the store. The door wasn't locked.

"They're gone," said Stokes as soon as he walked in.

Just beneath the bronze grate, Ally and Cary pressed to the sides of the drainpipe and tried not to slide. Cary's arms shook with the effort, but Ally was still as the wall itself.

"They must have gone straight through to the street before we got here," Mercer said.

Stokes examined the lock on the front door. "Don't think so," he said. "This is a double-keyed bolt. And it isn't scratched. But you're right. They're not in here. I wonder why the alarm didn't go off. I don't think we gave her enough time to disable it." He looked closer at the door. "No contacts. The place isn't wired."

Cary's palms were sweating. He slipped an inch, and Ally extended her leg to hold him in place. Cary's eyes widened. They'd be sitting ducks down here.

Cord breathed deep. "God, it smells great in here. *Fee fi fo fum.* I smell..." He examined the display cases. One of them had alarm contacts under the lid. "...*Cohibas.*" Hidden in plain sight—always the best way. He looked one more time at the alarm contacts. "Why the hell not?" he said, and lifted the lid.

"Noooooo!" Stokes said, but the alarm was already blasting.

Cord smiled and grabbed a box. "I guess that explains why old Almengual didn't have the door wired."

Stokes was already out the back door. Cord followed, casual as a man walking out of a theater.

The moment the door clicked closed, Ally released her tension on the pipe walls, and gravity took them down into the fetid underworld.

They came to a tumbling mess on a curved, wet floor.

"That was close," Cary said. "If that alarm hadn't gone off..."

Ally disentangled herself and pulled another flashlight from Cary's pack.

"Plan ahead," she said.

"What do you mean?"

"I chose that particular cigar store for a reason," she said. "That day we stopped at this place, I saw that there were no alarm contacts on the door. But I could see them on one of the display cases. That told me a lot. Plus, know your enemy." She laughed. "Ian Cord would sell his soul for Cuban cigars."

"If he had one," Cary said. He turned on his flashlight and played it over the walls. "Jesus!"

The slanted space that awaited them was not much larger than the pipe they had descended. They still had to brace themselves to keep their footing. The putrid scent of low tide permeated the dank air.

"You sure about this?" Cary asked. "What if the tide washes in here and we can't get out?"

Ally's sigh was audible in the confines of the pipe.

"Okay, okay. I know," Cary said.

They entered a huge room, 35 feet high, 80 feet long, and 40 feet wide. Safety lights hung along the walls at 12-foot intervals. Beneath each light was the entrance to another pipe like the one from which they had just emerged. Multicolored mosaic tiles decorated walls, floor, and ceiling in a repeating, three-dimensional illusion.

Cary found it difficult not to lose his bearings. He was floating in space, though his footsteps landed on solid ground. He pressed his right hand against the cold tile, and it passed through so easily that he almost fell over. *Is this happening?* His hand tingled and burned halfway up his forearm. *This can't be happening!* His eyes rolled back, and he smelled burning flesh, heard the sizzle of meat, heard a woman calling out to him. Urgent. Pressing. Merciless.

"Cary," Ally was shouting. "Cary." Her voice careened off the curved walls.

"What?" he said. "What's wrong?" He shook his head and rubbed his wrist.

Ally took his hand. "Come on, crazy man," she said. "Let's keep moving. I made a lot of noise waking you up."

Their footsteps echoed in the hollow chamber.

"But what is this place?" Cary rubbed his uncharred arm. "How could this be here?"

"All over the world," Ally said, "there are hollow places that nobody knows about. More than you could ever imagine, really. But these, I knew about. Most people don't think places like this could be so close to the water, but this part of the city is well above sea level. The mob used to run liquor through here during Prohibition."

"But who comes here now?" Cary asked. "Who uses this place now?"

"That," Ally said, "might be an interesting thing to know sometime. But not today. Today I think we'd rather not meet those people."

***

Stokes and Cord lounged at a sidewalk table in front of Carmine's. Between Stokes' thick, square bulk and Cord's tensile curve, each fidgeted in continual attempts to find comfort in the wrought iron café chairs. Neither succeeded. They drank steaming cups of *café con leche* from heavy white mugs. Cord puffed a freshly purloined Cohiba, his cell phone pressed to his ear. Their soldiers were back at the Harbor Island Hotel, clearing out of their respective suites.

Cord clipped his phone into the holster on his belt. Thick smoke oozed out of his mouth and drifted upward in front of his face.

"What'd he say?" Stokes asked.

"Not happy," Cord said. "Yours?"

"Also not happy." He sipped the half and half. "And he's here."

"Here?" Cord said. "In Tampa?"

Stokes nodded. "Well...almost. I have to pick him up at the airport in about half an hour. You want to come along?"

"Might as well. Not like there's anything else to do." He drained his coffee. "Hey. By the way...is this as weird to you as it is to me?"

"You mean, weird as in this-time-last-year-we-were-trying-to-kill-each-other weird?" Stokes asked.

"Yeah," Cord said. "That weird."

"Don't worry," said Stokes. "We may get the chance yet." He laughed. "You still watching the kid's place?"

"I've had a local P.I. on the kid since Walker and the girl slipped you in Burnsville. Guy named Luther Parker. He's a burn out, but when it comes to surveillance, he's a ninja. He'll call me if they show. But...damn...if they're stupid enough to go there, then the assholes deserve to die."

"Stranger things have happened," Stokes said. He finished his coffee. "Come on, let's go see my boss. Maybe it won't be as bad as we think."

***

Ally produced a compass from her bag.

"You have a compass with you?" Cary asked.

"Of course. Always. So do you. In the bag—duh. Come on. This way." She pointed to the path on the right. "This should take us where we want to go." She smiled back at him. "If it's straight."

The unlit tunnel was cylindrical, and, like the great chamber they had just left, lined with tiny tiles. They had only gone a hundred paces or so when a slight curve took them to the right. Another 50 paces, and they drifted back to the left. The MagLites provided plenty of illumination, but they could only see to the limits of the curve. The tiny tiles resembled scales. Cary wondered if maybe five years ago, he had been swallowed whole by that Indigo, or dragon, or whatever it was, and had been wandering lost ever since in the belly of the serpent. Would he ever get out?

Muffled traffic sounds reverberated above their heads.

"Getting close to downtown," Ally said.

"Turn your flashlight off," Cary said. A faint light glowed somewhere up ahead. Hard echoes of conversation careened past them against the tiled walls.

The chamber they entered was half the size of the first. Four men sat on wooden crates around a cable spool against the far wall. A Coleman lantern washed the room in white light, transforming them into ghoulish apparitions with stark, ashen faces and pitch-black hair. Their giant shadows danced upon the tiled walls.

Cary looked at Ally.

She shrugged. "It's not like we can go back," she said. They stepped out of the tunnel and into the light.

At the sound of her first footfall, three of them jumped to their feet. Cary thought the men would attack, but he soon realized that these men were frightened of them. Who knew, after all, what one might encounter down here in this dungeon?

Ally held her palms out. One of the men staggered back as if she had actually pushed him. "We only want to find our way out," she said. The men remained standing, still wary.

"Why you want to come in here?" asked one. He was aged and grizzled, and wore tattered clothing. But he was surprisingly clean. All of the men seemed particularly clean for being homeless. The fourth man remained seated, looking down at the table.

"We're lost," Cary said.

The standing men looked at one another and smiled. Cary was unsure whether the smiles were benevolent or feral. He turned his body sideways to them, though he did not know why. Ally had done the same. She moved while she talked, backing herself and Cary toward the nearest doorway.

"Is this the way out?" Ally asked.

Somewhere in the shadows, a raven rasped a single caw. The sound was a needle in Cary's brain. He slammed his eyes closed, and the world went black.

Before Time

~

Ksama

Ksama's eyes flicker open, and the predawn harbor comes to life. Flies swarm about her, having navigated along the drifting signature of fresh-spilled blood. Scattered and distant fisher sounds pepper the air. A barely formed song drifts to Ksama's ears on the shifting winds. Though she cannot quite make out the lyrics, the melody is beautiful. And familiar.

Her arm, now swollen to the size of a small melon, is a hideous, marbled combination of green and black. She desires nothing more than to remain here, doubled over on her knees amidst the carcasses of two Ugra and one assassin. Movement equals pain. In stillness she can manufacture the illusion of no-pain. Less than 20 feet away, the *Varuna* bumps against the quay in the shifting tide.

Twenty feet.

She does not know how she has risen, or how Sh'ele has found its way onto her back. Ksama staggers forward, each step a burning hammer-strike to her wrist. Fiery needles shoot up her arm and through her body. She stumbles into the rocking boat and slumps against the gunnels, her back to the quay. The gathering rain in the vee of the hull soaks the seat of her pants. She forces harsh and ragged breaths in and out of her mouth. The boat's naked mast stirs the sky with a gentle spinning.

Very soon, I will pass out again. Another assassin will find me. They will find me. I must untie the boat. Slip the moorings. Let the tide take me out.

But Ksama cannot will her legs to stand. Her eyes drift closed, and the face of her teacher, Dayate, shines on the screen of her mind.

"When all seems lost," Dayate says, "surrender. Let go of that which you cannot control. The solution is always at your fingertips."

Ksama hovers for a long moment at the edge of life's shadow. The distant song drifts closer, into her private darkness. The words "God's Tooth" float on the wind. Her left hand tightens on DevaRada.

In spite of the pain, Ksama laughs, though the croak is so pitiful, only Ksama knows it as laughter.

God's Tooth. At her fingertips.

With the vestiges of her strength, Ksama raises DevaRada straight up and lets the blade fall against the mooring line, surrendering the work to gravity.

Again and again DevaRada rises, each ascent like the slow, upward cranking of a drawbridge. On the 12th fall, God's Tooth bites wood, and the Varuna drifts free. Ksama drifts with it on the slipping sea as the sloop catches the ebb tide and slides silent and unseen from Q'Tal Harbor. She tumbles back into the inner worlds, and her soul floats safe on the pulse of the song that hangs just out of reach.

Present Day

A few minutes after nine, Simon cut the engine of his '65 VW Microbus. He rolled dark and silent down Edison toward the parking spot that would provide him full view of the apartment house and keep him behind the P.I. who was also watching the place.

"Simon's Survival Rule number 2358," he said, easing the VW to a curb beside an old bungalow. "You never know who might be watching you."

Two weeks earlier, Simon had abandoned his apartment at the Ponce and holed up in the Cockroach Bay Motel near Ruskin. Two days later he had read the headline: "Professor's Body Found Floating in the Hillsborough River."

Freddy.

Police were still investigating.

He'd emptied his bank account, traded his Volvo for the van, and resumed surveillance of the cemeteries. He wanted more than ever to get to the bottom of this.

Part of his daily routine included a search of Hyde Park for more of the zombies who had spooked him out of apartment and home. Most days, Woodstein stayed behind in the motel.

Sometime after midnight last Tuesday, Simon had spent a couple of hours updating his notes and fine-tuning his nerve strings with sugar, yeast, and caffeine at the vintage Krispy

Kreme on Kennedy. He decided to make one more pass through Hyde Park before calling it a night, and then he saw two young men half-dragging, half-carrying a barefoot man in red pajamas and a red bathrobe.

"Well if it ain't my old poet friends, Percy and Byron."

A pretty, dark-haired woman of about 20 seemed to be directing the show. Simon crept along in the shadows and tracked them to a two story, brick apartment building on Edison.

The first thing he'd noticed was that someone else already had the apartment staked out. A rumpled old trench coat of a fellow slouched in the driver's seat of a maroon Reliant K. So far, Simon had managed to stay under the guy's radar. The VW bus proved to be the perfect stealth vehicle for the area. Three others of varying colors were parked on the same street. He had come back every night since. Something was bound to happen here eventually.

Now, Simon poured a cup of fresh coffee and laid his binoculars in his lap. He didn't have to wait long.

"Hello there," he said. Two girls, the brunette he had seen the night he had found them, and a shorter blond girl left the apartment. Each carried a bulging, black garbage bag and a backpack. "Well, ladies," he said. "Either it's garbage night or you two chicks are flying the coop. Or maybe it's more like rats deserting a sinking ship." He followed them with the binoculars until they disappeared around the corner onto Platt. Seconds later an engine coughed to life, one of those Japanese jobs with the aftermarket muffler that made it sound like a lawnmower on crack.

"Goodnight, ladies," he sang. "Farewell, ladies…"

Simon poured another cup of coffee and settled deeper into his seat.

Michael Phillips Mann

SIXTH ARTICULATION

a raven song

a gumshoe

a bad guy constellation

death and Death and almost death

a feast of crimson snakes

a tower

Shangri-La

a new angel

Present Day

A raven cried in the darkness, and Cary felt his world shake. Someone was calling his name. Was it the raven, or something darker? Was it the light?

"Cary," the female voice said. The world shook harder, then pain stabbed at his hand. "Cary. Open your eyes."

He obeyed. For a moment he did not understand where he was. The raven cawed again, and a word flitted with dark, silent wings across his inner screen. *Underworld.* The catacombs. He was in the catacombs under Ybor City with Ally. There were men here. They might be in danger. He shook his head hard and rubbed his temples. The invisible raven croaked out three more caws that sounded like harsh laughter.

"You with me here?" Ally asked.

Cary nodded.

By now, the fourth man had risen, and the other three sat down.

"You never find your way out of here," the man said. His accent was Caribbean. Ally had edged Cary to the doorway now, and they were slowly backing into it.

"How will we get out, then?" Ally asked.

"You got to trust someone, don't you now, little girl."

That's funny. Now she'll have to trust someone.

In the shadows, perhaps behind the man, the raven spoke

once again.

"And that would be you?" Ally asked.

He nodded once. His piercing eyes remained on hers.

"And what do you require in return?"

The man looked them both up and down. "I'll collect later," he said. He held his hands far apart, palms up. "For now, consider it a gift from one traveler to another."

Cary was about to protest. Ally grasped his hand.

"We accept your terms," she said. "We will owe you."

Cary tensed. Ally pressed her thumb into the nerve between his thumb and index finger. Cary jerked his hand away.

"I am Murtaugh," the man said.

Ally nodded. "Of course you are."

Murtaugh released a dark, syrupy laugh. He was well over 6 feet tall and wore faded gray capris with a red stripe down each side, and a sleeveless, blood red, *Xibalba* T-shirt. A black watch cap clung to his head like an inverted tulip. His wrinkled face was true black, darker than the shadows from which the raven had spoken, and his skin looked tough and weathered. But when Cary shook his hand, it was soft as warm butter. Tufts of white beard sprouted from his face like random plumes of light. His abundant silver brows danced above his eyes when he spoke.

"That is not the way," he said. He walked past the entrance in which they stood and pointed his ancient finger to an opening concealed behind the spool table. "You must go farther into the west."

"And here I thought," Ally said, "that we were about as far as we could safely go in that direction."

Murtaugh digested her comment. "For most," he said. "Perhaps. But not for you."

"Excuse me," Cary said. "Have we met?"

Murtaugh's smile broadened, his white teeth a bright contrast to the shear darkness of his presence. "Not so stupid after all, this one," he said to Ally. He did not answer Cary's question.

His three companions stood to follow. The lantern projected their looming apparitions onto the tile wall. Ally looked to Murtaugh, but he had already shifted his attention to the three men. The gravity of his gaze forced them back into their chairs. Murtaugh led Ally and Cary into the small entrance.

"You are in danger," Murtaugh said.

"Someone is trying to kill us," Ally said. She cut a silencing glance at Cary, who was on the verge of elaborating.

Murtaugh guided them through more turns than they could count. Cary could only hope they could trust their guide. After nearly 15 minutes in the tortuous hallways, they rounded a corner and emerged into a small vestibule. A heavy steel door stood at one end. Beside it, a narrow set of steel stairs led upward into the dark.

Murtaugh pointed up the stairs. "You go this way. And be careful when you open that trap door, you hear? You never know what kind of creepy folks you going to find up on the surface." His laughter resonated in the chamber.

"You're not coming up with us?" Cary asked.

Murtaugh looked deep into Cary. "Don't get up on the surface much. Only in special circumstances. Besides, I got an appointment with a warrior woman." He looked at Ally and smiled. "Another time," he said.

Ally shivered, shook it off, and then pointed to the steel door. "What's through there?"

"Aahh," Murtaugh said. "You don't want to go there. Not yet." He looked at Cary again with a hint of compassion in his eyes. "You two got troubles enough ahead of you." He backed away until he reached the bend in the hallway. "Good luck to you, now. And don't be forgetting that you owe me." He laughed again and disappeared around the corner.

The steel stairs thudded like dull bells.

"Who was that guy?" Cary said.

"You wouldn't believe me if I told you," Ally said. "Here's the door." She pushed it open a crack and looked around. "I think it's safe."

The trap door opened into a park with small grass squares bordered by concrete walkways. The entrance was concealed by a bronze plaque commemorating the dedication of Mopheit Park. Crape myrtles and sabal palms rustled in the tender breeze. A cylindrical skyscraper stood at the southern edge of the park. On top of the giant cylinder, two spotlights cast focused beams into the sky.

"Okay," Cary said. "Now that we're safe, I have to go see my son."

"They'll be watching," Ally said.

"I don't care." Cary hesitated. Then he took in a deep breath and slipped the necklace over his head. "You take this. I'll go alone. I'll meet you back here afterward. If they don't catch me."

Ally weighed the necklace in her palm. She shook her head and handed it back. "I can't let you go by yourself." She pulled an iPhone from her bag.

"Wait a minute," Cary said. "You have an iPhone?"

"Hey. Just because I'm a thousand years old doesn't mean I'm not a kid, too." She consulted the screen. "Come on. There's another car in the Ashley Garage. Which, ironically, is right underneath us. That stairway we came up must have passed right through it." She headed for a set of stairs that accessed the garage beneath Mopheit Park.

"How many cars do you people have?" Cary asked.

"As many as it takes," she said. "As many as it takes."

***

Their newest land barge was a retired white '97 Crown Victoria P71. Ally idled up de Leon Street and pulled a left onto Edison. The sliver moon peeked between ranks of giant oaks that stood like sentinels. Cary scrunched down in the front seat, the top of his head barely level with the window.

"Yo. Ninja boy," she said. "You do realize that these windows are tinted black, right?"

Cary slid up slowly. "Oh." He squirmed to straighten his

153

shirt. "Do you see anything?"

"Not really," she said. "And that's weird. They should be here."

"Maybe they don't think we'll risk it."

"Possible," she said. "Not likely."

She parked in the shadow of a stucco apartment building. A white metal sign with black, block letters squeaked back and forth in the breeze: "Apartment for Rent." Someone played an acoustic guitar and sang "Kid Fears" by an open window. At the end of the alleyway and across Edison, soft lights glowed in the downstairs corner apartment of a brick octoplex.

"There it is," she said. "I'll be out here in case someone shows up." *When someone shows up.* "Listen to me. No matter what, you have to be ready to leave when I say. No notice. No questions. Can you do that?"

Cary nodded. He would have agreed to anything.

"Be safe," she said. "I'll be watching."

The apartment house was nearly derelict. Even in the darkness, the sad, dingy bricks sagged with resignation. Apartment A was on the downstairs right. The windows glowed with golden, flickering light.

***

Half a block away in a maroon Reliant K, Luther Parker poured another cup of tepid coffee from a red tartan thermos. He had been watching the apartment for more than a week now and had become relatively certain that his target was not going to show…until this night when he saw the surplus police cruiser casing the neighborhood. A car like that? The way it slunk through the streets? Dead giveaway. His night vision binoculars were on the passenger floor camouflaged by fast food debris. Parker activated them and tracked the man crossing the street to the kid's apartment.

Luther Parker studied Cary's face.

"Shit!" he said. "Shit! It's you! I don't believe it." He dug his cell phone from underneath several crumpled McDonald's bags and pressed the speed dial.

"*Ka ching*," he said. The phone began to ring. "Bigass bonus time."

***

Stokes drove the Express Van through Drew Park and into an old TWA storage hangar on the back side of TIA.

"There he is," Stokes said. He pulled the van alongside the sleek black jet just as Carver descended the still-unfolding stairs.

Cord's phone rang while Carver climbed into the front seat. "This might be something," he said.

Carver and Stokes waited.

"Got it," Cord said and hung up. He shook his head in disbelief. "Damn if they didn't go to the kid's place. Fifteen minutes here to there."

Carver nodded. Stokes was already accelerating the Chevy across the hangar floor. Within minutes, both Cord's and Stokes' men were en route to rendezvous at Olde Hyde Park Village.

The killing team was on the way.

***

Cary swung the door open, creating a long, creaking song. His only child sat in the center of a threadbare, red velvet couch. Taylor's wide eyes watched the door open. He wore a dark red cotton robe and the strangest smile Cary had ever seen. Some sort of writing, Hebrew or Arabic—Sanskrit maybe—loomed huge and black on the wall behind Taylor.

Candles burned on every flat surface in the room, even the floor. A dozen sticks of Nag Champa smoldered in the soil of a wiry spider plant on a small, round table. The scent of cloves dominated the room.

Taylor seemed thin. Attenuated. Almost transparent. And

then Cary noticed the glow. His son emitted golden light. Subtle, but unmistakable. At first Cary thought it was only an effect of the candles, but the light shining from Taylor was brighter than the flames.

They stared at one another from across the room, from across the universe. With each breath, the illusion of distance collapsed a little more. The whirlpool in Cary's chest warned him that, when that illusion had fully disappeared, he would not like what he found.

"Taylor?" Cary said. "Are you all right?"

Tears welled in Cary's eyes. Taylor's nod came from the shores of another world.

"Are you sick?" Cary asked.

Taylor shook his head. His half smile quirked higher.

Cary's feet finally moved, propelling him across the room. He would have run if there had been enough space. Taylor was light in his arms, like the child he had once been. So light.

Cary loosened his embrace, and Taylor sank into the sofa. The seed of fear that Cary had brought into the room blossomed to a poisonous flower in the flickering flames. Taylor's cheeks and eyes were deep hollows in the landscape of his face. Cary pulled open the robe.

***

Simon did not refill his coffee cup. The last few minutes had provided more stimulation than any amount of caffeine.

He had seen the PI slink down into his seat. Moments later, a surplus police cruiser with no headlights had eased up Edison and disappeared onto Platt.

"You're a hell of a lot better than you look," Simon said.

A man walked across the street and disappeared into the apartment. The detective watched through binoculars and then made a call. Then nothing. Something was up.

Simon scanned back and forth with his Nikons and caught a glimpse of movement. A woman was running…almost gliding across the dark street, silent and fluid as a shifting shadow. Her arm swung back and forth behind her like she was sowing seeds; muffled bells followed her footsteps. She slammed open the front door. A single glass pane shattered from the impact and tinkled to the floor. If Simon had not been looking at the right place at exactly that moment, he would never have seen her.

"Damn," he said. "What are you?"

Two white stretch vans zipped past Simon and jerked to a halt next to the Reliant. Three men exited the front van; two spoke to the PI, and one of them passed him a fat envelope. The third hung back and scanned the street. Then he looked directly at Simon and smiled.

"Ruh roh," said Simon. "*Tres* cree-pay."

***

Taylor's arms were sticks in Cary's palms; he looked like a poster child from Auschwitz. Cary lifted him to a sitting position. Tears leaked from Taylor's eyes. His face still held that strange expression. Cary shook him, but Taylor only smiled until Cary stopped. Cary had to do something, to say something. He had to help his son. Taylor shook his head and spoke before Cary could find his voice.

"I love you, Daddy," he said. "I love you. Tell Mommy I love her, too." For a moment, Taylor gazed into the vast distance. His smile morphed to…uncertainty. Then fear. And, finally, to cleverness. An unmistakable, clever smile teetered in Taylor's eyes. "I have a secret," he said. He giggled. "I know my true name."

"What are you talking about?" Cary asked.

Taylor cut his eyes left and right. He crooked his finger. "Come closer," he said. "I'll whisper it to you."

Cary leaned forward. Taylor whispered his secret into Cary's ear and then slumped against his father's shoulder; the effort had drawn his last drop of strength.

"Taylor," Cary said, shaking his son again. Taylor's subtle radiance faded. The whole world grew a little darker. Taylor's eyes opened wide. Then they slammed closed with a finality beyond hope. The last of Taylor's light died, leaving Cary lost and astonished in the darkness of the candles' flames.

"No!" Cary screamed. "No!" He squeezed Taylor's limp body and chanted a mantra of denial.

"No...no...no."

From a distant world, footsteps pounded on wood. A door crashed open. A glass pane shattered.

These sounds held no meaning.

Ally assessed the scene with a single glance: Cary on a wretched red sofa rocking his dead son. A dark sigil spray-painted in dripping Hebrew script on the wall behind him.

And then she was on him, shaking him.

"Cary! Cary! They're here! They've found us! We have to leave."

She pulled at his hands, but he would not relinquish his death grip on death. She slapped him hard, and he almost came back. She shook her head. Tears streamed down her cheeks. She pressed her thumb hard under Cary's ear.

"Aaaaaggghhhhh!"

His scream filled the house, filled the street, filled the world. He focused on Ally in disbelief. How could she cause him pain when he was already so raw? How could she touch him with violence when he had no skin?

"We have to go," Ally said. "If you want to live to do something about this, we have to go. Now."

She pulled him to his feet and walked him to the kitchen door. His eyes remained on Taylor until they had passed through the kitchen. He staggered out the back door and into the alley behind a shadowbox fence. Cary continued to stare into a world where Taylor's image lingered, a world that only Cary's eyes could see.

***

The PI pointed to the apartment, started his Reliant, and drove away. Four men stepped out of the rear van.

"Now that's some scary-looking guys," Simon said. "It's like a freaking bad guy constellation up in here."

His hand crept to the ignition switch. From somewhere in the night, he heard a scream that turned his chest inside out. The man who had looked at Simon nodded to the others, and all seven of the men rushed the apartment. Only when he saw their backs did Simon realize he had been holding his breath.

***

Cord was first through the door, then Stokes. The apartment was empty except for Taylor Walker's body. Carver stood framed in the open back door. The alley behind the house offered nothing but the night. From a couple of blocks away he heard the surge of a big engine.

"Back to the vans," he said, and took off at a run. The others followed in his wake.

***

Cary lay unmoving in the back seat, lost in his unimaginable world. Ally jerked the car to a stop in the intersection 30 feet in front of the vans just as Carver was climbing into the front passenger seat.

"My God," she said. "I don't believe it."

She powered down the driver's window, revealing herself. Her eyes met Carver's. She nodded. Carver nodded back. Ally raised her middle finger and punched the accelerator. The P71 roared, and the Crown Vic fishtailed away in a piercing, rubber scream.

"Do not let them get away," Carver said.

Stokes slammed the accelerator to the floor as Ally disappeared onto Platt. The van charged forward in pursuit. Then the front tires exploded with loud, pneumatic pops as they rolled over the first array of caltrops Ally had strewn into the street only minutes before. The front end dipped, and the rear van plowed full speed into them, tipping the lead van onto its side. When they finally came to rest, the street was completely blocked, and all eight tires were shredded.

Ally threaded the Crown Vic softly through a maze of back streets and empty lots until she finally emerged into Saturday night traffic on Dale Mabry Highway. They blended into obscurity among cars full of innocents and slipped out of the city.

***

Nearly a week later, Simon was still spooked.

He had been more than a little unsettled by the creepy Qellepoth kids. He had been devastated by the death of Freddy Blake. But he had been scared shitless by the look of the man who had stared at him that night on Edison. Not to mention the big, ugly guys with him.

After leaving Hyde Park, Simon had returned to his hidey-hole in Cockroach Bay and had not ventured into Tampa again for several days. But then he read the funeral announcement for Taylor Walker, found dead at age 20 of a drug overdose in an apartment building on Edison Avenue.

He was spooked, but he was also a reporter. His impulse to unravel the truth overcame his fear. So, five days after dodging bad guys at the Edison apartment, Simon mounted an expedition to Jose Marti Cemetery and the funeral of Taylor Walker. He spent nearly two hours scouting the West Tampa neighborhoods around the graveyard for scary people before he parked the van and snuck into the City of the Dead.

A small gathering of mourners clustered around Taylor Walker's open grave.

"Nobody too creepy," Simon said. "And it's an actual burial." Simon watched the black coffin sink into the ground. "Closed casket," he said. "I wonder, Taylor Walker, if you are even in that pretty box."

A middle-aged woman tossed a handful of earth into the hole. A twig cracked somewhere in the distance to Simon's right.

"Ruh roh," he said. Fifty yards up the hill, a man and a woman watched the funeral from the shadow of a mausoleum. Simon slipped behind the thin curtain of Spanish moss. Not much cover. If either of them looked in his direction, they would see him.

***

"It should be overcast," Cary said.

A handful of friends and relatives swarmed about the distant grave like dusky black scarabs. Slanted sunlight lit the graveyard with preternatural brightness, and a brisk wind swept away every mote of uncertainty. Cary's only child was dead. Ally pressed into him as if he were supporting her. Both knew the arrangement was quite the opposite.

Taylor's mother, her brother, Ed, and their parents stood on the far side of the casket. Cary had not seen Jennifer for more than a year and had only spoken to her twice, both times in attempts to locate Taylor. The grave was a canyon between them.

"This is your fault," Jennifer would have said. Cary flinched at the thought. A heavy cloud bank rolled across the sun, settling the entire graveyard into shadow.

"'Dark as a funeral scarf from stem to stern,'" Cary said.

"It's painful enough," Ally said, "without blaming yourself." Westerly wind lifted a few strands of Ally's hair across her eyes. She shook her head and let the breeze work them back into alignment.

She had not wanted them to come, but how could she expect Cary not to be here? And how could she let him come alone? She had taken every possible precaution, but this was such a risk.

Jennifer cast a handful of dirt onto her son's coffin. Cary dug his fingers into the earth and retrieved a thick clump. He slammed it back down to the ground.

"Not fair," he said, his voice dull and dead.

"No," said Ally. "It's not."

The mourners scurried away.

"Let's go," Cary said.

"Wait." She pulled them both deeper into the shadows. "Who's that?" She nodded toward a copse of trees on the far side of the grave. A bald, bearded man watched from behind a curtain of Spanish moss. Cary looked at him. The man turned and quick-walked to the nearest gate. He climbed into a VW Microbus and chugged away.

"Don't know him," Cary said. "He's not one of the bad guys?"

"No," Ally said. "Definitely not. They have a certain look about them. Like professional wrestlers. Only more lethal."

"Probably nothing."

"Nothing," Ally said, "is ever nothing."

"We can go for now," Cary said. "I want to come back when no one else is here. Tomorrow. Or in a few days. To say goodbye."

They took a slow zigzag back to the car, keeping to the shadows. Cary reached for the door handle. A split second later, he was flying through the air over the hood of the car.

Cary descended into dreamtime, and the play of the world slowed. By the time he thumped to the earth in front of the car, a bulldog of a man was pressing Ally against the passenger door and gripping her by the throat. He wore the same uniform as the men who had attacked them at Cary's house that first day. He was smiling. Ally's hands moved in a blur; the man's smile disappeared, followed by the life in his eyes. He hit the ground hard and did not get back up.

Cary pushed up to a crouch. Two more men emerged from the edge of the palmettos. One pulled a Sig from under his left arm and swung it back and forth to cover both of them.

"Don't move," he said. "Stay exactly where you are."

His partner tried to push the gun aside. "Are you crazy?" he said. "Put that away."

"I don't believe that magic crap," said the man holding the Sig. He waved the gun at Cary. "Stand up. Show me your hands."

Cary stood in front of the grill and raised his hands.

"You too," the man said.

Ally raised her hands. And smiled.

"You are a killer," she said.

"That's right, bitch," he said. He looked directly at her when he spoke. "I'm a killer."

"Idiot," said his partner. "Put the thing away."

"Shut up." His voice had become distant.

"You enjoy killing," Ally said.

The man nodded.

"You enjoy killing," she said again.

"Shit," said the other man. He shifted his weight to run, but his partner raised the Sig and fired in one smooth motion, putting a 9mm projectile into his head.

"Good killer," Ally said.

"I'm a good killer," the man said. He raised the gun to his temple and fired three times before the signaling mechanism from his brain to his finger stopped working.

"How did—"

Ally held up her hand. Then she somersaulted up onto the hood toward him.

The fourth member of the team had been nearly 50 yards away when he heard the first shot. Now he emerged from the palmettos at a dead run toward Cary. Ally tumbled over the hood and to the ground just as the man swung a right at Cary's ribs. Ally drove the tips of her fingers like a spear into the man's throat. He fell flat on his back and spent the last few moments of his life trying to breathe. He still gripped a curved blade in his lifeless fist. Its entire length was wet and pink.

"Oh God," Ally said.

"Wh-what?" Cary's eyes flickered back and up for a moment. A dark stain spread on his left side. Warm blood pulsed and turned cool on his skin. He pressed his hand to the wound and offered Ally an uncertain smile. His eyes flickered back a second time, and this time they stayed.

Before Time

~

Ksama

The deck of the delirious boat is alive with crimson snakes. They writhe in a seething bed beneath Ksama; they slither along the gunnels and twirl about the mast.

Be still, and they will not see you.

But her very thoughts alert the vipers to her presence. As one, the serpents turn their smooth heads and rush to engulf her. They spiral up her arms and legs; they spread their hungry jaws and seek her soft neck. Ksama opens her mouth to scream and scare them away, but no sound issues from her throat. Instead, the high lilting song of a flute vibrates through her every cell. The serpents pause and then turn their heads to locate the hateful source of the sound. They recede, exposing her skin to the warm sun. Across the deck, over the sides, and into the water they surge. Invisible ocean creatures rush to the boat from all directions, churning the sea to blood as they devour the venomous feast. Ksama curls into a ball to hide from the insane world.

When her delirium has passed, Ksama awakens. Q'Tal Harbor, the City of Light, and swarms of red serpents are but distant memories.

Perhaps the tide has saved her. Or luck. Her brain pounds

to escape through her skull. Her cheek aches where Sidra's short stick cracked it. A chunk of tooth rankles under her tongue, unnoticed until now. Nausea washes over her and then passes, only to be replaced by an emptiness that might signal hunger. The stench of rotting fruit drifts near. No, not fruit. Almonds.

Why do I smell almonds? In her hidden heart she knows the truth.

Near the bow, a brazier sits empty and cold. Flint and coals lie in one of the storage compartments underneath. No food.

"To one who has no teeth," she rasps, "God gives dried beans." She laughs. "At least I'll be able to stay warm."

Ksama braces her back against the mast. Ocean. Everywhere. In every direction. Her arm does not hurt as much as before. Snaky red tendrils extend up her arm under the skin. They almost look alive.

I was dreaming. Snakes. And a song. Was someone singing back at the harbor? Ksama closes her eyes and reaches for the thread of her dream and the song that seemed so important. She can almost hear it. For the slightest instant, she glimpses a wild-eyed man standing on the edge of a turbulent river. He aims a fully drawn bow at an unseen prey. Blood drips from his hand down the lower limb of the bow, and blood paints the razor tip of the arrow. He holds his mouth wide, but she cannot hear his voice. Perhaps his scream is only silence. Instead, she hears a different sort of voice, a woman's voice, much closer—behind her. Here. *Now.*

"You'll have to amputate your hand, or it will kill you."

Did I hear that? Or only think it? Did I say it myself?

The idea echoes in her thoughts, and the truth of the declaration floats at the edge of her awareness. She tries to push it away, but she knew as soon as she awoke and smelled almonds. Her eyes work hard to avoid her sword.

The voice will not let her hide.

"You will have to amputate your hand, Dear One, or you will die," says the voice. And Ksama knows this voice.

Perhaps if she opens her eyes the voice will go away. Instead, she sees the figure sitting at the point of the bow, a living figurehead turned backward.

"DevaSurya," Ksama says. The Queen of Light inclines her head once in greeting. A swift gust of wind whips a stormy strand of hair across her pale cheek.

"You know this, Ksama, do you not?" The Grace's voice retains the essence of song, though she does not sing these words.

"Yes," Ksama says, her gaze falling at last to DevaRada. "I...I don't...I don't think I can do it."

"Like all difficult tasks," DevaSurya says, "you must begin with the most simple and immediate element."

Again Ksama forces her eyes away from the sword.

"Can you help me?"

"Only with the sound of my words," DevaSurya says. "I am here. And I am...elsewhere. My presence is real, but it requires all my strength to create this vision you see. I cannot do even the simplest of tasks in this place."

"Are you saying," Ksama says, "that you are here *and* in the City of Light?"

The Grace holds Ksama's gaze for a moment and then looks out over the pitiless waves.

"The City of Light is gone," she says. "Apsara has returned to the sea from which it once arose."

The simple pronouncement crushes Ksama's heart. She presses her good hand to her chest, but she feels no relief.

"But how—"

DevaSurya raises her palm. "You have drifted upon the Nameless Sea for six days now. I have guided you in your delirium to drink rainwater from the bottom of the boat. That has kept you alive."

Ksama tries to draw the reality of this knowledge into her mind, and fails. The entire continent. Her world, fallen into the ocean. The icy wind of solitude sweeps through her.

"There is more you must know," DevaSurya says. "Many escaped. Vessels have scattered in all directions; they will build the empires of the future. Some have even set out across the Nameless Sea as you have done. These will find shelter to the south with the guidance of my Sisters and of the Scion. You have drifted true west, as was your intention. Syrgala fled to the east. Yet, even now he and a handful of followers mount an expedition to acquire Sh'ele."

Ksama struggles to her feet and looks astern. Her right arm dangles at her side.

"But, if he has captured the other crystals, then he already knows where I am!" Her wild eyes sweep the endless ocean, searching for landfall that is not yet there. "They'll find me before I can—"

"No," DevaSurya says. "Syrgala escaped. But his plan failed. The fire that grew under the earth burst first into the Temple. The crystals drew the destruction there. Do you understand? Their growing imbalance was always the source of this fall. Syrgala was but a symptom of a greater infection. When you removed Sh'ele, the disease quickened, inviting the inferno to rise. All of the other crystals have joined together, melted by the fire into a single abomination that lives now with Apsara beneath the waves. Only Sh'ele remains intact." The Queen of Graces pauses. "And understand this, as well." DevaSurya's eyes hold Ksama still for several seconds. "The power of all of the crystals combined has transferred into Sh'ele."

Ksama's knees lose their strength, and she collapses to the deck.

"This is my fault. I killed them all." She curls forward into a ball. "I'm responsible…"

"No, Precious One," DevaSurya says, and her voice almost breaks. Almost. "This is not your fault." The Grace's strength calms the spinning in Ksama's heart. "This fall was inevitable. Set in motion long before you were born. You are performing a role you agreed to play in a story that was conceived in the beginning moments, before the world was written. Your actions only served to prevent the abuse from continuing. Syrgala or his followers would surely have brought this same fate to other worlds. Or worse. This cataclysm could only have been delayed, never averted.

"Concerning Syrgala's intentions, though, you understand correctly. Already he sends out trackers and assassins. Unless you act with precise intention, they will find you. But, for the moment, you have more pressing matters. Remember your training. When the work before you seems overwhelming, attend to the most immediate task. Therefore, light the fire."

Present Day

Ally swerved onto a side road just past Lake Wales. Cary slumped against the window, listing left and right as the car leaned around soft curves up Iron Mountain. The gash in his side ached with each turn, but he barely noticed the pain. Inside his head, a soundstorm raged, all but eclipsing the outer world. They careened around a sharp curve, and a huge Gothic tower emerged into full view under the moon.

"Never fails to take my breath away," Ally said. "Even now."

Cary glanced up at the bright tower in the near distance, but said nothing. He held his pendant in his right hand, worrying it with his thumb. His outer shirt had slipped down over his shoulders. He leaned forward and let it fall the rest of the way down his back, leaving only a blue, blood-soaked T-shirt. Ally saw for the first time since she had met him that he had a black dragon tattooed on the inside of his right arm.

"Funny," she said. "You don't strike me as a person who would have tattoos."

Silence.

"Cary," Ally said. She shook his shoulder. "Cary," she said louder.

He forced his eyes to focus on her from where he hovered half inside the doorway to the land of the dead.

"Ally," he murmured. "What?"

169

She decided to let the tattoo go for the moment. "I'm going to take you somewhere you can rest."

"I can rest at Bok Tower?" he said.

"No," Ally said. "I'm going to take you somewhere you'll be safe. Somewhere no one can find you."

"Okay." His eyes slid away to focus on eternity. "Go ahead." He wanted only endless night and the water of eternal forgetting. Had he ever before been this tired?

Ally drove through the empty parking lot and onto a wide brick sidewalk. Bok Tower loomed in the night. She jerked the car to a halt in front of a padlocked, iron gate. Beyond the gate, a short bridge crossed a small mote.

"I'm going to take you through the tunnel. Like back at your house. Only I'm not going to make you forget this time."

"You made me forget? How?" The words barely escaped his lips.

"Never mind that now," she said.

"LightGates," he murmured. "Tangle of Light. Will there be aliens there? Fairies? I mean *the Ow-Sheeeeee*—"

"No aliens," Ally said. "Definitely *AosSidhe*. But you won't see them."

She picked the lock on the bridge gate and led him to a brass door that depicted the story of Genesis. Ally pressed her palm against a dark swirl in the marble to the right of the door. A section of the vestibule rasped inward, revealing a narrow stairway concealed within the walls.

They circled up and around the tower and emerged onto a balcony above the sundial on the south side. Cary's head vibrated with an inner roar. Ally pushed open the red door and drew him into the cool darkness.

Their eyes adjusted to the ambient light. Polished marble reached upward to a ceiling too high to see. The entire far wall shone with a Celtic design, circles overlapping circles within circles. Moonlight played tricks with Cary's eyes: the design seemed to be moving.

"That day when we went into the cave," Ally said. "Do you remember?"

He had told her they wouldn't be able to escape that way. *Trust me*, she had said, several times. In the cave. Damp. Dark. And then the bad guys were coming down into the cave. And then...

"Bright light," he said. His breath shortened in response to pain he did not feel, but to which his body reacted. The design on the far wall grew brighter. "Wind," he added. "A hurricane." *Spinning. Like my head.* He curled forward, trying to coil himself around his wound. "You hit me."

"Geez. Okay. Fine. You're right. I hit you."

He looked into her eyes and found his way to the momentary edge of clarity. "Please don't hit me," he said.

Ally choked back a sob. She kissed his forehead once. "I'm not going to hit you," she said.

She pulled his hand away from his body and walked him to the shining wall. The curves were filaments of gold and silver inlaid into polished mahogany.

"Why is it shiny?" he asked.

"It's reacting to me," she said. "It's a sigil. You know that word? Sigil?"

Cary's strength seeped from the slice in his side. He slumped against Ally to keep his balance. The ferocity of the storm in his brain increased, even though he was sure it was already as violent as it could get.

"Magic," he murmured, his voice all but lost in his own echoes. "Sigils are magical signs. No such thing. As magic."

"Magic," Ally said, "is nothing but science that hasn't been understood and appropriated by scientists. Don't let go of my hand." They approached the wall.

"What are you—"

Ally began to sing in a language Cary had never heard. And yet the song was intimate, familiar. He struggled to keep his eyes open.

"I know that song," he whispered. He hummed a quiet harmony.

"I expect you do."

Light pulsed along the curves so quickly that the entire

design shone with a steady brilliance. Ally continued to drag him toward the wall. When Cary was certain that they would crash into it, the sigil transformed into pure white light. They entered into the light and drifted, floating in a place where no shapes or shadows existed. A soft draft pulled at them, inviting them to go back. The breeze shifted, pushing them from behind—first gently, then harder, and then like a gale propelling them forward. Except there were no reference points, since light, and light alone, permeated this space.

In subtle increments, the white light separated into greens and blues, golds and browns. The blur of colors resolved into a meadow poised upon the edge of a cliff. Beyond the precipice, a smoky blue valley joined a deeper blue sky at the distant horizon. The line between heaven and earth was difficult, if not impossible, to distinguish.

Cary had never seen a greener place. A thick carpet of ground moss blanketed a large yard bordered by a wide swath of ferns and wildflowers. Gigantic boulders overgrown with dragon claw ivy enclosed the space in a circle of protection. At the upper end of the meadow stood a round, stone cottage with a thick, thatched roof. Enticing smoke drifted above the fat chimney.

His wound called to him once again. Or perhaps the enormity of these events became too overwhelming for his mind to accept. He dropped to his knees and teetered backwards, arms outstretched. Ally cradled the back of his neck and lowered him to lie on the carpet of ground moss. A door opened and closed; a rhythmic clop of footsteps, first on a wooden porch, then on stone, grew louder and then stopped altogether. His eyes flickered and tried to roll back to the land of oblivion, but he held on. Ally's face floated above him, an auburn-haired angel in the blue, blue sky. At the periphery of his vision, another angel floated. Her dark, curling hair danced on a rising breeze, and her full lips appeared almost bloody against her pale, soft face. The gaping pain in his side was shoved away by a longing in his chest.

What is that? It feels like being in…

"You have killed," the other woman said. Even when speaking those incongruous words, her voice reached inside his soul and comforted him.

"Yes, ma'am," Ally replied.

"We'll take care of that particular wound later," the woman said.

"Yes, please," Ally replied.

"Where am I?" Cary whispered.

"You are in Shangri-La," the woman answered.

Again, that voice, that ache…

"Shangri-La's from a movie," he murmured. "*The Far Country.*"

Is this a movie? Is this a dream?

"*The Lost Horizon,*" the woman said. "*The Far Country* is a book."

"Shangri-La doesn't exist," Cary said. He struggled to keep his eyelids from slamming shut.

"Nevertheless," this new angel said, "Shangri-La is where you are. Somewhere you will be safe. Somewhere that doesn't exist. "

"Good," he barely sighed. "Good. Exactly where I want to be. Somewhere that doesn't exist." His eyes rolled back, and he fell through infinite blue shadows, into a warm, dark, world.

Cary Slept.

He did not struggle to awaken. Still, he dreamed.

SEVENTH ARTICULATION

a demon and an angel

an ambush

a stand-up monk

healing and hope

a protector

breaking the Canon

union

the Beast of the YMCA

Present Day

Cary came to his senses sitting cross-legged on a flat, black boulder in the shadow of a slate escarpment. A quarter of a mile away, the sea beat against the shore. Salty wind swirled around him; sand battered his face. Magical waves of light played over the shoreline, turning the sand to pitch and the waves to shimmering rubies. Stars clustered high in the bruised sky. A brighter point of light, perhaps a planet, floated just above the center of the horizon.

He reached for his necklace, anticipating the comfort of the talisman in his closing fist; his back sank into the embrace of a down mattress. A presence hovered nearby, a woman, a healer. The alien shoreline shimmered and, for a filmy flicker of time, became a transparency superimposed upon a cozy bedroom. Against the far wall of the room, an abundant array of small bottles covered the top of a mirrored dresser. The woman floated nearer. Cary sensed danger behind her, a threat she could not see.

"Is this a dream?" he whispered. His fingers closed on the necklace, but found only air. The soft bed dissolved, the room faded to nothing, and Cary was once again sitting on the dark slab of rock. His eyes searched his chest and then the gritty rock surface; his talisman was nowhere to be seen. He was naked.

The wisp of a melody danced in the shimmering air.

From the ebony sand at the shoreline, a dark blue silhouette rose. A woman. An impossible, blue woman. She wore loose, green trousers that ended mid-calf. Nothing else. She faced the bloody ocean, her back to Cary.

And there was someone else. Someone even more impossible. Just beyond the shoreline, an angel floated above the red waves.

The angel wore the creamy-soft innocence of a young girl. The increasing wind buffeted her white confirmation dress. Lace collar stays snapped like small whips in the torment.

Cary pressed back deeper into the shadow of the cliff.

The angel ascended; her perfect, white wings swept the sky in a slow rhythm that, even at this distance, blew taut gusts across Cary's face.

The blue woman pointed up at the angel and spoke. The angel replied. Though Cary could not make out their words, the angel's voice comforted him. She was his guardian. She would protect him from this blue demon. And yet, with each sweep of the angel's wings, a storm shivered through his heart, rippling his skin with gooseflesh and chattering his teeth together.

The word-battle ended; the angel's eyes transformed into chasms of fire. She extended her arms, palms down, drawing the power of the ocean into her hands. The ocean responded. Far on the horizon, a great red wave arose and began its journey toward the shore. The relentless wall of water churned forward, a crimson tsunami driving new wind before it. Cary could only observe as the giant red wall advanced toward the blue demon. And toward him, as well.

What is this place? I can't die here. She has to have a plan. I can't die here.

But the wave did not hear him. The red wall rose higher and higher as it advanced.

***

A little past 3 a.m., a Gray Edge helicopter floated above downtown St. Louis. Plasmonic metacoating, noise-canceling rotors, and radar baffles that even DARPA had not yet seen made the air ship virtually invisible in the St. Louis sky. The chopper whispered above the Federal Reserve Building, crept over hotel row, and came to a silent hover above the Gateway Arch. A rectangular container, 8 feet by 4 feet by 2 feet, dropped from the bottom of the helicopter and adhered to the upper surface of the arch via an array of powerful magnets. The chopper went vertical for a thousand feet before angling to the south. The pilot keyed his microphone and said three words only: "Airmail package delivered."

More than a thousand miles away, in a mobile command post in Savannah, Leon Hess sat at a console with three dozen dark video screens. "Roger," he said. Hess typed a command into the console. A list of parameters lit up the left side of the top left screen. He swiveled his chair to the man standing behind him.

"Sniper's in place," he said. Gareth Stokes nodded.

While the silent helicopter was drifting away, a tractor trailer maneuvered into the parking lot of the Basilica of St. Louis. The driver positioned the refrigerated container north to south, as instructed, and climbed into his sleeping compartment. The Gateway Arch Park police had received official notification and authorization of the middle-of-the-night delivery. The action was in the system, so the truck's presence constituted business as usual. As the driver settled in for some sleep, he pressed the speed dial of the prepaid cell that had come with his instructions.

"Ground package delivered," he said.

"Thank you," said Leon Hess. He nodded to Stokes and typed again. Sixteen more screens activated. The team was in place. They were only lacking their targets.

Stokes didn't know why they had never thought of this before. Maybe because killing the Namayan had never been on the table until now. But the idea had been so simple; it seemed silly that it had never occurred to him. For longer than he had worked for Carver, the Namayan had been able to know when they were about to be attacked. And if the attack involved guns, then his soldiers might as well shoot themselves before they even deployed, because that's what they would be doing anyway once they got on site. Carver had told him the Namayan could read their intentions, whatever the hell that meant. Whatever they were doing, it worked. They always knew, either well ahead of time or just before an attack. Stokes had found this very frustrating. They all found it very frustrating. Then one day Stokes thought, "What if there were no intentions to read?"

Enter Leon Hess. Hess had been a coordinator of black ops for government organizations so secret they didn't even have names. Until he went entrepreneurial. He now operated a private team of Super Soldiers using technologies the government bad boys wished they had. He usually did this for the same people he had answered to before, only now for more money, and with even greater secrecy.

At this moment, 16 of those Super Soldiers waited in chemically-induced hypnotic states inside individual containers in the truck parked at the Basilica. They wore lightweight armor suits over robotic exoskeletons. A 17th lay alongside a Barrett M107 in the box atop the arch. This one wore an aerodynamic bodysuit with adjustable-on-demand magnets that would allow him to slide to any position on the metal arch he wished. Once he was awake, his only limitation was gravity. He could go down, but not up.

The sniper box and the truck container were equipped with scanning video that would track the arrival of the Namayan Council. Once all nine members were in place, Hess would type a simple command into the computer; simultaneous injections would awaken his entire team immediately, even as their individual containers propelled them forward. They would literally awaken in the air and hit the ground attacking. Hess estimated that the sniper would register two to three kills before the Namayan sensed danger; he could then pick off any others that the ground team failed to dispatch during the melee. Estimated time of attack from awakening to completion was 30 seconds. And no intention to read. Complete surprise.

***

Ally floated in a crystalline tub at the narrow apex of a large, granite canyon. The deep sky overflowed with stars; beneath the tub, blue and gold filaments illuminated the vessel. A recorded choir intoned a single word.

The lights faded; stars lit the canyon. The song fell to silence, leaving only the howl of wind. Ally rose naked from the warm pool and cloaked herself in a thick, white robe. Her eyes adjusted to the darkness, and the night sky revealed its secrets. Two lights, brighter than the rest, floated in opposition at the horizon's edges. A tiny slice of moon held the balance.

Cittam Puram, the Namayan City of Healing, had been carved from living rock in the 10th century. While its technology had maintained pace with the world, its methods of healing had remained the same: light and sound, when properly combined, hold the greatest powers of healing available in the universes.

Nelson had first told Ally of the Secret City when she was 9. It was the darkest memory of her childhood.

She had been watching the red and gold leaves dance in the backyard from her bedroom window upstairs. Lingering light filtered through bare branches. The front door slammed like a slap, and Ally rushed down the long stairs. Daddy had returned from his latest trip. But he was different, cloaked in shadows that Ally could sense but not see. Nelson avoided her searching eyes and disappeared into the kitchen with Mommy. Her parents spoke in muffled tones while Ally listened at the door. When they emerged, both had been crying.

"I have to leave again," he said. She opened her mouth to protest; Nelson had anticipated her question. "Right away," he said. "But not for long. Another week at the most."

"But Daddy," she said. "You just got home." Tears spilled from her eyes.

"I need to go to Cittam Purim," he had said. "The Secret City. When I get home I'll be…myself again."

"What do you mean?" Ally said. "You're yourself right now. I don't understand."

"I know you don't, Little One. One day you will."

Nelson had returned a week later. Ally perceived greater strength and greater wisdom in her father. And a darkness that had never been there before. The shadow she had sensed the week before had not really gone away; darkness had simply receded into the background. Though Ally had already begun her training, though she had learned things that other children her age would never learn, she still had not understood this.

Now, 15 years later, Ally had required the miracles of Cittam Puram herself. The life of service as a Namayan is taxing. Sometimes, only the greatest powers can restore what has been lost. For the first time in her life, Ally had killed. Now, standing in the desert air of the canyon, still wet from the healing pool, she truly understood.

At the far end of the canyon, a monk clad in a heavy maroon robe emerged from a hidden door. He was barely older than she. His deep blue eyes sparkled with secrets. And humor. He faced her, placed his hands together in prayer, and began to chant. His ominous voice echoed in the oval canyon.

"Stick a fork in you," he intoned, "for you are done."

He maintained a reverent poker face. Ally laughed.

"Are you sure?" she said. "Because I could go for another few days of the CP Hot Tub Jam."

"Sorry," he said, checking his watchless wrist. "But I've got Siva coming in today at four, and I've got to drain out this water and fill the tub with virgin blood, sooo…" He shrugged. Ally nodded and choked back another laugh. Still, reality awaited.

"Any news?" she asked.

"No word from the Council," he said. "They are to reassemble soon. Perhaps we will hear from them then."

"I miss my Daddy," she said. *And my Teo.*

"Memsalemn is still in Arcata; Nanoshe sailed to the Yucatán." He looked left, then right. "The crow flies at midnight," he whispered.

Ally rolled her eyes. "Doesn't he always." She looked into the sky. "Layton's in the Yucatán."

The monk nodded.

"Chichen Itza," she said. "Gathering intel."

"That would be my guess."

Ally looked to the vast sky. Venus and Jupiter floated in opposition a few degrees above the horizon. Overhead, Draco loomed like the skeleton of an eldritch god etched into the firmament. The monk followed her gaze. He placed his hand on her shoulder.

"There's hope," he said. "Always."

Ally closed her eyes and envisioned the face of her teacher on her screen of consciousness and spoke with her inner voice.

Pava, can you hear me? I need you. More than ever. I need your guidance. I need your strength. On her inner screen, swirling clouds coalesced into a thunderhead, then burst into a torrent of falling tears. The tears formed first small pools, then rivulets, then streams. A river. The river swelled and rushed to fill a boundless ocean. The ocean lifted her heart. She opened her eyes, looked at the monk, and nodded once.

"Yes," she said. "Of course. There is hope." As she spoke, a thought crept forward from her own shadows: *But wherever there is hope, there is also threat.*

***

The Old Courthouse in downtown St. Louis had been the site of two of the three Dred Scott cases. A few hundred feet to the east, the Gateway Arch curved into the sky. Neither the historical significance nor the architectural grandeur of this location made it appropriate for a rendezvous of the Namayan Council. But a dozen LightGates stood within a half-mile radius of the arch, and that made it perfect. Standard tactics for the Namayan Council dictated that they were never to meet anywhere with fewer gates than members. That way, if they were compromised, as they had been in D.C., they could scatter rather than amass at a bottleneck. Even though they could all join hands and enter a single gate at once, they would be jammed together in the same place for crucial seconds, and sometimes seconds were all that mattered. Still, because of D.C., the Council was being extra careful. First came the scout.

Teo Kirten emerged from a LightGate on the northeast side of the courthouse an hour before dawn. His initial read was that something was wrong. He shifted his weight to reenter the gate immediately, but whatever he had felt was not strong enough, or not close enough, to be a real threat.

He walked the perimeter of Gateway Park, then stood directly beneath the arch and spread his arms, fingers stretched wide. Nothing. He circled the refrigerated semi in the parking lot of the Basilica. Nothing. Satisfied that the site was secure, he sat on the wall at the edge of the lot, closed his eyes, and slipped his consciousness into the inner world. He recalled in great detail the images of his fellow council members. One by one, he looked into their eyes and envisioned the symbol that indicated the rendezvous was safe. Then he slipped off the wall and headed to the small peninsula on the western side of the south pond.

In Savannah, Leon Hess watched the video feeds.

"One," he said.

"Teo Kirten," Stokes said. "Advance scout. Probably just gave the all clear when he closed his eyes. He's one of the captures. Him, Tristan Warner, and the leader, Nelson Profett. Kill the rest. Be ready. They'll be there soon."

In nooks and crannies all around the edges of the park, lights flickered briefly like camera flashes. One by one, seven more members of the Namayan Council emerged from shadows and converged on the peninsula where Teo Kirten waited.

"I count eight total," Hess said. "You said nine, right?"

He pressed a button, and the images were suddenly much closer.

"Profett's missing," Stokes said. "We hold."

***

Apavarita Varsah, Hidden Rain, Warrior Princess of the Samudra Janah, walked in her LightBody along the dark shore between a red ocean and slate gray cliffs. The indigo sky rippled like a descending shawl. A cold planet floated above the far horizon; the Dragon Cluster held watch from the zenith. Pava, as she was known to her inner circle, regarded the glimmering lights above her and smiled her most secret of smiles.

Black sand clung to her feet and then slithered up to her knees. Silica tentacles pulled at her legs to drag her down. She closed her eyes, pressed her palms together in front of her heart, and inhaled more Light.

"Stop this foolishness." she said. "You are only sand." The grains lost their polarity and fell back to the shore. But this was not a good sign.

At the far end of the strand, a huge gryphon slouched from the darkness where the shoreline disappeared behind the precipice. Its lazy wings beat the salt air as it took flight over the water, stopping to float above the waves in front of her. The beast shimmered and became an Earth Daughter of about 7 years, a waif with translucent skin and ravenous, black eyes. She wore a tattered white dress with a lace overlay; two satin ribbons dangled from her unbuttoned collar.

Pava softened her gaze and glanced to the girl's left. The shape swam and shifted, flashed in and out of Pava's vision. A familiar visage emerged from beneath the mask of innocence. Then the waif's image reformed, smiling with

184

serene malice.

"Enough games," said Pava.

"You waste time here, Samudra," said Ripu Dasi. "As you can see," the child spread her hands, "you are too late. He has been mine for lifetimes. You'll never retrieve him."

"Speaking a thing does not make it so."

The girl inclined her head toward the water and closed her eyes. Wind swirled like an unpleasant surprise, drawing a fetid aroma from the horizon. Her eyes opened. They were tinged with blood.

"My speaking has not made it so, *pumscali*," said Ripu Dasi. "I have done the work. I am the God of his Secret World. He will never accept you. You are a virus. I am your antibody."

"He will recognize you for what you are."

"Ahhhhh," sighed Dasi. His girl-child voice shifted into lower rumbles. The angelic aspect shimmered again in the red air and transformed into a male warrior angel. "Behold! He already does." The angel ascended and spread his arms. Red wind whipped at his golden hair. "I am his savior." He glowed with brassy light. "I am his inspiration." White feathered wings unfolded behind his back. "I am his Angel. You are his Demon of Death. By the time he becomes fully aware of your presence, he will hate you to the depths of his heart."

"I will not harm him."

"You are the agent of his destruction," said Ripu Dasi. "It is already done."

"There is much yet to be decided."

Dasi's laugh surrounded the world. Wind gathered in a sudden rage. A giant wave rose on the horizon and rushed shoreward. Dasi rose higher. Red mist swirled about his angelic aspect; Pava gripped her feet into the black sand, pressed her hands together palm to palm, and turned her left shoulder to the shore. The crimson wall rushed forward. Pava held Dasi's gaze and then pulled her hands slowly away from one another until her arms were outstretched, the knife edge of her left hand confronting the approaching wall, the palm of her right hand facing downward to the sand. The wave filled the sky above them. Still Pava held Dasi's gaze. The wave crested forward, a wall of death. Then it split in two and crashed to the shore on either side of Pava. Water joined sand and hissed like rain on a furnace, surrounding them in an anemic fog.

The angel laughed. Its image blended with the swirling mist and then blew away over the churning waves. The sea calmed. The wind died, leaving behind only an echo of laughter. Ripu Dasi was gone.

Pava turned away from the sea. Cary sat curled on a boulder, trembling, naked, his eyes wide with fear.

How terrible he must have made me appear to you, Pava thought. She released a wave of compassion that swept over Cary. He wrapped his arms tighter around his knees and sobbed.

Pava closed her eyes to Cary's inner world and opened them toward her own. Nothing more she could do here and now. A familiar rush of wind embraced her; the roar of the AllSound filled her every cell. Pava opened her eyes, and she was once again sitting on her favorite cushion, looking out through the invisible barrier onto the molten landscape of Venus.

***

Eight Namayan Council members gathered on the small peninsula. They looked very much as they had in D.C.: a nondescript group of homeless men. Minus one. If the Park Police were out this early, the worse that would happen is they'd be told to move along, which was their plan anyway. Then they would find a nearby location, invisible to most of the world, where they could set up.

Pablo Tranh, the smallest in stature, bounced from foot to foot.

"I don't like it," he said. "Something's wrong. We've been out in the open too long. Where's Nelson?"

Warner scanned the park. Like Teo, the only danger he sensed was far, far away.

None of the council knew that only moments before, Nelson had stepped through a concrete wall on the third floor of the garage at the northern end of the park. Like Warner and Teo, he sensed the distant danger. Unlike Warner and Teo, Nelson had the ability to articulate to the thread of that danger and trace it to its source. By the time he reached ground level and exited the garage, he was moving at a dead run toward the northern base of the arch.

Nelson's body sprinted with the effortlessness of a machine, and he slipped his attention half into the inner worlds. The light-presence of objects became palpable. He saw the entire scenario in a single, 360-degree flash: the Council assembled on the peninsula; the dormant Super Soldiers in the parking lot; the sniper-in-a-box on top of the arch; Leon Hess at the console in Savannah; and Gareth Stokes behind him, waiting to pull the trigger to set the operation in motion.

Theoretical physicists are so close to understanding the nature of the inner worlds, so close to learning through technology what the ancients knew through direct experience. If they could see the world that Nelson now saw, they would understand at once. Nelson focused his will on the light that surrounded and permeated his body. He extended the energy fields of his hands and feet, charging the particles such that they would entangle their counterparts on the arch. A simple concept, really, one understood by Shaolin masters for centuries. Friction. Light. Energy. Just a matter of deploying them correctly. Of course, before you could do that, you had to believe such things were possible, and then spend a lifetime learning how.

***

"Tranh's right," Teo said. "We're over the limit here. We've been exposed far too long."

Warner kept scanning the park. The danger he had felt was still far away. But it was stronger. How could that be? On the screen of his mind, he saw a flickering image of a park in downtown Savannah. *Why am I seeing that?* But he knew from years of experience that it meant something. Teo was right. They should...

"What the..." said Derrick Fish, a tall, solid man standing directly behind Tranh. Fish was pointing at the northern edge of the arch. Something was moving about halfway up. They all looked.

"Good God," Warner said. "That's Nelson."

***

A good reporter follows every lead, and Simon Boon was a good reporter. A little more than two weeks ago, when he had noticed the man and woman skulking in the shadows at Taylor Walker's funeral, Simon had decided to follow them.

Maybe planning to steal the body. Though these two didn't look like any of the other Qellepoth he had so far encountered. Then the woman had seen him, and Simon had hightailed it back to his Microbus. Without falling. Simon's Life Rule number 741.2 slash B: Escape whenever possible.

He drove two blocks, then doubled back on foot and followed a soft carpet of pine needles through a maze of sharp, green palm fronds. Languid pines danced to and fro in the hot Florida wind. He crouched behind a stand of palmettos just as Ally and Cary reached the clearing where they had parked the Crown Victoria.

I know that car.

That was when Simon got his first surprise. Four big uglies in black BDUs ambushed them. He had not seen these guys at all. He could only hope they hadn't seen him. He'd crouched lower and watched the fray.

That was when Simon got his second surprise. The girl was 5-feet nothing and maybe a 100 pounds, but she opened a can of whup-ass on the first guy like he was a little kid. But the real surprise came when she had somehow forced one of them to shoot his partner, then himself. Simon was sure of it. By the time it was over, she had taken out all four of them. Killed them. Dead. Not, however, before the last one had sliced open her companion's side.

None of the dead men had carried ID. Or worn plaid. So they were okay on that last score at least. One of them looked like one of the men he had seen that night on Edison. Couldn't be sure. Maybe it was just the clothes. Put BDUs over a few shaved-headed bricks and they all look the same. Then he remembered. That was where he had seen the car. She had to be the ghost woman he'd seen running across the street. Who was she?

Simon retrieved the knife, a Spyderco Harpy, and dropped it into his jacket. He had just slipped back into the palmettos when, of all things, a FedEx van rolled up. Four more big uglies piled out of the back.

For the second time in a matter of minutes, Simon had crouched where he stood and let the palmettos embrace him. Simon's Life Rule number 741.2 slash B, sub-paragraph 1: When you can't escape, hide. None of the men had spoken. Two of them placed the corpses in the back of the FedEx Truck while a third used a broom—*Seriously, a broom?*—to sweep sand and pine needles over the blood spots. A fourth walked the perimeter of the glade, his right hand invisible under the left side of his coat.

Simon sank down farther, his head almost to the ground, as the man approached his hiding place. Gnats turned in holding patterns around his eyes, and mosquitoes dive-bombed his ears. He held his breath and studied the arcana of pine needles until he heard the man's receding footsteps. Simon remained unmoving long after the sound of the truck's engine had disappeared. It wasn't until he had begun to rise that he realized he had been crouched in a position of prayer.

***

Nelson ascended the arch like a human fly. Later, his body would experience fatigue from the exertion, but for the moment such feelings were unnecessary, detrimental, and therefore compartmentalized. He climbed quickly, and as he climbed he looked south at the collective light of the Namayan Council exposed on the peninsula. He compressed a thought into a tight ball, wrapped it and all its emotion into the sign and signifier of a single word, and flung the bundle of energy at the group.

Ambush!

"Something's up," said Leon Hess. "They're spooked."

"Put the sniper in play," Stokes said. "And put down the locals."

Hess typed. A colorless gas deployed throughout the arch facility, putting the third shift Park Police to sleep in seconds. A small hypodermic awoke the sniper. The lower end of the box on top of the arch slid open. A spring released and catapulted the sniper into position. He awoke, gun already in his hands, virtually invisible against the metal of the arch.

"Now or never," Hess said. He typed another command; his finger hovered over the *Enter* key.

Stokes saw Derrick Fish pointing at the arch. The angle was too low for them to have seen the sniper. But Hess was right. They were going to bolt any second. He wanted Nelson, but better to get the rest of them than none at all.

"Do it," he said.

Leon Hess executed the command, and 16 sleeping monsters came to life. Simultaneous injections brought the Super Soldiers to full consciousness as their containers slammed open and spit them into the air. They landed running, CTAR 21s locked and loaded. Atop the arch, the sniper was already taking aim.

Nelson's message hit each of the Namayan Council members at the same moment. *Ambush!* A speck of light flashed high on the arch, and Derrick Fish's head bloomed like a crimson flower. Half a second later, Tranh's did the same. Before either of the dead men had hit the ground,

Reverté launched backwards, his chest collapsing inward as he flew. The report of three quick shots followed. The sniper had taken down three of them before they heard the first shot.

Nelson heard the sniper fire just before he crested the arch. He reached into the man's thoughts and assumed control of his intention. The sniper shivered for a moment, trying to shake off the invasion, then resumed firing.

The remaining Namayan were all moving now, scattering in different directions. Another bullet shattered the tree behind where Teo's head had just been. He dove forward, and when he rolled to his feet, 16 giants charged over the hillock to the west. They were like a *Star Wars* nightmare: full body armor, including helmets, in high-tech urban camo. They covered ground in huge leaps, bringing their weapons to bear as they approached. Teo angled to the south, trying not to get boxed in by the pond. Three more of the council were cut down by gunfire. Only Teo and Warner remained alive on the ground. Warner charged to the north, but five soldiers closed in a circle around him. They swung their guns away on straps behind their backs. Five more pealed away from the group and bounded after Teo. He could hear servos whirring under their armor.

Two of the soldiers closing on Warner dropped, blood spurting from the small opening between their helmets and their body armor, and two more shots rang out from the arch. Two of the ones following Teo fell, and the report of two more shots followed. Three to one now, and Nelson had control of the sniper. Maybe Teo and Warner could get away.

"What the hell?" Hess said. He and Stokes watched four of the ground troops fall to perfectly placed gunfire.

"Shit," Stokes said. "Profett's there. Got to be. Take the sniper off the board."

"He's maybe the best sniper in the world," Hess said, but he was already typing. Inside the shooter's skin-tight suit, a needle deployed, knocking the man out immediately. The Barrett slipped from his fingers and dangled from the straps that secured it to his suit. The man hung limp, still magnetized to the metal surface.

"Send the chopper back in. And send some of those big dogs to the arch," Stokes said. "I want Nelson Profett."

Nelson felt the sniper go limp in his mind even before he saw the man's body relax. He checked his pulse. Still alive. Three of the ground troops had separated from the fray and were bounding toward the arch. Nelson left the man alive and retreated the way he had come. He stopped by the container and stared into the camera lens, but the camera deactivated before he could reach Hess through the connection. Nelson launched himself like a baseball player stealing home and slid down the side of the Gateway Arch. He let gravity do the work of acceleration until he was thirty feet from the ground, then he reapplied light-friction. He hit the ground running at full speed back toward the parking garage and the LightGate on the third floor. He could only hope he had given Teo and Warner enough of an edge to escape. Behind him, the three soldiers vectored to the left and closed the distance.

Teo circled back through the parking lot of the Basilica. The truck container was open now from the side, revealing a honeycomb of empty containers. The three soldiers drew closer with each leap. So close now that he felt the ground shake each time one of them landed.

Use their own strengths against them.

He rushed across Memorial Drive and onto the Market Street Bridge. Street traffic was still virtually nonexistent, but down on I-70, big trucks were roaring through. Teo executed a controlled stumble. The first of the soldiers was almost on him now. Almost. He sensed the approaching mass bearing down. Almost. He stumbled again and went down against the bridge wall, spinning to face the attacker as he fell. The thing landed in front of him with a ground-shaking thud, legs wide, arms already reaching forward. Teo pushed away from the wall, sliding between the armored legs and up to his own feet. He drove his shoulder up and under the soldier's armored butt with all his might. Jesus, it was like trying to push a

Humvee uphill. But Teo dug in and shoved harder. He was reaching the end of his strength when a second trooper landed, casting a shock wave through the street and lifting the giant up enough to topple him over the edge. The second soldier managed to catch his companion's wrist long enough to dangle him above the interstate for a few seconds. And long enough for Teo to sprint away. Then the grip broke, and the dangling soldier slipped free. He landed hard on the hood of a Peterbilt ambling along at 50. But that provided more than enough force to crush the man inside the armor, even though the armor remained largely intact. By the time the other two looked up from their fallen comrade, Teo Kirten was nowhere to be seen.

***

At a little past 5 a.m., Carver reviewed a flow chart on the transparent screen in his office. Since the failure at Taylor Walker's funeral, Cary Walker and Ally Profett had not been sighted. He had operatives in Tampa and in Burnsville, but that trail, as the saying goes, had gone cold. Probably hidden away at Shangri-La. How many years had he been trying to find that place? Soon, maybe.

At least their other operation had been successful. Stokes' plan had been genius, really. How could the Namayan read someone's intentions when they had none? By the time one of the council had figured it out, most of them were already dead. Only two were still unaccounted for. Hess' remote-control team had killed six of them. But they had captured one. An important one. One who knew secrets. They were tough bastards, hard as nails, especially this one, but all things break eventually. Everything was only a matter of time. Once he broke, all the Namayan secrets would be revealed, including their Sanctuaries. Then they would find Walker, and the plan would be back on track.

Dossey continued to press. A necessary annoyance, for the moment. And though Layton seemed to be more of an

193

ally than he had ever been, Carver was increasingly distrustful.

I should prepare the Benben, in case Layton has plans that I am not sensing.

A subtle shift in the air pressure of the office drew Carver's attention away from the screen. Miranda breezed through the open doorway. She carried a mahogany tray with two white porcelain cups and a red *YiXing* pot. A wispy rope of steam drifted aloft from the spout.

Did I not lock that? He waved his hand over a sensor in his desk, and a slide show of their vacation to Banff replaced the chart. The Canadian Rockies loomed gigantic on the screen.

"I woke up and you were gone," she said. "I couldn't get back to sleep. Thought you might like a cup of *Pu-Ehr.*"

Carver kissed her on the cheek and poured both cups. "Thank you, love," he said. "But let's go out onto the veranda. Easier to relax when I am not surrounded by work, even with these gorgeous images to distract me."

"You work too hard," she said.

They settled into the chaise lounges and sipped their tea in silence. The essence of the Pacific Ocean bathed them in mist. Dawn made its subtle entrance into their corner of the world. Stars faded until only the reflection of the sun on Jupiter and Venus remained in the sky.

It's only a matter of time. Patience.

Carver had much practice in the art of patience. He took his wife's hand in his own and watched the day continue to arrive.

***

Why did you leave me?

Cary's angel had abandoned him. The blue demon turned. Cary could just make out the curve of her hips and breasts against the red sky. His body cried out for him to jump down to the sand, to run away for all he was worth, but her dark green eyes impaled him, fixing him to his perch on the boulder. Queasy fear drove through him like the wall of red water that, moments before, had failed to crush the blue demon. Tears poured from Cary's unclosable eyes.

His body relaxed as he acquiesced, still tremulous, to his fate. The sickening fear faded as quickly as the ocean storm had calmed. A relieved sob filled his mouth, and he cried it out. His soul settled into the peace of a still pond. His thoughts resonated from deep beneath the unmolested surface.

Why is she staring at me? Why am I not afraid anymore?

The demon's blue skin lightened. Waves, sky, and one shining star all became visible through her fading aspect. And then she was gone, leaving only the strange red ocean, the lazy waves beating against the black sand, and the dulcet warble of songbirds.

To Cary's left, a square of blue floated in the red air almost close enough to touch. Birds flitted across the opening, singing to one another and to Cary. He reached for the blue square. A white frame surrounded the opening. He had not noticed the frame at first, or the curtains that reached for him with gauzy arms in the soft breeze.

The red sky darkened and coalesced to dusky solidity. Not sky, then. A red stucco wall with a white frame window. Through the window he could see the crystal blue sky. He was in a room, in a bed. A grosbeak cocked her head and sang a wake-up song from the windowsill. Her rosy chest flashed in the morning sun.

Cary tried to sit, but pain stabbed his left side and he collapsed back onto the feather mattress. The door opened and a woman swept in, her dark hair flowing behind her like a cape glittering with threads of silver. Probably in her late 30s. Dark jeans hugged her hourglass hips. Her breasts moved freely under a white, V-neck T-shirt. She took his wrist. He felt fire and sanctuary in her touch. She had dark-rimmed, golden brown eyes that swept upward toward the outer point of her brow to form an elongated S. Though they were not green, they reminded him of…

"Alethea…" Cary began.

The woman's laugh danced like wind chimes.

"Alethea's not here," she said. "I'm Emma." Her voice opened again the ache in his chest. Cary's head spun with the same vertigo he had experienced when he had first seen Ally. Then Nelson. She must be Alethea's sister.

What is it with this family?

"Finally," she said. "Waking up. Careful, now. Not too much too soon."

Her voice sounded like it was spiraling through a long tunnel. Cary blinked once. The walls and ceiling disappeared. Emma remained, solid, smiling down at him, but behind her the world became a protean panorama: a swirling, multicolored cloudscape, then a world of writhing forms in a red cloud, the ocean, a golden ziggurat, a shining river. He felt the current rush over his bare feet. For just an instant, Emma was gone, and the blue demon stood in her place. But before he could scream, Emma was back, her hypnotic eyes calling up that ache inside him.

He struggled to keep his own eyes open. His left side burned like tearing skin. His muscles were exhausted, as if he had just swum across a wide, dark river and then back again.

"I thought you weren't coming back," Emma said.

Her voice was a balm, and the longing in his chest doubled; despite his pain, he wanted her. *How can this be? I don't even know you.*

The feather bed enfolded him like a lover, inviting him back to the land of dreams. Inner landscapes beckoned.

"How long…" he said.

Emma reached into him with those dark-rimmed eyes. No judgment. Only kindness. And strength. And…desire? Cary sensed that she was assessing him. Evaluating. She shook her head, almost too subtle for him to see. Then she touched the center of his forehead with her index and middle fingers.

"Sleep now," she said. "Answers later." And with that simple touch, Cary was once again living in the world of angels and blue demons, though they remained concealed for the moment, deep in his shadows.

Before Time

~

Ksama

Alone now, Ksama lights the fire and binds her useless hand with a scrap of sail cloth. Under the helm seat, she finds salted fish and flatbread. She hoists the gray sail and ties off the boom and the rudder. Then, for the first time in a week, she fills her belly.

The *Varuna* rises and falls across long waves, finding its own way. Bundled in her leather sheath just forward of the mast, Sh'ele rocks back and forth in the vee of the keel.

If DevaSurya spoke true...

...as if the Queen of Light could speak other than true...

...then the entire power source of Ksama's dead continent lies next to her. Her mind cannot contain such a fact. If Sh'ele's energy is this vast, Syrgala will find it easily. But for the moment, only present circumstances matter. Ksama's life has come down to a series of essential tasks in a prescribed order. The most difficult is always the next in line.

Sea spray whistles across the pitching bow. The dark disk of the sun struggles behind silent clouds. Ksama has begun to think of her hand as an enemy, a former ally turned traitor, now sentenced to death. With delicate fingers she unlaces the bindings that press the traitor against her body. Slicing through muscle and bone will be difficult enough, but the true test will be remaining conscious long enough to cauterize the wound. If she passes out, even for a few minutes, she will bleed to death.

I doubt that I even have the strength to raise my sword.

A shard of light blinds her. She curls her elbow around the mast to keep from falling. The leather sheath has fallen open, exposing Sh'ele's uppermost facet, the same facet upon which Ksama had, only days ago, drawn a prophetic line across the reflection of Sidra's throat. The *Varuna* pitches on the long waves. Each time the boat tilts forward, the sun reflects off Sh'ele's surface, flashing into Ksama's eyes. She imagines for a moment that Sh'ele is trying to get her attention.

"Crazy," she says, but she pulls aside the leather sheath, exposing the rest of the crystal to the sun.

The Añucara are taught that the Stones of Uktenah are inanimate. Sacred, it is true, but not living. And yet they are grown, nurtured. The Cultivators empowered them with names. Could it be that her training was wrong? Unthinkable. Yet the question turns like a worm in her brain: Could Sh'ele be alive? Conscious?

"You're delusional," Ksama says. No one is present to hear. Except, of course, for Sh'ele. So now she is talking to her crystal. Perhaps the crystal is also speaking to her, has been speaking to her from the beginning. Her visions of Asita. This sloop calling to her. The blinding flash of insight that inspired her to take up the quartz dagger from Sh'ele's base and plunge it into Sidra's neck. Were these her own thoughts or...

Communication.

Ksama is Añucara. The Guardian of Sh'ele. Her title long ago became her identity.

"Can it be," she says, looking at the crystal, "that it is actually you who have been my guardian, and not the reverse?" Even as she speaks the words, she hears the answer to her question, not in words, but through direct knowing.

Can it not be that both are true?

A palpable, almost sexual heat flushes her skin. Sudden desire overwhelms her to dissolve the cloak of protection she has worn for most of her life. Her tentative hand moves on its own. She longs like a lover to press her palm onto Sh'ele's perfect skin and allow the crystal's power to flood into her. But fear stabs at her heart.

The Canons.

Never once has Ksama been tempted to draw on Sh'ele's energy. The power of the crystals belongs to God. Yet a cold awareness fills her. If she does not use Sh'ele's power, she will not survive. Her skin burns.

The First Canon.

She tilts her head back and cries out to the heavy sky. "I don't know what to do." She lowers her head and speaks more softly. "Please. Tell me what to do."

But the sky does not answer. Ksama has sworn to hide and protect Sh'ele, but she cannot fulfill that vow if she dies in the middle of the ocean. Her hand inches forward. She pauses, still uncertain, still needing help. The *Varuna* drops abruptly on a choppy wave, and Ksama pitches forward.

Her left palm presses onto the shining surface, and she gasps. For a moment nothing happens. She stares at her hand outlined on the quartz. She can see her bones through her skin—so great is the crystal's light. Still nothing happens. Then she remembers that the Pravarna was created and is maintained through her intention. Her eyes fill with tears, and she is uncertain whether these are tears of grief, shame, sorrow, or love. She does not even know exactly how she accomplishes it, but somewhere inside she releases her grip on a braided strand of light, like letting go of a cord that holds closed a purse.

Her hand tingles on the surface of the crystal. The ur-songs of existence, the sounds behind the sounds, shift down an octave and pulse inside Ksama's cells. Electricity crackles through her. A holograph blinks into view above Sh'ele. In the momentary image, Ksama sees herself lying on the deck of the boat, her arms and legs wrapped around Sh'ele, holding it close to her chest as a wife would embrace her husband. Just as quickly, the holograph is gone.

Did I imagine that?

The answer does not matter. Her arm throbs like a hammer. Scarlet snakes pulse and writhe anew under her skin. They slither up her arm, thirsting to mingle their venom with the blood in her heart. She lies down as the image had shown her and pulls Sh'ele close. The last layer of the Pravarna falls away, and, with a deep sound that must surely be the grandmother of thunder itself, her entire world turns inside out.

Present Day

After rising from prayer in the palmettos, Simon had driven directly to the Cockroach Bay Motel, retrieved Woodstein, and moved full time into the Microbus.

Since that day he had stayed mostly on the move, watching his rearview mirror constantly and shifting parking sites every few days. His latest hidey-hole was an old cotton shed behind a dilapidated Civil War mansion 10 miles out old US 92 near Ruskin. Brown-green mold had long ago consumed the white majesty of the manor.

Earlier today, Simon had driven to the nearest Circle K for coffee and the Tribune. The official word on Freddy's death had been released: accidental drowning.

Right.

In the afternoon, Simon drove to West Tampa. Now he crouched behind curly tendrils of Spanish moss in the dusky shadows of Freddy Blake's backyard. Broad swaths of yellow crime scene tape sealed the porch door. TPD apparently disagreed with the accidental death hypothesis. Or maybe they had floated the story to see what would pop up next to it.

Freddy had lived his entire life in this West Tampa bungalow. When his parents had retired and moved to Alaska while Freddy was at Georgetown, they had left him the house. He had come home immediately after finishing graduate school. Maybe Thomas Wolfe was wrong.

Simon knew the house almost as well as Freddy had. He had spent many a night here studying Spanish. Or algebra. Or unfolded glossy photographs. He had snuck a thousand times onto this back porch. The police had tied this crime scene up in a tight, yellow bow; they had padlocked the front and back doors. But Simon knew something they did not. The screws in the window lock in Freddy's childhood bedroom had been threadless for more than three decades.

Simon slithered through the window. The shoelace of his trailing foot snagged on the sill, and he tumbled forward in his inevitable unbalancing act.

"This would be where I fall on my ass," Simon grunted. But instead of the expected crash, he settled into a thick futon.

"Thank you, Freddy," he said.

He searched every room, sweeping his penlight across drawers and corners just to be thorough. He found what he had expected painted on the living room wall.

Qellepoth.

Simon shuddered, and his skin threatened to crawl right off his body. The floor creaked near the kitchen. Simon held his breath. Nothing. But he could not shake the feeling that every slight sound might mean death. A car drove down the street. Maybe a FedEx van full of killers? No. A TPD blue and white. The officer parked around the corner. Simon slipped out the bedroom window and followed a trail of shadows back to his van.

Woodstein curled up in Simon's lap all the way back to the mansion. Simon eased the bus into the old cotton shed and walked out under a thick night. The cat grazed furry figure-eights around his ankles. A billion stars, one brighter than the rest, peppered the sky.

"Too bad it's not Christmas time," he said. "We could use a good omen right about now."

***

Beneath the swirling clouds of Venus, on the far reaches of the Plains of Midnight south of the city of Retz, Apavarita Varsah kept watch over Earth from under the protective dome of Dalam Palace. Pava had guided and observed each Tellurian civilization as it grew, flourished, and then collapsed in self-wrought decay. Her apprentice and assistant, Rahni Sisyah, had served only for the last 50 years. A mere neophyte.

Dalam Palace was a simple white cube topped by a protective blue hemisphere shimmering like a cabochon sapphire. The surface of the cube was one vast room. Soft carpets lined the floor; pillows of various shapes, sizes and colors lay strewn about, alone or in groups. A marble dais marked the center. Three feet above the dais, a black pyramid known as the *Omphalos* spun clockwise in the lazy air. In front of the Omphalos stood a blue, rectangular stool, and to its left, a single blue spotlight illuminated a four-poster bed in which Cary Walker's LightBody lay pale and unconscious.

Pava sank onto a green cushion. She had a soft oval face, green, almond-shaped eyes, and black hair that tickled the border between neck and shoulders when she moved. Her loose-fitting pants and blouse matched her eyes. He skin shimmered golden-blue.

Rahni perched cross-legged on the stool in front of the Omphalos. He was thicker in body, and wore only blue-green trousers. His smooth skin was a dark bronze, and his hair hung between his shoulder blades in a tight braid crisscrossed with a strand of red silk. Rahni's attention was split between the Omphalos and Cary sleeping on the bed.

"He's been stirring," Rahni said.

"I am aware of Mr. Walker's travels," said Pava. "Tell me what *you* see."

Rahni sighed and returned his focus to the Omphalos. "Nothing," he said. "Only dark surfaces."

Pava unfolded herself and joined him.

"Concentrate, *Vatsah*," she said.

Pava passed her hand over the apex, and the black pyramid turned to pure light; another pyramid formed, upside down and identical to the first, touching at the tip. Their rate of spin increased until they became a glowing blur, drawing light toward the center point and forming a bright torus. A holographic sphere formed around the torus, then appeared to solidify. A perfect, real-time facsimile of Earth hung three feet above the floor where, less than a minute before, only the black pyramid had spun.

"So," said Rahni Sisyah. "Simple as that."

Pava laughed. "Don't worry, *Vatsah*. You'll get it." Pava angled her palm slightly and their perspective shifted. They were moving within the image now, flying toward Earth's surface as if they were in the sky. In seconds, they hovered a few feet above Ally. She stared up from the canyon at Cittam Puram, searching the sky for Pava, but unable to see.

"She calls out to you," Rahni said.

"And I answer," said Pava, "though she hears me only in symbols." Pava looked over her shoulder to Cary's LightBody. "This one hears even less." She turned her hand again. They flew at light speed above the Earth. Simon Boon shimmered into view outside the cotton shed, also staring directly up at them. "And this one hears nothing at all."

"What will you do about Mr. Walker?" Rahni said.

"I will speak with him, soul to soul. He is soon to return fully to his Tellurian body. Then I will be even less able to make him hear. He will remember little of what I tell him in any case. If only he knew how important he is. If only he could fully awaken to us, here and now, then perhaps I could remind him of his history, and we would be able to avert the struggle that is yet to come. But Ripu Dasi has a death grip on him. So much depends on Mr. Walker's vow. If only he could know what he knows."

She closed her hand and turned it toward her chest. The image disappeared; the torus flows converged into the center point. Only the dark, spinning Omphalos remained.

"I will tell Mr. Walker part of his story. Then we shall bring them all together: Alethea, Mr. Walker, and Simon Boon. Perhaps the three of them will be able to construct a useful version of the truth."

Pava settled on the edge of the bed and laid her soft palm upon Cary's forehead.

"You loved scary stories when you were a child, Zachary Walker. Awaken now, such as you can. I will tell you a bedtime story that will melt your bones."

***

The next day, Simon followed his own shadow along the south fence of Interbay Cemetery. He had a routine graveyard-lurking schedule now.

If this is Thursday, I must be in South Tampa.

But these days, lurking was a lonely, fruitless endeavor. He had not flushed a single Qellepoth kid or big ugly since the melee after Taylor Walker's funeral. Maybe it would be safe to come out of hiding. But his money was still holding out, and his Simon-senses said, "Wait." He at least felt safe enough to begin his Schedule of Lurk in late afternoon rather than waiting until dark. Though it felt less like lurking when the sun was still out.

Interbay was a bust. Simon drove north, all the way across town to the Starbucks on North Dale Mabry, a place he was unlikely to encounter anyone who might recognize him. He wedged himself into the back corner booth so he could watch the entrance.

Just in cases.

The dark-haired girl who entered with her head down looked vaguely familiar. When she raised her head to place her order with the barista, Simon recognized her as one of the girls he had seen abandoning the house on Edison.

Ding ding ding. Thanks for playing. You win the big prize.

He tailed her to the YMCA in Northdale and parked

across the street. Moments later, another car pulled up. Someone else was following her.

Two men in their early 20s conferred in the front seat. The passenger got out. He was the same age as other Qellepoth Simon had seen, but he moved with greater purpose. The kid walked toward the front door of the Y, then stopped. He scanned his surroundings until his eyes locked on Simon. Simon rested his hand on the ignition key.

The guy smiled, nodded. And then, for scarcely an instant, his aspect shifted. The transformation was unmistakable; for the tiniest of moments the man became...

No way! What now? The Beast of the YMCA?

Simon shook his head to cast the monstrous image out of his thoughts, but the vision appeared again. Wide. Square. At least 8 feet tall. And it had four arms. Monster shimmered back to man. Comprehension played across his now-human face: he knew that Simon had seen him for what he was. He smiled again, then launched into a dead run toward Simon.

EIGHTH ARTICULATION

bilocation dreams

a scary story

an evil overlord

beast vs. Microbus

Sisters of Mercy

surgery on the high seas

a boy in a shell in a box

a failed ostrich attempt

Present Day

Cary sat up. His lungs did not at first obey his body's scream for air. Darkness dominated the edges of his vision. His hand scrabbled at his chest and caught the necklace dangling at the end of its cord. Air rushed in at last. He could just make out his surroundings. The walls of his room at Shangri-La were fully transparent, barely there at all. Small shadows flitted past the darkened window, but he heard no birdsongs. A low, unmistakable hum of power emanated from nowhere and everywhere at once. A few feet away, a shadow-figure stood backlit by ambient, purple light that, like the deep hum, originated from no apparent source. Another figure hid behind the first, peeking around its left shoulder.

"Where am I?" he said. "What's happening to me?"

"Be at peace," a woman said. Her voice touched his soul, and though the voice was as frightening as it was soothing, he had no choice but to acquiesce. "Lie back; listen," she said. "I am going to tell you a story. It is crucial that you hear and remember."

The second figure stepped from behind her like a child who has decided that Mommy's friend is safe after all. This second one appeared to be male. Both remained silhouettes in the ambient light.

"Long before Tellurian histories were written," she said, "your people watched lights wander across the vast starscapes of night."

Her words washed through him. Skies of light and landscapes of sound took shape in his private universe. The more she spoke, the further his fear of her voice receded. Cary sank deeper into the feather bed that was somehow both in his room at Shangri-La and in this strange, purple place. The more she unfolded this story, the more his comfortable bed floated in the space and time of her hypnotic voice. Soon, the bed disappeared. Only Cary and the story remained. And then he was the story itself.

"One light burned brighter than the rest and, over the centuries, held many names. *Sathahrathah*, the Cunning Chariot. *Nibiru*, The Eternal Wanderer. Centuries later you called it *Jupiter*, after the King of the Gods.

"One day, an Englishman looked through his telescope and saw the gigantic storm you call the Eye of Jupiter. Your people have held that alien cyclone in awe ever since. And so you should.

"But your imaginations are so limited. You have always only conceived of Jupiter within the framework of your own, tiny solar system, just another planet, different than your own, to be sure, but a planet nonetheless. Therein lies your mistake. Jupiter is not a planet at all, but a vehicle that arrived in your backyard millions of years after your solar system had taken shape. Upon it, within the great cyclone, live the Grastar, a race of monsters who are the source of every terror you have ever conceived. The Grastar, and nothing else, are the source of all that you call evil on your planet."

Malign shadows moved at the edges of the light from which Pava wove this story. Cary's heart turned in upon itself and threatened to pull him deeper into the darkness that had always been waiting. Thick fingers plucked at the threads of the tale, unraveling the weave.

"Earth's Children have never understood that, from a time before your first coherent human thoughts, the seeds of your death have been waiting on Jupiter. Horrors that far surpass any you have ever created in books and films. The

Grastar are the true evil. They have been waiting for you for millions of years. And their wait is nearly over.

"Your fate choices were long ago inscribed upon your bodies. Every possible ending is contained in this single beginning. Your destruction lies at all ends of this story, save one."

The swirling terror in Cary's chest accelerated, pulling at his periphery, threatening to make him collapse in upon himself.

"Can you not feel that sickening seed of death within your soul?" she said. "Do you perceive how it drags you downward? The flowering of your fate is about to unfold in your universe.

"You have no conscious knowledge of this threat, but it lives within each of you as a tiny fear in your heart. Think of that terrible sinking that spins in silent, unguarded moments, as you fall asleep, or as you awaken startled into fearful alertness; the unknown terror, the depthless guilt, the shame with no horizon of redemption, the dread of a responsibility you know so well but can never name.

"You know this fear. Deep in your heart, you know it. You and your billions of brothers and sisters wander the skin of your planet, trying to stave off unnamed destruction, never knowing what it is, always mistaking it for something else—something more immediate, more local, more temporary."

The beast at the edge of Cary's awareness pulled the threads more quickly now, and though the darkness surrounding it grew, Cary began to discern its symmetry. Four arms swirled interweaving circles in front of its body. The torso stood upon two thick legs with great, square feet. Beneath its wide head, deep set eyes burned with cold darkness and searched endlessly as the arms continued to spin light into shadow through some arcane alchemy.

"Still Jupiter hangs in your sky," Pava said. "Tiny and vast, far away but oh-so-near, it spins with malign purpose, like a single cancer cell hiding in the liver, like a grain of asbestos floating in the lung. Upon that giant speck of destruction, seething in the Red Spot, the Grastar SoulEaters bide their time. Their name is their truth, for they will gouge out the meat of your soul like marrow from a stew-soft bone. Not only each corporeal soul, but that of your planet, as well.

"Their Warlord, Ras Graal, watches from his fortress on Europa, waiting to wield his army like a hammer that will shatter your existence to nothingness, to the absence of Being. Graal has watched from a time before time, waiting for the flower that is your planet to bloom into its magnificence. Only then can Earth be harvested, sucked empty of all joy, drained of all light and sound. This is what they do. This is all they do. And Earth's blooming is now at hand.

"You, Mr. Walker, hold the only key that may allow them to accomplish their purpose. Long ago you made a promise. Now you must honor that..."

The beast at the edge of the shadows sniffed the air and let loose a roar, drowning out Apavarita Varsah's last words. Back and forth the beast shifted its eyes until, in a single, swift movement, it squared its head and shoulders and focused a black gaze upon Cary. The Grastar's mouth opened into a chilling smile. Recognition filled its eyes. The four arms stopped their dark work and reached forward, elongating like tentacles reaching for Cary's heart.

***

Planet harvesting is patient labor.

From his fortress on Europa, Ras Graal, the Devourer, Lord of the Grastar, observed the terrible beauty of the giant red storm in which his Grastar Hive spiraled in a violent dance across the face of Jupiter. Over one hundred million SoulEaters raged in containment within that great storm that Earth knew as the Red Spot. Very few on Earth knew that this storm was Graal's generator, the source of Grastar power.

Graal cast a thread of consciousness inside the massive

whorl where Grastar SoulEaters seethed in hatred and famine. He tasted the rage of his warriors, tested the texture of their collective hunger, and found it rich and full.

Restrained within the huge red cyclone, confined to a gaseous state of existence for as long as they resided in Jupiter's atmosphere, the SoulEaters hungered for flesh: their own to inhabit, and that of humans to consume. They ached with the desire to tear away the skin of humans, to crack open their bones, to suck dry the souls that rested deep within, to consume the light of every earth being, until finally—when no more humans remained—to consume the light and life of the planet itself, leaving only a collapsing shell that would continue to consume all within its reach. Earth scientists theorize that collapsing stars are the source of black holes. The Grastar are their only true source.

Tens of thousands of years Graal had watched, waiting for these approaching moments. And during that time he had expanded the horde, generating levels of power that no Grastar had ever imagined.

A perfect architecture of destruction. Until that pesdeuk vesya pumscali Samudra bitch put herself in my path.

Apavarita Varsah stood there now, guarding the portal.

But there is still the other way.

Graal sent out another thought thread to an individual containment sphere at the edge of the storm, a sphere in which resided a single warrior, one with a special purpose.

Ripu Dasi, he said. *Come to me at Vinâsa. Coalesce to corporeality and come to me.*

***

Simon fired the VW to life. His hand was quicker than his foot, and first gear ground like breaking teeth. He shoved the gearshift harder. The changeling launched into the air from 30 feet away and soared across the parking lot in an impossible leap. The gears caught. The van lurched forward just as a great weight slammed into the rear quarter panel.

The Microbus tilted onto the right side tires, hung there as precarious as Simon Boon on a cemetery fence, then crashed back to all fours and squealed away, leaving the attacker sprawled in the parking lot.

"What the hell was that?" Simon yelled.

He made random turn after random turn through Northdale neighborhoods before navigating westward into Pinellas County and the beach roads, south across the Sunshine Skyway to Bradenton, then east and north, describing a great circle that led back to the old mansion where Woodstein waited.

The journey took more than three hours, but Simon had not yet stopped shaking when he arrived. The rear quarter panel of the Microbus was caved in where the creature had crashed into it, and the window above it was cracked. Even scarier, the sheet metal above the tire had been gouged open by an eight-taloned claw.

***

Ally opened her eyes with a start. For a moment she did not remember where she was. This world was too soft, too beautiful. Too safe. A hand reached from behind her and found her waist, slid around to her belly and upward, coming to rest between her breasts.

Teo.

His touch anchored her to the present, and she relaxed, spooning back against him. Teo Kirten—maybe the only surviving member of the Namayan Council—pulled her closer and nuzzled his eyes against the back of her neck. They yawned and stretched, rolling away from each other in the process. Dawn filtered through hand-sewn curtains and hand-crafted window glass to light up their brass bed. The box springs groaned when Ally sat up, and the thick quilt fell away from her shoulders. Cool morning air delighted her uncovered skin. She shook the morning cobwebs from her brain, flicking her auburn curls into a quick dance on her milk-white shoulders. Her fingers tightened in Teo's dark hair, and shook his head slightly.

"I know," Teo said. He sat up to join her. "I know. Time to get my ass moving."

"I like how your ass moves," she said, and giggled.

"Alas, no time for any more of that."

"Alas," she said with a heavy sigh. But they looked at each other and smiled. "Well, maybe time enough for just a little more of that," she said. Back into the nest she fell, pulling Teo down on top of her.

Locating Teo had not been difficult. They had begun this life-thread as stolen-moment-lovers nearly six years ago and had created contingency plans for events exactly such as these. When they had first begun, they had fantasized about the places they might escape to together. Over the years, they had assembled a list of bed and breakfasts and historic inns at which they might one day meet. Twelve in all, one for each month of the year.

Cell phones were always risky, especially now, since Carver and Layton had obviously known where to ambush the Namayan Council.

Still trying to figure that one out.

So Ally had left Cittam Puram by way of a LightGate and had emerged in a cave in Yosemite. From there, she hitched a ride to Sonora. Teo was waiting for her where she'd known he would be, at the Lavender Hill Inn.

They breakfasted in the downstairs dining room with the innkeepers and two other couples: a young, well-tanned pair of honeymooners from San Diego, and a couple of seniors from Baltimore who were traveling the country in a vast land barge.

After breakfast, Teo and Ally faced each other in green, Adirondack chairs, Ally's backpack between them at their feet. A soft breeze stirred the aromatic jungle of poppies, marigolds and lavender that surrounded them. Ally grasped heavy stalks of lavender in her hands and stripped away the blossoms. The air swam with clean-sweet perfume.

Teo slid his chair closer until their knees were touching. He held her hands, crushing the remaining lavender blossoms in Ally's palms and enchanting them both with the scent.

"I have always," he said, "hated these moments when we have to part. Especially now." He looked at their intertwined feet, then up to her emerald eyes. His own eyes brimmed with tears.

"It wasn't your fault, Teo."

"But I gave the all clear."

"Warner didn't sense it either," she said. "There was no way to plan for that kind of attack."

"Nelson knew."

"Yeah, well, he's different, isn't he?" She softened her gaze into the lavender jungle surrounding them. Maybe her father had escaped. *Maybe.*

"Where will you go now?" Teo asked, but he knew the answer.

"Shangri-La," she said. "Eventually. After a little research. I still don't know what Cary has, but whatever it is, the stakes are more and more desperate. We have to find out." She paused. "I thought it was his necklace, but now I'm not sure. And I haven't been able to reach Dr. Whitt." She pulled a water bottle from a pouch on her pack and took a drink. "Whatever they're after, I think it's back at his house in the mountains. We'll have to risk going back there. Eventually." She paused again and looked into his dark brown eyes. "And you?"

Teo sighed and closed his eyes. Clouds drifted slowly in front of the morning sun; when he opened his eyes again, the world seemed a little darker.

"I have to activate the recruits," he said. "Until I know whether Warner and Nelson survived, I have to consider the possibility that you and I are all that remain; we have to get the Nine back as a full matrix as soon as possible."

"You need to go to Cittam Puram first," she said.

"No time," said Teo. "No time. I wish there were."

Ally took his face in her hands. Her lavender fingers

nearly overpowered him.

"Listen to me, Teo Kirten. You need to heal your soul." She looked away, remembering the men she had killed in Tampa. "Believe me, I know. And…if you are the only one left…" she choked back a sob, "if you are the only one left besides me, then your full presence to your position is more important than either of us understands. You can't risk that. Contact the recruits. Tell them to prepare for your summons. But heal yourself first, or you will bring a darkness into the new Council that will undermine its strength even before it forms." Tears spilled from her eyes, but she did not look away.

Teo sighed and shook his head. He took her hands, first the left, then the right, and kissed each one with reverence. "Right," he said. "As always."

"I know," she said, and kissed Teo with her soft lips.

They stood, sliding the Adirondacks back in the process and held each other tightly.

"I love you, Ally Profett, " he whispered.

"I love you back, Teo Kirten," she replied. Always their parting ritual. Ally retrieved her pack, and they walked in separate directions—Ally toward the road that would take her to the cave in Yosemite, Teo back into the inn. He paused on the front porch and watched her walk away. Just before she disappeared around a boxwood hedge, she turned and blew him a kiss. And then she was gone, leaving Teo alone on the porch wondering now more than he ever had before if this was the last time he would see her.

***

Cary flailed his hands in front of his chest. A single word echoed in his head like a drumbeat: "…promise…promise… promise…promise…" He struggled to focus his attention.

Someone is speaking. A woman. I know this voice. I know this story. This story lives inside me. Why does this story live inside me?

"…promise…" the voice continued. "Long ago you made

a promise, Zachary Walker. A binding vow. So many years ago that you do not remember the making. I listened when your soul spoke those words. Your promise has come due. You must awaken now. Awaken and remember who you are. Awaken now and meet your responsibility."

"Does he hear you?" asked Rahni.

Pava nodded and held two fingers to her lips.

The beat of crashing waves washed through Cary's head.

A boat. I'm in a boat.

A beautiful, blue woman faced him from the prow; a heartbreaking smile played across her face. Then she was gone. The shadow of a craggy escarpment loomed over him, then the boat passed through an almost invisible inlet. In the darkness of the inlet, the beat of waves faded to the whisper of wind. And among the susurrations…voices. One stood out. "Hold the bow this way," she said. Cary knew that voice. He dropped to one knee, no longer in the boat, and aimed his arrow at the sky. "You're aiming at the wrong target," she said. He lowered the bow, but darkness rushed in to cover the vision. A thousand voices of madness called his name. He screamed and plunged his right arm into a fire. He reached for the pain with his left hand, but his grasp closed on emptiness.

"He is drifting," Pava said, "upon the Nameless Ocean and within himself."

These words echoed in the sky of Cary's mind. Pava passed her soft hand over him, and he was rising like an arrow. He flew high above the circle of islands into which he had sailed. The ocean receded. As he continued to ascend, the islands rose out of the ocean and became an oval of green mountains in the middle of a vast continent.

The most beautiful birdsong he had ever heard filled his ears. With the arrival of that melody, Cary's ascension reached its apex, and he plummeted toward the song. The verdant world rushed upward to meet him.

His feet splashed down in a shallow river. Two ravens watched from an ancient yew that towered, tall and powerful, above a thick copse of rhododendron.

Yggdrasil. How long since I planted you?

Birdsong ceased, leaving only the melodies of the river dancing all around him in the bright morning light.

"Do you think he understands?" croaked one of the ravens. It cocked its head toward its companion and closed its dark mouth.

"Yes," replied the other, turning one black eye to gaze at Cary. "But it is not the understanding that matters. It is the remembering at which he fails."

Cary looked past the two birds. His house stood 40 yards up the hill. The ground beneath it glowed with a pulsing blue light. Silver water rushed around his ankles and spoke to him. "Welcome home, One," it said. "I have many names. You have sung them all. Welcome home. Now awaken."

Cary's skin throbbed in perfect synchrony with the pulsing light beneath his house. He saw for the first time how the hillock on which it stood resembled a soft-edged ziggurat.

"Awaken, child," the world sang, and sang again. "Awaken."

Cary opened his eyes.

***

Ally's face floated above Cary.

No. Not Ally. Emma. Emma. Cary rose to her, but surrendered almost immediately to gravity. Still, he reached for her without movement.

"How long have I been here?" he croaked.

Emma did not answer at first. Cary's eyes flickered back to the shores of the unconscious and then focused fully on the face above him. Her similarity to Ally struck him again.

"A little over three weeks," Emma said at last.

The tension of Cary's attempt to rise drained away with the sound of Emma's voice, and he let the softness of the feather mattress completely support him.

"How did…how did I…"

Emma took his right hand and placed his fingertips over the knitting scar on his left side. Her face blurred and swam in Cary's vision. She looked into his eyes and reached out with the intention and power fingers of her right hand to touch him gently in the center of his forehead. A wave of warmth expanded from her touch, washing first over his skin, and then deep into his body. A sob burst from his throat.

"Remember," she whispered.

Even as waves of pain began to fade, images washed through him in a jumbled flood:

Ally crushing a man's throat in a blur of movement. An austere woman with tight braids breaking Cary's wrist. *Why aren't you dead?* The heft of a crystal shard in his hand as it pierces the skin of the austere woman's neck. *You should be dead.* Ally again, forcing a man to shoot his partner, then himself. A slender, red-skinned hand hollowing out a piece of bone, scratching out a design on its surface, dipping it in liquid shadow. The skeleton of a dragon floating in the deep night. Ally killing a fourth assassin, his bloody blade still in his slack hand. An underground ziggurat shining with blue light. *Beautiful.* Cary's blood pouring from between his fingers. No fingers on that hand. No hand. The other hand tamping down a mound of earth around a freshly planted sapling. *Yggdrasil, my love.* Droplets from a waterfall kissing his sunburned cheeks.

"Too much," Emma whispered from very far away. "Too far. Return now." But one more image burst through.

A cemetery, a funeral, and….*Oh my God. Oh my God! Oh my God. Oh my God! Taylor! My son is dead. Oh my God!*

A thunderhead bloomed in Cary's heart and fell from his eyes. The torment lasted an eternity. Eventually, Cary could speak through the rain, though his throat felt like a desert.

"Where…where's Ally?" he managed to choke out.

"She is with Kirten," Emma said. Her voice ricocheted in his head. "There was an ambush in St. Louis. The Namayan Council was devastated. Most were killed. Some may have escaped. Kirten survived. Things are not good out there. We don't…we don't know…who else survived. Ally will come soon, as soon as she can, now that you are awake."

"But how…" he began. "How will she know that I—"
Emma held up her hand; then she pressed gentle fingers to his forehead. Cary's own fingertips imagined the warm, soft texture of her face and the full curve of her hips. He was too exhausted to know what to do with those feelings.

"Rest again," she said. "The time for all this is not now."
His eyes grew heavy. He tried to speak, tried to protest, but Emma's hand was a sleeping potion.

Lethe should be your nickname, he thought, as he was cast adrift on a vast inner sea. Emma's eyes followed, gazing into his.

Was she Ally's sister? A sister of mercy…
Oh, the sisters of mercy; they are not departed or gone…
A different face, beautiful and blue, blinked into view, then disappeared into ambient purple light.

They were waiting for me when I thought that I just can't go on …
The lilting Leonard Cohen lyrics floated to the dusky surface of his consciousness. He fell again into the gentle bliss of sleep and forgetting. And again, Cary was flying in an unknown sky. Shafts of sunlight poured from behind muscular clouds ahead. Someone was hiding in there.

Here there be monsters.

***

Rahni gazed into the dark Omphalos, waving his hand over the apex. His breath grew short and impatient.

"What did you mean," Rahni said, "when you told Mr. Walker that he holds the key? How can he have that much power?"

"Patience, Rahni," said Pava. "I will tell you these things when you are ready to know them. For now, you must develop your skills. Turn to your training. Breathe. Full deep breaths. Relax. Let Samudra flow through you. The Omphalos only activates through the flow of Source. Source only enters the

Omphalos through its vehicle. Through its *calm* vehicle."

He was trying so hard. Too hard really, she knew. So much might depend upon his abilities. Rahni had developed faster than any of her previous students, but he was so young. He might one day be one of the greatest Protectors the Samudra Janah had ever seen. Great songs might be sung about his glories.

If he survived the next few weeks. If either of them did. She could not put off telling him much longer. But only what he needed to know. No more. If Rahni Sisyah knew the true extent of the Omphalos' power, if he knew the destruction Pava could rain upon the earth—upon this entire system—he would be afraid even to try to use it.

I can only hope this situation does not become so dire that I have no other choice. I have grown to love these Children of Earth more than I ever imagined I would.

Rahni took another deep breath and let it calm his body. His brow relaxed. He passed his hands over the apex again. The black surfaces disappeared to reveal the inner light of the Omphalos, the second pyramid formed, and the torus began to flow. The Earth shone like a living jewel. Cloudscapes larger than continents drifted across the surface with barely perceptible movement. Pava smiled, happy for Rahni's achievement. First Vision is a landmark. But she also smiled because she knew what was coming.

"I see it!" said Rahni. "I see it!" His heart pounded and his breath quickened. Earth disappeared, and only the dark, spinning pyramid remained. "I don't see it," said Rahni. "It's gone."

Pava placed her hands on Rahni's shoulders.

"Everyone loses First Vision to its joy," she said. "Do not be disappointed, Vatsah. I am proud of you. You have crossed a threshold today. Now your training can move to another level. Samudra will flow through you more easily. This is a good thing. You still have so much to learn."

And you must learn it so quickly. I need help. I am spread so thin.

Rahni floated up off the stool and drifted over to a cushion, where he landed, less than gracefully, in a seated fold.

Pava shook her head. "Don't waste your energy so."

"But I like flying." He smiled, revealing brilliant teeth.

"Practice focusing, Rahni. Use economy. I have work to do now."

Pava folded herself onto her favorite cushion and closed her eyes. It was time for an inner journey, one she knew might prove disappointing, one she did not wish to make.

***

When next Cary awoke, the sky was deep purple, and the bird songs had departed for the day. A heavy brown cup sat on the bedside table, steam spiraling above its rim. He wore a pair of loose gray sweatpants with an elastic waistband and a baggy green T-shirt. He had never felt so thin.

The door to his room was open; Emma's voice lilted in from the kitchen.

If your life is a leaf that the seasons tear off and condemn...

They will bind you with love that is graceful and green as a stem.

This was a strangely natural feeling. A world so sweet. Memories flooded him: Jennifer when they were still happy, Taylor toddling back and forth between them, proud of his nascent mobility.

How could the world still exist without his son in it? It could not.

This was a new world, then.

Cary forced himself to sit. Wide-mouth, ceramic jars stood in neat ranks on the oak dresser. His gray-beard face was gaunt; the shadows under his weary eyes were so pronounced that he looked like he had been in a fistfight.

Emma swept into the room, the skirt of her sky blue, sleeveless dress billowing behind her. "Drink your tea," she said. She carried a wooden tray with two plates of fruit. "This will bring your strength back." She set the tray on the foot of the bed and caught him assessing himself in the mirror. "You're not that bad," she said. "You'll be fit as a fiddle in a few days. But I thought we were going to lose you for a while. Somewhere in your darkness, you found the will to live. Nothing I was doing helped. But now that you're awake…" She cut her eyes to the cup.

Cary sniffed the tea. He assumed it would smell like old socks and taste like day-old liver, but the bright aroma lifted his spirits, and the sweet taste filled him with nourishment as soon as it passed his lips.

"What is this?" he asked.

"From my secret garden." Her smile could have melted a glacier. Perhaps it had. Perhaps such was the creation of this magical place. She pointed out the window. Green, purple, and red leaves swayed against a cliff wall. Just beyond the garden, a small waterfall dropped off the edge of the earth. "Do you feel up to walking?" she said. "Better if you sit at the table and eat. Strength returns more quickly if you use it."

"Yes, all right," Cary said.

He was surprised that he could walk at all, but his legs wobbled only a little as he made his way out of the bedroom. A heavy wooden table, shiny with the patina of many hands, stood at the center of the large kitchen. Emma placed Cary's tray in front of him, retrieved a deep red cup from the counter, and sat to his right.

"Is Ally your sister?" he asked. Emma laughed.

"Not exactly," she said. "But we are related."

"How then?"

She laughed again, her golden eyes twinkling.

"When you're ready," she said. "Or maybe I'll just wait and let her tell you."

Cary accepted her answer for the moment.

"Did you tell me earlier that the Council was attacked?"

"That was yesterday," she said. "Yes. So far we only know that Kirten has survived."

"I don't know who Kirten is," Cary said. Another shudder of grief ripped through him. He stared at the meaningless food.

"My son is dead," he said. Saying it aloud brought unexpected strength. "My son is dead."

"I am sorry," she said. She placed her hand on his shoulder. His tears began as a trickle, like the first runoff from a drizzle in the desert. Then the storm of sobs broke, and Cary curled forward, hugging his chest. Emma slid closer and pulled his head down to her breast. She stroked his hair and forehead as grief tore through him.

When the tide of his pain had turned, Cary left the table and stumbled back to bed. Emma followed after a few minutes with another cup of secret tea for him and a cup for herself. She sat cross legged at the foot of the bed.

"There is never reconciliation for the loss of a child," she said.

Cary sank into the bed. He cradled his head in the crook of his left elbow and stared into the infinity of the white ceiling.

"Have you lost a child?" He wasn't even sure if he had spoken the question or simply thought it.

"Oh yes," she said. "A daughter. A long time ago. My other daughter is in constant danger. And now, my son is missing."

"I'm sorry."

"But the thing is," Emma said. "We have to go on."

Cary took a deep breath. Emma held up her hand.

"I'm not talking in clichés here, Mr. Walker. I refer to the tasks before us. In any case, they must be done. But we, you and I, Ally…we no longer live 'in any case.' We live in a very specific case, long in the making and now unfolding whether you like it or not." Emma sipped her tea and then cradled the cup in her lap. "There is more danger here than either of us truly understands."

Her voice was a siren song, reaching to the basement of his soul. Cary drifted on the rhythm of her words, on the rise and fall of their sound waves.

"Our responsibilities call to us, Mr. Walker," she said,

"regardless of pain, grief, loss, or worry. They want to know if we are ready to meet them. They want to know if we will hide and leave their completion to those less equipped to face them, to those to whom they do not belong. They want to know if we will step up and play our parts in the worlds we have created. Are you ready to kill your own monsters? You will have to wade through Hell to do so. The death of your son, the possible death of mine…that may be only the first level of Hell."

Emma stared into the same infinity from which Cary's gaze had only recently returned. Cary nestled his head into the feather pillow. His eyes were growing heavy, and he had to gather his energy before he spoke.

"Doesn't make it any easier, does it?" he said. His eyes blinked once, twice.

"No," she said. "But the responsibility remains."

Then Cary was gone again, drifting in the inner worlds.

Before Time

~

Ksama

Ksama embraces Sh'ele, and her world turns inside out.

Light becomes dark. The fiery coals burn icy blue. Half-formed sounds echo from no clear source. Cool rainwater sizzles against her skin. Ksama rises in the darkness of the day and lifts God's Tooth to the sky. The silver blade gleams black. Power pulses in her head, an oscillating hum from unfathomable depths. A deep voice speaks from nowhere and everywhere:

"It is time."

Ksama wedges her right elbow against the bow. She raises the sword in her left hand. Strength pours through her like a river of cold fire, and she strikes hard and true. The blade bites through her flesh halfway between wrist and elbow. Blood and poison burst from the wound. Her hand and half her forearm slap to the deck. She regards the gushing stump as if it is an interesting sculpture, then confronts the blue fire.

"Not yet," the voice says.

The red snakes beneath her skin writhe and twist, swimming against the ebb tide of Ksama's blood, still struggling to find a way to poison her heart. She watches them wither and die, the last of their strength draining out onto the deck.

"Now," the voice says. Ksama staggers to the brazier. Without pausing for the luxury of thought, she plunges the bleeding stump into the cold blue coals. Her flesh sizzles like a song. Ksama spreads her jaws wide and sings with it, a lone voice, high, pure. Triumphant. She forces her arm farther into the flames, roaring her paean until the ice transforms to fire, the charred sky turns cloudy blue, and the black blood returns to red. Her hymn of triumph resolves into an eternal scream.

Present Day

Cary dangled his feet from the rock overhang beside the waterfall and looked into the distant valley. A gray-blue morning haze smoothed the edges of the hard world. Soft mist cooled Cary's face. Far below this secret place, people chased dreams, legal and illegal, wise and foolish, good and evil—always believing their choices were for the best, that they deserved more than they had, that their personal labyrinths of logic always led to the right conclusions. And somewhere out there, two impossibly ancient men wanted something from him. He still had no idea what or why. For the moment, Cary floated above it all in this secret oasis, only God, Ally, and Emma knew where.

The waterfall had become his companion, though not quite as close a companion as Emma. His heart had been hers from that first moment of arrival. It was ludicrous, really. A cliché, he knew. You crush on your teachers, your doctors, your nurses. He knew all of this, but still her dark lips haunted him. He would awaken in the endless night, thinking she had just pressed them soft and full against his own. Then he would lie awake with the memory of her dark-rimmed eyes burning through him like predestined fire. During the day, well, he just tried not to stare.

He stood, and the world swam for a moment. His bare feet gripped rough granite until his equilibrium stabilized.

Across the meadow, Emma tended her garden, talking in a low murmur to her herbs. She settled back on her heels and wiped the sweat from her brow, depositing muddy war paint across her forehead. She smiled, and Cary's breath caught in his throat.

She knows, he thought, not for the first time. He could see it in her eyes. She saw right through him. How did someone in—what—her late 30s…achieve the depth he saw there? In the short time he had known Ally, she had continually surprised him with her knowledge. But there was something more here in Emma's eyes. Was it wisdom?

Emma held up a thick bunch of greenery and beckoned; Cary recognized comfrey and calendula.

"Take these into the kitchen for me, will you?" she said. His breath caught again when his fingertips grazed her earth-painted palm. She pushed her hair back from her face with both hands and arched her back. Cary's pulse quickened, but he tried to hide it. Emma's eyes held a secret smile; the ache in Cary's heart grew as wide as the Nameless Sea.

He lingered a moment in her warmth, then turned away and released a longing sigh. He carried the bouquet of herbs into the cool dark of the kitchen.

***

True darkness enfolded Taylor in her arms. His hands explored the limits of his universe. Soft, plush contours surrounded him, contained him completely.

Where am I? Why am I here?

I have a name.

If I can remember my name, I will know why I am here.

I will understand.

His name floated almost to the murky surface of his consciousness. But a different name, stronger, more solid, shouldered it aside and shoved it deeper into the murky depths. His mind cast about, trying to grasp the thread of that first name, but each time he would come close, the other name would solidify. One of these was his true name. Which one? There was too much of him in this tiny body that he called home, and yet he felt so empty.

The contradiction swelled and pushed up against itself like a volcano against a containment dome. Fire coursed through his heart and down his arms and legs. He compressed his hands into fists and struck out, such as he was able, flailing and kicking against the close-set walls, producing a tremor of muffled thuds.

He tried to speak. The words filled his mouth. *My name is...I am...* But the name would not name itself. So he tried to scream, but even that sound would not be born into his world.

Exhaustion soon overtook him; the last of his strength drained away, and he slipped into a dark well that was deeper still.

And he waited. Empty. Waiting to be filled.

***

Simon's frustration was getting the better of him. More than two weeks had crawled by since the weird, ugly changeling...thing had played human demolition derby with his van. Not that *human* was exactly the right word.

The day after his close encounter of the weird kind, Simon had driven to Publix to stock up on food. He had managed to escape the enticements of the super market without even glancing in the direction of the news rack. Maybe if he played ostrich, the nightmare would go away. But then, only minutes later, he had whipped into the Circle K and snatched up a *Tampa Tribune* like a junky hunting down a fix. The headline had chilled him to his soul: *Girl Abducted from Northdale YMCA in Broad Daylight.*

At least there was no mention of Simon or the van. Apparently no one had seen the encounter between him and the...

What the hell was that thing?

So he had decided to lay low. The most dangerous thing he had seen in the last two weeks was a couple of teenagers who parked their beat-up Mazda behind the mansion, smoked a joint, and got naked in the back seat. Simon had tried not to look.

He'd failed.

They say old habits die hard, but in truth, usually they don't die at all. Simon's frustration had reached critical mass. He sat now on a sagging bench behind the cotton shed and scooped Woodstein up into his lap.

"Well, Woody," he said. "I guess even weird, scary, shape-shifting assholes are better than terminal boredom."

Woodstein looked at him like he was an idiot, but Simon chose not to heed the sage, feline advice. Instead he checked his cash stash. Nearly $18,000 remained.

"Time to get back to work," he said to Woodstein. "And we're gonna need a faster car."

By evening he had purchased a beat-up, green 1987 Dodge Diplomat police cruiser. Automatic. At least if some weirdling came charging at him now, he'd be able to get the hell out of the way without arm wrestling with the gearshift.

New vehicle disguise in place, Simon performed a cursory cruise of the cemeteries and Hyde Park. A little after ten, he saw a familiar Range Rover pass him going the other direction.

"Byron," Simon said. "How goes the world of romantic poetry and body snatching?" He whipped the Diplomat around in the parking lot of WMNF radio and followed him into downtown.

Byron drove the Range Rover into the parking lot under Mopheit Park. Simon parked just inside the entrance and watched through his trusty Nikons. The Rover pulled up to what appeared to be solid wall. Byron made a call on his cell.

"Well, I'll be buggered," Simon said in his best Johnny Depp-Keith Richards slur; a huge slab of concrete slid aside and Byron drove the Rover into a section of garage that, if Simon's sense of direction was to be trusted, was directly under Mopheit Tower. The wall rasped closed. Simon was about to get out of the car when he spotted the scanning video camera.

"Shit."

He waited a half hour, but Byron did not emerge. He slowly backed the Dodge out and exited the parking lot. He was pretty sure he had not been seen. And it had only cost him .75 cents.

NINTH ARTICULATION

a kiss

Kukulkan homecoming

shattered wonder

landfall

hollow

by my own hand

a granny

sage zombie counsel

parasites

Uktenah

Present Day

Time twisted and turned in Shangri-La. In this hidden pocket of forgiveness on the mountainside, the sun itself was never quite visible. Only the presence or absence of its diffuse light signaled the continued spinning of the planet.

Cary's sleep had abandoned circadian rhythms. He would awaken in midday, or in a twilight that might be dawn or dusk, or deep in the star-encrusted night. Then he would walk out to the meadow to lie on the damp grass and stare up at the sky, or sit on the rock overhang and gaze down at the world, small and removed.

In daylight, the world below became a part of the pale blue continuum of sky and mountain. At twilight, a misty haze suffused even the air around him. In true night, the flickering lights of the valley joined with the stars, forming a composite galaxy that included not only giant, shining worlds light years away, but smaller, individual universes circulating in dangerous proximity, their gravities exerting more immediate influences than those of their celestial counterparts. Day or night, twilight dusk or twilight dawn, from Shangri-La all horizons were indiscernible, all borders were arbitrary.

As his heart healed, Cary drew nearer and nearer to the border that separated him and Emma. He longed to meet her at the edge of the edge. In the silence of this unspoken longing, he had begun to think of her as an angel. A fancy, he knew, but one he indulged in freely, on purpose, knowing somehow that she could be angel and human, and that she would remain as such in his heart forever. For as long as forever lasted.

Cary awoke. The feather mattress embraced him through the crispness of white sheets. He rolled to sitting. The pain in his side was barely a memory. Outside, flickering stars struggled to illuminate the purple-red sky. The house was dark and quiet. A breeze rushed through the back door and stirred the hairs on his chest and arms. He was leaner now than he had been in perhaps 20 years. Lighter. He shuddered at the wind on his bare skin and the thought of Emma, lovely and warm, asleep in her down bed only a room away.

Dew soaked the clover. His bare feet left wet footprints on the granite slab. He hung his legs over the edge and looked out over the infinite world.

Dawn or dusk? Didn't matter really. Light itself would reveal the time soon enough. Sparks flickered in the valley and in the sky. He looked to the dark house. His heart struggled to contain the unbearable ache that had been born in his delirium weeks before when he had first collapsed on Emma's doorstep. Could he ever cross that threshold? Then he saw that a second set of footprints paralleled his own.

She sat on her heels, watching him from the far left side of the rock. She wore a sleeveless, cotton dressing gown. Her shadowy hair fell across the front of her shoulders. The breeze lifted a thick strand across her face. She let it stay. Her eyes hid in that shadow, but her gaze was as close as lips. Emma tossed her head and the locks fell back revealing eyes that glowed in the growing light.

Dawn, then. Not dusk.

Somewhere on the other side of the mountain, the sun was coming up. He looked into her eyes. They sparkled with moisture.

What he wanted most in that moment was to fully reveal the depth of his love for her. That would be enough. Almost as a surprise to himself, he stood, walked to her, pulled her to her feet and against his body. He did not remember the last time he had done anything this decisive. Emma caught her breath. He was hard against her belly. Their eyes met. Blood rose to Emma's cheeks, visible even in the nascent dawn. The spreading fire of her body pressed against him; his own fire responded to her invitation.

"Yes," she said, her voice at once a whisper and a growl. "Since you first arrived."

A sudden gust whipped her hair back, rippled the fabric of her gown tight upon the secrets of her curves, and set the chimes on the back porch singing. The kiss began soft and sweet, just the corners of their mouths grazing each other, then their lips barely touching. Their fire spread until they were lost in one another, mouth searching mouth, bodies vibrating with certainty. By the time the kiss ended, the sky bathed them in red. They held each other, breathless, panting, trying to press their bodies closer. Then Cary swept her into his arms and carried her to her room. They fell together into the depths of her soft, warm bed, and into each other.

***

Layton stepped from under the shade of an *alamo* tree. Yucatán sunlight washed over his bare arms. Yesterday he had anchored the *Nammu* off *Tulum* and motored ashore in an 8-foot Avon. The Range Rover had been waiting as arranged. He had driven inland and reached *Chichen Itza* by early afternoon. The Rover now lay concealed under the heavy branches of a *Chechen* tree a little over a mile north of the ancient city.

The entrance to the Path of Shadows was exactly where he remembered, though now overgrown with palmettos and sea grapes. He pushed through plush leaves and turned south, into the canopy darkness.

How long since I last needed to come here?

After nearly half an hour, he stepped off the path beside a

large mound overgrown with *Chaya* and coral vine. He rolled out a straw mat, removed his clothing, sat facing the mound, and closed his eyes. Inhaling deeply, he tightened his throat and focused the air into a tight vortex. Jungle-rich oxygen roiled in the pit of his lungs.

Ujayii. The Venturi Effect, modern science called it, but this breathing technique was already an ancient practice by the time Layton had first learned it over six thousand years ago.

He spent the next half hour slowing his respiration with each inhale, each exhale, each pause, until a single breath lived four full minutes. He rolled his eyes back and opened his deeper vision. The vibrations of the jungle caressed the edges of his awareness. Such was true of all people to some extent. But Layton was not like other people. His awareness caressed back.

The perimeter of his aura flowed out in tiny tendrils, touching sisal swords and elephant ears. He knew the wind's intent before it beat the emerald leaves of the *Chak Kuyché* into pendulum dances. Behind him—though such concepts as front, behind, above, and below held little context in Layton's current state—nearly 20 yards away, a female jaguar raised her nostrils once again to the drifting vapors. Layton allowed another strand of his own essence to slip into the jaguar's nose. The cat had been following the scent of her would-be prey since he had first stepped onto the path. Layton smiled. A game. He loved games. He tightened his grip on the cat's mind, holding her in pause, letting the creature feel that she was waiting for the right moment to pounce.

The mound in front of him was nearly 12 feet tall. The average jungle explorer, even the descendants of the Maya who lived nearby, would walk right past this lump of green, believing it to be a hill or a boulder. But Layton knew that beneath the vines and lichens stood a statue of Kukulkan wielding a serpent in his right hand. He knew this because he himself had decreed that this statue be carved and placed here. As a tribute. And for future eventualities such as this moment.

On the far side of the statue lay a pool, about 3-feet oval, fully obscured by the undergrowth. The small portal opened into the vast *cenotes* that honeycombed the limestone foundation surrounding Chichen Itza.

Layton clasped his hands into Bhudi Mudra: *oneness with water.* His breath had become still slower. Five minutes per cycle. With his true sight, he observed the perfect green reflections of the secret pool. Though he did not move the tiniest bit, his inner attitude shifted into readiness. Behind him the jaguar tensed and perked her ears forward. Her back legs began to vibrate. Layton convulsed his full lungs, releasing a small bit of the suspended stores of oxygen. His will caressed the thread of control that held the cat in check; he plucked that invisible string, and the restraint returned into the unformed.

The hungry jaguar reveled in the surge of freedom. Purpose launched her into the air. Layton remained still. He felt the cat fly: fur, fangs, claws. And death. The predator descended. Her forepaws swept inward to close on her prize. Layton drove his body upward in a spiral. His left foot pressed down on the ledge created by Kukulkan's outstretched left hand, and he catapulted over Kukulkan's head and down into the *cenote* while the big cat smashed headlong into Kukulkan's knees. The jaguar struggled to her feet, shook off the indignity, and padded away without a backward glance. She knew when she had been outmatched.

Layton's lungs extracted every molecule of oxygen from the rich jungle air they contained as he navigated the underwater maze of the *cenote.* Three minutes. Four. Five. His head broke the surface of a small room full of echoes and twilight. He climbed from the water into the secret chamber underneath *El Caracol*, the Observatory at Chichen Itza.

When Layton had built this structure some 1,100 years ago, his subjects had believed that the observatory's only purpose lay in its upper rooms. Only Layton knew of this chamber hidden three levels below. He had concealed its presence so well that, even now, with the popularity of

Chichen Itza as a Yucatán tourist destination, no one had discovered it. Of course, he had not been known as *Layton* then, or even as *Nanoshe*. His name had been *Kukulkan*.

***

Cary was flying. Sliding effortlessly through the air. Flows and eddies of wind pressed upward, holding him aloft, then sliding him along an invisible jet stream, as though the wind itself were guiding him. Miles below, the ocean rippled with endless waves.

He dove into a cloud bank. When he emerged, the ocean had disappeared, and he was gliding over a soundless, red desert. The Giza Plateau emerged on the horizon. Cary soared high above the Pyramid of Khufu and its two companions. White noise screamed both in his head and in the distance. The sky itself threatened to rip apart.

A black triangle shot past him. A B6 fighter bomber. Two graceful fledglings dropped from under its wings and began a lethal dive. Their dark mother banked into a vertical climb to the safety of the stratosphere.

The friendly wind abandoned him; Cary's gut swirled in a sickening spin, and he plummeted toward the earth. The three pyramids grew larger and larger until the wind found him again, halting his descent at the moment when the two missiles struck Khufu.

The world became a fireball. Cary flew higher, into the stratosphere, with a power greater than the wind guiding him now. Concentric energy pulses spread outward from the point of impact, tsunamis of light that rushed across the surface of the earth, engulfing the entire planet from its epicenter.

Cary feared that the rising fireball would blind him, but he could not turn his eyes away. The burning giant climbed into the sky in terrible silence.

Why is there no thunder?

The fireball rose, and the ground below glowed brighter

than the rising ball of heat. A great, swirling storm spun around ground zero, driving dust in all directions. The image became clearer. The Great Pyramid was gone.

And yet, somehow it had remained. But what before had been stone was now a pyramid of light. Above it was another—a mirror image, upside-down. The two, if two they really were, met at their perfect tips. And they were moving. The lower pyramid, the one that had moments before been solid, spun in a counterclockwise direction, while the inverted one spun in the opposite direction. The light storm emanated from the point at which they touched.

The lesser structures—Khafre, Menkaure, and the Pyramids of Queens—had somehow survived the blast. Now they trembled in the great photon wind that blew from that spinning center point. One by one they began to disintegrate until their stones turned to dust and they too revealed the light that had been masked by ancient stone.

With four-dimensional vision and the logic of dreams, Cary glimpsed in an instant every pyramid on the planet, ancient or modern, vast or tiny, transforming in the same way. The number was astonishing. Many were underground, hidden by mountains. For the dreamtime nanosecond that he held that glimpse, he knew the purpose, pattern, origin, and fate of these structures. He knew his role. He saw the many fates of the earth, lined up next to one another like shiny crystal marbles rolling along side by side. As quickly as this knowledge filled his being, it blinked away, and Cary was once again watching the devastation below.

Continuous waves of destruction burst from ground zero and disappeared in all directions beyond the curve of the earth, showing no sign of diminishing. The B6 continued its climb, barely more than a speck now. Colossal bolts of lightning, some nearly a mile wide, shot from the pyramids' contact point. One found the jet and popped it like a drop of water on a skillet. Giant ripples of energy undulated through the sky.

Just when Cary had successfully stabilized his flight, the

sound wave hit him. He knew, without knowing how he knew, that this sound was not the echo of the pyramid's destruction, but something greater. A terrible *déjà vu* drew him into darkness.

"My fault!" he screamed.

He curled into a ball and tumbled toward the inferno. As far as he could see, the white glow of death and destruction wrung out the planet. Then he saw a second series of waves that had originated somewhere beyond the horizon. On the far side of the planet, another explosion had ripped away the covering of another pyramid, one hidden beneath 10,000 years of green on an island in the south Pacific. These titan waves of light and sound collided with one another and set the earth trembling.

Cary struggled to stop his descent. Guilt clawed at him, dragging him deeper. He shook shadows out of his head. His body threatened to vibrate itself to pieces.

Emma shook him by the shoulders. His wide eyes still stared into Hell.

"Oh, God," he screamed, sitting half-way up. "What did I do?" He collapsed into her lap. Her warm, soft belly muffled his incoherent cries.

Emma leaned over him. Her breasts and her hips embraced his head in the safety of flesh. She rocked back and forth, tears streaming down her face.

"It's all right, my love," she said. "It's all right. You're safe."

Cary's body stilled. His breathing evened and slowed. Emma placed her hand on his cheek and turned his face up to her. She stroked his forehead, ran her fingers through his hair, and dragged her nails across his scalp.

Framed by the window, the night sky shone brilliant with stars. And there was Draco, ever present, keeping watch, protecting them with the terrible beauty reserved for creatures such as dragons.

Emma looked to the stars. Hope hung in those ancient symbols. And hope lay here in her lap. Hope unknown to its bearer, but hope nevertheless. Perhaps the only remaining hope. And that hope was under attack. She cradled him there until his breathing steadied, and she knew that he was once again sleeping.

Before Time

~

Ksama

Ksama awakens to a high sun.

Where am I? Why do I smell the ocean?

She rolls over and discovers the strangest artifact. A hand is wedged under Sh'ele. She reaches instinctively with her right hand, the hand that no longer lives at the end of her arm, the hand that, in fact, lies before her. Horror swirls in her chest. And then the pain hits her. She scarcely reaches the side of the boat in time; chunks of dried fish, flatbread, and bile splatter the clean waves. Ksama falls back against Sh'ele, curls herself around the charred stump of her arm, and sobs.

"Sit up," says DevaSurya. Ksama obeys, expecting to find the Queen of Light seated in the prow, but the boat is empty. She is alone, she thinks. Utterly alone. Her tears return, but the Grace speaks again, harsher, stronger, and pitiless.

"You have work to do. Stop feeling sorry for yourself and do it."

Ksama shakes her head and looks again. Still, no one is there.

"I have only one hand," she says. "I don't know what to do." She chokes down a sob. "I'm all alone."

"Even when you believe that lie," says the voice of DevaSurya, "you must go on. Through the loss, through the pain. Through sadness, through trial. Through madness. Through Hell. You must go on. Even when you doubt, continue to do the work. Empty yourself of who you think you should be. Become..." The Queen of Graces lets the statement hang empty and unfinished.

"Hollow," says Ksama. She looks again to her severed arm.

"Exactly," says the Queen of Light. "Hollow. Like a scraped-out bone. Then who you truly are will flow through you. You will never be alone. You will always do what you need to, because only then can you be who you are. And remember, One, remember your true name. Remember what it means. Remember who you are. Become that again."

Ksama hears a cry then, and another. She is certain that the sound must signal an escape of her own hidden weeping, but these cries rain from the sky.

Birds. Land birds.

A green-black wall of trees looms a mile off the port bow. Two red-tailed hawks describe spirals above the opening to a narrow inlet.

Asita.

"Thank you," she whispers.

"You have earned your destiny, One," says the Grace, her voice growing more distant. "Let this moment sustain you. But remain strong. Your struggle is far from over."

Ksama's severed hand still lies wedged partially under Sh'ele. It is a monstrous thing. Pale and limp. Bloodless. But somehow beautiful. She imagines tossing it into the sunlit sea and watching while creatures of all kinds swarm to fight over the morsel. But another idea displaces the image.

"Oh my," she says aloud. "Yes, of course."

She struggles to keep her body from shrinking into a ball of pain and self-pity. DevaSurya is right. She has work to do.

"And so I begin," she says. She bathes the hand in sea water, washing away the remnants of blood and infection, then wraps it in the sheath with Sh'ele. With her good left hand, the hand that, as she has been taught, receives the love of God, she reefs the sail and takes the tiller. The loamy perfume of land fills her lungs. She brings the *Varuna* to port and makes for the inlet. Through it all, her body shakes with sobs of grief.

Present Day

Simon searched 11 days before he spotted the exit from the lot underneath Mopheit Tower. He hung around downtown, playing tourist or eccentric artist, sketching and taking pictures of the Solstice sculpture, watching the underground entrance to Mopheit Tower all the while.

He had to be careful though. Downtown Tampa crawled with former colleagues. One day while Simon sat before the giant metal spiral, sketchbook on lap, pencil in hand, his editor, Charley Daysfield, had walked right past him. Only then did Simon realize how different he must look.

He had noticed that his pants hung looser around his waist, and he hadn't shaved in at least six weeks. In an even more radical move, he had stopped pretending he had hair, abandoning the combover—*how the Hell did I ever think that was a good strategy?*—for a self-inflicted buzz cut. He had been tempted to test his incognito, to ask Charley what time it was, but he decided not to push his luck. Besides, he might endanger Charley in the process.

Two days later, Simon saw the Range Rover emerge from a hidden alley beneath the Cube on the south side of the tower. He trotted down the ramp just in time to see a metal door close.

Whatever was going on with these missing bodies, whatever was going on with the weird-ass Qellepoth, the key to it seemed to be underneath Mopheit Tower.

I didn't even know there was an underneath to Mopheit Tower. Now all I have to do is find a way to get in there. And, of course, a way to get back out.

***

Cary swung his feet back and forth in the air and let his spirit drift with the mist of the waterfall. Emma's footsteps approached, and he smiled. He turned to her as she sat and almost leaned in to kiss her. But it was not Emma. Ally had returned at last, no doubt to take him away from paradise and back to the world.

She settled without a word, leaned against him, and laid her head upon his shoulder. They sat that way for several minutes before Cary became aware that she was crying. An occasional seismic sob shook her like a tiny earthquake. Cary let his arm slip behind her back, and he drew her closer. The soft roar of falling water filled the air; her body relaxed into his. After a few minutes, her breathing steadied. He thought she might have drifted off.

"I always cry when I come here," she said.

"Why?" Cary said.

Ally shifted to face him, cross-legged, elbows on her knees, chin resting in the double cup of her palms. A sheen of mist glistened on her face. Tiny droplets of water adorned her hair like pearls of light, illuminating her as if she were some mythical creature. One of the *Sidhe*, perhaps.

"I think maybe this is the only place in the world I've ever felt safe, at least since I was old enough to understand the world. So when I come here...well...it's the only place I feel secure enough to really let down."

Cary tried to put off his question, but it burst out of his mouth before he could stop himself.

"What the hell's going on out there?"

Ally stared into the waterfall.

"Pretty dicey," she said. "Carver and Layton ambushed

the Council in St. Louis. We still don't know how they managed it. We've always been able to…know if they're going to attack us."

"I don't understand."

"We've learned how to read their intentions," she said. She held up her hand before he could protest. "I know. I know. But it's not that fantastic, if you think about it. Just a matter of knowing how to tune in. It doesn't matter. We can all do it. You could, too, if you wanted to. If you believed it was possible in the first place. It's not that hard. Especially when their feelings are intense. And if they have bad intentions and guns…well," she looked almost embarrassed, "you know what happens then."

Cary remembered all the times she had seemed to know what he was thinking, what he was going to say before he said it. "Okay. I guess I can buy that. Based on what I've seen, anyway. So what happened in St. Louis?"

"Somehow they managed to attack without anyone having anything but the slightest uneasiness. They killed six for sure. The only one I've actually seen is Teo."

"I don't know who that is," Cary said.

"Remember the man in D.C. who thought the attack might have been accidental?" Cary nodded. "Teo," she continued. She swallowed away the tears that were trying to come. "He's my…"

She paused and looked toward the house. Emma was washing dishes, framed by the kitchen window. Cary's gaze followed Ally's to the house. Emma smiled and waved. Fear and worry seemed to float away with the drifting mist of the waterfall.

"Oh my God," Ally said. She looked at Cary, back at Emma, and then back at Cary again.

"What?" Cary said. His cheeks flushed to pink.

"I knew somehow you were different," she said. "But I didn't think…oh my God!"

"What can I say?" Cary said, his face fully red by now. He looked down at the ground, then back up to Ally's eyes.

"She's amazing. I mean, at first I thought that, well, you know, I just had a crush on her because she was taking care of me. But...wow. I thought she was your sister or something, but she said she's not. So what? Cousin? Something like that?"

Ally laughed so long and so hard that Cary started to get uncomfortable. He looked up to the house where Emma remained, framed like a Vermeer, only prettier. Emma shrugged and blew him a kiss before disappearing into the shadows of the kitchen. At last Ally's laughter died away. Her tears left twin tracks down her soft cheeks.

"Not your cousin, then?"

"Remember the cave?" Ally said. "Remember when I said everything is going to change?

Cary nodded.

"The rules you thought you were living by—you've already seen they don't really apply?"

Cary nodded again.

"That's even more true here," she pointed to the ground, "than out there." Ally took a deep breath, giggled. "She looks really young for her age. This place does that to you."

"So what are you telling me? She's your mother?"

"Actually, no," she said and laughed again. "She's my grandmother. And she's 78."

Cary looked to the kitchen window. Emma moved back into view. She waved again, blew another kiss, and tilted her head to the left, her countenance asking the question.

Seventy-eight? He thought about the last few weeks he had spent with her. No wonder she was so amazing. And suddenly her age just seemed to make it better. He blew a kiss back to her and laughed.

"Oh," he said, suddenly realizing. "Emma said her son was missing. Nelson. Oh my God, you don't know if he escaped. You don't know if he's still alive."

"I haven't heard from him," she said. Her voice threatened to break. "But the last time Teo saw him, he was alive, so I can still hope. Anyway...I have to go on. Even if the worst is true." She pressed the heels of her hands to her eyes, rubbing away tears that wanted to fall, but had not.

He looked closer at Ally. "You're different, too," he said.

"Yeah," she said. A soft breeze danced across the tiny, green field of grass. "The cemetery. It happened so fast." She looked into the gray horizon. "I had to react so fast." She looked directly into his eyes. "I killed all four of those men. I hoped I'd never have to kill anyone." She spat out a mirthless laugh. "So much for that plan. Movies make it look so simple. You kill the bad guys, crack some jokes, and have a beer with your buddies. But it's not like that. Not like that at all. It changes you. Takes something from you. You're never the same. But that doesn't mean you can't be healed. And you have to be healed if you want to go on."

***

Layton assumed *savasana* on the amethyst altar in the sub-chamber of *El Caracol,* and the Tangle of Light became visible to him. He directed his intention to the pyramidal quartz point hidden atop El Castillo. An all-seeing eye. In that moment, he became a transmitter and receiver of thoughtforms, capable of reading any living vibration anywhere on the planet. Provided, that is, that the originator of that vibration had not learned how to mask its presence. The Namayan had long ago learned techniques with which to conceal themselves and their sanctuaries in the Tangle, and it had been many lifetimes since Layton had been able to read Carver's presence without his consent. But that did not mean that he could not read those of Carver's operatives.

From the apex of the pyramid, Layton extended his will into the Tangle, a fisher of minds casting lines into the vast ocean of thought that enmeshes the atmospheres of the earth. And very soon—in no time at all, really—he felt the tug of information as it began to flow back up the lines.

***

Emma made *caldo gallego* and popovers. They ate on the porch and watched the stars brighten against the deepening sky. Emma insisted on cleaning the kitchen by herself so that Ally and Cary could continue to catch up. Ally told Cary about Cittam Puram. She told him about Teo. How much she missed him. How he would now activate recruits and form a new council. How much danger he was in.

"It's really bad out there," he said.

"Worse. I haven't been able to get in touch with Dr. Whitt, either. I can only hope that they haven't killed him, too. And...I don't want to pull away your scabs too soon but..."

"It's all right," Cary said. "Just tell me."

"I know how your son died."

Cary waited.

"There's a drug. The street name's Nirvana, but it's a pharmaceutical. I don't know the real name. I managed to get some, but I haven't had a chance to research it yet. Taylor took one. Just one...and it killed him. It kills everybody who takes it, but they're taking it anyway. It hasn't hit the media for some reason."

The growing awareness chilled Cary's heart. "Show me," he said.

Ally handed over a small Ziploc that held six yellow tablets. The Lilly logo screamed accusation. The baggy slipped out of his hand and landed in his lap.

"What's the matter?"

"Praboda," he whispered.

"What? How do you know that?"

"Have you forgotten what I used to be? Where I worked?" Cary stared at the pills. "It was supposed to cure Alzheimer's. But they wanted to push it through. I wanted to test it more."

"What are you saying?"

"I made this," Cary said. "This is what I was working on when I left Lilly. It's why I left. I was never sure about it in the first place because…"

"What?"

"It's crazy," he said. "Or…I don't know…I thought it was crazy. Now I…"

Ally's voice was gentle. "Just tell me, Cary."

"I was never sure about the formula because it shouldn't have worked. But it did. And because I didn't figure it out the usual way."

"Then how?" she said.

Cary looked at the pills for a full minute before he answered.

"In a dream," he said. "I got the formula for it in a dream."

Ally stared at him. "Cary," she said. "Look at me." Cary managed to pull his eyes away from the pills. "When was this? When did all this happen?"

"A little over five years ago," he said.

"Five years. When you built the patio. And found the necklace."

Cary nodded. "Just before I came to the mountain. When my nightmares started," he said. He rubbed his thumb over the surface of his necklace. "When I started going crazy." His wrist ached for the first time since he had arrived in Shangri-La. He struggled to pull the words out, to speak them out loud. "I have these nightmares," he said. "I never remember them." Emma appeared behind him and put her hands on his shoulders. Cary released the necklace and placed his hands on top of hers. "And…I hear these sounds in my head. And voices. I can't hear what they're saying. It sounds like arguing." He laid his cheek against the back of Emma's hand. She kissed him on the crown of his head; warmth spread from the kiss and flowed over his body. "But," he said, suddenly brightening, "I haven't heard them since I've been here. Not the voices anyway." His brow furrowed. "The sounds are still here."

"It's this place," Emma said. "It's protected."

Ally nodded.

"Then why do I still hear the sounds?" Cary said.

"Because," Ally said, "you don't need to be protected from them. They're there to help you. I hear them, too."

"Me too," Emma said.

Cary nodded his head and shifted to something more tangible, anything concrete enough to wrap his mind around. "What was the weird writing on the wall behind Taylor?" he asked.

Ally paused a moment before answering. She'd have to return to the sounds later, when he was ready.

"It's Hebrew," she said finally. "Qellepoth. From the Cabala. I still don't know what the connection is."

"How did you find all this out?" he asked.

Ally looked out into the blue horizon. She nodded once. "We have a source in Carver's organization."

Cary digested this news in silence.

"I have to go back to Tampa," Cary said, finally. "Especially now."

"Too risky," Ally said.

"I don't know how well you'll understand this," he said "because you don't have children of your own. But I have to see Taylor's grave one more time. It's like…like I was shoved under water at the time I needed to be most aware, in the middle of dealing with his death."

Emma leaned forward to kiss the top of Cary's head again. Ally smiled at her.

"He's the one," Emma whispered.

"Whodathunkit?" Ally said.

Emma shrugged. Both women giggled. Ally turned her attention back to Cary.

"Sorry," she said. "Go on."

Cary regarded them for a moment, then shrugged. More new information that he could digest later.

"I know Taylor's dead," Cary continued, "but I have to go there and say goodbye. It's…it's like his grave is still open. I have to close it."

"You're right," Ally said. Her voice took on an edge. "I don't understand."

"I do," said Emma.

She slid her arms around Cary's neck and laid her cheek alongside his. Ally sighed, nodded, and turned back to Cary.

"I don't think it's the best idea in the world," she said. "But I can't say you haven't earned the right. We'll have to be very careful."

***

A dead, naked man hung spread-eagle against the cold concrete wall. Bruises and dried blood painted his body like a Goya sky. His head rested on his left shoulder. Two men stood before him.

"Shit!" said one.

"He was never going to talk anyway," said the other. "We should have known better than to even try this. Should have let him escape and then tracked him."

"Too late now," said the first. "You going to call Layton?"

"Already tried," he said. "Haven't been able to get through. He'll find out soon enough."

One of the men pulled down the lever on an electrical box, consigning the room to darkness. The door clicked shut behind them. They climbed to the floor of the mile-long cave that would lead them back to the world. All three flights of metal stairs rattled and rang. The room behind them was now nothing more than a lost tomb, the last resting place of a former senior member of the Namayan Council.

***

The amethyst altar was proportioned according to the sacred ratios, the same as the box at the center of Cary's courtyard. Layton now sat at the center of the slab. Most of what he had learned he had already known. Carver was still pulling strings from his home in Arcata. He had operatives in

Tampa and Burnsville; Layton already knew this because his own men were with them. But Carver had another team on the way to Tampa, one that not even Carver's other operatives knew about, much less Layton's. They had been directed to retrieve a chest from a safe on the top floor of Carver's tower in downtown Tampa.

The Benben. It has to be. He's making a move.

He and Carver had agreed lifetimes ago that the Garal seed would remain buried at Ubai, where they had found it. At first, when the seed had taught them to become demigods, they had kept it out in the world, sometimes on display. The legends had grown around it among their subjects, who believed it to be the Benben, from the ancient myth of Atum.

And, in a way, it was.

The danger of the stone's overt presence in the world had first become apparent to them when Alexander had guessed that it was the source of their power and had stolen it. They had been forced to remain in hiding for more than 15 years while Alexander used its power to conquer the world. Finally, Layton had managed to infiltrate his camp kitchens in Babylon and poison him. Only then had they been able to steal the stone back. After that they had created a false version of the Benben and hid the true seed in a chamber in their first temple, the ziggurat at Ubai. The false Benben was still on display at the Museum of Antiquities in Cairo. The original had remained all these years, hidden away at Ubai.

Until you took it out!

And now, Layton had to admit, it looked like his ancient brother was planning to break their most sacred pact, their most fundamental agreement, and would, for the first time in their history, use the power of the Benben just for himself. He put thoughts of that aside for the moment. He could do nothing from here but observe. Action would come in due time.

Layton had been, as always, unable to access the Namayan girl, or any of the Namayan Council. He smiled at that thought.

Not many left to contact anyway.

Walker, too, was inaccessible.

At least these visits to Chichen Itza had the added benefit of recharging his batteries. He always came away from these treks feeling stronger than ever. He would need that strength now.

Layton cast his consciousness outward in a final scan of the Tangle. He suspended the tips of the light threads at the edges of his consciousness and released his hold. But, before he could rise, power surged back into the dwindling threads; thick vines of light twined around him, cutting into his subtle bodies, fixing his physical form to the spot. A flicker emerged in front of him and began to grow. Slowly, slowly, it took on the shadowy silhouette of a man standing before a flame.

"Mr. Layton," the man said. "I have been expecting your answer."

Though the man himself remained obscured in shadows, Layton recognized the voice.

"Dossey," he said. "How did you…"

Dossey waved his hand in dismissal. "This parlor trick of yours? Do you imagine you are the only one able to walk the Tangle of Light? You should see how Mr. Carver accomplishes the same skill. There are a thousand ways and more. You are novices. Both of you.

"But this is all irrelevant. The longer you wait, the more he plots against you. And thus, the more likely he is to succeed. I trust your partner even less than you do. I offered the two of you a triumvirate through which we could rule this planet. Instead of accepting, he plots against both of us. But I have found that two can rule as well as three."

Dossey's aspect fell silent, letting the implications hang in the air. Layton paused only a moment before nodding.

"He appears to have left us no choice, Mr. Dossey. You and I, then. My…information specialist…has one of the Namayan. We will soon know where Walker and the girl are hiding."

"No," Dossey replied. "Your man has already failed. If

you had bothered to scan your own operatives' thoughts, then you would already know that. But it no longer matters because they are no longer hiding. You must act quickly now. Leave your boat here and fly back. Very soon, Walker will return to his mountain home. Contact your brother. Tell him you were able to learn Walker's movements from your prisoner.

"The Sh'ele is buried on Walker's property. You and Mr. Carver must be there when Walker returns. Let Carver continue to believe he is in control. Once the Sh'ele is retrieved...kill him and all of his men."

"And where will you be?" Layton said.

"You will see me."

Dossey's apparition disappeared, and with him the threads that restrained Layton. He climbed a narrow stairway that dead-ended against a slab of stone. The hidden doorway opened inward on the north wall. He crawled through and stood in the warm sun. A woman screamed. Layton turned, expecting to defend himself. Only then did it occur to him that he was still naked. The woman continued screaming. Layton smiled and nodded to her.

"Afternoon, ma'am," he said. "I hope you are enjoying your visit to my little city."

He turned and walked to the nearest wall of trees.

"Bloody tourists," he said. The Mayan jungle swallowed him up before anyone else saw.

***

Pava passed her palm over the apex of the Omphalos. The torus took shape, and the cloud-covered earth resolved into view. Her body phase-shifted into a rarer span of vibrations. She no longer merely sat on a stool observing the Omphalos, though to Rahni it still appeared so. Pava had entered the vibration of Earth in her LightBody, invisible to most Earth beings, but present nevertheless.

She plunged into a cloud bank and passed through a

moment later. Mountains lay before her. Cities. Towns. A river. A house by the river. Cary's house.

Pava alit on the wooden deck. Two gray squirrels chased each other up and down an old oak that rose through a hole cut in the weathered planks. Chickadees and Carolina wrens chirped and flitted about, checking for black sunflower seeds that might have fallen from the long-empty bird feeder hanging from the eaves. High above them all, a single raven hopped short flights from treetop to treetop, witnessing the newly arrived, ethereal being.

Pava wandered through the empty house and the deserted grounds. Trace vibrations of violence, recent and ancient, lingered in the rocks and trees. The land spoke histories to her. She had witnessed many of these skirmishes, some through the Omphalos, and others present as she was now. Most recently, she had balanced upon the spine of the peaked roof, invisible to them all, and watched as Ally had led Cary into the darkness of the hidden cave, escaping from Carver's men into the LightGate that opened into the Tangle.

Pava knew the secrets of this place. She knew what lay beneath the cave, beneath Cary's house, beneath the perfectly proportioned arc in which Cary had found his necklace. She knew who had built that arc. She knew why it was positioned and proportioned as it was. She knew exactly what Memsalemn and Nanoshe were after, even though they did not fully understand it themselves.

Graal and Ripu Dasi had been busy here in the minds of Earth.

Pava walked along the stone pathway that Cary had laid. Rhododendrons, tulip poplars, and an occasional hemlock surrounded the brickwork: nature's border between the known and the unknown. *If Cary knew how many times he had stepped upon this ground, and in how many different lifetimes, he would probably faint.* She smiled. Even Ally had no idea of the enormity of these events, though Pava had inscribed their importance in her heart.

The Grastar plan was beginning to bear dangerous fruit.

Poison apples, the Earth fairy tale said. *I have tried to tell you in so many ways. So many ways.* The result of tasting this fruit would be more sinister than sleep, and a mere kiss would not bring about the cure. This was a disaster that must be averted, because once it occurred, the damage could never be undone, only abandoned for a new fight.

This apple was ripe. And Graal was ready. He would set Memsalemn and Nanoshe in motion again soon to retrieve Sh'ele. And if they succeeded, the deepest darkness that hearts on earth could imagine would come to pass. Even worse, if Graal attained Sh'ele, he would have a weapon that would make him virtually unstoppable. More than just the Earth would fall.

Poor, dear Children of Earth. All your speculation about earth changes and harmonic convergences. Your morbid fascination with 2012 and Armageddon. You have no idea, really. But you're trying. You are trying so hard.

Shafts of golden sun struck the courtyard at sharp angles. Pava stepped onto the ArcStone at the center of the great circle. With her singular intention magnified by the power of the box on which she stood, she rose above the Time Track. Ethereal lines of probability waved in the air, connecting pasts to futures. She gazed into the past as it existed and watched the events of five years ago: Cary laying this patio and finding the ArcStone on which Pava now stood. She watched her Messenger take solid form and emerge from the Arc. Through it all, Ripu Dasi lurked in the shadows of Cary's mind. He had been there for so long, almost from the beginning, hiding and manipulating for so many lifetimes.

She shifted her gaze to the future. The strongest threads revealed the most likely outcomes, while attenuating branches of less likely events swam gently in the currents of shifting probabilities. Ally and Cary would return to this place. A virtual certainty. Memsalemn and Nanoshe would be waiting. And...someone else...

Impossible.

But the probabilities were strong. Clear. Only one course

of action was available to her now.

Pava stepped off the ArcStone and back into mundane time. Thoughtlines dissolved into the air, leaving only the beauty of the mountains.

"Worse than I ever imagined," she said aloud.

Perched high above her in a tulip poplar, the raven cocked his head and squawked once in answer. Pava looked up at the great bird and nodded. When her LightBody took flight, the raven spread his dark wings and ascended into the air. He had important information to report to his brothers and sisters, and to their allies. Soon would come The Gathering. They must all prepare.

As Pava flew, she focused her intention on Cary and Ally, and she whispered a single word to them.

***

Cary rolled over in the soft bed and stretched, the contours of his body pressing against Emma's back. She rolled over to face him and blinked sleep away.

"I hate that I have to leave," Cary said.

He stared into Emma's eyes. They seemed more beautiful, more mesmerizing now than ever before. She snuggled closer, and her lips grazed his.

"I know," she said.

He searched for words, opened his mouth to speak, but closed it again. Finally he said, "Everything is a cliché. Nothing comes close to describing what I feel."

Emma pressed her hand to his chest. "I know exactly how you feel." Warmth spread from her fingertips. "Like this."

They held each other for as long as they could. Then reality spoke like a parent.

"Hello?" Ally was just outside the door. "If you two teenagers are ready to get out of bed, we really have to get moving."

Ally and Cary left Shangri-La by the same LightGate through which they had arrived. The moment they emerged into the upstairs room of Bok Tower, Cary slapped both hands over his ears and dropped to his knees.

"The voices," Ally said. "They're back?"

Cary nodded; ragged breaths rushed in and out of his mouth.

"Put your attention on the other sounds," she said. "The ones you could still hear in Shangri-La. They're still there. They've always been there between the voices." Cary shook his head. "Listen," Ally said. "Concentrate. Find one. Just one. Tell me what you hear."

Cary curled forward over his knees. His hands squeezed his head to force the voices out. He listened for the inner soundscape that had roared in his head for the last five years. The more he listened, the more he distinguished separate sounds within the roar. And then he heard it.

"The ocean," he whispered. "It sounds so far away." He concentrated on the rhythm of the waves; gradually they washed away the voices. Ally extended her hand to Cary, and he glided to his feet in one fluid motion. He was leaner now, stronger, and he moved with more grace.

"Whenever you think you are going crazy," she said, "just put your attention on that sound. It will center you. Now, come on. We have to go to Tampa and put ourselves in unnecessary danger." Cary shrugged and offered a half smile.

They managed to slip out of the tower without being noticed and then insinuated themselves into a gaggle of tourists waiting for the afternoon Carillon Concert. Ally chatted up an English professor from Gettysburg. Just like that, they had a ride to Lake Wales. Cary and Ally sardined into the back of the professor's minivan with three kids, two boys and a girl, all under nine. His wife turned around in the front seat and kept watch. Cary felt a tug at the sleeve of his shirt. Ollie, the 4 year old, looked up at him with large, serious eyes.

"Have you ever seen a zombie?" he asked.

"Not yet," said Cary.

Ally raised her hand. "I have."

Ollie executed a wise nod. "You got to watch out for zombies these days." He glanced up to the front seat, then leaned closer to Cary and whispered, "My dad's a expert."

The minivan spit them out in the parking lot of a Publix in Lake Wales.

"Remember," Ollie said. "Zombies." Ally and Cary waved goodbye.

"Here's our ride," Ally said.

"You're kidding, right? A Gremlin? I had one of these when I was a kid. Slowest and ugliest car on the planet. Until the Yugo."

Ally popped the hood. It would have been difficult to slip a sheet of notebook paper between the engine and the firewall. "Ugly, maybe. That's an asset. Slow? Never. You drive."

Cary climbed into the mustard-colored beast. "But how did they know to leave this here? In this particular parking lot."

"Granny takes care of that," Ally said.

"Don't call her that!"

Ally laughed. "Okay, but that's not gonna change the fact that—"

"I know, I know," Cary motored the Gremlin onto US 27. "Doesn't really bother me. Just joking. Damn, this thing is really is fast."

"Told you," she said. "Take it easy, Earnhardt. We don't want to get caught because you think you're in NASCAR, even if it did start in your back yard."

"You know where NASCAR started?"

"Never know what info's gonna come in handy," Ally said.

They drove due west on 60 and had just passed through Mulberry when Ally grabbed Cary's arm. "Pull over," she said.

Cary eased the Gremlin onto the shoulder. The skeleton of an abandoned concrete structure lurked in the distance to their right; its square, brownish columns were decorated with malign symbols.

"Whoa!" Cary said. "That place looks creepy."

Ally's eyes had taken on a distant gaze.

"What?" he asked.

She held her hand up and closed her eyes.

"Uktenah," she whispered. Her eyes remained closed.

"Ook-what-a?"

"Huh?" Ally said. She opened her faraway eyes. His question had startled her into the present. "Uktenah," she repeated. "Say it."

Cary opened his mouth. Seconds drifted by before the strange word formed deep in his throat. "Uktenah," he said. Strength filled his mouth. "Where is this coming from?" he asked. "Does it have anything to do with that creepy building over there?"

Ally noticed the old factory for the first time. The moist wind carried a hint of rotting flesh. "Yuck," she said. "That place *is* creepy." She shuddered away the morbid feeling. "Let's get out of here."

Cary pulled the mustard-mobile back onto the highway.

"So?" he said.

"I just heard it." She smiled and shrugged. "I was thinking about your necklace, about where you found it. Trying to figure out what's inside it. Why Carver and Layton want it. That reminds me…we should try to find out what's up with Dr. Whitt while we're here. Anyway, the word was just sort of there, in my head. I didn't even know I had said it out loud until you said 'what.'"

"Weird," Cary said. He was trying to articulate the unnamable. "It feels…good. Like it belongs to me. How could that be?"

"Sounds have power," she said. "Did you ever read *Dune?*"

"Yeah, but—"

"Remember how they used words as weapons, the…whatchyamacallems…the *Fedaykin?*"

"But that was only a book. Fiction. It…"

"No book is only a book," she said. "How many times do I need to tell you that? Frank Ebert was…"

"Herbert," he said.

"What?"

"Frank *Herbert*. Not Ebert."

"Right. Ebert's the movie guy. Anyway, Frank Herbert was tapped into something, whether he knew it or not. All writers are, really. Stories don't just come from imagination. Imagination helps you find them. Helps you shape them. But the story is actually out there somewhere, or maybe *in there* would be a better way to say it."

Cary looked at her in silence.

"Doesn't matter," Ally said. "This is your word. It has power for you. Keep it. And keep it safe. One day you'll need it."

"How the hell am I supposed to know that? When will I need it? What does it do?"

Ally shrugged. "You'll know."

They cut west on Turkey Creek Road to get off the main highway and then caught old US 92. They were still a few miles from Tampa when Cary jerked the Gremlin onto the shoulder.

"Look at that place," he said.

An old mansion stood a hundred yards back from the road. Its tall, white columns were so green-brown with mold and lichens that it very nearly merged with the Florida undergrowth.

"Wow," said Ally, not only because of the energetic pull she felt from the place, but because Cary had felt it, too.

"Do you think we should check it out?" he asked.

"Definitely." The place didn't feel dangerous. Just…alluring.

The rutted dirt driveway curved to the rear of the house where an old cotton shed sagged in the shade of Florida live oaks heavy with Spanish moss. A gray tabby cat emerged from the shadows. Cary rubbed the cat's cheeks while Ally looked in the shed.

"Someone parked here recently." She bent forward and swiped two fingers through the sugary dirt. "Fresh oil."

Woodstein broke away from Cary and bounced over to rub against Ally's legs. She picked him up.

"No tag," she said. "But he's well taken care of."

"*Meow*," Woodstein said, most likely in contradiction to Ally's last statement.

They explored the property for another half hour; Woodstein kept them company, but they found no more signs of human habitation. Eventually they climbed back into the Gremlin and rumbled up Old 92, toward East Tampa and Taylor's gravesite.

***

The Omphalos spun dark and impenetrable. Rahni sighed. Across the floor to his right, Pava rested on a throne of soft pillows. Her eyelids flickered in contemplation.

Rahni focused as Pava had taught him and struggled to allow Samudra to flow. He imagined his inner body as a pipe, a flute, the banks of a river, but he experienced only frustration as energy drained out of him. He sighed and gave up. At the moment he surrendered, all of the energy he had been trying to channel for the last few minutes rushed through him in a single surge, jerking a sob from his throat. He shuddered off the stool and onto his feet. Pava remained seated, her eyes still flickering in contemplation. A sad smile graced her full, dark lips. She held up her hand to stem Rahni's tide of questions before it could begin. Rahni settled back onto the stool, his body still tingling with energy.

How did that happen? Which of the visualizations worked? He tried each again. Nothing.

He waved his palm again over the apex. To his complete surprise, the torus formed and the Earth resolved into perfect clarity. Rahni steadied his breathing. The image wavered, then resolved. He shifted the view, navigating with his hand as he had watched Pava do countless times. He rushed through clouds and approached a small town.

An old clapboard house in the middle of a block of similar homes. A young man in a chair. The pale sheath of light surrounding his body glowed sickly brown. The man smiled with the bliss of an adept, but Rahni could see things the Earth Man could not.

A shadowy parasite was attached to the man's aura. Countless, squirming tentacles extended from the creature's chitinous body and surrounded its host, caressing him, hemming him in.

The parasite's dark brain hovered above and behind the man's head. A sticky, dripping thread extended from the creature into the base of the man's skull, projecting a perpetual stream of beautiful lies into his mind.

The young man lifted his hand and massaged the hollow at the back of his neck. The fetid cord pulsed thicker, and the man's body shuddered with pleasure.

Horrible! Rahni thought; the image flickered, almost disappeared and then resolved.

But a more sinister knowledge was soon to be revealed. Rahni now saw that another pulsing cord extended upward from the parasite's carapace and disappeared into the ethereal dark. This creature was only an appendage of something more sinister and far more intelligent, wielding this man like a marionette. Rahni's perspective shifted higher, and he saw that this man was only one of thousands; all over Earth, young men and women were tethered to a sinister darkness that lay somewhere beyond the scope of Rahni's vision. An abrupt shudder raced through Rahni's body.

"Ugly, is it not?" Pava said. She laid her palm on her student's shoulder, and his body stilled.

He had been so engrossed in the horror that he had not sensed Pava's approach, but he kept his focus, maintaining the loathsome vision. The beatific glow on the young man's face did not waver. Manufactured bliss. Only illusion. More illusion than any created by the humans themselves. And perhaps even worse, this was illusion with a purpose, illusion that controlled, persuaded, manipulated.

"This is Graal's work," Pava said. "This is how he prepares his vessels."

"What do you mean?" Rahni said. He turned to Pava; the

Omphalos darkened to its dormant state.

"Graal has created a poison. A drug. When the Children of Earth take it, they believe they have achieved enlightenment, a state of consciousness so euphoric that they take the drug even knowing that they will die in the process. They are so lost in the dark, you see, that even the hope of enlightenment is worth death to them. So they take the drug anyway. But this enlightenment is false, powered by the minds of the Grastar horde, Graal's army on Jupiter. This is the part of his strategy you have just observed.

"Ripu Dasi has been at work in Cary's mind for a very long time. For lifetimes. I have tried to hold him off, but I am spread so thin. This drug. It's Cary's work. He walked away from it when he realized it might be dangerous. But, through Ripu Dasi's manipulations, it was Cary who created this drug."

Rahni opened his mouth to speak, but Pava held her hand up and shook her head.

"The Children of Earth take the drug, and they die. Their bodies shrivel almost to collapsing, but they do not decay. And, again through the work of Graal's network of followers, their bodies are not destroyed. They become empty vessels, each one waiting to be animated by the presence of the Grastar SoulEater who controls it.

"Graal's followers have formed an underground religion; they call themselves the Qellepoth, from an ancient earth myth. Shells of the Dead. Those who have not yet taken the drug believe they are being prepared to accept a sacrament. Thus, the Children of Earth, in their quest for a shortcut to enlightenment, unknowingly prepare the path for Graal's invasion. Each Grastar uses the parasite to enter the EarthChild's consciousness disguised as a higher being, a spiritual guide. Instead they create pathways through which they may enter the bodies of their hosts, and thus walk the earth in human form.

"But, to make this journey into the waiting shells, they must pass through the LightGate that articulates Earth to

Jupiter. There is only one such gateway. With very few exceptions, all pathways must pass through this one." She paused for only a moment, letting the enormity of this information, and of the information that was still to come, take root in Rahni's consciousness. "I," she continued, looking into Rahni's eyes, "and I alone, guard that gateway."

A tingling of admiration rippled across Rahni's shoulders, and his eyes welled with tears.

"This is the true importance of what we do," Pava said. "Over 100,000 Qellepoth are already prepared and waiting all over the planet. If the Gate were unguarded, they would begin to pass through. Millions more wait in the Grastar Hive on Jupiter."

"My God!"

"When the earth is ripe, Graal will unleash the first wave into the Shells of the Dead. These prepare the way for the rest to arrive in their true form. They harvest the souls of Earth, and then they harvest the soul of the planet itself. The earth will collapse upon itself, creating another vortex of darkness in the fabric of SpaceTime, another void in the Universes of Light. Darkness takes another step forward. The balance shifts again in the direction of that which we call evil."

An immense wave of terror washed over Rahni, and suddenly he understood his newfound skill with the Omphalos.

"You let me see this," he said.

"I guided you to it, yes," Pava said, her voice a soft song in the comfort of the dome. "Not everything in the universe is beautiful, One. It was time for you to know what we are facing."

"And where were you?"

"I was meeting with the Samudra High Council," Pava said. "You see, Vatsah," she paused, took a deep breath, "I need help. This Grastar Hive is the most powerful I have ever faced." Pava looked at the beautiful swirl of threads woven into the carpet at her feet. "I do not know how much longer I can hold them back. And...there is the Sh'ele."

"The crystal?"

Pava nodded. "This is the key that Cary holds. If Graal obtains the Sh'ele, he will be able to open alternate portals at will. Whenever and wherever he wishes. And then there will be no way to stop the Grastar from taking Earth. Even worse, he will then have a weapon that will allow him to do the same on any planet. The spread of the Grastar will be unstoppable."

"But...surely the High Council will send someone to help," Rahni said.

Pava walked to the edge of the dome and collapsed onto a pile of cushions. The stunning mists of Venus danced and spun only a single molecule away. She turned back to Rahni.

"No," she said. "There is no Protector who is not already fully engaged elsewhere. This has been Graal's plan all along. The Grastar want Earth badly. Even more, they want Sh'ele. It is their primary objective, so on all other fronts their assaults are at full aggression. Their plan all along has been to isolate me, and they have succeeded. Only the two of us can face this."

"What about the Masters across the valley?" Rahni pointed to the misty atmosphere. "Retz, the Spiritual City."

"No," said Pava. She shook her head, smiling. "The Masters of Retz are beyond these skirmishes. They will guide and they will advise, if we ask. But they will not get involved. In a different way, they are already involved, more so than we can understand. The battle we now engage in is a small part of what they watch. But they leave us to our own devices. They are as far removed from the wars of the Samudra and the Grastar as we are from the squabbles of Earth.

"We must deal with this evil ourselves. It is our responsibility. The responsibilities of those Masters are above concepts of good and evil, in realms we cannot begin to understand. It will be you and I alone. Can you help me?"

"Of course," Rahni replied. "I will do whatever you ask."

Pava sighed. "You have so much to learn. If only we had

more time. We must simply intend that there will be enough."

"I will train twice as hard. What do I need to learn first?"

"First, you must learn to be the pure vehicle for Samudra. That is the key to everything else. If you learn that, then all other tasks will fall into place. Are you ready to learn that?"

"I am ready," said Rahni.

Pava smiled, and her heart filled with love for her student. "Good," she said, "because there is more."

Rahni waited. Pava closed her eyes, reliving in a single moment her recent petition to the Samudra Council, remembering the probable, almost inevitable future she had witnessed while standing on the ArcStone behind Cary's house.

There was no other way. She let her eyes fall open of their own accord. Diffuse sunlight filled her head. But the shadow of her decision remained. Rahni stood before her.

"I must go to the earth," she said, "in physical form. It is our only chance. You will have to learn to hold the Gate closed by yourself."

TENTH ARTICULATION

a coffin warehouse

a triumvirate

a plot

a burning bark

a ziggurat

a journey

a reunion

a dragon, again

a spy

a thud…

Present Day

Taylor's gravestone was a simple black slab in the Garden of Memories. *Taylor Walker. Beloved Son.* Dates. Nothing else. A terse testament to impermanence.

Cary rocked foot to foot on the grass facing the grave. Behind him, a fat, red moon climbed into the sky. Ally kept lookout only a few feet away. Oblivious traffic whined by out on 50th Street or crept along Martin Luther King Boulevard toward Seminole Heights.

"I can't believe my son is under this dirt," Cary said. "I can't make it make sense."

Ally had driven the perimeter of the Garden of Memories and scouted the streets of the nearby neighborhoods for more than an hour before hiding the mustard-mobile in a copse of palmettos behind a vacant lot. They'd walked through growing shadows to find the gravesite so that Cary could, in whatever way was necessary, say goodbye to his son.

Ally looked down at the grave. Something seemed wrong to her, too.

"I wonder," she said. But that was as far as she got. The sweep of approaching headlights lit them, and they both hit the ground as one. Ally raised her eyebrows at his speed. Cary smiled.

"I exercised a little while you were away," he said.

"Don't lie to me," she said. "I know that move. Granny's been training you."

Cary was about to respond, but Ally slapped her hand over his mouth. "Humor later," she said. "Survival now." Cary nodded, and they both rolled into the shadows.

The car was an old, green Dodge of some sort. It looked like a beater, but the engine throbbed with power. Ally and Cary stayed low in the shadows. The car paused as it passed them, but then moved on.

"Something familiar about that guy," she said. Cary nodded.

The old Dodge followed the inner driveways of the Garden of Memories. The driver slowed to a crawl as he passed each mausoleum. When he appeared to be reaching the end of his run, Ally popped up to her feet.

"Let's go," she said.

"Where?" Cary asked, right on her heels.

"To follow him, of course. I don't know where we know that guy from, but he's involved in this somehow."

They ran to the Gremlin and had just pulled up to the street when the Dodge—Ally saw now that it was a Diplomat—passed them. She eased into traffic and followed at a distance, first down MLK and then Florida Avenue into downtown. He parked near the Kennedy Bridge and walked into the raised park above Ashley.

"Remember this place?" Ally said. They watched from the car, but as soon as the man disappeared from view, they took off across the street.

Cary nodded. "I recognize it from when I lived in Ybor, but it looks more recently familiar..." his voice trailed off. A warm breeze shook the leaves of the crape myrtles. "This is where that creepy guy—"

"Murtaugh."

"Right. Murtaugh. This is where we came out after he showed us the stairs. Just before..." he trailed off again, but took a deep breath and forced himself to speak the words. "Just before my son...just before Taylor died."

The bronze placard was exactly where Cary remembered it. He looked at Ally. She raised her eyebrows and shrugged. Cary worked his fingertips under the edge of the plate and pried it up. The trap door fell back into place above them with a soft clang. The harsh steely-ringing of their footsteps echoed off the smooth, concrete walls.

At the bottom of the stairs, the tunnel led back toward Ybor, and the metal door stood to the right.

"Do you think he came down here?" Cary whispered.

Ally shook her head. She was digging into her pack. A keypad with an LED readout was mounted on the wall to the side of the door jamb.

"Was that here before?" Cary asked.

Ally nodded. She drew a tiny device that looked like a small flat, flashlight out of her bag and pressed it to the bottom of the keypad.

"Umm, isn't this the door that Murtaugh told us not to go in?" Cary asked.

"Mmhmm," Ally said. "But he's not here now."

Numbers flashed on the device's small screen. Ally nodded and keyed in the code. The metal door popped open with a soft rush of cool air. Ally smiled, raised her eyebrows, and cut her eyes toward the door.

"Where do you get this stuff?"

"Traded in my Namayan decoder ring for it," she said. "Come on." She took the Maglite from her backpack. Cary did the same, and they entered the cool hallway.

They followed a smooth, white corridor that looked like a long cleanroom for 50 or 60 feet before they came to another metal door. This one had only a traditional handle lock, and Ally made quick work of it with her picks. They killed the flashlights and stepped into a vast, dark room.

***

Ripu Dasi yearned for solidity. He navigated eddies and flows of gas to the transfer matrix that would transmit him in a concentrated beam of particles to Mount Vinâsa. Once there, his body would coalesce for his audience with Graal.

The gaseous form that the Grastar maintained on Jupiter offered a certain freedom of movement. But the Grastar are a corporeal race. They relish carnality. Dasi longed to feel once again the rush of hot blood through his veins. Even more, he missed the perfume of fear, the cries of anguish, and the sweet savor of blood gushing from the broken shells of his victims. Frequent forays into Cary Walker's inner worlds had provided Dasi with the illusion of the physical, but this had only fueled his hunger for flesh the way a carcass turning on a spit fuels the appetite.

The lip of the whirlpool drew him to its edge and downward into the point of concentration. A familiar, exquisite density swirled at his core and pulled the rest of his molecules inward. A momentary sensation of sinking and rising at the same time, of being everywhere and nowhere at once, an instant of flight, and Ripu Dasi stood, for the first time in tens of thousands of years, upon his thick, wide legs. He flexed his four arms, wrapped them tightly around his broad chest, then slapped his sides hard. "Aaahhhh," he growled. The sting of pain was exquisite.

Soon he would inhabit an earth body. The shell was already waiting. How did they manage with only two arms? Combat must be so mundane, sex so boring.

Graal sat on the Lord Stone, his thick legs tucked underneath him. His lower hands were folded, index fingers pressed together and pointing upward, his other 14 fingers interlocked. A focus mudra. In his upper hands, Graal held a LightScroll. He stared into the lucent document.

Graal transmitted a command with his thoughts. "Submit." Dasi abased himself and waited, head bowed, all four palms pressed to the floor. After a moment, Graal spoke aloud. "Approach." His voice was a deep, malignant rasp. Dasi obeyed.

"You have an assignment for me, Lord," Dasi said.

"The Samudra bitch." His voice hissed out the name,

"Apavarita Varsah…"

"I know her well, Lord. She has continually confronted me in Walker's DreamWorld."

Graal stood on the Lord Stone. The gravity in the chamber doubled. Ripu Dasi had to struggle to remain standing. Among the Grastar Horde, it was rumored that Graal could kill with *drismirtu*. Truly, the warriors of the horde, formidable as they were, had no idea of Graal's abilities. The Death Gaze was among his lesser powers.

"Yes," Graal replied. "Her strength in the inner worlds is formidable. So we must fight her with other strategies. I will not…" he spread all four of his arms, and his voice rose to a roar, "*you* will not allow her to keep this prize from me."

"Yes, Lord," Dasi said. "Other strategies?"

"You shall materialize upon the earth," Graal commanded, "in a human body." He revealed the scroll to Dasi. A holograph floated above the surface, a likeness. "As this human. You will manifest a facsimile of this body and oversee your Sumerian pets when they capture Walker. If they fail to learn his secret, extract the information yourself. Then take possession of the Sh'ele and bring it to me. The Apsara had no idea what a treasure they were creating for me. I will be unstoppable. When it is done, do as you wish to the Sumerians. I will have no further need for them."

Ripu Dasi laughed. "That last stratagem," he said, "is already in play. They are a delightful game."

Graal nodded. "And we have the additional benefit that your presence upon the planet will draw Apavarita Varsah to the earth. That will leave only her acolyte, Rahni Sisyah, to hold The Gate."

"It is against Samudra Law to walk upon the Protected Planet, my Lord," Dasi said.

"I know this one well," Graal said, waiving the objection away with both of his left hands. "She cannot abide defeat. And she hates to lose to me. This is her weakness, her sin of pride. She will break her laws. And when she walks the earth, you will crush her. She may be able to withstand you in

Walker's DreamWorlds, but in the physical world, her strength will be no match for yours."

Dasi half raised his thick brow before he responded.

"Unless," Dasi said, "she is able to draw on the Samudra Source through her disciple on Venus."

"Exactly," Graal said. "But the acolyte is untrained and untested. He will have to hold the gate and channel Samudra to his teacher. He will be spread too thin. This will leave the Gate vulnerable. While the acolyte's attention is divided, send your most fell warrior to Dalam Palace. The Gate will become unguarded, and the *AtmaAsurahs*, my army of SoulEaters, will fill their Qellepoth hosts." Graal's guttural laughter echoed through the chamber. "You will have the added pleasure of devouring the Samudra bitch. Have you ever tasted a Samudra? It is a savor you will not soon forget." He laughed again. "But do not indulge yourself too much among the EarthKine. Not yet. I know your hungers. You must wait until we are ready. Then we will all feed in abundance. Do you understand?"

"Yes, Lord," Dasi answered. "I will not fail you. I shall have Panii Viisam ready to attack. She is most lethal."

"She had better be. The Gate must fall. And we must retrieve the Sh'ele. Then no amount of Samudra Protectors will be able to withstand me. Go now. You have your orders."

Ripu Dasi stepped backward into the transfer vortex and was drawn away in an instant. Graal settled onto the Lord Stone and folded all four hands into a killing mudra. He spread his wide mouth in a predatory grimace. "Death is good," he said. "Death is good."

***

"The Council told you to go to earth?" Rahni said.

Pava gazed into the mists beyond the dome. The Venusian atmosphere had darkened to the color of bruises.

"I have not told them," she said. "I have decided on my

own. It is the only way."

Ranhi's eyes widened. "But…" he almost sputtered, "but that is forbidden. You know the Laws. You taught them to me. You'll fall from grace. The Council will remove your mandate. You will be branded as a renegade."

Pava rose and activated the Omphalos. Earth hung, a glowing jewel suspended in the chamber.

"You must understand this." Pava fixed her gaze on the Earth as she spoke. "Graal's strategy has advanced too far. My own state of grace can no longer be a factor in my decisions. Graal has set his earth pawns in motion; until now, Alethea has managed to keep Mr. Walker out of their hands, and Sh'ele has remained hidden. But Ripu Dasi intends to walk the earth in human form. Do you understand what that means? He can kill with a touch. A word. He can literally draw the life and light out of Cary and learn the location of Sh'ele. If Dasi takes control of the crystal, the Gate will no longer matter. Graal will use Sh'ele to open an alternate gate. Earth's darkest dreams will come true. And Graal will have Sh'ele to use on other planets. He will be unstoppable. This entire system, this entire galaxy is in jeopardy. I must set my feet upon the planet. No one, save me, can face him. It's the only way."

Rahni rose a few inches off the floor and floated to the far edge of the dome. He settled into a pile of soft cushions, legs folded, rocking forward and back, hugging himself tightly. Pava followed him across the thick carpets and sank into the pillows beside him. Motes of dust rose and caught the light. She watched them float in the air, as she so often watched Earth float in space.

"There is still more," Pava said. "Look at me now, Dear One. This is crucial." Pava took a deep breath before she continued. "You will have to learn to hold the Gate by yourself, as I have said." Rahni waited.

"And," Pava said, "you will simultaneously have to be a conduit of Samudra to my Earth body. I will never be able to face Dasi without the power of Samudra flowing through me, and that power becomes so attenuated in an Earth body that I must have your help."

Rahni stood so abruptly that he continued to rise into the air. He realized as he drifted uncontrollably upward that he was breaking the rules. Never had he been so disrespectful as to gaze down upon his teacher. Yet, he could not stop himself. The words poured out of him.

"But…I'm not ready." His voice broke. "You know I'm not ready. How can you expect… You told me I had so much more—so much more to learn." Rahni fell silent, floated slowly down to the carpets, and stared at the floor waiting for the reprimand that was certain to come.

Pava rose to float a few inches above her cushion. She gently placed both of her hands on his face and tilted his head upward until their eyes met.

"They have a saying down upon the earth, *Añujah*," she said. "'Necessity has no rules.' We have arrived at that place now, you and I. You *are* ready, because you have to be. Necessity demands it. There is no other way. You must hold the LightGate closed. And you must be my conduit to Source."

Pava returned to the Omphalos. She gestured once, and the perspective shifted farther back to reveal the entire planetary system. Earth followed its path around the sun in perfect cosmic balance. A beautiful, shimmering ball of blue and green and white. Jupiter waited, just as beautiful, only two valence shells away.

Perhaps I am falling into the traps of attachment. Perhaps my love is no longer pure. No matter.

She glanced at Rahni Sisyah, her most gifted student. So much depended upon him now. She created a secret thoughtform, set it to orbit around Rahni's heart matrix, and gave it the command to blossom at a precise moment. She could only hope that, when these images and feelings burst upon him, Rahni's training would show him what to do.

"Now," Pava said. "Let us prepare. There is so much that you have to learn. But there are shortcuts. It begins in the vibrations of your heart. Come. Sit. We begin."

***

Ally pushed the metal door shut behind them. Cary could just make her out standing next to him.

He whispered, "Do you think there's anyone in here?"

Ally placed her finger vertically across Cary's lips and waited. The room felt cavernous. She heard the muffled street sounds above them from Kennedy Boulevard, but nothing else. Not even a rat.

"I think it's okay." She turned her flashlight back on. Cary flipped his on a second later.

"Jesus!" he said.

Huge racks of heavy scaffolding extended in every direction into the darkness. The racks were filled with identical black coffins. It was impossible to tell in the shadows beyond their flashlights how many there were.

"I don't suppose this is a coffin warehouse," Cary said. Before Ally could answer, a large concrete door at the far end of the room began to slide open. They killed their flashlights and backed into the shadows. A white, windowless van drove in through the opening and came to a stop. The concrete door slid closed. With a loud click, stark halogens buzzed to life. The room, they could now see, was larger than either of them had imagined. There had to be at least a 1,000 coffins in there. Ally nudged Cary's shoulder and pointed. Ladders were built into the sides of the racks.

Two men in blue coveralls and Devil Rays caps exited the van. They slid a coffin, identical to the others, from the rear compartment and onto a lift. One of the men got back into the van and pulled it forward to what must have been an exit door. The other used a remote control at the end of a thick wire to operate the lift. The coffin rose with a whir and slid into an empty slot. The man jumped into the passenger seat, the metal exit door rolled up, and the van rolled out onto Kennedy Boulevard. They had been in and out in less than three minutes.

Cary was about to step out into the light when Ally grabbed his belt and pulled him back. She pointed to the descending door. A man was running down the ramp, trying to get into the warehouse before the door closed. He dove at the last minute and slid headlong into the room as the door clanged shut and the lights clicked off, leaving only the residual glow of the bulbs.

They waited, listening as the man got to his feet and crept forward in the near darkness. His path would lead him directly to them.

Ally held her palm up. Even as Cary was shaking his head in protest, she disappeared into the shadows. The man drew closer, almost on top of him now. Cary braced for an attack. Light flooded his eyes. He could just make out the shape of the man, a dim silhouette behind a spotlight. He was reaching under his coat. Cary knew he could never get away in time.

Why do these assholes want to kill me anyway?

Cary uttered an unintelligible howl that might have transformed into words if there were only enough time. But the flashlight beam was already shifting away; the man had become a human propeller. For a moment his head was where his feet were supposed to be, and then he smacked onto his back on the concrete floor. The flashlight clattered to the ground. Cary scrabbled to scoop it up.

It was the man they had just followed from the cemetery. Ally knelt over him, gripping his impossibly bent hand between her thumb and first two fingers. He thrashed back and forth on the concrete, fighting to draw air into his body. Ally pressed her other hand to the man's chest, and his eyes widened, clearly fearful that she was going to force even more air out of his lungs. But when she pushed down, his chest filled. She stood and let him gasp on his own. In her left hand, she held his wallet.

"It's all right," she said. "He's just a reporter." She glanced at him. "Can you sit up?" He nodded and struggled into a sitting position. "What's your name?"

"You've got my wallet." He sounded like he had been hit by a train. The Alethea Express. "You tell me."

"Tell us anyway," she said.

"Simon Boon."

"What are you doing here, Simon Boon?"

"Look," he said. "I don't know what you guys are doing here. I must have gotten the wrong information. I'm doing a story about drugs, and I don't see any crack dealers here. So let's just call it a mistake, and I'll be on my way."

"Wait a minute!" Cary said. "Now I recognize you. You were at my son's funeral."

Ally took a closer look at the man. "Skinnier," she said. "No more combover. But you're right. The guy who got into the VW."

"Of course. Now I remember," Simon said. "You were hiding in the shadows up on the hill at—what was his name? Oh…you said it was your son. Oh. I'm sorry. I didn't know. And…I saw…"

"Saw what?" Ally said.

"I was…I was hiding in the palmettos when those men attacked you." He looked at Cary. "I thought you were dead."

"Yeah," Cary said. "I get that a lot."

Ally looked at him, mouth open.

Cary smiled back. "Call me *Snake.*"

For a moment, no one seemed to know just what to say. Simon reached toward his jacket pocket. Ally performed a subtle shift, but not so subtle that Simon didn't notice. He held up his other hand and moved like a snail.

With two fingers he pulled a Ziploc from his jacket. It contained the Harpy that had sliced Cary's side open.

"Been carrying this around ever since," he said. He held the bag out and Cary took it. Cary's dried blood was still on the blade. "Why were those guys trying to kill you?"

"Maybe we'll answer your questions later, Mr. Boon," Ally said. "But first, what exactly are you doing here? And what were you doing at Taylor Walker's funeral in the first place?"

Boon looked from one to the other. "It's going to sound

pretty weird," he said.

"I doubt it can get any weirder than it already has," Cary said.

Boon sighed in resignation. "Grave robbing," he said. "I'm following a story about grave robbing."

Cary and Ally exchanged a quick glance.

"Looks like you hit the jackpot," Ally said. She pointed her flashlight to the racks of coffins.

"Jesus." Simon looked around for the first time. "I thought they were in here. I just had no idea there'd be so many."

"You said before you were working on a story about drugs," Cary said. "Was that true?"

"Not at first," he said. "But now…well, maybe. I'm not sure yet, but I think there may be a drug angle, too." He walked over and put his hand on one of the coffins.

Cary looked at Ally and back at Simon. "What drug?" he said.

Simon looked over his shoulder. "It's called Nirvana. And there's something even weirder."

Simon told them about Freddy Blake and the Qellepoth. "The main thing I haven't been able to figure out is *why*."

Ally joined him by the wall of coffins. She looked back at Cary and then at Simon. "I think we should look at one of them."

Cary operated the lift. They set the coffin on the floor and released the six latches that sealed the lid. Cary stood at one end, Simon at the other, and Ally in the middle. She raised the lid on its hinges.

"My God!" Simon whispered.

A sob escaped Ally's throat before she even felt it coming.

"What's wrong?" Cary asked, taking a step toward Ally before he got a good look at the girl. "Did you know her?"

"No. It's just that…she's…perfect."

Cary looked at her for the first time. The girl had been 19, maybe 20, and had probably been plain in life. You could see that she had been plain. But in death she was beautiful. More than beautiful. Beatific. Though she was thin, barely there really, she glowed the way some women glow in pregnancy. And she wore a smile that said everything was right in the world.

But nothing was right. Nothing was right. She was no longer part of the perfect world. Her life had been wasted, prematurely extinguished. Just like...

"Taylor smiled at me exactly like that," Cary said.

They put the girl back and left through the door they had come in. A dark figure waited in the hallway, leaning against the wall by the stairs.

"My friends," said Murtaugh. "We meet again. And you have a new playmate with you."

"Murtaugh," Ally said. With a smooth sidestep, she inserted herself between Murtaugh and Cary, but Cary found the man's dark eyes, and the voices he had not heard for so long returned. He staggered against the wall and felt the here and now spin away.

Before Time

~

Ksama

The tide spits the *Varuna* from the narrow inlet, and Ksama emerges into an inland sea bounded by green cliffs. Miles away, on the far side of the gulf, a cataract falls from the clouds. Tiny droplets of mist kiss Ksama's tear-washed face.

Across the water, beside the waterfall, she discovers a quay hewn into the bedrock of the island. She steps onto land for the first time in more than a week, and onto the Island of Dreams for the first time in her life. But clearly she is not the first to have come here. The edges of the quay are precise. Beside the falls, uniform stone steps zigzag up the mountainside, changing direction every 12 steps. These are the cuts of master artisans.

When she has offloaded everything of use, Ksama opens the door of the brazier and tilts it forward. Scarcely more than a day before, she had found the will to plunge her arm into this inferno. Now, red coals spill from the open mouth. Steam rises from the gray planks until the mast succumbs to true fire. She shoves the stern hard with her legs, and the vessel of her deliverance drifts burning into the bay. The fire lives for a long time, and the *Varuna* floats farther and farther from the shore toward the center of the inland sea. Ksama dangles her languid feet back and forth in the cool water, ensorcelled by the orange flames until they disappear beneath blue waves.

Before the last wisps of smoke have joined the sky, she straps Sh'ele to her back and begins to climb. After an hour, she enters the cloud bank and ascends in thick fog, her only companion the roar of a waterfall she can no longer see. Darkness falls. She tries to press on, but though the steps are firm, there is no hand rail. She ties herself to the trunk of a huge cedar and sleeps in the white noise of falling water.

In her dream, a faceless assassin has found her. He closes his hand on her throat. Her feet dangle and kick above the floor. Ksama can do nothing but scream; the scream strangles away to a rattling hiss in his iron grip. She awakens on the stairs and finds her own hand squeezing her throat, but the dream escapes into shadow and mist. Exhaustion casts her back into the dream world where the assassin still waits. Again he closes his hand on her throat, and again she starts to wakefulness. And so she passes the night. When at last she rises to the dawn, bruises paint her neck purple.

Midway into the second day, the clouds thin before disappearing altogether. The top of the waterfall waits only a hundred steps higher. The stairs open onto a large courtyard of red stones. To the left of the courtyard, a swift river rushes to its cataract destiny. To the right, a large circular pool reflects the morning sun.

For a moment, Ksama is back in Tirtham Commons, moonlight shining from the surface of the reflecting pool. The water turns black with fresh-spilled blood. Sidra kneels before her with empty eyes.

I have become death.

And just as quickly, Ksama is back to the present, sitting by this new pool that reflects the new light of the morning sun.

I should be grateful.

She searches inside her aching, empty chest for gratitude that she is still alive, that Syrgala has not found her, that Sidra did not kill her, that she has found the Island of Dreams. Her mind replays the arguments of the Parisad; Syrgala's words hold far different meanings now that she understands him for who he truly is. Instead of gratitude, she mines a rich vein of deceit and betrayal. She replays the scene in which she had come so close to death at Sidra's hands, the events that culminated with her taking a life. Instead of gratitude, she finds guilt.

I have become death.

Ksama's rage shakes her, and she pounds her left fist into the ledge of the pool until her blood paints the stones. A scream gestates deep inside her, and she struggles to push it out, but the scream is not yet powerful enough to rise.

When she has exhausted her anger, she rinses her hand in the water, seasoning the pool with the vitriol of her blood. She bandages her hand with a scrap of sail cloth. A difficult task, since it is the only hand she has.

"Not much of a strategy," she says. "Damaging the only good hand you have left."

She looks out across the cloudscape far below.

"And now, you are talking to yourself." She turns away from the clouds, away from the warm pool. Her face is crusted with the salt of dried tears.

And then she sees for the first time the secret that looms before her. It is so vast, and its shape blends so perfectly with its surroundings that at first, Ksama thinks she is looking at the slope of the mountainside. But there before her, as if it has risen out of the land itself, stands a ziggurat. The polished, outer walls reflect the surrounding forest, making the temple appear and disappear depending on the perspective and position of the viewer.

Her thoughts of betrayal and guilt swirl together and coalesce into an amorphous, unrecognizable mass. Ksama shoves this storm down, not beneath a layer of gratitude, but one of relief.

Present Day

Cary focused on the ocean sound that lived in his head and, with great effort, forced the madness away. The world was still a blur, but he sensed someone was holding him up against a wall. From the distance of his madness, he heard more local voices. Ally. And Murtaugh.

"Are you here to collect your debt?" Ally asked.

Murtaugh's laugh was thick and smoky. "No, little girl," he said. "Just a reminder. Just wanted to say hello. I'll be finding you when the time is right."

Cary opened his eyes. The light of the white corridor was almost blinding. Simon Boon had pressed Cary up against the wall to keep him standing. Cary shuddered and broke free with a growl. Simon backed away and held his hands up in a placating gesture.

Murtaugh's laugh was thick as syrup. He pushed off the wall and walked down the tunnel. "Be seeing you," he said over his shoulder.

After Murtaugh had disappeared beyond the curve of the hallway, Ally turned to Cary.

"Are you okay?"

Cary nodded, but shook his head to try and clear away the cobwebs. "God, I am so tired of that shit," he said.

The three of them climbed the stairs to Mopheit Park. The late night breeze carried the putrid fish smell of Tampa

Bay at low tide, but it was a refreshing contrast to what they had just left.

"Okay," Simon said. "That scored an 11 on my weird shit-o-meter."

Ally shook her head. "Nothing we have to worry about," she said. "Not yet, anyway. Right now we need to figure out what to do next."

Cary's head was almost clear. He turned to Simon. "But why are they stealing bodies?"

"How should I know?" Boon said. "I just noticed something weird and started chasing it down. My editor thought I was crazy. Probably thinks I'm dead now. But shit, when the police bust this place, I'll get nominated for a Pulitzer."

"We can't tell the police about this," Ally said.

"What do you mean? We have to tell the police. Do you realize what these people are doing?"

"No, Mr. Boon, I don't. And neither do you. But I do know that this is much bigger than it seems. Can you even be sure that the police aren't somehow involved? This isn't simply about grave robbing. There's something much more dangerous going on here. Those men you saw try to kill me and Cary? That's all related to this somehow. He has something they want, but we don't know what."

Cary felt for the presence of his necklace.

"All the more reason to tell the cops," Simon said.

"No," Cary said. "She's right. I don't know exactly how she's right, but you just have to trust her. Believe me, I was right where you are when this all started, but if you'd seen the things I have in the last six months, you wouldn't doubt her. So let me save you the trouble of a lot of arguing that you will never win anyway. We're not going to tell the cops. Or your editor. Sorry."

"How do you plan to stop me?" Simon asked. Cary looked at him, then at Ally.

"You're kidding, right?" Cary said.

Simon sighed. "Okay," he said. "Sorry. Just a reaction.

What do we do, then?"

"I don't know." Cary looked at Ally.

"Well, Mr. Boon," she said, "how would you like to go to North Carolina?"

"You're saying I'll find the answers to all of this in North Carolina?" Boon said.

"What do you mean?" Cary asked.

"We have to go back to your house," she said. "I don't think it's just the necklace they're after. Whatever you have must be back there."

"But where?" Cary said.

"I'm not sure," Ally said. "Maybe under that patio. Maybe there's an entrance in the cave."

"Cave?" Simon asked.

Cary laughed. "Oh, you're not going to believe this cave," he said. Ally shot him a fierce look, but he continued.

"And," he continued, "there are fairies. And aliens." He smiled and shrugged.

"It doesn't matter if you believe me," she said. "And I don't really know much about them anyway. Except that they're real. And they're dangerous."

"Well," Simon said. "He may not believe you. But I do. One of them attacked my van." He pulled out his phone and scanned pages until he came to a picture of the claw marks. "Did this. I'm pretty sure they have something to do with the Qellepoth."

***

"Make no mistake," Dossey said. "Your brother plans to kill you and your men before the Sh'ele is ever in your hands. You must be ready."

Carver pressed the cell phone hard against his ear and leaned back in his Aeron Chair. He nodded. "How do you know this?" he asked.

"Quite simple," Dossey said. "He told me. He no longer trusts you. Said you've…'taken the stone'…whatever that means. He asked me to be his new partner. He said, 'Two can rule as well as three.'"

Carver laughed. "Layton has always lived by fear," he said. "It's time for him to die by fear."

"He will soon contact you with information his torture squad took from the Namayan General before he died. He will tell you that Walker is returning to the mountain. This is true. Go there with him. Let him think he is in control. But he will not know that it is you who really are. You and your men simply have to be ready to kill them before they kill you."

"That will not be difficult," Carver said, "since my men are superior."

"Indeed," Dossey replied. "As are you. This is precisely why you and I are having this conversation. Layton is correct, you see. Two can rule as well as three. He simply does not know that he will not be one of the two."

"And where will you be during all this?" Carver said.

"You shall see me."

The line went dead. Carver placed the phone in its cradle and left the office.

Miranda was in the den, reading *Vanity Fair* and listening to her iPod. She smiled and removed the ear buds.

"What are you listening to?" he asked.

"*Bush of Ghosts*. Want me to put it on speaker?"

"No. I have to pack."

"Again?"

"Afraid so," he said. "Have to work every once in a while to keep you in the style to which etc. etc."

Within the hour, Miranda was waving to him from the front window as he pulled away in a new toy, a black Bugatti Veyron. She watched until the little scarab of a car crested the last hill a little over a mile away. She watched for another 20 minutes. When she was certain that he would not return, she took a first edition of *Idylls of the King*, signed by both Tennyson and Doré, from a glass display case on the mantle. A first anniversary present from her husband.

Miranda opened the leather cover and let her fingers play over the signatures. She had considered it a shame to desecrate such a treasure, but a necessary one. She thumbed to the end of *Merlin and Vivien*. The remaining pages were hollowed out. A blue velvet bag holding a sleek, black cell phone was wedged into the cubby. She knew the number by heart, and always deleted it after she made this call. The line rang for nearly a minute before it was answered in silence.

***

Simon had dumped his Dodge in Hyde Park and climbed into the back seat of the Gremlin. He had used all of his powers of persuasion to convince Ally to let him call his ex-girlfriend and beg her to drive out to the old mansion and pick up Woodstein. Then, at nearly one in the morning, they hopped on I-75 and headed north. By 1:30 the next afternoon they were rolling into Spruce Pine, half an hour east of Burnsville. Ally was driving. Simon dozed in the back.

"Turn here," Cary said. "There's a place downtown where we can get great coffee." He reached blindly into the back seat and slapped his hand around until it hit cloth. "Yo, Simon," he said. "Wake up. Coffee."

They turned onto Lower Street in downtown Spruce Pine.

"That's original," Ally said. "Where's Upper Street?"

Cary pointed up one of the alleys to the left. "Duh? We were just on it," he said. "Park here."

DT's Blue Ridge Coffee House lived in a small storefront across the road from the old train depot. Plate glass windows on either side of the door offered Goodwill sofas and Salvation Army chairs. They had arrived in the aftermath of the noon rush. Carcasses of sprout sandwiches and BLTs littered bistro tables.

Cary scanned the room, saw no one familiar, and let relief escape with his breath. But he knew she would be here. She was always here. It was, after all, her place. As always, his hands trembled just a bit with the residue of excitement, trepidation, wistfulness, and a dozen or so unidentified feelings.

Simon ordered them large, white mugs of steaming coffee from a roundish redhead with ultrapink skin; her name tag appropriately labeled her as *Rosie*. Cary didn't know her, but the staff was always in flux.

Ally tracked the remains of the lunch crowd and settled for a nano-moment on a dark wildman hunched over a book-laden table in the window to the right. He wore a rumpled, brown tweed three-piece that might have last been pressed sometime prior to the Depression; his abundant, chaotic black hair could have turned Medusa to stone. The guy rocked fore and aft, humming and glancing this way and that as he scratched ink onto paper. Ally's eyebrows drifted upward. Not a threat, but...there was something about him.

Hunted. That was how he looked. Hunted. Who knew from what. But she understood the look.

Ally shrugged and plopped onto a soft green sofa with its back to the left side window. Cary settled for a plush, threadbare armchair against a wide, wooden pillar facing Ally and the outside. A black and white photograph of steam rising from the rim of a coffee cup hung on the pillar behind him. Cary had a clear view of the street. He was surprised to see Ally sitting with her back to the window. He had become used to her always taking the seat with the most strategic view of her surroundings.

Simon arrived with their coffees and set them on the old cedar chest that performed double duty as a table. He took the chair against the weathered brick wall to Cary's right.

"So, let me get this straight," Simon said. "We're going back to your house to try and figure out what might be there that these bad guys want from you."

Cary nodded.

"But you don't know what it is? Or where it is? Or even...if it is?"

Cary nodded again.

"And you think your necklace has something to do with it."

Cary took the talisman in his hand. He looked to Ally.

"That's what I think," she said.

All three fell silent when a woman arrived and bussed the table behind Cary. As the woman bent forward, Ally caught a glimpse of darkness on her lower back.

"Nice tattoo," Ally said.

"Thank you," she said. Her golden hair swung back and forth above her shoulders, and her pale green eyes sparkled in the shadow of her brow. Cary had not seen her, but his breath caught a little when he heard her voice. He leaned around the pillar.

"Renee," he said.

"Cary!" she said. "My God. Where have you been? I've been so worried about you!" Cary stood and they hugged.

"Oh," he said, his voice coming from far away. "Just some abrupt business out of town."

After introductions, Ally said, "Can I look at your tattoo, Renee?"

Renee turned around and lifted her shirt to reveal an arcane symbol that spanned her lower back.

"What is it?" Ally asked.

"Ask Cary," she said. "He got it for me."

One of Ally's eyebrows quirked up.

"Found it in a book," he said. "Renee was looking for a symbol for a tattoo. I was just drawn to that one. So was she, once she saw it. Book said it was some kind of ancient symbol used to refer to a Buddha, but it was much older than that. I can't remember what it's called."

"Vamh," Renee said.

"Give me your necklace," said Ally.

Cary hesitated only a moment before handing it over. Ally looked at the necklace, then at the tattoo. Slowly, she turned the pendant sideways and held it up to Cary.

"My God!" he said. The pattern was formed only of dots, but the comparison was unmistakable. The two images were virtually identical, as if the dots were the skeleton of the tattoo image.

"Looks a little like a dragon," Simon said. Cary and Renee cut their eyes to each other, then to the floor. Simultaneously they pushed their right sleeves up. Both had identical dragons inscribed on the inside of their forearms.

"We got a little hokey with the tattoo thing," Renee said.

Ally passed the necklace back to Cary. The cedar chest began to vibrate. Everyone was silent for a moment, not sure what to do. Ally picked up her pack and the table stilled. The buzz came from her pack.

"Excuse me," she said. "I've got to take this." From what appeared to be a hidden compartment under the bag, Ally extracted a small phone and stepped through the front door into the afternoon sunlight. She raised the phone to her ear and waited.

***

When the Grastar had first arrived in the Earth system, Graal labored with great patience to craft vortices that articulated Jupiter to each of the planets. These manufactured connections were separate from the LightGates and the Tangle of Light. In the early days, Graal had used the vortices to travel about the solar system with impunity. But, one by one, Apavarita Varsah had found and destroyed each of the portals. In fact, this was precisely why Graal had moved so openly, so that Pava would believe she had found and closed them all. But, deep below the surface of Jupiter, near its dense core, several had remained unused and untouched for nearly 50 millennia in anticipation for moments such as were now approaching. Planet harvesting is patient work.

Now, Panii Viisam called forth the image and frequency that Ripu Dasi had imprinted in her mind. A swirling tunnel of gasses formed before her, and she relaxed her own atoms into it, letting it take her. She was simultaneously Panii Viisam, a matrix of awareness, and the vortex itself. She gathered speed, riding the flow that terminated somewhere near the center of the planet, at the secret field vortices and the thread that articulated Jupiter to Venus.

To feed again on soul.

For centuries, Viisam had resided in the Horde body, fighting, spinning in virtual nothingness, generating heat and energy for the attack, growing hungry. She and all the SoulEaters of the Horde ached to devour the succulent, warm flesh of humanity. Now she would have a chance to feed before all others.

Viisam's atoms reached stability and hovered above the mouth of a gigantic whirlpool. Multicolored particles spun in a great spiral dance, inviting all surrounding energy to condense into a single point. She had never experienced such power.

Ripu Dasi had instructed her to remain here at the edge until he flooded her mind with another image, a destination. She need only to concentrate fully upon the image to instantly transfer herself in a particle beam to Dalam Palace, taking Rahni Sisyah by surprise.

Viisam would need to generate a tremendous amount of energy to materialize her body on Venus, so her time would be limited. When the energy ran out, she would be drawn back into the vortex, and then back to the Horde body, like an electrical charge releasing. But the acolyte was undeveloped and unprotected. There would be more than enough time. More than enough time to accomplish this mission, and more than enough time to feed.

And once I have sucked the soul out of this Samudra morsel, the Gate will open. The vanguard will enter their hosts, and we will walk the earth. Then the feast will truly begin.

***

Ally rocked from foot to foot in front of DT's, phone to her ear, and waited. Across the street, a slow freight train clacked by.

Click... clack...

"Is it you, Little One?" said the familiar voice at last.

Click...

"You have news?" Ally said.

Clack...

"They'll be waiting for you when you get to the mountain,"

said Miranda. "Be very careful. It's going to be a bloodbath." The caboose rolled by, and the train receded into the east. "He's planning to kill Layton."

"This is more out of hand than I could have imagined." Ally took a breath and let it out. Three goth teens strolled by paying her no mind. "Are you okay?" she whispered into the phone.

"I hate this," Miranda said. "You know how I hate it. I always have. But, yes, I'm all right."

"Perhaps," Ally said, "it won't be much longer before you can abandon this post."

"Or until he figures it out," Miranda said, "and kills me."

"You've made it almost 12 years," Ally said. "Even the most powerful men have blind spots."

"Thank the Goddess for that," Miranda said. "There's something else. Layton's men captured one of the Council. I don't know who." Her voice trembled. "They tortured him, sweetie. I'm sorry. He's dead." She descended into quiet sobs. When she spoke again, her voice was barely a whisper. "It may have been Nelson."

"I still haven't heard from him," Ally said, her voice small. She swallowed, calling on reservoirs of courage to displace her fear. When she spoke again, her voice was stronger. "Are you sure you are willing to keep this up? No one would blame you for bailing under the circumstances."

"'Have I not sworn?'" Miranda said, her voice still barely more than a whisper. "'Am I not trusted?'"

"Umm," Ally said, "I think I speak for the whole world when I say, *huh?*"

"Private joke," said Miranda. She squeezed the faded book still in her hand, and laughter returned to her voice. "Apparently we neglected crucial elements of your education."

Ally laughed. "Yeah, instead of practicing *Neijing*, *Seamm Jasani* and *Aikido*, I should probably have read more Shakespeare."

"Tennyson, actually," Miranda said. "But, point taken. Try not to worry about your father. We still don't know it was him that they caught. Nelsie's always been a very resourceful boy. And if Teo got away, it's possible that he did also."

"Why wouldn't he contact me?" she asked.

"Maybe he has," Miranda said. "Maybe you just haven't

gotten the message. He'd never use this line. Only me. Tell me this, Little One. Have you felt his absence, or is it the fear of that possibility that you feel in your heart?"

Ally took a deep breath and scanned her body. Plenty of tight swirls of tension, but none of them felt like father-death. "No," she said. "It doesn't feel like he's dead."

"Pay attention to that," Miranda said. "And be careful. I'm not ready to lose you."

"I'm not ready to be lost," Ally said. "You be careful, too. I don't want to lose you either."

Miranda laughed. "Don't worry. As you said, I've made it 12 years. I can play this game a little longer. As long as necessary."

"I need to go. Take care of yourself. I love you, Aunt Miranda."

"I love you, too, Little One," Miranda said. She deleted the number and placed the phone back into *Idylls*. She pressed the worn, leather storybook to her heart.

"'Doubt not,'" she whispered. "'Go forward.'" She gently placed the treasure back into its display case. "'If thou doubt, the Beasts will tear thee piecemeal.'"

***

Ally settled back onto the sofa.

Do I tell them? They already know it's dangerous. Maybe telling them would just make it worse.

"Hello?" Cary said. He knocked three times on the cedar chest. "Anybody home?"

"What? Oh. Sorry. Preoccupied."

"I was saying I thought you had an iPhone," Cary said.

"Oh, well," Ally said, shaking her head to clear the cobwebs of fear. "That's mostly for getting information. This one is special. Secure. Only for emergencies."

"We have an emergency?" he said.

Out on the sidewalk, a tall, thin man in a dark suit walked past the entrance to the coffee shop and stopped directly behind Ally. He reached under his coat with his right hand. Cary opened his mouth to warn her, but she cut him off.

"If you're worried about that man in the suit," she said, "he's not a threat." Even as she spoke, the man tapped his cell phone and began speaking into it.

"How…" he began, but Ally pointed to the photograph on the wall behind him.

"Reflection," she said.

Cary squeezed the necklace in his hand. He had still not placed it back around his neck, and he had forgotten, for the moment, about any potential emergencies.

"Can I take a look at that thing?" Simon asked.

Cary handed it to him, and Simon turned it over a couple of times in his hand. He studied the dots. "This kind of looks like a constellation," he said. "Have you shown it to an astronomer?"

"Damn," Ally said, sitting forward. "Dr. Whitt. Everything's so crazy, I keep forgetting." She turned to Renee. "Is there a payphone in here?"

"You can use my cell," Renee offered.

"Thanks," Ally said. "But a payphone would actually be better."

The phone was in the middle of its fifth ring before anyone picked up.

"This is Dr. Whitt."

"Thank God," she said. "Harvey, it's Alethea."

"Good God, girl! Where have you been? I expected to see you after that weekend in March. What happened? "

"But I tried to call you. Several times. They said you had decided to take a sabbatical."

"What? No. I've been right here. I've even spoken to your father, and we both know how rare that is. Who told you I was… Oh, never mind that now. You won't believe what I found out. Your friend has no idea what he's walking around with. I have to see that piece again."

"Oh my God, when?" Ally said. "When did you talk to Daddy? How long ago?"

"Two weeks, maybe two and a half. He was worried about you."

A sob escaped from Ally's heart. *Alive!*

"Did he tell you how to get in touch with him?" she said.

"You're kidding, right?" Whitt said. "Have you met the man? But he did leave a message for you. He said to tell you that Selu holds the key."

"That's it?" she asked.

"That's it," Whitt said.

"Who in the wide world of sports is Selu?"

"Corn Woman, of course," he said.

"Of course," she said. "*Not.*"

"Corn Woman. Selu is the First Woman. From the *Tsalagi* creation story."

"*Tsalagi.* Like Cherokee?"

"Exactly. There's a statue of her at the Casino in North Carolina. What do you think it means?"

"No idea. So tell me about the necklace?"

"Oh! Oh! Right," Whitt said. "Very exciting! Very exciting! Let me get my papers." The phone hit the desk with a thud, and Ally heard papers being shuffled around. Something broke with a splash.

"Are you sitting down?" Whitt said when he returned to the phone.

"Actually I'm at a payphone in a hallway," she said. "So I'll have to take my chances. Go ahead."

***

Ally rejoined Cary and Simon by the window, a faraway smile on her face. Renee was at the espresso station making a vanilla latte for a bald mountain of a man in Carhartt overalls.

How could I not have been able to tell what it was? Why can't I feel its vibration?

"So?" Cary asked. "What did he say?"

Ally extended her open palm. "Gimme."

Simon passed the talisman to her. Ally held it in her left fist, closed her eyes and took a deep breath. Nothing. No sense of its vastness whatsoever. How could that be? She opened her hand and pointed to the end. "This part," she said, "the composite on the ends. Whitt says this is white tail dear antler mixed with pine resin. It's about a 150 years old."

"Sounds about right," Cary said. "I always figured some Cherokee made this and left it there. Thought maybe I'd do some research one day, but I never got around to—"

Ally held up her hand. "That's not all," she said. She looked at Simon. "He was right about the markings, too. What do you know about astronomy?"

300

"Just the usual," Simon said. "Big Dipper. Little Dipper, Seven Sisters. Orion's Belt. That's about it."

Cary nodded. "Me, too."

She turned the talisman over so he could see the design better. "This is a constellation. Draco. The dragon."

Cary looked at the still-exposed dragon on his arm, then across the room at Renee. She smiled and rippled her fingers.

"But," Ally said, "there's an extra star in it. Right here." She indicated the next to last spot on the tail.

"So? Does that tell us anything?" Cary asked.

"Why would a constellation have a star in it that's not there?" she asked.

Cary thought about it. If this was a quiz, he was failing. He held his palms up in question.

"Maybe the guy that carved it just got it wrong," Simon said.

"Or maybe," she said, "that star used to be there."

"Okay," Cary replied. "So?"

"There's more." She shook her head. "The rest of the piece is bone, all right. Human bone. A small section of a wrist. Probably female. But not a 150 years old. That's just the stuff in the ends."

Time hovered above them like a cresting wave.

"The wrist bone," she said, "is somewhere near 500,000 years old."

Cary tried, not for the first time since meeting this woman, to wrap his mind around the enormity of information she revealed. "You mean I have been walking around with a...an artifact...that predates recorded history, just dangling from a piece of leather around my neck."

"No wonder those guys are out to get you," Simon said. "Jeez! That thing must be worth..."

"I don't know." Ally looked down at the necklace.

"What?" Cary said. "What do you mean you don't know? It has to be. What else could they want from me? I don't have anything else." Ally shook the pendant around in her curled hand.

"Heavy," she said. "Remember what Dr. Whitt told us.

He said it was heavy. Too heavy for bone. Maybe what they're after isn't the necklace, but what's inside it."

Cary took the necklace back. "I can't open it up," he said.

Ally weighed the finality of his statement.

"Why?" Simon asked.

Cary couldn't pull his gaze away from the dots marking the smooth surface. His mouth shaped to form words, but none would come. He had been able to keep the voices buried beneath the calm ocean sound, but now they barked out like angry dogs.

Cary closed his eyes. The whoosh and flash of flying blades assaulted his inner vision; a hurricane of knives, swords, axes, and spears blew toward him, clanging and ringing in a deadly gale. Like a Loony Tune. Like Roger Rabbit. Except these were terrifying. He shook his head, and they scattered to mist.

"Cary?" Ally asked. She shook him by the shoulder. "Cary!" He looked up.

"I don't know," he said. "It makes me feel sick? Like crying?" He lowered the necklace back over his head. "Like dying." They sat in silence for a moment. Renee brought three large to-go cups to them.

"We should get moving," Ally said. They stood, but Simon pulled up short.

"Whoa," he said. "What the hell is that guy?"

His gaze had fallen upon the raggedy man in the other window.

Ally shook her head. "Saw him when we came in. Not a threat." She looked into the distant shadows over the man's head. "But there is something…unique…about him."

"That's just old Maddy Shope," Renee said. "Nothing dangerous about him. He's in here all the time. And I mean *all* the time. Always scratching away in his notebooks. Writing. Making drawings." She laughed. "Sometimes I think he might have been here writing in one of those notebooks before I even opened the place."

They said their goodbyes. Cary held Renee before they left.

Their passion had long departed, but love remained. Now, when he held her, it was a reminder of a contract fulfilled.

"Something's terribly wrong, isn't it?" she said.

Cary nodded. The voices in his head tried to rise again; he closed his eyes and concentrated on the ocean. "But it's nothing for you to worry about."

Renee remained inside and watched from behind the front door glass as the Gremlin slipped away with Cary behind the wheel. She released an encyclopedic sigh and turned, almost in a daze, to the wildman in the front window.

"You need a refill, Mr. Shope?" she said.

Maddy Shope jerked upright, arms flailing, ready to defend himself. Even as his face relaxed in recognition, a tower of Moleskin notebooks, each cover labeled in perfect white letters identifying it as the property of one Madeg Shope, each dated and identified by a different title carefully inscribed in the same white ink, cascaded to the floor. Renee scooped several into her arms and deposited them onto the table.

"*Gray Star*," she said, her index finger *tap tap tapping* the curlycue letters on the cover of the topmost book. "What's that?"

Madeg Shope leaned back in his chair and took her measure. He turned the book over to expose the darkness of the back cover. Then he cut his gaze to the end of the street where the Gremlin idled at the intersection, waiting for permission to proceed. Shope's deep and haunted eyes softened into something like compassion.

"Gray Star's coming," he said. "Ain't nothing they can do about it." He tugged on a silver fob, and a dead pocket watch tumbled out of his vest to land with a soft slap in his palm. He stared for a moment into the face of time. The hands were frozen at 11:11. "Be here any minute."

"What do you mean?" she said. "Nothing *who* can do about it?"

Madeg Shope raised a furtive eyebrow at the window. Red changed to green; the Gremlin eased through the intersection.

"Them friends of yours, of course," he said. "Don't need to tell you nothing. Already know, don't you. They're in for trouble. Big trouble." He looked at the ceiling. "Gray Star'll be here any second."

***

They were almost to Burnsville before anyone spoke.

"So," Ally asked. "Who was she?"

"Oh," Cary said with a long sigh. "Just someone I once thought was the love of my life." Emma's eyes filled his thoughts, and a warm smile rose from his heart. "Doesn't matter anymore. Now she's a friend."

"And a messenger," said Ally. "It's no accident that you found a representation of Draco and that she had it tattooed on her back."

"Maybe it was subconscious," said Simon. "Because the image on the necklace was so present in your mind. Stuff like that happens."

"No," Cary said. "I mean, yeah, it does. But it couldn't have here."

"Why not?" Ally asked.

"Because. I got her the tattoo more than 10 years ago. Five years before I found the necklace. Renee was the woman I went to Tampa to forget."

***

Ripu Dasi saturated his atoms with the image of the human Ras Graal had shown him. In the ethereal presence of his being, the architecture of a human body constructed itself as an idea.

He hovered on the lip of one of the remaining vortices that articulated to Earth. Only Dasi, Ras Graal, and the handful of Grastar who were already walking the earth in human form knew of this particular portal.

The gravity of the whirlpool unraveled his borders,

inviting him to spin into its center.

Not yet. He coalesced the matrix of the human in his mind. When the corpus was fully realized, he fell into the wide mouth of the transfer vortex.

In the space of a few nanoseconds, Ripu Dasi transformed into a stream of pure energy that touched both Jupiter and Earth, connecting the two giants by a luminous filament a million times thinner than the finest spider web. With the power of a thought, he disattached the terminus that held him to Jupiter, and the Grastar warrior slammed to the earth with a thud. Dust rose in two tiny swirls where his feet impacted the dry gravel parking lot in Burnsville. Soon it would be time to rendezvous with Carver and Layton, though neither of them knew that yet.

Ripu Dasi stretched his two human arms and took a deep breath. The first true air he had breathed in 50 earth centuries tasted delicious. But not as delicious as the hot splash of blood that was yet to come.

ELEVENTH ARTICULATION

...and a thud...

Selu

a drunken master

dark dreams

new guys and new beasts

promises remembered

deva footprints

an assassin

...and yet another thud

Present Day

Cary took the left fork into Burnsville. A minute later, they passed Winter Star Trading Post where Cary had first seen Ally in the parking lot only a few months before. The billboard announcing the Appalachian Storytelling Festival had long since been papered over with the list of last summer's Playbill for the Parkway Playhouse. Cary turned on the left blinker. A heavy thump shook the ground.

"What the hell was that?" Simon said. Ally pressed her hand to her chest.

Cary pointed to a stony gash in the mountains to the south. "Strip mines," he said. "Probably blasting. Happens all the time. Used to knock my pictures off the walls."

None of them noticed the man with outstretched arms in the Winter Star parking lot.

"Wait a minute," Ally said. "Turn right. Go into town."

Cary circled the town square and parked in front of the old, brick library. A faded poster for *Unto These Hills* hung diagonal from a single thumbtack.

"So?" Cary said. "Are we not going to my house?"

"They'll be coming," she said. "They might already be waiting for us there."

"Umm, didn't we already know that?" Simon said. Cary nodded.

"It's worse than that," Ally said. "We knew they'd

probably be there, but the call I got…it's going to be ugly…I think they're planning to kill each other, too. I'm not sure what we should do."

"We have to go anyway," Cary said. He pressed is fingers to his lips. The words had escaped his mouth before he knew he said them.

Ally smiled. The wind kicked up and set the poster swinging back and forth on the library wall. "I think we should wait. First, we need to go to Cherokee."

"Cherokee?" Simon and Cary said in unison.

Ally nodded. "I got a message from my father. He's alive." She smiled at the thought. "I think he left a message there for us. We've waited this long. One more day won't matter. And maybe we'll be able to go into the bear's cave with a little more wisdom tomorrow than we have today."

They drove to Asheville, high on the reprieve of at least one more day before having to face big, ugly, scary guys. Simon treated them to rooms on the Club Floor at the Grove Park Inn, and they spent the evening basking in the luxury of spa pools and room service.

Simon got a facial.

"Might as well enjoy it today," he said. "Don't know what the hell might happen tomorrow."

At dawn the next day they checked out and dropped the Gremlin off in Montford, where a faded, midnight blue '67 Impala was waiting in front of a '20s apartment building called The Francis. Cary looked at the window on the top floor. A score of gaunt nuns pressed pale faces against the murky glass. Their covetous eyes plucked at his edges, trying to catch a strand of his mind and unravel him into their world. Cary clenched his own eyes like a desperate fist and shook his head. When he looked again, they were gone.

Almost two hours later, Ally pulled the Impala into a dirt and gravel parking lot near Harrah's Casino in Cherokee. Thick clouds obscured the October sun, and the tourist traffic was low. Selu's statue stood at the other end of the lot atop a truncated pyramid in the center of a low mound.

***

Elias Carver eased a rented, gray Chrysler 300 into the Ingles parking lot in Burnsville. He carried a Glock 19 in a shoulder holster under his left arm and a folding *karambit* clipped lengthwise to his belt. He did not remember the last time he had felt the need to arm himself, but these were special circumstances.

Stokes waited behind the wheel of a black Suburban; four operatives sat silent in the back. Carver looked them over as he climbed into the front. One was unfamiliar.

"Who's this?" Carver asked. He spoke to Stokes, but looked directly at the soldier. This guy was truly black, as black as anyone Carver had ever seen, and Carver had seen and worn all varieties of dark skin in his time. The man held Carver's gaze for only a few seconds before looking away. Business as usual.

"Arnie Booth," Stokes said. "Replacing Boyette. Flew in and met us here this morning."

"I thought Boyette recovered," Carver said. He continued to stare at Booth, who glanced up briefly every few seconds.

"He was okay up until a few days ago. Then he just dropped dead." A hint of a smile almost flitted across Booth's mouth.

"Dropped?" said Carver. "Dead?"

Stokes nodded. "Maybe that Profett bitch learned the *dim mak.*"

Carver waved the notion away. She was good, but probably not that good.

"You trust him?

"Got him from Goons 'R' Us, just like the rest of them," Stokes said. He waited a beat for the laugh that didn't come. "Yeah. I trust him. You know I check everyone out."

Carver nodded. "You know what you're doing, Mr. Booth?" Carver asked.

"I get the job done," he said.

"Good enough," Carver said. He turned back to Stokes. "Where's Layton?"

"Just talked to Cord," Stokes said. "We're going to meet behind the old Avondale plant west of town. What's the plan?"

"We'll send in a recon team through the woods. The rest of us will go in after we know what's up." He paused.

"I'm getting the sense," Stokes said, "that there is more?"

"Do you remember a few months ago when I told you we may find it necessary to return to our old arrangement with Layton?"

Stokes nodded. He failed to hold back his smile.

"Assign each man a counterpart from Layton's team. When I give the order, I want them put down before they can blink. I'll take Layton myself." He turned to the back seat. "Understood?"

The men nodded as a unit.

"It looks like you picked a good day to join us, Mr. Booth," Carver said. "It's going to be rocking and rolling. Now, let's go meet my erstwhile partner and his walking corpses."

***

Ally looked at the statue.

"Dr. Whitt said 'Selu holds the key,'" she said.

"Maybe the answer's corn?" Simon said.

They both gave him the idiot look.

"What?" said Simon. "You two geniuses have a better answer?"

"Not really," said Cary.

They all noticed the old Native American man at the same time. He was watching them from the other side of the lot.

"You think we're safe here?" Simon asked. Ally took the man in with a glance. His clothes were old and stained with the uniformity that comes with constant wear. She scanned the surroundings. The lot was still almost empty. No one else was in sight.

"Probably safer than most places," she said. "He wants something though. Just keep checking out the statue. I've got this."

The man tacked toward them like a drunken schooner. A lazy dust trail stirred behind his footsteps and drifted west on the slight breeze. Ally slid her right leg behind her left and cocked her hips. She waited until the man was in the process of stepping up onto the mound before she spun smoothly to face him. He stopped, teetering for a moment, one foot on the ground and the other on the rise.

Maybe, thought Simon, *somebody else is going to fall on his ass. Cool.*

The man's equilibrium stabilized, but if he had been planning anything aggressive, he was at a disadvantage. For a moment he offered only a glazed stare with bloodshot eyes; a sour fog of rum-soaked pheromones cloyed the air. Then a quick gust pushed aside the clouds. The stench of alcohol sweat disappeared.

Sunlight reflected off Selu's outstretched hand and into the old man's face. He put a palm up to shade his eyes. When he took it away, his vision was clear. More than clear. Bright. Wise. Ancient. He held up both of his hands, palms forward.

"I am no danger to you," he said. His voice was strong, his speech unslurred. He eased his other foot up to the mound and focused on Cary. "You have enough of that without me, I think." Ally and Cary exchanged a quick glance.

"How do you—" Cary said, but Ally held her hand up, just slightly, just enough.

"We're all in danger sometimes," she said.

"Sometimes," said the man, his ancient eyes still locked onto Cary's, "the danger is closer than others. Your danger is very near. You are traveling to it. You are walking into the mouth of the bear."

His hand snapped forward and took hold of the talisman. Again a flash of sunlight reflected off Selu's hand, into the old man's eyes and, this time, into Cary's. He fought the urge to back away. The moment teetered on the edge of sanity.

"Uktenah," said the old man. His voice was barely a whisper, but it echoed like a thunderclap. A roar grew in Cary's inner world; behind it, voices screamed unintelligible war cries. Cary sought the calm of the ocean, but it was nowhere to be found. In its place he heard the soughing of a high wind, the tinkling of a thousand bells, a single flute. The old man was talking. Cary struggled to anchor his attention to this one, earthly sound. "You carry within you," he said, "the strength of the dragon." A series of images flickered across Cary's inner screen as the old man spoke. *His and Renee's tattoos.* "But the dragon is eating you up." *The indigo snake walking on four legs.* "Because you resist him." *Draco shining in the night sky.* "Stop fighting your dragon and..." *The talisman.* "...become him so you can kill the real monsters."

The inner sounds and the barrage of images stopped. The ensuing silence was deafening. It took all of Cary's will to keep looking into the bright chasm of this man's eyes.

"Do you want to ask me anything?" the man said.

Cary remained lost on the borders of the world that lay behind those eyes.

"How will I know what to do?" he asked, finally. The man looked into him for a long time, perhaps measuring his answer, or perhaps finding the answer to Cary's own question somewhere deep inside Cary himself.

"You do not have to know what to do," the old man said. "Only do what you must."

"But how will I—"

"Be a hollow bone," the old man said. He released his grip on the necklace so that it fell against the center of Cary's chest with a soft thump. "Empty yourself of who you think you should be, and who you *are* will rush like wind through a hollow bone. Then you will always do that which must be done."

Cary took an involuntary step back, but his eyes remained fixed upon the old man's. Clouds scudded back together to block the sun.

Before Time

~

Ksama

People have been busy here on the Island of Dreams. But whoever they were, they are long gone now, for Ksama finds not a soul, or any evidence of recent habitation. She does, however, find workshops, tools, a scullery stocked with dried goods, sleeping chambers, and a library that dwarfs even the Grand Library of Apsara. She might be alone, but she has enough knowledge at her fingertips to keep her learning for many lifetimes.

Still, large sections of the temple remain inaccessible. The many rooms she has found comprise the outer edges of the structure, but the central area seems to have no entrance.

That night she chooses her sleeping quarters, a large, domed chamber on the third level with a huge window that offers up the night sky. Ksama lies in the soft bed, experiencing the first comfort she has felt in weeks. Her body aches from toil. Her right arm burns as if it remains in the fire. Her left fist throbs with fresh bruises. Her heart aches with loneliness and abandonment. She sobs until sleep overtakes her and dark dreams sweep her into an inner world.

She lies naked on a sacrificial altar of rough stone, surrounded by a mob of more than a million souls. They scream her name. Pointing. Accusing. They hunger to tear her to pieces. Within the din of the crowd, two voices quietly debate her disposition. All night the mob rails and the two contenders vie for her soul while Ksama curls in a ball on the altar, trying to cover her nakedness with her inadequate hands, awaiting judgment, awaiting a fate beyond her control. In the morning the dream flits away like the wrens and chickadees outside her window. But a sinkhole has opened in her chest, and Ksama walks one step closer to the abyss of madness.

Each night the dark dreams return, and each day her shadows creep further into the bright day. Her forgotten vow lives just beyond the borders of her memory. Sh'ele and her severed hand remain in the abandoned leather sheath in the entry chamber.

One night she awakens to the darkness of a new moon. Dawn is less than an hour away. The stench of rotting flesh fouls the air of her sleep chamber. She sits up and presses back against the wall, pulling quilts and pillows around her. Something is in her room. Whatever this thing is, it brings with it an absence of light deeper than the moonless night. Rasping breaths scrape at the silence. Ksama can almost imagine the thing's outline, almost sense its contours. The creature raises a feral face to the ceiling and sniffs. It takes a step in her direction, then stops.

Ksama is paralyzed on her soft bed. Her right hand throbs, and she reaches with it to take up DevaRada even though the hand is no longer there.

The beast is stalking now, searching. Hunting. In a flash of insight Ksama realizes what the creature seeks.

Sh'ele!

Her reality shifts. The here and now blink away, and Ksama trembles in an inner pocket of reality where nothing exists but her own thoughts. The events that had brought her to this moment collapse into a single point and explode, assaulting her with memories. *Syrgala. Sidra. The Varuna. Dissolving the Pravarna. Amputating her arm. The holographic vision floating above Sh'ele. Her guidance. Her duty. Her destiny. And the*

Queen of Light.

DevaSurya's words flash like lightning on the sky of her mind. She hears and sees them at the same time. "You have work to do. Stop feeling sorry for yourself and do it." And Ksama's own words follow the flash of insight, echoing like distant thunder.

I promise to hide you and protect you, now and forever, until you rise. How could I have forgotten this promise?

Back in the *Varuna*, when Ksama first heard the Grace's pronouncement, she was so certain that doing this work would be a simple matter. Just begin and continue. What could be easier? But the accomplishment has been far from simple. She carried more than Sh'ele up the mountain with her. She carried anger and resentment. The weight of her own self-pity pressed her face to the gritty floor, where no work was possible.

And now I cower in the nascent dawn behind soft pillows on my soft bed like a spoiled, frightened child waiting for Myrtu to come take me.

A scream stirs in her soul, a scream powerful enough to sustain her for lifetimes. She lets just a portion of it loose and dives from her bed, taking up DevaRada in her good left hand as she flies.

"Enough," she says. "I have had enough!"

She arcs DevaRada forward, hilt first, blade back. Ksama is not well-trained in the art of the sword, as her encounter with Sidra brought home so clearly. She is not trained at all with her left hand. Nevertheless, she advances.

The beast's stench still cloys the air. Ksama tilts on the balls of her feet to drive forward, but when the half light of dawn reaches its tipping point, she finds her bed chamber empty. She searches the adjacent rooms. Checks the outer doors. Nothing. All is secure.

Her search delivers her at last to the entrance chamber, where Sh'ele waits, wrapped with her hand in the leather sheath. Ksama kneels before them. She reaches for the lashings twice and draws her hand back until finally, on the third try, she pulls the leather straps away, untying the bindings. She places her sword within easy reach in case the phantom beast turns out to be real.

How could she have lost her vision? How much time has she wasted, crawling from day to day, feeling sorry for herself, doing nothing but surviving?

Ksama shakes her head and hopes that she has not waited too long. She peels away the wings of the leather sheath. Only at this very moment does she own that she has been cowering from this task. A sticky ball of anxiety lurches in her belly. She fears that seeing her hand will make the loss more real somehow than simply passing each day with only one hand.

When she last looked upon the thing, it seemed monstrous. She pulls the flap away, expecting to find rot and putrefaction. But her hand is beautiful. Encrusted in sparkling salt. Perfectly preserved. She knows suddenly that it is not just the salt water; it's Sh'ele. The energy of the crystal has preserved it.

She takes her hand into the workshop and works all that day and into the night. She peels away the skin and sews it into a small pouch with the sign of Uktenah displayed on the front. Muscle and sinew strip easily from the bone. A small section of ulna has separated from the wrist.

"Become hollow," she says. She can almost feel the heat of DevaSurya's smile.

She scrapes out the marrow with a narrow chisel and polishes the surface with fine pumice stones. Using a sharp awl, she scratches from memory a series of dots onto the smooth bone and presses inky paste into the depressions. Ksama hangs the piece around her neck on a leather thong, then assembles the bones of her hand into the Anucara sign of blessing and mounts it vertical on a wooden base.

Sh'ele remains exposed on its leather bed in the entry chamber. Another baby crystal has broken away from the base. Ksama reaches for it, and a sob catches in her throat, for lying next to this small crystal is the spike with which she took Sidra's life. Dried blood still clings to the point. Her hesitant hand takes up the crystal and presses it to her heart.

The blood-stained tip knocks against the wrist bone hanging around her neck, and flecks of Sydra's blood flake away to land upon the sweaty skin between Ksama's breasts. She sobs once, but this sob is no cousin to the self-pitied weeping she has known since she arrived. This is a cry of respect. Though this spike is an instrument of death, it deserves a place of honor in her history. She lays the spike alongside Sh'ele and places its small sister in her pocket.

A word shines in her thoughts like a fire beacon signaling a vessel long lost at sea. Her mouth opens, and she releases the word into the world.

At first she thinks the dancing lights are fireflies, but the more Ksama sings her word, the more the lights take on human form. The *AosSidhe*. Tiny creatures of light fly in from every direction, summoned by this secret word. They assemble on the stone wall behind Sh'ele until the entire surface is a solid sheet of light. Then, with a sound like the bowing of a million violins, the lights blink out, and the wall returns to normal. Except now there is an arched entryway through what, only seconds before, had been solid stone. The *Sidhe* are gone, having performed their duty. Ksama rises, cradles Sh'ele in her arms, and passes through the portal.

The Inner Sanctuary is one gigantic room. Crystals and gemstones of all shapes, sizes, and colors form sigils that write an esoteric narrative on the walls, creating a vast chamber of protection. At the center of the room, an altar stands on a dais directly beneath a circular window in the dome ceiling. Upon the altar, an elegant gold and silver frame waits empty.

"How can this be?" Ksama says. The frame is identical to the one that held Sh'ele in the Temple of Uktenah.

Present Day

Rum and sweat once again floated on the slight breeze. The glow behind the old man's eyes faded, and he stumbled backward a step.

"Spare some change?" he said. His voice was shaky and rough. Cary dredged up a handful of bills and change from his jeans and passed them to the old man.

"Hey!" The shout came from behind Cary, and was followed by the approach of running boots. The old man hastily stuffed the treasure into his dirty jeans. "No! No!" the approaching man shouted. He, too, was Native American, about 35, dressed in an expensive tan suit and shiny brown boots. "How many times have I told you, Billy? No begging from the tourists." He gripped the old man by the upper right arm. Billy stared at the ground.

"We aren't tourists," Cary said.

"What?" said the younger man.

"What he means is," Ally said, "Billy wasn't begging. He gave us a gift. And we gave him a gift in return." The younger man released his unsure grip on Billy. "I thought," Ally continued, "that it was your tradition to revere your elders."

"I'm sorry," he said. He looked down. "It's just that...I'm sorry." He turned and walked away.

"Thank you," Ally said.

Billy nodded.

"Yes," Cary said. "Thank you." He shook Billy's limp hand.

Cary was opening the passenger door to the Impala when he felt the hand on his shoulder. He spun quickly, sweeping his arm to block the attack. But there was no attacker, only the man who had interrupted their encounter with Billy. He stepped back, easily avoiding Cary's hands. Ally stood at the driver's side. Simon, already in the back, watched through the open window.

"I wanted to apologize," he said. "Sometimes old Billy hits the tourists up for spare change." He shrugged. "It's a problem." He held out his hand. "I'm David Johnson, David Two Feathers. I run the museum." He pointed to the large, modern building across the parking lot from the Casino.

"No problem," Cary said. He reached behind him for the door handle.

"What's it mean to be a hollow bone?" Ally asked. Cary waited, suspended between question and answer.

"We are different from you," David said. "We believe Spirit is present in all things, not separate from us."

"Not so different," Ally said, and shrugged.

David nodded.

"All right," he said. "Maybe not so different from you. But different than most."

Ally nodded back.

"Spirit doesn't just live inside things," David said. "It moves through things. Everything. But people? We have choices. We can stop...no, not really stop...but limit...how Spirit moves through us. Or increase it. There's a saying. 'Let Spirit flow through you like wind through a hollow bone.' It's a very old belief."

"How old?" Cary asked.

"Some say it's from our people. Some say the Lakota. But really, if you go back far enough, it's all the same. Lakota. Cherokee. Aniyunwiya. LeMurian. Whatever you got."

"All that rises must converge," Ally said, her voice barely more than a whisper.

"Exactly," David said. "All the same." He watched Cary's

hand cradling the pendant. "May I see that?" he asked.

A gust of wind lifted particles of dirt and sand in a spiral dance that swirled around the three of them for a moment.

"It's all right, Cary," Ally said. "Let him see it."

Cary looked over the faded roof of the Impala at Ally. She nodded. He looked back at Two Feathers and slipped the necklace over his head. Ally walked around the car to join the two men on the passenger side. Simon hung his head out the window like a curious puppy.

Two Feathers received the piece with reverence. He turned it over in his hand several times, examined the ends, and rubbed his finger over the markings. When he spoke, his voice was low and far away, almost a whisper, but filled with the presence of a landscape larger than the mountains in which they stood.

"Uktenah," he said.

"What?" Cary asked. "Billy said that, too. Why did you say that?"

David stared at Cary, not understanding the question. He seemed to be somewhere else.

"You said, 'Uktenah,'" Ally said. "Is that right?"

Two Feathers nodded and returned to the present. "Yes," he said, tapping the pendant. "Uktenah. This is Uktenah."

"What?" asked Cary. "The pendant?"

David Two Feathers nodded, then shook his head, then nodded again. "The pendant. No. Not the pendant. The design. The dots." He held up the piece and traced his finger along the dots, then pointed up. "In the sky. Europeans call this 'Draco,'" he said. "But to us, this is Uktenah."

Cary looked at Ally, smiled, and shook his head. Ally's eyebrows said, "Told you so."

"Tell us about Uktenah," Ally said.

"The legends get all mixed up," he said. "Uktenah became the boogie man. 'Go to bed, or Uktenah will get you.' Like that. But in the true legend, Uktenah is the Horned Serpent God that has lived in Hourglass Mountain since the beginning of time, when these old mountains were young islands. The Islands of Dreams. They say our whole continent grew from the Islands of Dreams. Well, really, from the Sacred Crystal hidden in them. One of Uktenah's titles is Protector of the Sacred Crystal."

"The Sacred Crystal?" Cary said.

David nodded. "You know," he said, "you are the second person I've talked to about Uktenah in the last few weeks."

"What?" Ally said.

"He told me you'd be coming. I didn't realize it was you. He said there would only be two."

"Nelson," Ally said.

David nodded. "He's your father, isn't he? I can see it now."

Ally nodded. Her eyes teared. She knew Nelson was alive, but talking to someone who had actually seen him made the reality even more certain.

"But why here?" Cary asked.

"The statue," Ally said. "Selu. Did you see her hand light up?"

David nodded. He smiled. "People walk by that statue every day. They look at her hand hovering over the corn stalk, the symbol of creation. Very few people know that she has a design imbedded into her hand. A serpent. Uktenah. But your father knew."

"But still," Cary said. "How could he know—"

"He didn't know what would happen," Ally said. "Just that something would. He learned about your necklace from Dr. Whitt. I have no idea how he knew about Selu's hand, but he did know that the symbol on her hand would speak to the symbol on your necklace, and that something would happen. He just didn't know it would happen through Billy."

David nodded again. "You know," he said, "there are many legends of Ancient Ones borrowing bodies in order to speak to someone in need. Maybe Billy is more of a hollow bone than I thought."

***

Three-tenths of a mile from Cary's home, the narrow driveway passes an old, clapboard house, then takes a sharp right turn, hugging sheer rock on the right and pulling farther away from the Cane River. Adjacent to the house, a smallish field stands overgrown with chest-high weeds gone golden in the death of autumn.

Carver pulled the empty black Suburban into the field and waited. Stokes and his team had already hiked in across the back of Turkey Ridge. Layton eased an identical Suburban behind him. Cord sat in the passenger seat; four of his men waited in the back.

A rusty screen door creaked at the back of the house. The old woman who stepped halfway out wore a faded blue, hand-sewn cotton dress with a full, white apron. Ninety-five if she was a day. Her lank, white hair caught the sunlight and lit up like a halo. She sniffed the air once, tossed her head, then disappeared into her kitchen. The long spring slammed the screen door with an indignant slap. None of the men flinched. All had been aware of her presence.

Soft wind rippled golden waves across the tall grass. Carver sensed Stokes' presence in the cover of the weeds a moment before he popped up next to the window.

"How's it look?"

"Walker and the girl aren't there," Stokes said. "Someone else though. Some old man. About 70. Looks harmless enough."

"Vehicles?"

"Only Walker's. I think it's been there since last time we were here."

Carver thought for a moment. "You think it's a trap?" he asked.

"No way," Stokes said. "He's a sitting duck, whoever he is."

"All right," Carver said. "Take Cord and his team and assume positions around the house. Layton and I will drive in and pay the old guy a visit. Wait for my signal." Carver made sure Layton was still in the other Suburban. "And remember your other instructions."

Stokes nodded. "All in place." He looked back to Cord and twirled his finger in the air. Cord and his men climbed out of the truck. Within seconds all six of them had disappeared into the grass. Layton climbed into the first Suburban with Carver.

"Who do you suppose it is?" Layton asked. Carver eased the Suburban back onto the driveway. Inside the old house, white cotton curtains fell back into place.

"Doesn't matter," Carver replied. "How much of a threat could some old guy be by himself?" He threaded the SUV through a tunnel of rhododendrons until they emerged onto a long, wide driveway.

The old man was tall and barrel-chested, with a full head of gunmetal hair and gray-blue eyes. He leaned against the barn-red deck railing and watched Carver back the Suburban up to the end of the driveway. Carver waved. Everybody waved up here in the mountains, Carver had learned. Made them trust each other. The old guy waved back.

"Help you?" the old man said. His voice was deep, rich. For a moment, he seemed to shimmer in the morning light. The energy was high up here. Carver could not feel the presence of the Sh'ele. Something must be masking its location. A spell, or a special container. Still, even without the object's activity, lines of energy were popping in all directions.

"This your place?" Layton said.

"That's a real nice truck you got there," the man said. "What do you call that thing?"

"It's a Suburban," Layton said. "Chevy. So, is this your place?" The old man took his measure, but when he found Layton's eyes, they slid right by. Carver and Layton were climbing the short stairway up the deck. The man leaned over the railing and watched their ascent.

"Them fellows up there in the woods with you?" the man said.

Mountain men, thought Carver. *A lot sharper than they look.*

"Bring it on in, Mr. Cord," Layton shouted. Ten men

324

emerged from the wall of foliage a few feet from the house. In seconds they had climbed over the railing and taken up positions on the deck. Arnie Booth hung back, almost invisible in the shadowy overhang where the deck railing met the rear wall of the house.

Layton raised his eyebrows at Carver. Carver shrugged. Time for a more direct approach.

"I am Cyrus Layton," he said, extending his hand. "This is my associate, Elias Carver." The old man hesitated a moment and then shook both of their hands.

"And these fellows?" he said.

"They're our assistants," Layton said.

"You folks got a lot of assistants. What you need so many assistants for?" The man looked up at Carver's face, and then quickly away. But his eyes met and lingered on Cord and Stokes. Layton ignored the question.

"We're looking for Cary Walker," Layton said. "I was under the impression this was his place."

"Thought you must be," the old guy said. "I'm Arthur Walker. Cary's my son. Call me Art." Layton exchanged a quick glance with Carver. This might be useful. "So, what you need Cary for?"

"We want to help him," Layton said.

"That what all them guns are for?" Arthur said, cocking his head toward the men. No guns were visible, but each man carried an MTAR-21 suspended from a strap under the back of his jacket. The straps were virtually invisible against the black shirts the men wore.

"Believe it or not, Art," Carver said, "those guns are almost never necessary." *And*, he thought, *sometimes they're a liability.* "We just bring them as precaution. The fact is, we think Cary may be in trouble. We believe he is traveling in the company of a very dangerous woman." He produced a picture of Ally from his jacket pocket. "Have you ever seen your son with this woman?"

Arthur took the picture. "Don't look dangerous to me," he said.

"I suspect that I don't look dangerous to you either, Mr. Walker," Layton said. "But looks can be deceiving."

"No, Mr. Layton, Mr. Carver, you're wrong." Arthur studied the weathered grain of the deck. "I wouldn't say you don't look dangerous. Fact is, I'd say you two are about the most dangerous things I've come across in my short time on this here earth. But you're right about one thing. Looks can be deceiving. You're damn sure right about that."

"Then we understand each other," Layton said.

"Yessir, we understand each other all right," Arthur said. "But I don't know where Cary is. Or this little girl you say is so dangerous. I was kind of expecting I might find him here myself. I was just planning to wait right here until he come along home."

"Well, Art," said Carver. "Your son will be coming along home any time now. Mind if we wait?"

Art looked the men over. "I got a choice?"

"There are always choices," Layton said. "It's just that sometimes some of them produce consequences that aren't very pleasant."

Arthur Walker paused. "All right then, Mr. Layton," he said, still not meeting Layton's eyes. "Let's just make it pleasant then. I'll put on a pot of coffee, and maybe you can tell me just what kind of trouble my boy is in. And how I can help you get him out of it."

***

Ally, Cary, and Simon followed a winding dirt road up Coxcomb Mountain and hid the Impala in some trees across from a weather-worn tobacco barn near the peak. They had decided on the drive in from Cherokee to try to get into the secret cave before Carver and Layton even knew they were there. Then, even if they couldn't find anything hidden there, they'd be able to escape through the portal Ally and Cary had used before.

"Who's that?" Ally asked, cutting her eyes to the right.

Cary and Simon stopped. A lanky explosion of color had just stepped from behind the tobacco barn. Red pants. Bright green shirt. Blue vest covered with sunflowers. A safety-orange ball cap. Neon purple rubber boots.

"Dru Cuervo," Cary said. "We're about as close to him as we want to get."

"Jose's brother?" Simon said.

"No joke," Cary said. "You think that guy in DT's was weird..."

"Shope?" Ally said.

Cary nodded. "This guy's his own universe of weirdness. This ridge line marks the border of his property and state land. We stay on this side of the line and follow the ridge down the mountain. Cuervo's land leads right up to the edge of mine." He looked directly at Ally now. "Comes to a point right at the edge of my patio."

"A point?" Ally said.

Cary nodded. "Cuervo's land's triangle shaped. Well, sort of. More like an arrowhead, complete with the little curved indentations at the flat end."

Ally raised her eyebrows, but said nothing.

Cary half-nodded to Cuervo. Cuervo touched his orange ball cap in response, then stepped sideways and was gone, a riot of color vanishing beyond the edge of the gray barn.

They followed the trail northwest along the ridge that would bring them to the point of Druid Cuervo's arrowhead, above and behind Cary's house. The hike was a rough five or six miles, even if it was downhill, but it was the only way to be relatively safe. Eventually, they emerged from the tight trail into an old cemetery.

"Well," Simon said. "This looks familiar."

"You've been here before?" Cary asked.

"No, no," Simon said. "Just spent a lot of time in cemeteries over the past few months."

Thunder echoed down the mountainside from the west. Cary trailed fond fingers over the dusty tops of gravestones, and then pointed a smudged fingertip at the darkening sky above Point Misery. A huge thunderhead loomed behind the mountains. Ally found herself smiling unexpectedly.

"What's wrong with you?" Cary said. "You look like you just won the lottery."

"Yeah," said Simon, trying to catch his breath. "What's there to smile about?"

"I don't know," Ally said. "Just got this feeling that everything's going to be okay. Like when you're a little kid and your mommy walks into the room."

Cary and Simon looked at her like she had just beamed in from from Mars.

"No," she continued. "It's something more. It's like I feel when I'm with Pava, only…more real." She shook her head, still smiling. "I can't really explain it."

Lightning crackled across the western sky, and thunder rumbled again a few seconds later.

"Do you think it'll get us?" Ally asked.

"Never can tell, really," Cary said. "Sometimes they just sit there, and other times they slide between the mountains and travel along the valleys. Just depends which side of the mountain it decides to take. One thing's for sure though. Wherever it falls, it'll make the river rise."

"We'd better stay focused," Ally said. "If we're where I think we are, this is the crest of Turkey Ridge."

Cary nodded. "My house is just a couple of hundred yards down the mountain."

***

Thunder boomed behind Pava as she materialized at the bubbling source of the Cane River, just below Point Misery. She looked very much as she did in her natural state, but her skin was dark golden rather than blue. That would be a little too difficult to explain. She wore blue jeans and a heavy maroon sweater.

Wispy clouds cloaked the shoulders of the Black Mountains like a filmy shawl. The vibrations of countless gemstones overwhelmed her for a moment. Scattered clusters of quartz, garnet, and emerald sparkled in her inner vision like distant galaxies in the firmament. A thick vein of Serpentine ran like marrow through the backbone of the mountains. Pava let her thoughtlines ride the waves of energy, spreading in all directions. So much power here. She never would have guessed, even having visited this land countless times in her LightBody.

She felt a familiar presence about 10 miles northwest, high on the mountain ridge, almost at the same altitude as where she now stood. She focused her thoughts and viewed Ally walking with Cary and the reporter, Simon Boon. They were nearly to Cary's home. Pava was still over eight miles away. This was no inner landscape. She would have to find a ride, but that shouldn't be difficult for a resourceful Deva like herself. She cast out an enticing thread and hiked out of the wilderness to the nearest road.

She had only been on highway 197 for three or four minutes when a weathered blue, 1959 Chevy Apache pulled up next to her. The driver was a thin, wrinkled old man in his 70s. He wore faded bib overalls, a white thermal shirt, and a wide grin that revealed a lifetime of chewing tobacco.

"Offer you a lift, young lady?" he asked. His voice was rich and rough as freshly turned earth.

"Thank you," Pava said, opening the door. *Young lady. If you only knew.*

"Name of Clovis," he said, extending his hand. "Clovis Plowright."

"I am…Pava," she said. *Why not?*

"You a Indian or something, Miss Pava?" Her deep eyes took him in, seeing in an instant more than he would ever know of himself before he passed into the inner worlds. A kind man. A man who loved animals; a man who had been to war twice and still carried the stain of killing, even though the mountains had healed much of his sorrow. A man who had devoted most of his life to growing tobacco. A father, a grandfather. A faithful man. She let her aura shrink into the luminance of Clovis Plowright's presence, allowing his vibration to mask her own. She would need as much of the element of surprise as she could afford herself.

"Yes," she said. "Something like that."

He let the Apache glide like a leaf, falling this way and that along the switchbacks that led down the mountainside.

"It's funny, you know, miss," Clovis said. "I was just sitting to home on the porch when I got the funniest hankering to take a drive. Ain't got nowhere to go. Just thought I'd drive a while. Ain't done that in maybe 40 years. Me and the Mrs. used to drive out to Mt. Mitchell for a picnic of a Sunday afternoon. And there you was, just walking by yourself in the middle of nowhere." He stopped talking long enough to muscle the pickup around the last hairpin. "Kind of funny though." He straightened the truck out and picked up speed.

The Cane River came into view on the left, and the highway mirrored the river's meander.

"You are most kind, Clovis," Pava said. "And I am very grateful."

"So, you going into Burnsville?" he asked.

"Not that far," she said. "I am visiting some friends. I will show you where."

***

Ally visualized Pava's image and slipped a thread of her consciousness into the inner worlds. She was sure now that her surge of well-being had been a result of Pava's presence. If she had felt her that strongly, then it should be easy to make contact. She formed a vision of the chamber where Pava had instructed her for so many years, but...

Strange. She's not here.

She sensed the other presence, the one she sometimes felt hovering in the background. But no Pava. Ally focused on this other person. For a moment his face came into view. He started like he had seen a ghost, and then contact broke. Ally refocused her thoughts. Though she could no longer see the young man, and though she could still not feel the presence of her teacher, she managed to keep the thread of connection open. But the effort was draining.

Then her elation began to turn. Or rather, her joy was joined by another, more threatening sensation.

"Are you all right?' Cary asked.

"What?" Ally said, shaking her head.

"You gasped," Cary said. "Did you see something?"

"No," Ally said. "It's nothing. I'm fine." But something was amiss. Such a strange combination of feelings. Elation and well-being still hovered near like the mist hugging the mountains, but underneath the mist, an unknown danger hid.

They were nearly to the upper edge of the patio when Ally staggered and held up her hand for them to stop. "Something's wrong," she said. "Something dangerous."

Cary looked at Simon.

"No shit," Cary said.

"No," Ally said. "Something's really wrong."

"No shit," Cary said again.

"No," Ally said. "Not here. Not here. Something worse." Her eyes blinked rapidly. "Someone...someone...is...in danger. *She's* in danger." A clap of thunder echoed up river, closer now.

"*We're* in danger," Simon said. "What's wrong with you?"

"Ally!" Cary grasped her by the shoulders. Her eyes held a faraway glaze, and she wobbled on her feet. "Ally, what's wrong with you?" He shook her, and her head lolled to the left.

"Cord," Ally whispered from deep in her dreamworld. Her eyes rolled out of sight and she collapsed where she had been standing. The voice took them completely by surprise.

"Welcome home, children," Cord said. "Carry her, Mr. Walker. Time to come inside, to return to the fold, as it were." He laughed. "We've been expecting you."

"Wait just a minute..." Simon began, but stopped when Cord swung an efficient-looking automatic weapon from behind his back.

"Well, we've been expecting two of you, anyway," Cord said. "Whoever you are, you're part of the party now. Let's go."

Cary cradled Ally in front of him. He was astonished at how light she was, this woman he had seen kill four men, and who had kept him alive over the last six months. Simon led the way and Cary followed, Ally's all but lifeless body in his arms.

***

Panii Viisam hung above the vortex. A blur of light took rough shape in her thoughts and then resolved into a clear vision. *Venus. Dalam Palace. A single figure cross-legged on a prayer rug. Rahni Sisyah.* The message was clear. Time to attack. She released her hook on Jupiter's gravity and experienced a sensation of traveling in all directions at once. Then the imagined image became real.

Panii Viisam filled her lungs. She extended her arms and reveled in the rush of hot blood animating her flesh.

Weight.

Her coarse soles gripped the soft carpet.

Density.

She pressed her two sets of hands together, roughness caressing roughness, and crouched in the shadows behind Rahni Sisyah.

Blood.

Panii Viisam opened her mouth in a feral grimace.

Perhaps I will play with you a bit first. Soul seasoned with terror tastes much better than when taken by surprise.

***

When the old Apache passed the east end of Bolen's Creek Road, Pava felt Ripu Dasi's mind scan the area. She shrank further into the radiance of Clovis Plowright's aura,

332

but it was only a matter of time before the Grastar knew that she was here. She did not wish to place Clovis Plowright in any danger.

"Here," she said. "You can let me out anywhere along here."

"You sure?" he said. "Ain't nothing here but river on one side and mountain on the other."

"I am sure," she said. "I will cross here. But first I would like to give you something."

"Awww, now that ain't necessary at all, Miss —"

Pava leaned over, kissed him softly between the eyebrows, and whispered a word in the First Language.

A wave of forgiveness flowed from her heart, through her lips, and into the soul who was, for the moment that was this lifetime, Clovis Plowright. The tide of grace anointed him, washing him clean of a lifetime of guilt, filling him with absolution. And just in time, for he would not walk the earth much longer. Clovis stared into the blissful distance.

"Thank you," he muttered.

"You are welcome, Clovis Plowright," said Apavarita Varsah.

She descended a gentle slope and crossed the Cane River on stepping stones. Several minutes passed before she heard the Apache rumble to life and drive away.

The muddy path wound upward through rhododendrons and saplings, then followed the embankment all the way to the house. Dark groundwater seeped into Pava's deva-footprints, flooding a string of tiny lakes where she walked. She slipped off the trail and watched the play from a cluster of Mountain Laurel, still using most of her energy to conceal her presence. A small group entered the clearing above the house. First came the reporter, Simon Boon. Then Cary. In his arms he cradled the limp, unconscious Alethea. Ian Cord followed, his weapon trained directly on Cary's back.

What is wrong with Alethea? Can I risk contacting her in the inner world? Pava cast a thread of consciousness out to Rahni. *I hope you are observing this. I'm going to need all the help you can give me.*

The center of her forehead tingled. Rahni was responding.

Then, with no warning, a concussion rocked her where she stood, though the trees around her remained still. Her knees buckled,and she smacked face first into the thick trunk of a shaggy bark walnut. When she pulled away, her nose was bleeding.

What in the name of the Samudra was that?

***

Rahni sat on the floor, legs folded, hands clasped in the Mudra of Purpose. The sudden increase of the flow felt surprisingly familiar. He realized that he had always known this sensation. He had simply not known it in such abundance, or with this much certainty. It felt like reconciliation.

Under Pava's instruction, Rahni had assumed guardianship of the Gate, a shining oval suspended in a non-space defined by the absence of all other matter and energy. A thin membrane covered the opening. He more than felt or saw this membrane: he *was* the membrane, because he was its conduit. On the other side of the barrier, only a thin molecule away, the Grastar Horde roared and seethed, glaring, challenging.

How does she do it? How does Pava walk around so calmly with these creatures constantly staring her in the face?

Rahni put his attention on the tasks at hand and let the horrible visions of the Grastar fade to background noise. The pulsing surge of Samudra vibrated him like a perfectly tuned string; he tasted the fluctuations of its strength and thickness as he balanced and distributed the flow.

Pava had taught him how to split the stream of Source as it flowed through him, how to direct a portion of it to her, and how to subtly strengthen that thread when Pava most needed it. This would be her emergency lifeline on Earth. Rahni could increase the flow to her as long as he retained the minimum amount required to hold the Gate closed.

Sitting here now, the strength of the Samudra flowed into him, and he touched with his mind the SpaceTime where it split into two cords as it flowed outward.

For the second time in only a few minutes, a tingling on the back of Rahni's neck alerted him to another presence in the room. Probably Alethea again, trying to make contact with Pava. Rahni had been startled by her near materialization just moments before. But she had faded before fully taking form. If she only knew how close her teacher was to her now. Soon Alethea might be actually talking to Pava on Earth.

But this presence was not Alethea. Its edges were not soft and receptive, but hard and sharp and…

Dangerous…

Rahni dove to the right and rolled to his feet. A clot of darkness flew through the air and shattered the stele next to where he had been sitting. The Grastar was female, with greasy, dark gray skin. Six leathery dugs swung slightly as she circled to Rahni's left. Her thick legs and arms were well-muscled, but he knew that the strength of her body was not her greatest weapon. She crouched and continued to stalk Rahni Sisyah, all four of her palms glowing. The eerie hiss of a laugh slithered from between her gray lips.

Rahni focused on maintaining the twin streams of Samudra as he moved.

"Who are you?" he asked in the ancient language, trying to stall. He knew, if not who, at least what she was. "What do you want?"

When the Grastar spoke, the same slicing hiss lay under each word like knives sliding on a whetstone.

"I am Panii Viisam," she said. "And you know what I want. I will have it with or without your consent." Thin lines of black saliva oozed from the corners of her mouth.

Rahni hesitated.

The Gate. I must hold the Gate. That is my first task. And I must protect my teacher.

But Pava had taught him well. "In battle," she had said, "always confront your most urgent priority." To defend himself against this monster, Rahni Sisyah would have to withdraw his attention from Pava and leave only enough upon the Gate to keep it guarded. Dangerous. A great risk to leave his teacher unprotected. But if he did not gather all of his strength to fight this…thing…he would most certainly die, and then he could not hold the Gate at all. Or help Pava.

I will have to risk it.

Rahni circled to the right, keeping distance between himself and Viisam, and began drawing energy into his body and away from Pava. Each moment that his body grew stronger, his connection to Pava weakened. Viisam's lips twisted sideways in a satisfied grimace.

"We will fight, then," she hissed. "Good."

Panii Viisam launched herself forward, cartwheeling on all four arms. Her thick legs crashed to the floor where Rahni had just stood, shaking the foundation of Dalam Palace. Rahni slid to the right and stepped back, his left leg in front of his right. He shaped his hands into Fire Lotus; heat surged into his palms, and he released a ball of burning light that shot across the room toward the Grastar beast. Viisam slapped it aside like a pebble and circled left, cutting off Rahni's escape. Rahni edged farther to the right; Viisam clapped her upper hands together, launching a clot of shadow. Rahni dove to the floor and the dark missile struck the dome membrane, making a sound like a dampened, plucked string. The dome surface undulated and absorbed the malign energy. Rahni rolled forward, trying to slip past, but Panii Viisam grazed his back with her fingertips.

"Aaaaagggh!"

Rahni screamed out the agony even as he rolled to his feet. His back burned, ripped open by wire-thin streams of acid from the Grastar's fingernails. Viisam smiled and circled all four of her arms. Dark lightning crackled in the surrounding air and gathered in her rough palms. She clapped all four hands together; a shaft of black flame shot out and struck Rahni in the chest, driving him up and backward through the air and then down to the floor. Rahni lay paralyzed, unable even to scream, barely able to keep his attention on the Gate.

"Now you are my meat," Panii Viisam said. She stalked forward, four hands reaching for the Samudra acolyte.

Rahni could only watch the beast approach. He focused on his point of connection and opened his heart to Samudra, the Source of All, as Pava had taught him. But it was too little, too slow. His skills were not developed enough for this severe a test. He might be able to resist another attack, maybe even two, but the life force could not fill him quickly enough. He lay there, trying to gather his strength, waiting to die, and felt the last of his waning strength slipping away from the Gate. On the opposite side of the barrier, Grastar warriors roared in the anticipation of triumph. They were coming, and the Gate was threatening to fall.

My teacher, I have failed you.

TWELFTH ARTICULATION

impossible Sumerians

impossible patriarch

sacrifice

masks removed

dreams made flesh

when worlds collide

runaway

choices

surrender

my name is Forgiveness

the scream

death and Death again

Light

Present Day

"I don't know what you're talking about," Cary said. "There's no crystal here." He sat on the deck, his back against the weathered railing. At his left, Simon cradled Ally's head in his lap. She had remained unconscious since Cord had found them.

There were 12 bad guys in all. Two Cary recognized from Tampa as Cord and Stokes. But the two men in charge really set his skin crawling because he had learned their history before ever seeing them. Now, seeing them in the flesh, he finally believed: Memsalemn and Nanoshe were real. Their power virtually rippled about them in the air.

Layton had been questioning him; Carver stood a little behind. Cary watched them all. Cord and Stokes cast covert glances at one another. All the men did, for that matter. The atmosphere on the deck crackled like a schoolyard just before a fight breaks out.

Through the sliding glass doors that led into the house, Cary could just make out a strangely familiar head of silvery gray hair above the back of the recliner in the living room. Cary's neck tingled and a shiver coursed up his spine.

Impossible. He shouldn't be here.

But after the events of the last six months, anything seemed possible. Even this. Two goons stood in the kitchen, and a third drank a cup of coffee, making himself at home on

Cary's sofa across from the gray-hair in the recliner. Carver stepped in front of him and took over the interrogation, blocking his view of the interior.

"Mr. Walker," Carver said. "It's very important to us that we find the Sh'ele. You know it's here. I know it's here. You are the only one who knows where it is and how to get it."

"And I'm telling you," Cary said, his voice rising almost to a scream, "you're making a mistake. I've never even heard of a...*shuh-alay*? You people have been harassing me for the last six months. Leave me alone. I don't have anything of value here." He resisted the urge to hold his necklace; instead he lowered his head to rest in his hands.

What was it? He still had no idea beyond what Carver and Layton had just told him. A crystal? Sh'ele? And yet, hidden somewhere in the recesses of his mind, Cary could almost see the thing. Whenever his mind approached the memory, as soon as his thoughts closed on its reality, the idea flitted away like a ghost. It was like trying to grasp water. But none of that mattered at the moment. His intuition told him that, whatever the Sh'ele was, these men must never have it. He knew to the depths of his being that it must remain hidden, even if he had to die to keep it protected. When this last thought took shape in his mind, a sense of destiny joined it. This was his job, his responsibility. His purpose.

He tried harder to focus, but it was always so hard to focus with the voices... And he suddenly realized. The voices were gone. Not a whisper of them remained. When had he last heard them? He did not remember. Earlier today? When had they gone away? Why?

"Well, Mr. Walker," Carver was saying. "If you don't wish to tell us, I have someone here who will, perhaps, help to jog your memory." He nodded to Layton.

"Cord," Layton said. "Bring him out."

The glass door rolled open behind Layton. He and Carver stepped aside, revealing Cord holding Arthur by the arm. The nubby barrel of Cord's automatic was pressed hard up against the base of Arthur's skull.

The momentary shiver that had shimmied through Cary's body when he first saw the silver hair in the living room now returned in full strength. His entire body broke out in chill bumps, his hands shook, and his eyes filled with tears. Cary observed, despite the overwhelming revelation that was taking place, that Carver had slipped a hand gun out of its holster and was concealing it behind his back. Layton was turned in such a way that Cary could not see his hand, but he too seemed to be hiding a weapon. All the men on the deck shifted subtly; they were squaring off against one another without having spoken a word. The air itself threatened to explode.

Arthur remained unperturbed, like being held hostage at the end of an automatic was all part of his plan. Cary felt a combined sense of protection and danger from the old gentleman. And so he should.

"What is it?" Simon asked. "Who is that?"

Cary's shivers had subsided. He wiped the remnants of tears from his eyes. "It's my father," he said. He chuckled softly and shook his head.

"I don't get it," Simon said. "What's funny about this?"

"Not much," Cary said. Then he leaned forward and whispered into Simon's ear. "Except that my father has been dead for 10 years. I spread his ashes in that cemetery we passed on the hike in here."

As Cary spoke these words, Ally sat up and cried out, attempting to scream from the unknown depths in which she was moving. Her eyes flew open and she stared into nothingness, yet they burned with fierce purpose.

***

The sensors on the back of Rahni's neck rose again, perhaps in anticipation of death. But then he sensed another presence. A familiar presence. Viisam roared in anger and staggered forward a step. Rahni glimpsed movement on the other side of the beast. And then he saw Ally, fully present in her LightBody, dropping to the floor from where she had kicked Panii Viisam's back.

She must have left her earth body completely to be here with this much presence, Rahni thought.

Ally flew into the air a second time and struck Panii Viisam with three kicks dead on her face in rapid succession. Viisam staggered back and roared again. Ally hit the floor, rolling quickly away. The beast chased her across the room, but Ally was fast. Viisam's four arms reached for her several times only to close on empty air. Ally dove to her right; Viisam cartwheeled on her thick arms. When Ally rolled to her feet, Panii Viisam was already waiting, dark death catching fire in her palms.

***

The tension of a standoff hovered on the deck. Cary watched helpless as dangerous hands inched toward hidden weapons. Only the dark man in the corner failed to move. This one leaned, arms crossed, in the shadows of the eaves; he observed the unfolding drama, taking in the actions and movements of the characters like a director watching his creation play out. Cary thought he was familiar, somehow. Most likely, he would be the first to die.

Carver began to swing his gun from behind his back. Layton turned to Carver, his own hand moving forward. The soundtrack had reached its climax in this slow motion dance of death. Critical mass. The deadly dancers hung in suspension, waiting for the next beat to propel them into a killing frenzy. And then, a most unexpected thing happened. Slow laughter filled the air. Fingers relaxed on triggers. Carver and Layton turned, instead of to the work of killing each other, to the source of the humor: Arthur Walker.

"What is it," Layton asked Arthur, "that you find so amusing, old man?"

Arthur fixed his gaze on Layton and held it steady. For the first time in more than 500 years, someone other than

Carver or a Namayan held his gaze for more than a few seconds.

Layton now realized that Arthur's earlier failure to meet his eyes had not been an effect of fear or intimidation, but a tactic of subversion. Arthur had not wanted Layton to see his own power, for then Layton would never have taken him so lightly.

"I don't think I am quite ready yet to risk the death of this one," Arthur said, his eyes cutting to Cary. "So forgive me for stopping you from killing each other long enough to accomplish what we have really come here for."

"Who the hell do you…" Carver began.

"In good time, Memsalemn," he said.

Carver's breath caught in his throat.

"Now," Arthur said, "if you or your brother, Nanoshe, will have a couple of your soldiers sweep the area near the southern corner of the house, I believe you will find the final player in our little drama has arrived."

Layton hesitated a moment, then nodded to Cord.

"But, just a caution," Arthur Walker added. "I would be careful about attempting to bring her in by force. An invitation would work much better. Tell her that Ripu Dasi has requested her presence."

I know that name, Cary thought. *Where have I heard that name?*

"Dossey?" Carver said. "You're Dossey?"

Ripu Dasi laughed. It was a very human sound. "You have no idea, Sumerian, who I am."

He turned to Cary and gestured upward with his palm. Cary jerked to his feet, not of his own volition, and approached the man who somehow looked exactly like his father. But this man was familiar beyond that. The voice was not his father's, but Cary knew it nonetheless.

"And now, Mr. Walker," Dasi said, "let us see if we can extract from you this curiously secreted knowledge of yours. I believe it may be as well-hidden in the labyrinth of your mind as the thing itself is in the labyrinth of these mountains."

You should be protecting me, Cary thought.

For a moment, not more than the blink of an eye really, Ripu Dasi's aspect shimmered and transformed into that of an angel. Cary's angel. Taylor's memory flooded Cary's thoughts. Holding his son as he died. Something Taylor had said...something about his name...his true name...

The power of Dasi's gaze bored into Cary's mind, and that memory skittered back into the shadows. Cary tried to look away, but Dasi's will became a cyclone behind Cary's eyes, forcing them open. The cyclone moved deeper into Cary's head. Bright pain ripped at the inside of his skull, threatening to shatter it into slivers and shards. But it was his mind that was quaking, not mere bone and flesh. Dasi's thoughts penetrated the layers of protection in Cary's mind, deeper and deeper, until they reached the borders defined by his pineal, and found...

A wall? Dasi thought. *A blank wall? The Samudra bitch was here before me!*

From worlds away, footsteps echoed above the rush of the river and the roar of the approaching storm. A woman's voice, terrifying and beautiful, clear and present, rang like a temple bell. Cary knew this voice, as well.

"Ripu Dasi," she said. Her words were soft, but her voice shook the world.

Again Cary thought, *Why do I know that name?* And again, Taylor's image floated to the surface of Cary's consciousness.

Cary forced himself to look at the woman. She approached from the back of the deck, two goons flanking her. She was so small, and astonishingly beautiful. Perfect. She appeared to be from India. Her skin glowed golden brown, and her eyes were as bright as a gathering of stars. Then, for the tiniest of moments, her skin flashed blue, and the points of her ears peeked out from her dark hair.

The demon is here!

Cary screamed.

Ripu Dasi laughed and tightened his choke hold; Cary's scream strangled in the air.

Apavarita Varsah stepped forward and spoke a single

word: "No."

Dasi released his grip; Cary slumped to the deck and tried to claw his way back into the present. Thunder boomed in the west, and wind chimes rang under the eaves. Living particles of light described a circle around the deck, paused for a nanosecond, and then disappeared into the trees. Cary scrambled to the railing and gathered Ally into his arms. Harsh and ragged breaths forced their way in and out of her slack mouth. She was still unconscious.

A familiar torment filled Cary's head. He suddenly understood the absence of the vitriolic voices that had screamed just below the surface of his consciousness for the last five years. They had emerged into his world. They were with him, here and now in the form of this angel who could not be his father and this demon in the guise of a beautiful young woman.

Pava stepped up to Dasi. Cary glimpsed an image of the two of them fighting at the rivers edge. He saw them standing on the dark shore in front of a great, red ocean. And here they stood on his deck. All of his nightmares had come to life.

Layton backed into the house; Stokes and Cord were poised just inside the sliding glass doors. Besides Ally, Cary, and Simon, only two humans remained on the deck: Carver, who still had illusions of taking control of this battle, and Booth, who continued to watch the drama from the shadows of the corner, a half smile playing across his face.

"I told you," Pava said, "that I would not let you have him."

"And I told you," said Ripu Dasi. "He is already mine."

"I never imagined we would do this here," she said.

Just inside the door, Layton sensed the shift in Cord's aspect. Layton turned to stop him, but Cord was already charging onto the deck. He rushed Pava from her left. She held her hand out, palm facing him, never breaking eye contact with Ripu Dasi. Cord's body moved as a mirror image of itself. One moment he was driving forward and the next he was flying backward, gathering speed. He crashed through both glass doors, coming to rest in a shower of shards and fragments. The left side of his face looked like a roadmap until blood covered it in a thin, red mask. Booth turned an avaricious eye to Cord and then returned his attention to the main event.

Halfway between Pava and Dasi, along the line of eye contact, the air shimmered like water flowing over rocks in the sun. A rough sphere formed, dark on one side and bright on the other. Cary pushed back against the railing, trying to escape the radiation.

Dasi raised his hands together and a beam of shadow shot from his palms, driving the sphere toward Pava. She raised both of her palms, inner wrists pressed together, palms out like an opening flower, and forced the tiny sun back toward Dasi. A steady stream of energy poured out of each of them, meeting in perfect balance, perfect standoff, at this impossible place in the air.

Bolts of electricity discharged from the sphere and found the tops of nearby trees. One struck a tulip poplar, boiling its abundant sap in an instant. The tree exploded like a blocked canon; scalding sap rained onto the house, the deck, and the rushing river. Tiny puffs of steam rose from the icy water.

***

Rahni witnessed with awe Ally's battle with the Grastar beast.

How fearless you are! he thought. His heart swelled in the presence of her courage, and Source poured through him with renewed strength. Inner waves of light turned his eyes golden. In another moment, he would be able to stand. He would be able to save Alethea, crush the dire beast, and redirect this strength to Pava. Though he was still unable to move, Rahni felt the limitless energy fill him. His arms tingled, and he tried to push himself up off the floor.

Alethea faced the Grastar, fearless, magnificent. Panii

Viisam cocked her head, curious that this frail human would choose to fight a battle she could not possibly win. Almost as an afterthought, Viisam whipped out her arm so fast it was a blur. Her index finger pressed into the center of Alethea's chest. Ally's skin rippled like a pool of water. Concentric waves spread from the point of contact. When the first wave reached Ally's face, her eyes rolled back in her head, and her hair whipped upward, caught by the waves of death spreading through her. Then the ripples returned, focusing and converging at the center point. Ally collapsed to the floor, her body convulsing in the tide of death.

Panii Viisam smiled and turned to her other victim.

"This day," she said, "I shall dine twice."

***

Back on the deck, Ally choked out ragged breaths. Cary shook her, but her gasps turned to coughs, and her body convulsed in rhythmic waves.

He shook Simon's shoulder. "Help me! She's choking." Simon tried to stand, but Carver kicked the back of his knees, sending him sprawling to the deck. Carver pressed his boot to the back of Simon's neck.

"Somebody help me!" Cary shouted. "She's dying!"

Ally's convulsions subsided into a series of short breaths. The tiny sun shifted toward Pava. At the same moment, both Pava and Dasi began to speak in a language no human had ever heard. The fireball moved another inch closer to Pava, then another.

Inside her consciousness, Pava called out to Rahni. *Now! Connect me to Source, or Dasi will destroy me.* No answer came, no contact, no replenishment. Pava had directed a precious thread of her lifeforce to Ally, and Dasi had seized the opportunity. But she could still prevail if Samudra would only flow through.

Alethea cannot die, she thought. *She must not die. What is killing her?* She exhibited all the symptoms of the Grastar

DeathTouch. But that was impossible. None of the Grastar were here, other than Ripu Dasi. She continued to call out to Rahni in the ancient language, while Dasi continued to chant his death spell. And death was pushing closer. The sphere was not yet touching her, but its weight pressed her down. In a moment, she would be forced to her knees.

Cary inched back from the battle. His wrist burned like fire, and his skull felt ready to explode.

I have to do something, he thought. But he did not know what to do. A word forced its way to the surface of his thoughts, and he tried to push it back down.

Escape.

He shook his head, but he could not dislodge the idea.

Run away.

Simon was face-down, a boot literally to his neck, and Ally was dying in his arms, but every ounce of Cary's being was telling him to slide under the railing and run into the woods.

I am not a coward!

He looked into Ally's tortured face. For a moment he was back in Cherokee. They were all fine. Nightmares had not yet come to life. Billy was holding his necklace, looking into his eyes.

"You do not have to know what to do," the old man said. "Only do what you must."

Cherokee slipped away. Cary remained on the deck; the impotence of ambiguity brought tears to his eyes. He looked to the two beings engaged in battle. The woman, the demon, glanced back at him with certainty. She spoke to him across space and time, though her mouth remained closed. Her words washed over him like a fable recalled from a childhood dream.

"You have work to do," she said. "Stop feeling sorry for yourself and do it."

I know you! he thought, but recognition flitted away.

For a moment Ally's face relaxed, and she almost— almost—smiled?

Pava dropped to one knee. Dasi loomed over her, intoning those strange words, his hand pushing her down into Hell. All eyes focused on their battle.

Now or never.

Cary swallowed his self-loathing and lay back. His head slipped under the lowest piece of the railing. He dragged his leg out from under Ally's head, letting it settle softly to the deck. Simon's eyes widened. Cary shook his head once, pressed his finger to his lips, and pulled himself over the edge with one smooth motion.

He flipped backward and hit the ground running. Through thick spider webs under the deck, over the stone retaining wall behind the house, and up the embankment to the courtyard. He had no idea where he was going or what he was doing, but something tugged like a taut string at his memory.

Red and golden leaves shimmered in the high wind. Ally's face formed on his mind.

"Remember when we met," she said.

"Is this really happening?" he said.

"Trust me."

Cary pushed through the underbrush to the trail that circled back to the driveway. He passed behind the two SUVs in a crouch and continued to the river. The driving current was just cresting the lower bank, washing away bits of dirt and ground moss. A fine spray rose from the rocks and kissed his cheeks. He emerged into a clearing near the wooden staircase that led up to the house. This clearing, this very spot, was exactly where he had been just before Ally had walked into his life, changing it forever, just—my God—just six months ago. It seemed like lifetimes.

The river's roar filled his ears down here, but he could still hear the crackle of energy between the two...what were they? Certainly not humans...up on the deck. Over the din of the river and the battle on the deck, Cary heard the throbbing hum of an engine rounding the last curve of the driveway.

What was I doing down here? he thought. *I had lost something. I was looking for something.*

Across the small clearing, the weathered fishing shack stood at the base of the stairs. He almost locked onto the memory. Then, blinding pain pierced his breastbone and pounded the center of his forehead. He slammed to earth.

The world fell silent. Cary rose out of his body, above the constraints of time. He watched himself six months ago, on one knee, at this very spot, bow aimed at the sky. The Cary of six months past released the arrow, stood, closed his eyes, pressed his heart to the sky, and strangled out a sound that was trying to be a scream. The arrow disappeared, blue feathers into blue sky, then reappeared, falling, finding its way home, finding its way to the center of Cary's heart, piercing his breastbone, knocking him flat on his back in the wet sand.

Cary floated above his corpse. Never had he been so calm, so at peace, so detached. This feeling was as close to bliss as he had ever imagined. He need only intone the sacred "yes," and he could remain in this ecstatic space. He need only accept this fate. Then it would all be over. No more scary men with guns. No more angels. No more demons. No more screams in his head. No more walking on the razor edge of madness. No more pain. No more responsibility.

From far, far away, muffled war cries still echoed through his being. Woven like a golden thread through those echoes, Cary heard the mantra that had brought him across thousands of years to this moment.

I promise to hide you and protect you, now and forever, until you rise.

Cary floated above his corpse, killed last spring by his own hand. He opened his mouth and said, "No. I do not accept this." The scene looped back, the arrow fell again, and his own ethereal hand snaked out from the shadows of eternity and closed around the shaft. The point barely scratched his chest. The arrow dissolved in his fist. Then his hand was gone, and with it, that probability loop turned to smoke, and the present rejoined itself.

His back was cold and wet from the sandy riverbank.

Where am I? No. When am I?

Cary jumped to his feet. The river was higher now. Louder. Thunder crashed again to the west. Pava and Ripu Dasi remained at impasse on the deck.

A momentary gap in the clouds let through a bit of sunlight, lighting a tiny speck of blue among the yellow, red, and orange of fallen leaves.

A blue feather. The arrow. The last arrow.

It stood only an arm's length away, head buried in the sand, where it had landed six months ago. Just beyond it, now partially obscured by the undergrowth, the bow, still in its case, leaned against the embankment. Without fully knowing what he was doing, or why, Cary retrieved the weapon.

Do I even remember how to string it? He bent the bow around his leg, not even sure what he intended to do.

***

Up on the deck, Clovis Plowright rounded the corner of the house before anyone realized he was there. He held a 10 gauge, double-barrel shotgun aimed at Dasi's throat. Though his knees trembled, his voice and the shotgun were steady as stone.

"I don't rightly know what the holy Hell is going on here," he said, "but you best stop putting your bad medicine on that pretty girl, lest you want a hole in you big enough to drive a train through."

Dasi ceased his incantation. His eyes flickered toward the gun, and Pava shifted forward a few inches. The heat of Dasi's attack nearly surrounded her now.

All in the space of a second, Dasi separated his left hand from his right and flicked it in Clovis' direction. Pava drove to her feet, pressing Dasi back a half step. Clovis' fingers squeezed down on both triggers. Pava cast a line of protection toward Clovis. But she was too late. Both barrels of the shotgun exploded in a deafening roar, splitting the gunmetal up to the stock. Clovis collapsed in a heap, blood streaming from his weathered face and hands. Dasi clapped his hands back together, took a step forward, and resumed the ancient song of death. Pava fell once again to one knee.

"This will be over soon," Carver said. "Then we can get back to the real business at hand. You hear that, Walker?" He looked over his shoulder. Ally lay completely still, alone at the edge of the deck. Carver dragged Simon to his feet. "Where's Walker?"

"Gone," Simon said. "He ran away."

***

Panii Viisam turned to kill her second victim. But Rahni was ready for her now; his entire body glowed golden with the full light of Samudra. Rahni struck the Grastar in the chest with both palms. Viisam tried to bring her arms forward to force the shadow of death into Rahni's body, but they were so heavy, too heavy to lift more than a few inches. Her fingertips, then her hands, then her arms turned to particles and swirled away to nothingness. In a blink she was back in the vortex, screaming as the last of her energy drained away and the whirlpool sucked her back toward the Hive.

Rahni watched the Grastar beast disintegrate and disappear. Ally's LightBody lay silent in death at his feet. He choked down his grief and rushed to the Omphalos to check on his teacher. Pava was on her knees; an Earth man stood over her, forcing her down with a ball of dark fire.

My teacher or the Gate, he thought. But Pava's instructions had been very specific on such a choice. Rahni Sisyah leaned all of his attention into the porous membrane that still barely covered the portal. The Grastar Horde slammed into him like a battering ram. The impact knocked him to his knees. Again he pressed, and again the Grastar crashed into him, laying him out bodily on the floor. A fetid gale rushed through the Gate, and he was almost sucked in behind it. Ethereal, triumphant screams filled his ears. Grastar SoulEaters poured through and into their Qellepoth bodies on the earth.

Rahni Sisyah had failed.

Despair pulled him down into a dark abyss, and still the SoulEaters poured through the Gate. The last shred of Rahni's hope evaporated. A choking sob rattled in his throat. And that was the moment that Pava's thoughtform, set to orbit around Rahni's heart matrix days before, burst in a flash of inspiration. Suddenly he felt Pava's presence, guiding his every move. He knew exactly what to do. More important, he knew exactly how to do it. He emptied himself of all expectation, all attachment, and became a hollow channel through which true power could flow. Pava's wise eyes urged him on. Despair flew away and died. He sat up where he had been knocked down, folded his legs underneath him, and folded his hands into the Mudra of Intention. Failure no longer existed. He took a deep breath and began to sing, as Pava had taught him, in the First Language.

"I am Rahni Sisyah, Protector of the Earth. I am here. I am now. I hold this Gate." He repeated the mantra over and over, shaping the vast, unformed reservoir in his heart into a matrix strong enough to reseal the portal and stop the onslaught of Grastar.

Rahni had no way of knowing how many passed through before he closed the Gate. The blistering rage of the remaining warriors burned red against the membrane. Their screams resumed, but they could no longer pass.

When Rahni was certain that the Gate would hold, he once again split the stream and turned his attention to Pava. He prayed that he was not too late.

***

The thunderous crashing upriver was like a faraway dream. But even at that distance, Cary recognized it.

Flash flood. Death by water.

In a matter of minutes, possibly seconds, a wall of water would sweep through here, washing away everything in its path. Trees, boulders, the shack…and Cary. But he could not, *must* not, let his mind engage that distraction. He must instead concentrate on how to shoot this arrow straight, this arrow that he had lost half a year before because he was shooting at… what?…who?…himself?…God? He could not let his mind embrace that madness.

He dropped the arrow and the bow. Without fully understanding why, he slipped the necklace over his head and held the talisman in his right hand. The texture of the bone felt different now, and it throbbed in his palm.

A dozen ravens wheeled on the wind and lit in the ancient yew. They spread open their black beaks, and Cary heard a beautiful choir.

> *Crack open the world;*
> *you can no longer hide.*
> *Crack open your heart;*
> *the answer is inside.*
> *Break bone.*
> *Spill blood.*
> *Surrender.*
> *Surrender.*
> *Surrender to the flood.*

His wrist was on fire. His palm tingled where he held the talisman. Electricity shot up his arm, and a convulsion whiplashed through his body once, twice, a third time. The aroma of the ocean overwhelmed him, and for a brief instant he saw a young woman lying in a boat, her arms and legs entwined around a huge crystal. A holograph floated above the crystal, and in that holograph, he saw himself; he saw exactly what he must do. The clarity and simplicity of the image brought tears to his eyes.

No time to think. No time to worry that he may have left Ally to die up on the deck. Cary moved with one purpose: to accomplish that vision.

He laid the necklace on a flat stone. With a familiar sweep of his hand, he retrieved a sharp-edged rock, struck down on the end of the talisman, and shattered the sealed end in one clean motion.

Dim light flooded into the bone and emerged brighter. Cary shook the talisman, and a quartz point dropped out. He pressed the razor edge of the arrowhead into his left palm and clenched his trembling fist over the crystal. Blood dripped like red rain on its shining facets. A final, crimson teardrop detached from his fist and began its descent. Halfway between his hand and the crystal, the drop slowed...and slowed...and the world stopped. The single drop of blood hung in the silence.

Before Time

~

Ksama

The nearer she approaches the altar, the faster Sh'ele and the crystal in her pocket vibrate. Ksama pauses at the bottom step of the dais. Sh'ele seems to move of its own accord, pulling her toward the frame on the altar. She stops resisting the attraction and climbs the three steps. When her foot makes contact with the dais floor, the beautiful frame clicks open and the chamber walls burst to life. Light pulses through amethysts, emeralds, garnets, and sapphires, illuminating the sigils, defining a matrix of protection. Directly above the altar, a stone door rasps over the eye in the ceiling, closing the chamber to the outside world.

Sh'ele slips from her grasp and flies the last two feet to float, suspended in equilibrium between the two poles of the frame. The sigils steady to a constant glow. At the same moment, a low hum of power fills the room, so deep and thick that Ksama can almost touch it.

A shock rips through her. The weight of grief and self-pity that had held her down, crushed her to the ground for the last twelve months, the shadow that she had just cast off long enough to find the opening to the inner chamber of the temple, now crashes back over her like a red wave. She collapses, face pressed to the floor. Blood pools in her mouth and drips onto the stone. She tries to push herself up, but the pressure of it all holds her down.

The crystal in her pocket has fallen out and now vibrates on the stone floor in front of her face. She cannot even move her hand to touch it. Her story floods through her, looping, building strength.

Ksama begins to wail. Her voice rasps inarticulate tales of suffering and sacrifice. Somewhere in the ache and longing of her screams, she finds the strength to form words. Before her eyes, the tiny crystal glimmers bright blue. Screaming gives way to singing. Ksama sings her life: Being chosen as Anucara. The years of training. Her dreams. Her service. Her commitment. Her sacrifice. Killing Sidra.

I have become death.

She sings her life back into existence, back into relevance. The more she sings, the less the weight of resentment holds her down. Anger and self-pity melt and fall away. Soon, she is able to sit. She picks the crystal up and it glows brighter. She sings her story into the crystal, and the tiny piece of quartz, small in size but vast in capacity, absorbs it all. For the rest of the day, she sings. Through the night and into the next day.

When she comes to the part where she is sitting on the floor of the inner chamber of the temple, when she comes to the here and now, she sings into the crystal and simultaneously to DevaSurya. "I know my true name," she sings. "I am Ksama. My name is Forgiveness. Now, I have become Forgiveness." And then there is silence.

Ksama's eyes grow heavy. One task remains, but she has no strength left for it now. The exhaustion of the day, of her song, of her story, of her life, descends on her. Again she presses her face to the stone floor, now from fatigue rather than despair. The blue light of the tiny crystal consolidates into a single point, and then winks out. With her last sliver of strength, she cradles her polished wrist bone in the palm of her left hand and presses the crystal that now holds her story into the hollow space. The crystal fits perfectly. Almost done.

She will craft the final touches onto her artifact later. She closes her fingers and her eyes. The weight of her life rests now, fully protected in her capable hand.

Then Ksama sleeps, and dreams the future into being.

Present Day

The scream was almost here, but a sound and light show preceded it, echoing off the curved walls of the past as it rushed upward into Cary's ragged consciousness.

Memories of thousands of lifetimes erupted into his mind. He watched Ksama and was Ksama at the same time. He observed and participated as she prepared the place of concealment for Sh'ele in the heart of an ancient ziggurat that lay buried directly beneath his patio. He listened and sang as she crafted the patterns of sound with which to release Sh'ele. Together they hollowed out Ksama's wrist bone and shared the use of her left hand as she scratched Draco onto its surface. He sang with her, holding this very crystal in their only hand, recording her history into the glowing facets. He knew in the space of a lightning flash the hundreds of other lifetimes in which he—they—had opened the necklace, relearned their history, and deposited the latest life chapter into it before returning it to the ground.

In nanoseconds, he lived a lifetime on the harsh steppes of Scythia as a master bow maker, the life in which he had crafted this very bow in preparation for this moment.

Cary heard the song of DevaSurya, the Queen of Graces, harmonize with the song of Sh'ele, reminding him of the responsibility of Ksama's promise.

And in a dark morning, he knelt with Ksama before

Sh'ele. Her right arm was shattered. She was so scared, in so much pain. Together they found the strength and vision to retrieve a crystal spike from the base of Sh'ele and drive it into Sidra's neck. Into Ally's neck. Death and forgiveness in a single gesture. A contract written in the perfection of that moment.

Another song was calling to him, as well. This one was closer, more urgent, and more beautiful than any he had heard in thousands of lifetimes.

He raised his head, in the past as Ksama, in the present as Cary, in all the lifetimes in between. He saw, here and now, the choir of a dozen ravens perched in the ancient yew, singing like a seraphim. They sang one word over and over, in transcendent harmony.

Uktenah...

The last drop of blood completed its descent and splashed upon the tiny crystal. The wave of the past broke into the now; images and sounds of the present crashed against the shores of his senses.

Cary scooped up the hollow bone and the crystal and dropped them into his pocket.

He joined the choir. "Uktenah," he sang. He grasped the bow in his bloody hand and nocked the blood-tipped arrow.

***

"Layton," Carver yelled into the house. "Walker's gone." Layton rushed out onto the deck. Arnie Booth still watched all from the corner. Simon Boon performed CPR on Ally. The battle between Dasi and Pava looked to be nearly over, but that would matter little if Walker had escaped.

Carver and Layton looked first toward the woods, then back up the driveway.

"There," Layton said. "By the river."

"What's that?" Carver asked. "What's he doing? What the Hell..."

Cary stood at the river's edge, holding a bow in his hand.

And he was singing. A dozen ravens squawked and croaked above him in the branches of a twisted tree.

***

Cary nocked the arrow, drew the taut string to his cheek, and sighted down the shaft.

Get out of your own way. Be a hollow bone.

Ksama's wrist bone pressed against his thigh. He stopped thinking about the fact that he had never held a bow before last spring. He stopped thinking about how the arrows had flown everywhere except where he had aimed. He let go of the anger and despair that had caused him to aim death at himself, at God. He focused instead on the feeling of the bow in his hands, and the word singing through him, escaping from his chest through his mouth to join with the choir of ravens and the raging stormsong of the world around him. How perfect it felt. How familiar. Such a perfect straight line the shaft of the arrow formed. He exhaled the song slowly, slowly, and as his breath left him, an arc of light materialized in the air, beginning at the tip of the arrowhead and terminating where he was aiming, at Pava's heart. The demon, disguised though she might be, was in his sights.

He relaxed his fingers on the bowstring.

***

Panii Viisam flowed backward through the transfer vortex, but she did not reach the Hive. Instead, she slammed headlong into the Grastar Vanguard as it surged toward the Gate, picking her up and carrying her through. Her consciousness slipped away.

When at last she awoke, she saw only darkness. Her hands thumped against soft walls. She still had hands, then, though only two of them still worked. Far away, muffled voices shouted. People were trapped and trying to escape. She pressed her two good hands against the walls that contained her. The voices outside were increasing in volume and number.

Then she remembered. She had been taught that it would feel like this. She was in a coffin on Earth. The transfer had been successful.

She pounded on the walls of her box, and shouted. Her coffin shifted a little. A series of snaps resounded all around her, and then the lid swung upward. A young man stood above her.

"Welcome," he said.

***

Cary loosened his fingers on the taut bowstring and sang the word. His dreamworld demon was alive in the world and centered in his sights. His mind assured him that this was the right course of action, but something was wrong. This woman might be the demon who had hidden in his dreams. But this woman was no demon.

You do not have to know what to do. Only do what you must.

Without thinking, Cary turned to aim the arrow at the one who looked like his father. Again, the man's image shifted for the blink of an eye and took on the aspect of Cary's angel. The angel turned to Cary in that instant. His eyes were blood red. Cary heard the words "Kill the demon bitch." And then the angel was Arthur Walker once again. He still chanted in some ancient language; the woman was on her knees before him. Cary lined the arrow up on his father's throat. His mind tried to hold him back, but his entire body relaxed into the synchrony of the moment. Louder he sang the word. Louder still. The word became a primal roar filled with purpose and passion held at bay for thousands of lifetimes and finally, finally set free. Louder. Cary's voice filled the entire world.

The scream was here.

Cary opened his hand and let the arrow fly, letting it sing its own song, letting it find its own destiny. Cary's voice fell quiet. The twelve members of the dark choir joined him in the silence. They turned their heads to follow the arrow's flight. The shaft flew along the arc of light and slammed first through Dasi's right palm, and then through his throat. The razor tip emerged from the back of his neck. Cary's blood mixed with the body of his father, with the blood of Ripu Dasi.

Arnie Booth straightened and took one astonished step out of the shadows.

"I know you," Cary said. "Murtaugh." And though the river and wind were too loud for anyone to have heard, Booth turned his head in Cary's direction, smiled, and nodded.

The ravens took flight and wheeled above the porch. They turned a dark vortex in the tormented sky and transformed. The dark choir became darker, and their voices, which had moments before rivaled the seraphim, now screeched a chorus of caws. Blue-black wings beat the sky in a shadow-spiral above and behind Murtaugh. They now belonged to him.

Ripu Dasi clawed at the back of his neck, reacting with human instincts he did not know he had. Pava rose to her feet and forced Dasi back one step, two. The burning sphere of death hovered between them, now retreating from Pava. Dasi pulled the arrow through his neck and hand, and out through the back in one single motion. Blood pulsed from the wound. He opened his mouth to resume his incantation, but only managed a gurgling cough. Still, he stood his ground and brought his hands together once again. A powerful thunderclap shook the ground, but there had been no lightning.

His power is enormous, Pava thought. *Far more than I had imagined.* And far more than she could withstand without Rahni's help. The sphere burned brighter and moved closer again. The arrow had been her last chance, she knew. And still Dasi's power pressed down upon her. Clovis had died for nothing. Ally had died for nothing. Everyone would die for nothing. The earth was lost. Graal had won. Weakened from the siege, Pava lowered her hands and let the fire engulf her.

***

With gentle hands, Simon lowered Ally's head to the deck. His anger was a volcano, and it erupted at Carver.

"You've killed her!"

Carver laughed. Simon's rage clicked up another notch, and his hands closed on Carver's throat. Carver was so astonished that, for a moment he just stood there, laughing and getting choked. Then he broke the chokehold, pushed Simon back a few feet to the deck railing, and pulled his Glock.

This would be where I die, Simon thought. He teetered against the top rail. The wood groaned and separated with a soft snap. Simon fell backward through the gap as the Glock pumped out five rounds.

***

A dark blue wall of water bore down on Cary. He scrambled up the embankment with the bow still in his left hand. With his right, he caught the exposed root of the yew as the first surge of the flood crashed into him, lifting him sideways. The weight of the water threatened to pull him free of his hold, and then he was submerged in the cold, driving rush of the Cane, his own river of forgetting. And now of remembering. The water continued to rise, sweeping all before it.

***

Deep inside her heart, Pava felt the heat grow. Fire burned at her center and expanded like the heat of a thousand suns. She had often wondered how death would feel when it finally came.

I have served Samudra for hundreds of thousands of years, she

365

thought. *My life has been honorable.*

The fire raged on, but, to her surprise, Pava did not disintegrate in the heat. She became the fire itself. A familiar fire. And then she understood.

Rahni.

Rahni had somehow reconnected to her. The fire of Samudra burned from within Pava, and with it, the knowledge of all that Rahni had witnessed: his fight with Panii Viisam, the passing of several hundred Grastar through the Gate before Rahni could get it closed.

And Ally. Ally's supreme sacrifice. Pava's heart filled with awe for her charges, and the flow of Samudra doubled.

Dasi pressed the darkness forward, certain of imminent conquest. Then Apavarita Varsah rose to her feet. Dasi raised his hands against the divine fire that poured unfocused out of his enemy. Pava brought her hands together in an elegant mudra, one taught only to the most advanced of the Samudra Janah: the Petals of Flame. The fire concentrated into a beam only microns in diameter. Ripu Dasi's body turned in on itself, burning from the inside out. He collapsed onto the deck, his body glowing white hot. And then he was gone. Only a Hiroshima shadow remained.

The vehicles at the head of the driveway coughed to life and roared away. Carver, Layton, and all their soldiers had retreated the moment the battle turned in Pava's favor. All except for one. But this one was not truly one of their soldiers. Pava knew this one well. And why he was here.

Cary ran up the driveway, soaking wet and carrying a bow. Simon Boon climbed the back stairs to the deck, rubbing the back of his neck with one hand, and checking with the other, even now, for bullet holes in his chest. But his gift for falling had, in this case, saved his life. Ally lay on the faded wood near the far railing. Dead.

Pava eased back into the shadows against the wall and watched. Cary rushed to Alethea's body.

"No," he screamed. "No. It's not fair."

"Fair got nothing to do with it," said the dark voice.

Cary turned to the remaining soldier, the black man they had called Booth, the man he had recognized.

"Murtaugh," Cary said. "Why…what are you doing here?"

"I told you I would find you when the time was right. And now the debt is due." He looked at Ally's body and then spread his arms wide like wings. "Come to me, my dark darlings," he said. The murder of ravens tightened their wheeling spiral and came to land, a living cape upon his shoulders and outstretched arms. He began a slow march toward Ally's body. Though there was still no visible sun, his shadow advanced before him.

Apavarita Varsah, Warrior Princess of the Samudra, stepped away from the wall and into the light.

"Cease, Myrtu," she said. "You may not have this one."

Murtaugh, or as he is also known, Myrtu, turned. His dark companions shifted and murmured on his outstretched arms.

"But there is a debt," he said.

"And it shall be paid," Pava said. "But not today. Not yet. Not by this one. I still have much work for her." She closed her eyes a moment, looked within, and then opened them. "I invoke the right of the Samudra," she said. "This one belongs to me. For now." She turned to the body of Clovis Plowright, which still lay bloody on the deck. "You may take this one."

"Ah, Princess," he said, shaking his head. "But this is not fair. He was mine already."

"Fair," she echoed back to him, using his own words and his own accent, "got nothing to do with it. Don't despair, Dark King." In her mind she saw hundreds of reanimated Qellepoth rising from their coffins, fresh hosts to the Grastar. "You will find much to harvest in the coming storm."

"Very well," Myrtu said. "But I will collect in time. It is my right." He shrugged his arms and the ravens took flight around him. They widened their spiral to engulf the body of Clovis Plowright, flying so fast that they became a blur of shadow. The shadow slowly dissipated, and when it was gone, so were Myrtu, the ravens, and the corpse of Clovis Plowright.

Cary and Simon continued to watch in silence.

Pava nodded to Simon Boon, and he felt the wave of her gratitude pass through him. And a tingling in his forehead. Simon stumbled where he stood, then sat down before he fell. The tingle expanded to fill his skull, and he eased onto his side and fell into a deep sleep. As he slept, memories of the past few minutes drained away. Pava turned her attention to Cary and smiled.

"You did well, Child," she said. In the silence between her words, he heard another message: *Tell no one of our meeting.*

"You're real," he said.

Pava laughed, and the sound of it brought tears to Cary's eyes. Pava knelt beside Ally. "And you, my Child," she said, "were beyond amazing."

Pava pressed the palm of her right hand against Ally's chest, and the palm of her left hand over her own heart. She sang again in the First Language. Golden light shone from beneath Pava's left hand. It grew until it surrounded her. Cary could see nothing but the blinding glow that engulfed Ally and Pava.

Her song continued. Slowly, the light and the song waned. When both had faded to nothing, Ally lay on the deck alone.

A stream of particles emerged like an army of fireflies from the treetops. They descended to Ally, swarmed about her, and lifted her body to a sitting position against the railing. They spun her a cocoon of light until she gasped and her eyes opened wide. Then the lights formed into a spiral that danced only a few feet away.

"Oh," Ally said. "My goodness. The *Sidhe*. When did they get here? What happened?"

The tinkling of tiny laughter filled the air, and the lights streamed away into the trees.

***

"I failed," Rahni said. They faced one another, each upon

a soft cushion. Steam ascended from the spout of a small, earthenware teapot on the pedestal between them.

"No, One," Pava answered. She poured tea for Rahni, then herself. "You were superb."

"But, the Grastar," he said. "They got through." His eyes studied the powdery swirl of tea in his cup.

"Yes," Pava said. "But not all. Only a few hundred. That will make things on the Earth difficult. And, understand this. Graal could still prevail. This small invasion has given him a foothold. But only a sliver of the one he needed. The Grastar who walk the earth will have to remain hidden. They will have to blend in and try to find another way to bring in the rest. They will still attempt to obtain Sh'ele. But Cary no longer walks deaf and blind. The task of the Grastar is much more difficult now. We have not won. But we are far from losing."

"But what about the Council? Surely they will punish you for your transgression."

"There are those who would like to, yes," Pava said. "But the reality is that there is no one to maintain this outpost but you and me. They will censure me, but that will be all. Now, drink your tea, and then we shall return to your training. Just because you managed singlehandedly to reseal the Gate during the full onrush of a Grastar Horde does not mean that you don't still have much to learn."

***

Ally, Simon, and Cary sat on the bench at the edge of Cary's patio. Cary's left hand was wrapped in a clean gauze bandage

"It's underneath here, like we thought?" Ally said.

Carry nodded. "It's funny," he said. "The things I saw when I opened the necklace...so many of them are gone now. And the rest are slipping away. Like it wasn't real at all."

"The mind can only hold so much information," Ally said. "You remember what matters. You remember what you have to do."

"But," Simon said. "I don't get it. Why don't the bad guys just come in with an army and a backhoe?"

Cary offered a half smile. "It's hard to explain. I don't even know how I know this. But there are...layers upon layers of protection. Over and over again. Lifetime after lifetime. If they were to try without my consent...then things would just...I don't know...go wrong?"

Ally nodded. "Things are going to get better," she said. "But I'm afraid that first they are going to get a lot worse. Memsalemn and Nanoshe haven't given up. They're not going to stop trying. Neither will the Grastar."

"I miss my Emma," Cary said, and smiled fully now.

"You won't be able to stay there forever," Ally said. "But I think it would be nice if you went to visit her."

"Where does she live?" Simon asked. Ally and Cary laughed.

"And what will you two do?" Cary said after his laughter had subsided.

Ally looked at Simon. "Simon is coming with me. In a few days we'll go to meet Teo and my father. They've already started reforming the Council. We'll see how Simon best fits into that structure."

"I think," Simon said, "my days as a journalist are over."

"But," Ally said, "your days as something much more important are beginning."

***

Ripu Dasi waited in the patient darkness. In time, he heard the telltale snap of the coffin locks. The lid was lifted, and light once again filled his eyes. He sat up and let the two human Grastar help him step out onto the ground.

Only a few hundred of his vanguard were here on earth, but that would be enough. He would gather them together and retrieve the crystal. He had chosen the perfect vessel as his earth body, in case this very contingency became necessary.

"Lord Dasi," one of them said, "we have a car waiting. Quarters have already been arranged."

"Very well," he said. He settled into the back of the limo and leaned back against the plush, leather seats.

Such limited bodies these EarthKine have, he thought.

"But be sure to only address me as such in private," Dasi said. "We shall have to remain covert for the time being. Use my earth vehicle's name. I shall be known to you as Taylor Walker."

From a deep, dark well, Dasi felt a stirring as he invoked the name. A vestige of the older consciousness trying to assert itself. He pressed that impulse deeper into the darkness.

Its presence should not be a problem.

EPILOGUE

…Oh…

the hanging arrow

a hanging thread

things that go bump in the ceiling

…my…

the King of the Corvine

a zombie horde

facing reality

a secret song

Sanctuary

…God…

Present Day

Before daybreak, Cary sipped coffee in the dark. The bathroom light had already been on when he had come downstairs. He listened for a moment at the door, then tapped out three soft knocks.

"You okay in there?" he said.

No one answered. Simon or Ally? He was about to try the door when he heard a small voice.

Fine," Ally said. "I'm fine."

"Just checking," Cary said. He slipped outside in the fading darkness and climbed down the embankment to the river's edge. Venus and Jupiter hung in the lightening sky like pinpricks in the film of reality.

Had any of this really happened? He had seen it; he had watched the impossible become real, and still he doubted.

The arrow he had launched into the sky last spring hung in the eternal present of his thoughts; Cary shook his head at the memory.

"What the Hell was I thinking?"

Behind him, perched in the yew, a raven croaked an indecipherable reply. Cary spun to look at the thing. The raven cocked his head and stared back with a single eye.

***

Ally sat cross-legged on the bathroom floor, her face

pressed into the bowl of her palms. Above her, the ceiling groaned as Simon tossed about in fitful sleep. She stared into the dark corner behind the claw foot tub. Something was moving back there. Hanging by a thread. A spider spinning. Ally watched the tiny thing work, then looked at the dark window above the tub, then the wall, then back to the spider. Anywhere except for the pee-stick on the floor in front of her.

***

Simon was back on Davis Islands, running down Aegean Boulevard, a horde of Qellepoth kids in pursuit. He used to call them zombies, but these were not like typical movie zombies. These guys were fast! He looked up to his apartment. Faces gathered at the window watching his pursuit with glee. In fact, now that he looked, Qellepoth faces filled every window of the Ponce. Simon was the entertainment *du jour.*

He approached the corner, just as he had done months before in his car. But now he recognized the person who stood there.

Taylor Walker.

Taylor Walker smiled. And he began to change.

***

"Are you even a bird?" Cary said.

The big corvine let loose a chain of caws that almost sounded like a laugh. At that moment, day broke, and a piece of the sun reflected off the top of the raven's black head, lighting it like a crown. Then the dark creature took to the sky, a rising shadow that disappeared into the darkness that still clung to the forest's heart.

Cary found the comfort of his necklace. His thumb traced first the well-worn constellation, then the temporary seal he had placed on the end. His wrist no longer ached, but he rubbed it anyway.

He hadn't told them everything, of course. While the memories—or were they just fantasies?—of most of his past lives had faded, his knowledge of the ziggurat beneath them, the temple that literally formed the foundation of his home, remained very present in his consciousness.

And now he knew how to get in.

He stood before a dark boulder lodged in the embankment behind the remnants of the fishing shack. Lichen and river silt camouflaged the rough stone surface, but the sigil, exactly at eye level and just the size of his hand, shone clear in the dawn light. He had lived here most of his life. He had leaned countless times against this very rock, but he had never seen this mark before today.

Cary pressed his hand to the symbol, and the necklace began to vibrate. He took a deep breath, then whispered a soft name, a name that had remained in his thoughts since the day he had opened the necklace. Her name. His name.

"Ksama."

Nothing. He tried again, a little louder. Still nothing.

Cary shifted his weight to turn away, and the raven called out again from the shadows of the trees. Then a fluttering sound caught his attention. Over the river, a single crow was flying in a tight circle over and over. The raven in the trees continued to speak. The crow over the river gathered speed, flying so fast that for a moment it appeared to be a hole in the sky. Then the raven went silent. The crow angled away and flew upriver. That was when Cary remembered the song he had hummed with Ally when they entered the LightGate at Bok Tower. And suddenly he knew. The song was the key.

He poured his intention once again into the sigil on the rough, stony face. With his other hand he took up the pendant. He sang the word to the secret melody.

"Ksaaaaaaaamaaaaaaaaaa."

***

Teo Kirten's smiling face filled Ally's thoughts. Lavender.

When she had last seen him, they had sat together holding hands in a sea of lavender, then said goodbye. She laughed aloud at the memory.

Above her, Simon thumped the wall. Then again. And again. What the hell was he doing up there? Whatever it was, he'd have to deal with it himself.

She let loose a sigh. She was a warrior. She faced things. That was what she had been trained to do. That's what she had done day in and day out for most of her life. She could face anything. Even this. She turned her gaze to the pregnancy test. She stared at it for a long time. Simon's thrashings in the room above increased, but Ally no longer heard them. She picked up the stick and stared at it.

"Oh my..."

***

Simon slid to a halt. Taylor Walker was no more. In his place stood the creature that had attacked Simon at the YMCA. No. Not the same creature. One exactly like it.

Behind Simon, the wall of Qellepoth continued to advance. One by one, they transformed into monsters. Simon no longer had anywhere to run.

The monsters closed in. Simon lurched to wakefulness in his bed.

"Oh my..."

***

Cary's breath stopped for a moment. An arched doorway had opened in the rock. He thought he heard the tinkle of laughter on the wind, but when he looked over his shoulder, only red and gold leaves oscillated in the morning breeze.

The long tunnel led through solid rock to an ornate antechamber, and beyond that, a vast, domed sanctuary lined with glowing gemstones. A low throb of power coursed through his body the moment he crossed the threshold.

"Oh…"

A stone slab at the apex of the dome rasped open, letting in a focused shaft of morning light. At the center of the sanctuary, a raised dais supported a stone altar. And upon the altar, glimmering in that spotlight of the sun…

"…my…"

***

Though these three could not hear each other in the traditional sense—Simon in his bed, freshly escaped from dream zombie death, Ally on the bathroom floor staring at saturated proof of life, and Cary in the heart of the temple witnessing his handiwork and his destiny—each and all spoke the final word together as one:

"…God!"

THE END

ACKNOWLEDGEMENTS

Many hearts have contributed to the creation of this book. More than I can name. More than I can count. This is a partial list.

Thank you...

...first, to the One for whom I choose carefully each word...

...to my publisher-editor-friend Jennifer Chesak, the madwoman juggernaut driving the unstoppable train that is Wandering in the Words Press, to all my fellow writers at WWP, and to Assistant Editor Victoria Shockley for her linguistic insights, her hard work, and her tireless tweeting. You conspire to make a community of us...

...to the insightful friends-first-readers-second who combed through manuscripts in various stages of repute and provided valuable feedback. Steve, Maggie, Sherita, Lolo, Tracey the Mermaid, Brittany—many changes herein are born of your insights...

...to the amazing Bryan Holland, whose painting graces the cover. With your brush you brought Ksama's essence into the Light...

...to my Dear Friend, who sees me like no one else...

...to Baraka, a midwife of dreams, and Todd, a teacher of the center, both living archetypes of hope...

...to Kevin, a good man whose counsel I have always treasured, and who lends me names...

...to the Glowing Girl for, among many other things, the best read of my life, many results of which are to be found in these pages...

...to Kara, who helped me build the best bonfire ever...

...to Jane Hollister, who taught me how to breathe, and why...

...to Marilyn, who validated and nurtured my feminism...

...to Bobby, who might be surprised to find herself on this page, but who belongs here in the Halls of Gratitude, nonetheless...

...to Jan, whose Love and Light make her a constant reminder of Life's Blessings...

...to Hannah, within whom lives the Spirit of the Sidhe and the Graces...

...to David and Rhonda, who forever teach me by example how to Love, and to Frank, who does the same... What is writing if not Love?

...to my brother, Bill, fellow traveler on this larger journey for more years and lifetimes than either of us can name...

...to Jean and Bill, who now must read this from other worlds...

...and finally...to my beautiful children, Dylan and Holland, my inspirations.